BUTTERMILK ROAD

BUTTERMILK

McGraw=Hill Book Company, Inc.

ROAD *by Thomas Turner*

New York ~ Toronto ~ London

Library of Congress Catalog Card Number: 62-21577

First Edition

65585

TO MY MOTHER AND FATHER

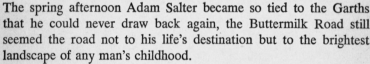

The spring afternoon Adam Salter became so tied to the Garths that he could never draw back again, the Buttermilk Road still seemed the road not to his life's destination but to the brightest landscape of any man's childhood.

The Buttermilk Road linked two valleys, one of which contained the houses and factories of the town of Mercer. The road left Mercer by the saddle point of a high ridge to the east and looked down from there on a green valley of farms and woodlands. The Garth house was on a rise at the left. Except in winter, trees concealed the house, so that anyone driving down the mountain could see it only for an instant.

Late that April afternoon Adam watched for the house as he always had, and when he saw it from the curve, the shadow from behind him was just drowning out the coppery light on its white columns.

At the foot of the mountain he turned his car in between two brick pillars. The house was a quarter of a mile beyond. It was a long driveway to pave, but there it lay, a black asphalt serpent winding through the trees.

As he drove, the brown brick and white woodwork of the house flashed between the dark tree trunks. The house was the only one Adam remembered vividly from childhood, not always accurately but with nervous dark illumination. He thought of a night a quarter of a century ago when the trees were struggling in a high wind, making the lighted windows blink, and the house itself seemed to be in motion, sinking like an ocean liner.

He emerged from the wood into an open lawn through which the driveway curved, and the house and its big oaks filled the windshield. The bricks were earth brown with a purple tint; Adam's great-grandfather had soaked them in water to prevent crumbling. The house did not look old: the landscaping was modern; the old shutters had been removed and the windows hung with aluminum screens. Dr. Garth was not one to preserve the house reverently against his own convenience, for he had the present industrial glories of Mercer and the fortune he had made there to offset any paralyzing dream of antebellum grandeur.

The freshly cut grass smelled like watermelon. Anyway, it costs a fortune to keep a place like this up, Adam said to himself, glancing at the acres of lawn. Even if we could have gotten our hands on it, we couldn't have held it.

"The servants will have gone when you get there," Dr. Garth had said on the telephone, "so just come in and back to my study. I'd come to your office, but I want to keep this business secret."

As Adam mounted the steps, he put on his jacket and tightened his tie. The cut of his suit emphasized his height and minimized the considerable width and depth of his shoulders and chest. He swung the door open and stepped inside. Down the hall a dim chandelier glowed like a phosphorescent deep-sea animal, and beyond it a graceful staircase turned from a cherry newel post into the gloom overhead.

Adam moved into the parlor and turned to the portraits of Adam and Rachel Garth. Their faces were yellow and webbed with lines of cracked varnish. Rachel was dark-eyed, gentle, and withdrawn as though already surrendering to the early death in childbirth she had suffered. Her husband, the builder of this house, had an excess of nose, mouth, and chin, and a look of disagreeable keenness in his eyes.

Their great-grandson turned from them with a smile. He had thick brown hair, a large handsome nose, and blue eyes. With a beard he would have been considered a handsome man, but clean-shaven, his mouth seemed too big like his scowling male ancestor's with a hint of brutality in the lips, and his thick neck reinforced this impression.

An ancient pier mirror was mounted between the front windows. The silver was flaking off the back, and the golden flowers etched into the border were fading. The glass received and transformed Adam's image as though the mirror were a cistern to blend the phosphenes of the past. His face by daylight was a reddish brown

2

farmer's color, but the reflection before him seemed gray like a face in a daguerreotype.

Behind this room lay the library, its windows more shaded than these of the parlor, so that it seemed later in the day there, an hour later perhaps, and dark enough now for Adam to see the rim of light around the door of Dr. Garth's study. He moved toward it, the deep rugs muffling his tread, the house seeming to ring with silence.

He knocked, and the door swung open away from his knuckles, and Dr. Garth, a dark silhouette in the lighted doorway, extended his big hand. His neck and bald head rose from his massive shoulders in a thick column like a torpedo. He too had the Garth mouth, thickened by age, and a fine face—like the face of a hanging judge.

"I was looking for you, Adam, but you came in like a cat." His oversized hand gripped Adam's and drew him into the room.

"You're looking vigorous, Uncle Ive."

"I feel vigorous," said Dr. Garth, but he moved slowly with the care of age, and his slowness gave him an aspect of formidable mass.

The room they entered had been added to the house as a plantation office. The trees and shrubbery outside were so thick that every day seemed overcast, and dark oak paneling and built-in bookshelves turned the room even darker. Adam's gaze swept over the leather-bound sets of classics, paused for an instant on the gilt letters of Mommsen's *History of Rome,* and quickly passed an enormous dull-looking medical library. The room had the smell of Dr. Garth's tobacco, his books, and his leather chairs—a blend which Adam as a child had thought was Dr. Garth's personal smell.

They sat on opposite sides of the desk, and Dr. Garth inquired about Adam's sister and her family. "I've owed her a letter for some time," said Dr. Garth. "She wanted some information about our ancestors which I'm afraid I'm not going to be able to help with."

Adam flushed. "I hope she hasn't been bothering you. Men don't keep up with that kind of thing."

"You'll find that matters of family seem more important as you grow older." He regarded Adam with a mild benign expression. "How old are you, Adam—twenty-nine? And still a bachelor. Well, your sister shouldn't give up about you. I didn't marry until I was forty."

Abruptly Dr. Garth took a cardboard folder from a drawer.

3

"How would you like to make a good bit of money in a hurry, Adam?"

"I'd like it fine."

"It will involve a lot of hard work under intense pressure. Knowing you, I was persuaded that you wouldn't mind that."

"You're right, Uncle Ive. Is there a catch?"

"Not just one catch, but two. First you'll risk making an enemy of the most powerful man in town."

"Bascom Olin?"

"He's the richest. I suppose that makes him the most powerful and he's probably the most vindictive."

"Does this have anything to do with that Taurus Company material you sent me?"

"It does. How do you like the company?"

"I like its product. Their four-dollar towel is beautiful. Big as an overcoat and soft as silk. And the way the volume of sales is holding up looks good. I don't like the earnings' trend, of course, but I simply didn't have enough information to decide whether that's temporary or whether the tide had gone out for good. Incidentally, you didn't send any figures for last year."

"Last year the company sold ten million dollars' worth of towels and lost one hundred and ninety thousand dollars. It's still losing money. One reason is we've got a weak president, Hubert Quigley, and the reason he's still running the company is that Bascom Olin has blocked me and General Myerson every time we've tried to make a change. Why should he do that? After all he has more stock in the company than I do. Now I know why. He's keeping Quigley until his son can get back here and run the company. The boy's working for Sutherland Mills in Birmingham. That company is being merged with a national firm, and evidently young Olin thinks his future is brighter here. What kind of president do you think he would make?"

Adam hesitated. Even though he was talking with a relative he trusted, he felt cautious out of habit about expressing himself too plainly about the Olins. "I've only seen him once," Adam said. "If you want a snap judgment, I'd say he's not the man you want for president."

Dr. Garth nodded, his head gleaming against the slowly fading light of a west window. "He would ruin the company, and I plan to keep him out."

"That might be expensive."

"I know it. Here is your interest in the matter. I'll buy all the stock you can turn up for seventy-five dollars a share. Get it for less and pocket the difference. You'll make more this way than if you work as my agent. I'll buy it from you in six months and it'll be taxed as capital gains." Dr. Garth was watching him with keen interest. "How does it strike you?"

"I'm delighted of course. I'll have to get Mr. Chisholm's permission since I'm in the securities business with him."

"Can you ask him without mentioning my name or giving this thing away? If Olin buys much through him, Chisholm will feel closer to him than to me."

"Yes, I can put it so he won't have any idea what or where the company is."

Dr. Garth's gaze was fixed on Adam's face. "Some stockbrokers wouldn't want their men dealing on their own. What if Chisholm says no?"

"I can talk him into it. All I want is your permission to tell him about it."

"Then go ahead. As soon as you've tried to buy the stock, it won't be a secret anyway. But I don't want Olin to know beforehand."

"I assume Olin doesn't have a majority of the stock."

"Almost. So I need as much stock as I can get. What prompted me to act now is that John T. Cutter died in January, and his heirs have offered to sell Myerson and me his Taurus stock, which will put us even with the Olin interests. In addition we'll need another 3,001 shares for a majority."

"Will people sell stock to me?" Adam said. "They may figure I'm buying for you, an insider with some good news about the company."

"They'll think you're buying as a broker rather than as my cousin. If I went directly to them, they'd ask a higher price."

"I'm going to have to borrow to swing this, so I'll be asked to go into detail with whoever lends me the money."

"Just don't go to any local people or any out-of-town people with local connections. Anything I can do to help? That is, short of going on a note for you?"

"If anybody asks, just say you think I'm a good credit risk," Adam said with a laugh.

"How much can you raise without borrowing?"

"I've got stocks worth ten thousand dollars."

"You've saved that much, have you? That's a good sign in a young man."

"Seven thousand of it is profit on investments. Everybody's a genius in a bull market."

"You'll need more money than that. An offer of sixty thousand dollars a share will buy a thousand shares easily, perhaps two thousand. That's fifteen to thirty thousand pre-tax profit to you."

"You mentioned another catch, Uncle Ive."

"Yes. Do you see any way you could lose on this project?"

"No, sir. You're being very generous."

"Think about it for a minute, Adam."

Adam gazed at Dr. Garth's hard face.

"If I should die before buying the stock from you, disposing of it would be your problem. I could provide in my will to buy it, but that would drain off cash which ought to remain in my estate. Josephine is my only heir, and she has no inclination to take a hand in affairs at The Taurus Company, and the man she marries may not either. So I don't want her to have any more capital tied up there unless I can settle this before I die. If I begin to look sickly to you, you don't have to wait six months—you can go on and sell me the stock and pay regular income taxes on it. I'm seventy years old, and I've had some warnings. You still interested, Adam?"

"Yes, sir."

Dr. Garth laughed softly. Adam had never really had an opportunity to see how Dr. Garth's mind worked in business matters. The offer was flattering, yet it filled Adam with peculiar misgivings, not because he was afraid of being stuck with the Taurus stock but because in spite of the clipped words, it sounded less like an ordinary business proposition by which someone intended to make money out of his services than a test like the labors of Hercules. He suddenly felt very much interested in the question of Dr. Garth's age, not so much regarding his health as his general faculties.

"I'd think the Olins would try to buy the stock themselves," Adam said. He studied Dr. Garth's face. The bald head and heavy features shone with igneous hardness, the voice was firm and deep.

"Olin has had his way so long, he doesn't expect any trouble, but when he learns what I plan to do, he will go after the stock with

6

great energy. I'm not going to try to outbid him. He has too much money."

"Do you have a list of stockholders?"

"Here," said Dr. Garth, indicating the folder. "You'll have to do some research to locate out-of-town stockholders. The company has their addresses, but I don't want to stir things up by asking for them. I knew you were a hard worker and wouldn't mind going to some trouble. That's another reason why I picked you for the job."

Adam accepted the folder and rose to leave.

∽∽∽∽∽∽∽∽∽∽∽∽∽∽∽∽∽∽∽∽∽∽∽∽∽∽∽∽∽∽∽∽∽∽∽

The sound of a car in the driveway reached them. "That must be Josephine," said Dr. Garth, getting up.

"I thought she was in New York."

"Just been back two days." Dr. Garth opened the study door eagerly. The brisk steps of a woman wearing high heels sounded in the hallway. "Josephine?"

"Hey, Daddy."

Dr. Garth turned to Adam. "Don't mention this business to her."

A tall brunette walked quickly into the study and kissed Dr. Garth on the cheek. She looked around, and her face brightened. "Adam!" Smiling after a moment of hesitation about whether to kiss or not, they shook hands. She had evidently just come from a party, for she wore a small flowered hat and a white woolen coat. Adam remembered her as a mature-looking girl of seventeen. She had changed only for the better.

"Am I interrupting anything important? I'd better not be! Daddy's retired."

"That was a long luncheon today," said Dr. Garth. "You must have eaten a great deal."

"Four of us played bridge at Blakely's afterward."

"I hope you're in Mercer to stay," said Adam.

"I don't know yet," she said with a quick glance at her father. "Aren't you going to have a drink?"

"Yes, won't you?" said Dr. Garth. "I have some good sherry."

Though he was pressed for time now, Adam accepted at once, for he was eager to talk with Josephine. Dr. Garth led them into the library and poured one glass full of sherry and another glass a third full from a glittering decanter. "Excuse me. I have to make a telephone call."

As soon as the study door closed behind him, Josephine handed Adam the full glass of sherry and filled up her own. She tasted it and said: "Good sherry, my eye. This is some of that California sherry that's been here for ages. You know what all that was about?" She glanced at the study door and lowered her voice. "Daddy doesn't think I should drink hard liquor. And you saw him pour out my child's portion of sherry." Adam lighted her cigarette. "Guess the first time I ever had a cigarette in front of him? Last summer—and I've been smoking for six years. I wish I were as young as Daddy thinks I am."

"Your father takes a drink, doesn't he?"

"He used to drink about this much sherry two or three times a week, but he's given that up now and tobacco too on account of his health, and he doesn't think a young lady ought to drink at all. Or smoke."

"Is that why he picked this time to make his telephone call?"

"So he wouldn't have to sit here and watch me be improper? I wouldn't be at all surprised. I hear you're living at the Oakley Court, Adam. Those are nice apartments—so modern and convenient. This big old house is a nightmare to keep up."

"But it's worth it!" His hands in his pockets, he looked enthusiastically over the room. "One of the things I remembered a lot when I was in Japan was the smell of the scuppernong arbor. It hasn't been cut down, has it?" He walked to the window before she could answer and said: "No. Good. I hear it's the fashion to cut them down now. Every time I taste certain wines I think of that arbor. The stepped-on scuppernongs must ferment on the ground."

"I don't think it's like wine," she said. "That damp ground smells like a grave to me."

"I guess for a hundred years it's been too dark under that arbor for grass to grow." He took a deep breath. "And I love the mellow smell in here. You remember my grandfather sold his right to the house to your grandfather to use the money to speculate in cotton? I've never forgiven him for that."

She shook her head. "You know why the world isn't overrunning with monstrous unlivable houses like this one? Because every generation or so most families have a fire. Well, the Garths haven't had an effective fire in over a hundred years."

"Josephine! It would break your father's heart if this house burned," Adam said. "And mine too. I love it. If you ever get ready to sell it, I'll pay you whatever you ask."

"I believe you're serious." She watched him over the rim of the wineglass. "I've tried to keep up with you, Adam, but it hasn't been easy. The last time I saw you was, let's see—when you were at the seminary. Why didn't you finish? You'd have made such a good minister."

"No, I wasn't suited to it. I'm no preacher. But it was a fairly complicated decision as you can imagine. Some day I'll tell you all about it."

"Don't you ever feel you made a mistake?"

"I did what I had to do. Tell me about New York. Did you live at that hotel—what's the name of it—the one for young ladies?"

"No, I lived in an apartment with two other girls at first, but it didn't work out, so I got an apartment by myself. I didn't tell Daddy. He would have worried about me."

"Let's see. You went there to study—what was it? Music or painting?"

"Close enough," she said. "It was the theater. But I wasn't really stage-struck, and when I saw all the bright-eyed young things from the provinces who'd give a right arm, or anything else, to be an actress, I got a job as a secretary. But it was a good year—year and a half—and I learned a lot. You feel so free in New York."

"I've found that cities are fun only if you have money to spend."

"Speaking of fun, I hear you're the most eligible bachelor in Mercer. And that you've been taking out Blakely Myerson. See how everyone knows your business in a town this size?"

"I come from a smaller town than this."

"I'll bet they don't watch you any more closely there than they do here. They couldn't."

"It's a cold world, Josephine. Be thankful they care."

He had thought as soon as he saw her that afternoon that she was an unusual beauty, and the conviction grew as he looked. Her cheeks cast soft crescent shadows, which deepened when she smiled. Her coloring seemed creole, as though she had just returned from the tropics instead of New York, and against this dark skin her teeth were very white. Her mouth was large but pretty, not the Garth mouth, for it had been her good luck to take after her mother.

Watching her and feeling the gentle warmth of the sherry in his empty stomach, Adam found the house even more mellow and comfortable, the smells of spring even stronger and sweeter.

He glanced at his watch and sat up with a start. "I have to go. The time really got away from me," he said, standing up. "I wonder if your father is still telephoning."

"I'll see." She walked to the study door and put her head against it. "Yes, but it's just some business with General Myerson."

"Don't interrupt him. I'll call him tomorrow."

"I hope I haven't made you late for your date. Tell Blakely it was my fault," she said as they walked to the front door. The late afternoon was pink with sunshine on a towering thunderhead, and it softened and rounded the curving surfaces of Josephine's face. He was surprised to see by daylight that she had a look about the eyes he didn't like and wondered if she were not getting enough sleep or coming down with a cold. She had entertained him cheerfully enough for the past half-hour, but the way her smile faded as he left her convinced him that Josephine was a very unhappy young woman.

3

Blakely Myerson sat against the right car door, her legs folded under her, a gauzy dress of baby pink in a cascade around her legs. She was a small girl with pretty features and skin the color of honey. Moonlight shone through the windshield on her little hands folded in her lap. Her blond hair looked white against the moon-bleached landscape.

"It's so nice and cool," she said to Adam. "Just right." The fresh smell of the countryside came in the windows of the car and mixed with Blakely's light sweet perfume. "Do you know this is the first time you've ever been late for me? I usually keep you waiting. I'm bad about that."

What had made him late was a call to Mr. Chisholm arranging to have the next day off for personal business in Atlanta. Adam had taken Blakely to dinner that night at Mammy's Log Cabin, about fifteen miles from Mercer. Mammy's served charcoal-flavored steaks and fried chicken, eaten by the light of candles stuck in wine bottles, and patrons could bring whisky, which was not allowed in any respectable restaurant in Mercer.

"I'm so glad Josephine's back," Blakely said. "I just love her. She was a wonderful roommate."

"I'd forgotten you two were roommates. She seems a couple of years older than you, Blakely."

"We're the same age. Uh-oh. Now you know how old I am."

"Twenty-four."

"Isn't that horrible?"

"Too horrible to contemplate."

"Josephine was just about a perfect roommate, I guess, except that I couldn't wear her clothes, not being the same size. She always had such pretty clothes, but she's so broad-shouldered and long-waisted anything would look good on her." Blakely talked in a high slow gentle voice. "She has a wonderful figure. And such good posture. Momma is always getting after me to stand up perfectly straight." She squared her shoulders at the thought. "Josephine is five feet eight inches tall. Now tell me the honest truth—don't you think Josephine has an unusually good figure?"

"She was wearing a long coat this afternoon. I really didn't see enough of it to tell."

"She was kind of skinny until the year we went to Miss Wycherley's. Then she filled out. She was so smart. She was the president of the honor council, good athlete, good student. I was scared to death to room with her."

"Why?"

"She was so *religious*. Every mother in town would always hold her up as an example. Momma'd say, 'Look here, Sugar Baby, you've got to do so-and-so. Josephine Garth does.' That's one reason we were so glad when she poured the whisky out."

"What was that?"

Blakely laughed a little soft laugh. "You don't know about that? Dr. Garth was so strict, and he made such a churchgoer out of Josephine. The year before we went off to Miss Witch's, this Sunday school teacher—Miss Carrie May McEachern—was so hipped on the subject of drinking and she got Josephine hipped on drinking too. Which is it—hipped or hepped? Josephine and her mother were visiting her uncle and aunt in South Carolina. They got a couple of cases of good whisky in for a cocktail party, and when Josephine couldn't talk them out of giving this old sinful party, she poured all the whisky out in the sink." Blakely laughed delightedly until she saw she was laughing alone. "Don't you think it's funny?"

"Yes, sort of. Was Josephine a puritanical roommate?"

"Yes, and when she was elected to the honor council, she was supposed to report anybody else who broke the rules. So I had to be real careful about my smoking. She knew I was smoking, but for a long time she never saw me do it. I mean, she could smell the smoke in my clothes and hair, specially if a bunch of us had been smoking in one closet. She pretended like she didn't smell anything. Then one day she came into the john when I didn't expect her, and there I was smoking this big fat king-sized cigarette. Well, of course she was supposed to report me. But she begged me to report myself. That way they'd probably keep me campused for the rest of the year, but they wouldn't kick me out. Well, I wouldn't do it. I hated the school anyway—it was hard as the dickens—and I said to myself, Sugar Baby, if it's a choice between being shipped home and staying on the campus, I'd rather be shipped."

"Did she turn you in?"

"No, she resigned from the honor council instead. When I heard what she'd done, I told her I wouldn't let her do it, I'd turn myself in, I'd drink a bottle of ink—if she didn't go and get her job back. She said I ought to turn myself in since I'd signed a pledge that I wouldn't smoke at school, but anyway she was off for good for not reporting me.

"That was the only thing that kept Josephine from getting the Silver Trefoil, the highest honor the school gives any graduating senior. Instead they gave it to this girl with great big old legs. Here's the thing about Josephine. She didn't hold that smoking against me. A lot of holy girls would have given me the silent treatment or anyway made me feel bad about it, but she didn't."

"She doesn't seem particularly holy now," he said.

"Yes, I guess she really started changing then. It was the summer after that she pulled that thing I never could understand."

"What thing was that?"

Blakely sat for a moment in silence. "I thought being a cousin you'd know all about that."

"But I don't. What is it?"

"I can't tell you. I'm not going to spread that story. Not many people know about it."

"You've gotten me wild with curiosity."

"I know I have, and it won't do you any good."

She settled back against the seat and hummed. Already the city lights of Mercer were glowing on the horizon ahead of them. The lunging giants of a drive-in movie screen appeared in the landscape, and Blakely twisted to watch them until they were out of sight.

"What was that about Josephine?"

"Are you still thinking about that?"

"Yes." Adam pulled the car over into the entrance of a farm road, stopped, and cut off the headlights. "I really need to know, Blakely."

14

Blakely shifted her position nervously. It was quiet here with no traffic. The stationary air in the car felt warm and close.

"Drive on, Adam Salter!" she cried suddenly. "What are you *thinking* about, bawy, parked out here in the middle of nowhere?"

"I'm thinking about the story about Josephine."

"Don't make me tell you that. You get so serious about everything." Her voice fell to a whisper, and he leaned close so that her breath was warm on his ear. "Since you're her cousin and all, I'll tell you. Josephine disappeared. She was gone for two nights."

"Where'd she go?"

"That's what nobody knows. Her mother and daddy took her to Europe with them the summer after we graduated from Miss Witch's, and they were in Rome, and Josephine went over the hill. Since it happened over there, Dr. Garth managed to keep it secret."

"How? I'm surprised there wasn't an international manhunt."

"I hadn't thought of that. Now you've made me feel bad because I swore to Josephine I'd never tell a soul. You made me tell. I'm just too agreeable."

He slid over and took her in his arms. "Now, hold on, bawy, I'm not that agreeable!" she said, closing her eyes and putting her lips against his.

She stiffened and pulled away as headlights glared in their faces and swung toward the road they were blocking.

Adam got back under the wheel, and once more they rolled down the highway.

It made him feel good to be with Blakely. She was always sweet tempered, and the more he saw of her the less important seemed the qualities she had seemd to lack at first. What had he missed in her? Depth? That was too snobbish a word, and it was only on being with someone like Josephine that he felt dissatisfied with Blakely.

Blakely hummed, and now and then broke forth in a true but piercing voice with a line of song and which went something like: "We'll ever honor thee."

"Is that the alma mater of Miss Wycherley's School for Girls?" Adam asked.

"How d'you know?" Blakely slid down until her head rested on Adam's arm. "Josephine seemed kind of sad this afternoon. Adam, I really do feel awful about telling you that about Josephine."

"Forget it." He was surprised that he felt bad about it too.

~~~~~~

4

After he took Blakely home, Adam drove out the Buttermilk Road, as he often did when he was too restless to sleep. From the curve on the mountainside he saw that the Garths' house was dark.

As soon as Dr. Garth had outlined his plan, Adam had decided on his strategy, and now he worked out some details. First he would borrow the money in order to be able to pay for the stock on the spot. Those stockholders most likely to sell would be retired persons or widows to whom the passing of the dividend meant a painful cut in income.

As for raising the money he needed, Adam had spoken with more assurance that he now felt. He had a connection in Atlanta—a bank vice-president who was under obligation to him. On the telephone he had asked Mr. Chisholm not to mention that Atlanta was where he was going. When he returned, he would ask permission to take part in this deal. Such timing would suggest that the company involved was in Atlanta.

If the banker wouldn't let him have what he needed, Adam had one or two rich friends he could turn to. This started him thinking about something peculiar in Dr. Garth's proposition: that a millionaire should turn to a young man of modest means to put up his money and credit. Dr. Garth had smiled when he made the remark about not endorsing his note, but he had meant it. If someone else had made such a proposition to Adam, Dr. Garth might have been the man to whom he would have turned to borrow the money. Also, if the proposition had come from anyone else, Adam would have demanded a rigid legal contract to sell the stock at seventy-five dollars a share.

As for Adam's own holdings, Dr. Garth's proposition could not have come at a better time. The market seemed to be topping out after a long advance, and Adam had already considered liquidating most of his stocks.

He would try not to excite the wrath of Bascom Olin, and with a more reasonable man he would have been fairly confident of success. As Dr. Garth had suspected, Olin was a good customer of Mr. Chisholm's, his best customer in fact, and that would make Adam's own position delicate.

Olin was a shrewd independent trader—quick to take losses when a trade went bad and indifferent to tips. Often he had a half million dollars riding on securities which he held for less than a year. He never sold short and rarely took a profit in less than six months.

Although Adam saw him every day, Olin had acknowledged Adam's existence on only one occasion. Usually Olin would deal only with Mr. Chisholm, but once when the latter was away, Olin had caught Adam's eye in the board room and, holding up two fingers, said: "BS."

"At the market?"

"Yes, at the damn market!"

Adam started writing the order. "Two hundred Bethlehem Steel, Mr. Olin?" Adam had asked and thought he had an affirmative nod. By the time the transaction was confirmed, Olin had left the board room, and Adam had been unable to reach him by telephone.

The next day Olin had stomped in, thrown down his invoice, and said: "I told you two thousand, God damn you!" The other eighteen hundred shares had cost Olin an additional twelve hundred dollars.

As for having him for an opponent, Adam in spite of common sense began to relish the thought. He doesn't know who I am, but he will.

The Buttermilk Road, shining in the moonlight, wound through the valley before him. Now and then Adam passed an old mansion, often with a family on one side of the reception hall and chickens or pigs on the other. There had once been lordly Magowans, Fraziers, and Chobots here, all of whom had died out or faded into genteel poverty. Now of the four families who had owned the valley only the Garths had successfully turned into city people.

An elusive pain was bothering Adam, and he realized that it came from Blakely's story of Josephine's disappearance. That had happened just before Josephine's mother died. She had been pretty and dark like Josephine, and she had lived the life of a great lady— graciously and generously—the kind of life Adam's mother had dreamed of.

The best memories of his childhood centered around Mercer and the Garths, and his mother had always looked forward to these visits and was happiest here. Adam's family had visited his grandfather, a widower, every summer while the latter was alive. After the rash speculations of 1893, he had been a conservative county tax assessor in Mercer until his death fifteen years ago. Grandfather Garth's house was small, so Adam often stayed with Dr. and Mrs. Garth when the family was visiting in Mercer.

For years before Josephine was born, Dr. and Mrs. Garth had wanted a child, and some of their feeling had spilled over Adam. At the age of four he had drawn a rhinoceros and sent it to Dr. and Mrs. Garth as a valentine, which they had framed and hung on their bedroom wall. Over a period of years during Adam's childhood Dr. Garth had put two thousand dollars in a bank account to help with Adam's education.

Adam had troubled memories of how as a child he had known that his father was not respected in Mercer, that the Garths, his grandfather's family, had no interest in his opinions, and even departed from their usual courtliness to interrupt or ignore him when he became very garrulous.

Dr. Garth was an exception. He listened with respect and interest to the professor, asked his advice on educational problems, with which he was concerned since he was a trustee of a university. Yet Adam had a fear he could not shake off even now that Dr. Garth was secretly contemptuous of his father and of him. Dr. Garth was one of the principal reasons his father continued to come to Mercer. The doctor was a formidable man, toward whom one felt gratitude because his kindness was unexpected, and Professor Salter had been overeager to please him, laughed too much in his presence, and contradicted himself in order to agree with him.

Adam's father had taught at McFall Falls State Teachers' College, one hundred and forty miles west of Mercer. Its site was a town of four thousand, and the redundant name had embarrassed Adam, when asked his home town, well into manhood. It was dusty and poor, not like a college town in appearance, and it had nothing to offer but a job to Ira W. Salter.

Adam still found his father puzzling. He had some of the qualities of the village atheist, full of scorn for the jerkwater town of McFall Falls, into the face of which he flung the only Republican vote in the county. As Adam grew older, he felt that his father had missed his calling, a favorite opinion with his sister Rachel, but it was an imaginary calling. If he had been a lawyer, people would have said he would have made a great economics professor, and when he did become a businessman at last, all Adam's doubts on this subject were resolved. He lacked the ability to discriminate among ideas, to use his time in sensible proportions, to carry on a conversation without talking down to people and antagonizing them.

Adam's mother died when he was twelve, and his sister, eight years older than he, had raised him. She was now thirty-seven, handsome, restless, and inflexible. She was married to a professor who taught on the West Coast and had three children, but she had enough surplus energy to teach school and do extensive civic work.

The Buttermilk Road ended at the river, and Adam turned there and started home. He was driving fast when he passed the ruined church, and he stopped the car and backed up. The tombstones there gleamed in the moonlight. This was where his mother had asked to be buried, and Adam had arranged for his father to be laid beside her.

The burned shell of the old church was still there. A hundred years ago Adam Garth had given the land for the church, and his slaves had built it. When it had burned thirty years ago, a few older people had hoped Dr. Garth would rebuild it, but a rural Presbyterian church could not survive in Sweetwater County, and the Garths had already turned to Mercer for community life.

The moonlight was bright and he felt an urge to get out and look. He would never visit McFall Falls again. Mercer had always been home to his mother, and he and his sister felt the same way. The graves in the moonlight stirred up weakening memories of childhood, and in protest, he started his car. These memories had enough happiness in them to tempt him, and he felt too much loyalty to his past to risk trifling with it now. He pressed hard on the accelerator.

His speed increased until he reached the saddle point in the range of western mountains. The scattered lights of Mercer twinkled below, and he rolled slowly downward, casting glances along the railroad to see if he could pick out the lights of The Taurus Company. Jeremiah Mercer for a few years of glory had made this town the horseshoe capital of the world, just as for Adam the town had always been the capital of his own private world. Descending into the valley at night reminded him of taking a ramp into the basement of a vast hardware store. He knew he might have a better chance of making a fortune in a larger city, and certainly he wanted that, but he felt that money would not mean so much to him away from Mercer.

~~~~~~

5

The following morning Adam stopped at a gasoline station before the trip to Atlanta. The sun was already hot and glaring on the white concrete, and Adam went inside the station to escape it. While he stood gazing abstractedly through the blue-tinted glass wall and planning what he would say to his banker friend, a man pushed past him to the telephone booth.

Afterward Adam had only an impression of a fat middle-aged man with unshaken jowls who wore a soiled coat and mismatched pants, the kind of man who spent his days hanging around the courthouse or bus station. He closed the door of the telephone booth, but the heat made him open it, and Adam heard him say: "That's right, that's the one. Big strapping black-headed girl. No, she just done bought it. Brand-new hard-top, white and tan, two-door. It's still got the dealer's plates on it."

Adam glanced at his watch impatiently.

"No, I ain't seen him, Jamie," came the voice from the telephone booth. "I don't believe he's here yet."

"Eighteen gallons ought to do it," Adam called through the door.

"They is only two kinds of titties I like, Jamie," said the voice behind him. "Good old biggerns and big old gooderns. She's got bofe kinds."

Adam signed the ticket for the gas and was about to drive away when he noticed a new tan car with a white top at the Mercer Motor Company across the street. A man in a shop uniform was taking the license plates off with a screwdriver. It occurred to Adam that it must be the car the strapping black-haired girl had bought. Just then the girl herself appeared. It was Josephine Garth.

Adam returned at once to the telephone booth. It was empty. He asked the station manager if he knew who the fat man was. No, was the reply, he had seen the man hanging around downtown, but he was not a customer, had just come in to use the telephone. Adam stepped outside. The man was gone, and so was Josephine.

Two and a half hours later Adam's banker friend was extremely anxious to do Adam a favor, but he could not lend much money for such a speculative venture, so Adam turned to Corwin Carson, an eccentric idler loaded with soft-drink money. Carson was about fifty, red-haired, and freckled. He listened to Adam's request and with Adam's help telephoned Dr. Garth. After several more bourbons and branch waters and a lot of silent inscrutability, he said yes. He would let Adam have ninety thousand dollars.

With Carson's lawyer present, Adam signed a bristly contract. Any Taurus stock Adam bought would go into escrow and if Adam did not pay the loan off in seven months, Carson could sell the stock without taking legal action.

"I know 8 per cent seems high," said Carson, clapping Adam on the shoulder, "but it's not real money with taxes and all. More like playing Monopoly. You can deduct interest, and I could get as much from a gilt-edged municipal bond. But you are my buddy, Adam. You saved my butt on that dog of a mining stock."

"You used to want a sweetener in any deal, Mr. Carson. What makes this one sweet?"

"I got a hunch that stock's gonna be in demand later on," Carson said in a singsong voice. "And you're not going to be able to pay me when the note comes due, so for once I'll get some stock off you without paying any brokerage."

Duncan Chisholm and Company's board room contained thirty folding chairs in rows facing a blackboard on which young women posted prices of stocks. A stag gathering of regulars spent five mornings a week there. Over their heads the smoke of their cigarettes formed a blue collective ghost, and all these men, no matter how successful in the market, were haunted by the trades they might have made, the Goodyear Tire or Boeing Aircraft they had almost bought in 1949. These unconsummated trades were joined by those of the present, which seemed to beckon like dream children waiting on the shores of eternity to be born.

This Thursday the market was inactive, and they talked about the weather. It was a hot day for April, and the air had a swamplike smell that it often had before a summer rain.

Adam's glass-walled office faced the board, and so did that of the other customers' man in the firm, Bob Reamer. Mr. Chisholm's office was separate with a plastered wall and a wooden door between him and the board room. It was a door he could lock, for Mr. Chisholm liked to be able to shut out the world.

As Adam telephoned various customers, he watched for Mr. Chisholm.

Even over the glass wall, Adam could hear Reamer talking on the telephone. It was harrowing, for Reamer spoke a bastard kind of market-letter English delivered in an earnest resonant voice. "The market shows promise on the upside . . . *if* the rails confirm, there should be a general movement . . . otherwise strong selectivity with emphasis on particular issues should prevail . . . trees don't grow to the sky, you know . . . on the other hand, although the volume is dropping, you should never sell a dull market short . . ."

Some fertile Reamer had come here from a nearby hamlet two generations ago, and Reamers were everywhere. There was Reamer Motors, Reamer Hardware, E. T. "Ed" Reamer Insurance Company. In fact, it seemed one of the beauties of civilization that it provided outlets for the Reamer energy. Some Reamers were rich, some poor, but they all seemed to be of one mind. They all wanted to get ahead.

So Reamer's most irritating quality was that he dramatized a similar ambition of Adam's. This ambition had always been the mainspring of Adam's energy, which he had expended with calculation, even in high school in McFall Falls and afterward in the Army Air Corps. His officers' training and the war with Japan had ended the same week, and his failure to experience combat had been at the time a tremendous disappointment.

He had gone to a large Middle-Western university, served as president of the undergraduate Christian Association, and broken the university record for shotput and hammerthrow. He had great powers of concentration, he was a fast reader, and he approached his academic work with machinelike efficiency. He took shorthand notes on lectures and reading, and transcribed them at high speed on a typewriter the same day. This efficiency and the Garth mouth had made him seem ruthless and fanatical to some other undergraduates. Once a roommate had remarked resentfully, angrily, after looking at Adam's notes: "Why do you have to do stuff like this? You got a damn photographic memory anyway." After his GI money was exhausted, his grades got him the best-paying scholarships, and he graduated first in his class.

The following September he had entered a theological seminary in Richmond, and by Christmas he knew that he would never be able to give either the seminary or the vocation of clergyman his best efforts. The air of the seminary was so saturated with a feeling alien to him that he could not live in it, and afterward it seemed to him that he lacked some spiritual quality that the others had, that he had not been truly religious but simply a conscientious man who had taken ideas too seriously. His father had invented a philosophy for his students and family called Ethical Positivism, but he was at heart a puritan, and Adam wondered if he himself had gone to the seminary to restore the old armor of puritan ideas which his father had discarded. He became aware that his own interest in ideas, his ambition, and some inarticulated personal religion were separated by iron chambers, and no effort of will would bring them together.

All his life in reaching a decision, Adam had imagined as a moral test what Dr. Garth would do under similar circumstances, and Dr. Grath had influenced him more than he knew at the time in his decision to go into the ministry. Adam's mother had always pointed to Dr. Garth as a bulwark of the church. Not until Adam came to Mercer a few months ago did he see with a profound feeling of irony that Dr. Garth kept the church at arm's length, had refused any office in it but that of trustee, and shunned it except at eleven o'clock on Sunday morning. Still he was a bulwark of the local church in that he was by far its heaviest contributor.

When Adam was trying to decide whether to leave the seminary, he wrote Dr. Garth a long letter asking his advice. The reply was disappointingly brief. As Adam expected, Dr. Garth said that it was a matter of individual inclination; he had gone on to say that the church was a great foundation of the republic, and he found its Scriptures an "inspiring monument of literature." Adam was astonished at the implication of this statement, which placed the Bible beside the *Iliad*.

As the year dragged on, Adam realized that for once his thoroughness and tenacity were working against him, for he could not make himself leave the seminary. It would look too much like failure.

During the spring his father got into a quarrel with the McFall College authorities when he was passed over again in promotions to full professor. He resigned, expecting the authorities to yield and beg him to return on his own terms. Instead he received a polite letter thanking him for years of faithful service. So he looked to the people of the town, the faculty, his present and former students to join in a chorus to demand his reinstatement and advancement. Only one voice was heard. That was Adam's. He flew to McFall and asked the college president to take his father back on the old basis. He was told with regret that all positions were filled.

That was the crisis Adam had needed for leaving the seminary. It was the summer of 1950. Without his ministerial exemption Adam was recalled to the Air Force, as he knew he would be, and sent to Japan.

He made no effort to avoid combat, but he did not have the craving for it he had felt in the Second World War. He was five years older, and he did not want to kill or be killed. And this was a different war, for which the public had no stomach, and the armed forces felt it. For Adam it was an interruption of his life rather than part of it.

This time his service was entirely on the ground. It had been divided between days of concentrated sleepless exertion and total idleness. He had tried studying law during slack times but rejected that profession because he did not want to use any more of his life in college.

His career was chosen for him by his father. After leaving the college, the professor had not found a job to his liking, lived with his daughter, grew morose and homesick, quarreled with his son-in-law. Late in 1951 he wrote Adam about a real opportunity, a small webbing mill just fifty miles from McFall. It would make a fortune. Enthusiastic letters about the progress there reached Adam at intervals.

Then after a silence, in August 1952, Adam received an urgent plea from his father for "whatever money you can spare."

Two weeks later Adam was discharged a captain, twenty-five years old with seven thousand dollars saved, and the world before him.

He went to McFall and found his father overworked, confused, haggard but optimistic. He had put his life's savings into what was known as the Salter Webbing Company, which ran seventy-five converted hand looms in a leased rotting building.

Professor Salter had worked out standard costs to show how the mill could return forty thousand dollars a year. Now he needed a little money to put the looms in good shape. Adam studied it and became convinced that the mill could make money and that his father needed his help badly. So he put three thousand dollars into it and became executive vice-president. During the first few months he couldn't get enough of it. He worked fourteen hours a day seven days a week, and though they were not making money, it appeared they would in a month or so.

Adam's three thousand was consumed quickly, then another three thousand, then the rest of his bank account.

Adam tightened every phase of the operation: shimmed up looms from sagging floors, bore down on preventive maintenance, fired the incompetent and insubordinate. In a few months he had cut labor turnover a third, weaving seconds in half, loom supply costs 40 per cent.

He could live on thirty-five dollars a week, less than anyone else in the mill made. Before he was through he could feel a shuttle and look in the quill can and tell how the loom settings were off. He could sell their entire production at prices set by larger and more modern mills. He could do all these things until he lost twenty-five pounds and was as pale as the lint in his hair, but he could not force the mill to make money.

He had no trouble locating the original error. His father's projected costs had allowed too little for repairs, maintenance, and shutdowns of these ancient looms. They were too old ever to produce efficiently.

The company fell behind on payments for yarn. It was either shut down or be shut down by suppliers in a few weeks. Adam's father would not face this. Just twelve hundred dollars from the bank and we'll be over the hump. When Adam tried to persuade him to give in, the older man would recite some canon of economics which was irrelevant to the creaking rusting dragon that was eating them alive.

So Adam tried to sell it. One textile man whom he approached laughed and said: "You know where your looms came from? They came from here when we modernized. Even if they were new, we

couldn't use them. We're operating at 65 per cent of capacity."
Other prospects he approached gave him even less conversation.

So Adam went back to his father with an ultimatum: shut down,
or he would throw the company into bankruptcy. His father resisted, but Adam's threat disheartened him, and though he continued going to the mill, the business immediately came to a halt.

After liquidation the corporation still owed thirty-four hundred
dollars. Adam had persuaded some suppliers to extend credit not
on the balance sheet but on his own personal guarantees. They had
no recourse against him, but he told them he would pay them off
in full.

A year and a half of overwork and defeat had put his soul into
retreat and fear. He wanted a regular pay check and a routine,
and he considered going back into the Air Force.

He took stock brockerage because he liked the complexity and
the action and because it represented opportunity without capital or
great risk. The house got its cut no matter what happened to the
market.

Why hadn't he gone to Wall Street? He knew no ambitious young
broker should have been satisfied anywhere else, but he was not
just looking for a job; he needed a refuge, which Mercer had been
for him all his life. Two stockbrokers maintained offices in Mercer
—a moribund national firm with an entrenched local manager and
no future, and Duncan Chisholm and Company. The latter's Mercer
office had two young salesmen—Bob Reamer and Mr. Chisholm's
nephew, who seemed in a sure trajectory toward the resident
partnership. So Adam went with Selburn Warden and Stone in
Atlanta to acquire capital and experience for an assault on Mercer
later.

Two months after the webbing mill closed, Adam's father was
found dead at his desk of a heart attack. The checks Adam had
sent him from Atlanta were in a drawer uncashed.

For months Adam had a feeling of horror about the webbing mill,
and shame at the memory of all that was foolish and pitiful in their
early hopes for it. He was more ashamed that he was sitting in this
clean office wearing a new tweed suit talking with this reasonable
customer and no broken-down machinery to sweat over until four
a.m. and no payroll checks to kite, while his father had died in
defeat, his head down on a battered roll-top desk.

Adam approached stock brokerage with his customary energy

and expended lavish homework on stocks he was trying to sell. He developed five new prospects every day and set himself a number of telephone calls and visits to make. This approach was scorned in some circles as used-car-lot procedure, but Adam made it pay. By living close he paid off the Salter Webbing Company's creditors before he left Atlanta.

After two and a half years there Mr. Chisholm telephoned Adam to say that the nephew hadn't worked out, and he had an opening. It was a sign that Adam was recovering from the blow of business failure to leave a job where he was already making over a thousand dollars a month. He had created such a market for his services that Mr. Chisholm had departed from his policy and permitted Adam to be partly on commission. He had previously kept his men on salary altogether to obviate the temptation of switching their customers' accounts for personal gain, but Adam had persuaded him that he could be trusted.

Now Adam was in a hurry. He felt that he had wasted time in the Air Force, in college, in the seminary, at the webbing mill, and now he was nearly thirty years old, with little capital, no family, and no home. Yet sometimes he would wake up at three in the morning and feel that he was throwing his life away on money-getting, that he might do something really important like reading *The Critique of Pure Reason*. He snorted at the idea, but it still haunted him. In the corner of his mind's eye was the shape of a super-college professor and statesman—someone like Woodrow Wilson. And once when he had seen Bascom Olin come into the board room, the disdainful phrase, "wordly success," had leaped to mind.

Adam had learned that the town and his profession did not mix well. A town of fifty thousand was simply not large enough to absorb an unlimited amount of stocks and bonds, and Adam, chafing at this limitation, was tempted at times to sell by high pressure to people who lacked the resources to invest in stocks. Mr. Chisholm had made his first fortune selling securities, but his success meant that the securities business here was fully exploited. He had over the years won the confidence of the town, and now he had the help of a long bull market to reinforce this confidence.

Adam's childhood visits had been too brief, and he had settled here too late to have any really close friends in Mercer, but for business reasons he exerted himself to know as many people as possible. Most of them now seemed to be duplicates of others he had met. Only five or six years ago, when he was in his early twenties, he had been aware of change—of new friends, new experiences, books he could get excited about. Now his own ambitions and little else excited him. He thought his growing inflexibility might arise from too strong a feeling of duty about his work. He had the responsibility of investing other peoples' money, and he could not afford to be distracted from it.

Adam was telephoning a customer when he saw Mr. Chisholm's silhouette reflected in the glass wall before him. Mr. Chisholm spoke to customers as he moved toward his office. He was about fifty, slender, nearly bald, with a fine worried face and an air of aristocratic awkwardness. He had been a Rhodes scholar, and his voice still sounded markedly crisp and correct.

Despite Mr. Chisholm's success he seemed to be an unhappy man. His childless marriage was often blamed for this. Adam sensed also that he wanted more solitude than his way of life permitted. His business brought him into contact with people almost constantly, and his wife demanded incessant social activity.

Adam caught himself unconsciously acquiring some of Mr. Chisholm's mannerisms. For example he would swear a listener to secrecy before giving him some not altogether vital information. Mr. Chisholm, Adam realized, had gotten into this habit because his wife talked indiscreetly. Reamer had picked it up too because he thought Mr. Chisholm used it deliberately as a promotional stratagem. "I'd as soon you didn't tell anybody this," Reamer would say to a customer, "but Allied Chemical looks mighty good today."

A half-hour passed before Adam could arrange to see Mr. Chisholm alone. "I'd rather this be confidential, Mr. Chisholm; a party has asked me to handle a stock purchase for him apart from this firm. I'd like to get your permission before going ahead with it."

"Sit down, Adam." Mr. Chisholm sat back and looked at him. "Stock in a local concern?"

"I'm not permitted to say where the company is, Mr. Chisholm."

"How can I give my permission, Adam? There are certain ventures which I wouldn't want anyone in this firm to undertake because they might be bad for public confidence."

"It's a completely honest business, Mr. Chisholm."

"I'm sure it is. But I have to be concerned with appearances."

Adam got up. "I see what you mean, Mr. Chisholm. I'll ask if I can tell you something definite about it."

"I appreciate your not just going ahead with it on the sly."

Adam returned to his desk and once more telephoned the Garth house and was again told that Josephine was out. He had called her several times that day, for the conversation he had overheard about her worried him. He hoped to see her when he went to confer with Dr. Garth that afternoon.

6

〜〜〜〜〜〜〜〜〜〜〜〜〜〜〜〜〜〜〜〜〜〜〜〜〜〜〜〜〜〜〜〜〜〜〜〜〜

Driving up the mountain, the Buttermilk Road tilted so that it seemed to Adam that he was rising into the sky. New honeysuckle bloomed along the roadway, which the hot weather made powerfully sweet.

A slim young colored man opened the Garths' door for Adam and said that Dr. Garth was lying down.

"Cato?" Josephine's voice came from upstairs.

"Josephine, it's Adam."

"Hey, Adam. I've just gotten out of the shower. I'll be right down."

"Take your time."

The windows were shut in the southwest parlor, and the room had an air of grottolike coolness and quiet. As anxious as Adam was to talk with Josephine, he was glad to be alone here for a few minutes.

On a big table he noticed a book, the only book in the room. The title was *The Cathexis of the Organon* by Walter Silberner, M.D. "Amazing man, Dr. Garth," Adam said to himself, "still keeping up with his profession." Adam leafed through the book and recoiled from the stretches of psychoanalytic exposition. Dr. Silberner, he discovered, was also author of *Vilification-Dreams and Affect-Energy* and a half-dozen monographs still to be translated from the German.

"Adam, it's so good to see you!" Josephine greeted him with a magnificent smile, and this time he believed her high spirits were genuine.

"Something happened I wanted to tell you about. But you're going out."

"Later. Let's have a drink first."

"Listen, before I went to Atlanta Tuesday," he said, embarrassed at the memory, "I stopped at a filling station across from the Mercer Motor Company. A man was talking on the telephone in there, and it turned out he was describing you and the car you'd just bought to someone he called 'Jamie.' Does any of that ring a bell?"

She frowned and shook her head. Adam described the man and concluded by saying: "I'm sure you wouldn't know him. That's what's puzzling. I thought it might have something to do with trying to sell you a car, but they talked about license plates and generally that doesn't fit."

"Don't tell Daddy about it," she said. She got up and dodged around the peninsular curve of the piano with a sidewise motion of her hips, and without touching the curtains which hung down like a bank of icicles she peered out a front window. Blakely was right: his cousin Josephine did have a splendid figure. "Adam, I've had the idea yesterday and today that somebody's following me."

She gestured toward the window, and he looked down the green lawn, across which the shadow of the mountain had risen. "Can you see an old logging road over there?"

Adam looked. The trees on the mountainside made a solid wall of green. "No."

"It's about halfway up. A couple of times I've seen a car up there." While she talked, she fiddled with her wrist watch, turning it as though it were uncomfortable, and he saw that it had a dazzling crust of diamonds on the band. "The sun flashed on the windshield, or I'd never have noticed it. I think someone's been parking up there to watch this house. It's the only place where you can watch it really.

"Sometimes a car—the same one, I think—drives past here very slowly. I saw it in the rear-view mirror yesterday more than once. But as you know, I have the feeling that everybody here's staring at me anyway."

"What does the driver of the car look like?"

"I haven't gotten a close look at him yet."

"What kind of car?"

"Old and faded. Sometimes it looks green and in some lights gray or blue."

"I'd notify the police."

"I'm afraid they'll come around asking questions and get Daddy upset. Daddy's why I came home. You heard about his fainting. You hadn't? Well, I'm afraid it may have been a light stroke." As she talked, she leaned on the grand piano and pinched petals from a skillfully arranged group of flowers in a vase. "Anyway he ought not to have any excitement."

"Still if this person's up to no good—let me do some checking. I've got a friend on the police force."

"Really, Adam, I don't want the mess if there's nothing to it."

"I'll do it quietly."

She turned to the window and looked out at the mountain again. Then she made a slow circuit of the parlor and library windows. Adam followed, groping for an image of this dim man and his chameleon automobile, and looking over her shoulder and seeing nothing where she seemed to see something, for she would stop and stare for several seconds. "Let's go out on the patio. The air's fresher out there," she said. "Would you turn on that light by you, Adam? On the piano there." He turned and felt for the lamp switch, and at the same moment he saw her in the mirror pull open the heavy drawer of a mahogany table and make a hurried movement with her hands. She's hiding something in the drawer, he thought. As she leaned over, the reflection of her dark shiny hair mixed with the faded gold flowers etched in the mirror. She pushed the drawer back with the pressure of her palms and thighs.

"This way," she said as he turned to her.

She led him through the dining room and opened some French doors on a patio paved with brick and enclosed by a boxwood hedge.

"Do your servants live on the place?"

"No, Daddy had the last servants' quarters torn down about four years ago."

"It seems to me I remember the young colored man who answered the door."

"That's Rutherford. He's not so young as he looks; he's forty-five and he has seven children. His wife, Willie May, cooks for us. When Rutherford came back here after he got out of the army, he told Daddy he was going to Detroit some day because he ought to earn good money for his children's sake. He didn't know when he was going, but he just wanted Daddy to know he wasn't permanent. That was eleven years ago. Daddy hasn't held that against him exactly, but he's been cool toward Rutherford and hasn't taken a personal interest in him since then."

"You're pretty isolated here. Look, Josephine. It doesn't sound frightening, but it doesn't sound right. Better let me look into it."

"All right, the next time I see that car, I'll get the license number."

"Good. Then I can see if the owner has a police record or—"

The sound of chimes interrupted him, and Josephine got up at once. "There's the doorbell. Excuse me," she said and hurried inside. "I'll get it, Rutherford," she called on the run.

Adam heard the front door open and low voices. Silence followed. Then came a burst of talk, and Josephine reappeared through the dining-room doors followed by a stranger.

"Adam, this is Cato Herold. My cousin, Adam Salter."

The man was shorter than Adam and seemed about his age. His hair was blond, thick, and cut close in a style which suggested a gentlemanly athlete. He had a broad forehead and a bony humorous face. Moving slowly, he took Adam's hand in a strong handclasp.

"Cousin? I'd have known you anywhere from the portrait. Is your full name Adam Garth Salter?" Adam nodded. "There is an amazing resemblance between you and your ancestor in there," Herold said, gesturing.

"I don't feel that fierce though. He was a colonel under Forrest and like Forrest he was supposed to have kept a razor edge on his saber in violation of the laws of war. He lost an ear at Brice's Cross Roads."

"We still have the ear, Cato," said Josephine. "In a little teak chest. Would you like to see it?"

Herold laughed heartily. "If it's in mint condition, yes. I can tell from your expression that I'm early, Jo, and I'm sorry."

"You can tell no such thing from my expression. I'm glad you did come early so you and Adam could meet. You two call each other by your first names."

Adam noticed Josephine's low neckline with a fleeting glance. She doesn't know how much it shows, he said to himself uneasily.

"Let's have cocktails," she said. "Gin and tonic?"

"Just ginger ale for me," said Adam. "I have some work to do tonight."

"I'll get Rutherford to bring it out," said Josephine, moving toward the door.

Herold stopped her. "You look lovely, Jo," he said, inspecting her. "You really do." Her blush and delighted smile made her look very young.

When she had gone, Herold turned to Adam and said, indicating the view: "Isn't this magnificent?"

"My favorite."

"Buttermilk Road. Where'd that name come from?"

"Before it was paved, farmers said the road was so rough that if you started in with a can of milk by the time you got to town it would be churned into buttermilk. Not long ago some real-estate man wanted to give it a name with class like Avalon Terrace, but Dr. Garth got the measure defeated."

"Good for Dr. Garth!"

Josephine had joined them again, and she added: "We haven't very much that's quaint in Sweetwater County, so we treasure what we have."

"You must be visiting in Mercer," Adam said to Herold.

"I'm staying with an old family friend, Belle Wriston."

"Mrs. Wriston is a customer of my firm's."

"What do you do? Wait, wait. You're a stockbroker. Jo's very fond of you, it seems. In fact she once had a crush on you when she was in her teens. Isn't that right, Jo?"

"You shouldn't have told him that, Cato."

Adam colored. "You should have told me yourself, Josephine. After all, how else would I know?"

"You'd have known if you'd looked at me twice. But I was fourteen, and you were a glamorous Air Corps lieutenant." She sat down, and the men drew up chairs around her.

"Of course we aren't accustomed to taking the romantic feelings of a fourteen-year-old seriously," said Herold. "How strange it is to consider that in earlier times, even in the Western world, it was not at all uncommon for a woman to marry at fourteen or younger. Venetian girls of the Renaissance married at twelve, and one still single at sixteen was pitied as an old maid."

Adam listened coldly and stiffly.

"It is curious too," Herold went on, "that opinions about the ideal age for a woman—wife or mistress—should vary so widely. You can see that I have made a study on this. We have Plutarch's observation that when Antony met Cleopatra, she was the perfect age for a mistress. She was then twenty-eight. That isn't far out from the result of a recent Gallup poll which indicated that on the average Americans believe that a woman reaches her peak of beauty at the age of thirty."

Rutherford brought out a tray of bottles, glasses, and ice, and Josephine mixed their drinks.

"Théophile Gautier has one of his characters express the view that twenty-six is best, and a creature of Maupassant's says that the 'right age' is eighteen." Herold accepted his gin and tonic and sipped it. "And our own Benjamin Franklin swears that for physical and other reasons a woman past middle age is the best mistress. Balance against that the conviction of Arab slavers, backed by the cold cash of their customers—slavery still flourishes in the Middle East, you know—that a female child of twelve or thirteen is worth several times as much as a woman in her twenties."

"And which one is right?" Josephine said with a teasing smile.

"It all depends on the woman. I'm sure, for example, Jo, that you must be lovelier now than ever before. Isn't that so, Adam?"

"Yes indeed." Adam got up. "It's time for me to be going."

"Wait," said Herold, glancing at his watch. "We're just going to Belle's for a very informal party. Buffet supper or some such. Why don't you come along?"

"Do come," said Josephine.

"Thanks, but I really can't tonight," said Adam. "I'd like to use your telephone before I go."

"Let me show you." Josephine led him through the hallway to her father's study and turned on a light over the desk. She stood close enough for him to catch a whiff of light perfume. "Here, you can shut all the doors."

"He calls you Jo. Is that what you want to be called?"

"Josephine's so long," she said almost apologetically. "It doesn't matter though. How do you like Cato?"

"He's very entertaining."

"I think so too." She stood looking at Adam, the light overhead reflected in her sparkling eyes, her earrings, and her wet lips. "Adam, I'd love for you to come with us if you'd care to."

"Another time, thanks."

She put her hands on his shoulders lightly and kissed him on one cheek. "Goodnight, Adam," she said and whirled away.

He knew his way very well, and she had shown him to this study to ask for an approving opinion of Herold. He reflected on this, rubbing the moist place on his cheek where she had kissed him. He was becoming aware of a powerful aversion to being alone that evening.

He dialed the Myerson's number. The line was busy, and he hung up and swiveled impatiently in Dr. Garth's chair.

On the desk was a photograph of Josephine taken when she was about fourteen years old. Her hair was lighter then, and her face looked soft, vague, and sweet. This was the Josephine he felt he knew.

Through the window he saw Josephine and Cato walk to an open convertible in the driveway. He had just enough light to see them. The car did not start at once, and Adam deliberately looked away.

He dialed the number again. Mrs. Myerson finally answered the telephone and told him that Blakely was out and not expected home until late.

He was turning out the light over the desk when it struck him that Blakely was probably going to Mrs. Wriston's party. The thought filled him with a dismal feeling of being left out, and the unsuccessful telephone call made him feel foolish besides. He had not felt this way for ten years.

He stood up and saw that Herold's convertible was still outside. He decided to accept Herold's invitation and went to the open window to call to them.

He saw them more clearly from the window. Herold was lean-ing over Josephine, her head thrown back exaggerating the curve of her throat, and he was kissing her on the mouth. His mouth moved to her cheek, and Adam saw that her eyes were closed and her lips were parted in a smile.

He stared in dismay, then tore himself from the window, and walked through the library to the parlor. He heard the motor start, and a moment later headlights swept along the side of the house, made a swooping curve down the driveway where they seemed to flicker in the intervening tree trunks and then disappear.

Adam kept staring. The headlights flashed in the opening at the curve of the Buttermilk Road and were gone.

He turned then to the big mahogany table to find out what Josephine had taken the trouble to hide. He opened the drawer and found inside only *The Cathexis of the Organon.*

From the corner of his eye he saw a great black silhouette and turned hastily. Dr. Garth stood in the doorway. His eyes shone with reptilian glassiness, and his pupils were enormous, as though he had been looking into a pit.

"Uncle Ive? It's Adam."

Dr. Garth lowered himself slowly into a chair. "What do you want?" He spoke in a remote husky voice.

"Sir, I've got the money, but Mr. Chisholm says he has to know more about this project before he can approve it. Can I tell him?"

Dr. Garth did not answer, and Adam drew closer in alarm. "Are you ill, sir?"

Dr. Garth shook his head. "I'll talk with you about this later. I don't feel up to it now."

"Of course."

Adam started for the door and was stopped by Dr. Garth's voice, which sounded hardly human—more like a branch scraping against the side of the house. "You think Chisholm can keep it from Bascom Olin?"

"I'm sure he can."

"Tell him what he has to know."

When Adam got behind the wheel of his car, he realized that he was unaccountably exhausted and streaming with sweat.

~~~~~~~~~~~~~~~~~~~~~~~~~~~~~~~~~~~~~~~

7

Bob Reamer greeted Adam the next morning with the words: "Did you hear? Liberty Mills is shut down. They're going to sell the equipment to the Japs for practically nothing. The textile business in this town is really shot to hell." He sat on the corner of Adam's desk and took a small feminine envelope from his pocket. "Did you get yours?"

"What's that, Ream?"

His face triumphant, Reamer slid from the envelope a folded piece of gaily colored stationery. "Invitation to the Chisholm's party? Oh yes," said Adam. "I'd forgotten all about it. That's not today, is it?"

"No, it'll be a week from tomorrow," Reamer said, disappointed. "I guess that means you're taking Blakely."

"It sure does. By the way, is Mr. Chisholm back yet?"

"Yeah, but he's on long distance. Wheeling and dealing." Abruptly Reamer made a pantomine of mock panic and said from the side of his mouth, as he stepped out of Adam's office: "It's a raid. Don't give your right name."

The man approaching Adam's office was a city detective, Clyde Lavender. This inappropriate name seemed to excite him to a perpetual expression of belligerence. He was Adam's age but looked older, for he was getting fat and bald. "That fellow that was bothering Miss Garth," Clyde said. "Up on that logging road you told me about. I got him. He had binoculars and a camera and all. You ever know James Sizemore? Used to be a claims-chaser for a used-car lot here. Big, blond-headed fellow. He got in trouble once for sending dirty pictures through the mail. Anyway he's a private detective now. He was hung over, smelled like a brewery. Sprised the hell out of me that he was a detective. Works out of Birmingham. He knew his rights, and I couldn't scare him into telling me anything."

"What did you make of it, Clyde?"

"It beats me," Clyde said. "I told him to stay away from Miss Garth. If he keeps bothering her, you make a complaint, and I'll run him in."

As soon as Clyde was gone. Adam telephoned the Garths' house. Once again Josephine was out.

Adam looked over the board room. Before him he saw the usual backs of heads and hats of customers who were torpidly watching the tracks left by the market on the Translux screen. He inquired to see if he could interest anyone in buying securities, then made a series of telephone calls to customers.

He was between calls when he recognized the back of a head which did not belong in the board room. It was Cato Herold.

Hatless, and wearing a light cotton suit, he was smoking and looking over the Translux screen and the customers, and seemed entertained by what he saw. He hasn't come to buy stocks, Adam thought.

Adam was signaled to the telephone, and when he hung up, Herold was waiting, very relaxed, outside his door and still absently surveying the board room. "Come in. Sit down."

"Tell me," said Herold, smiling, "do these men all buy stocks or are some only loitering as I am?"

"They all have some stocks. Otherwise it would be dull—like playing poker for matches."

"I like your simile."

Adam tried to think of some small talk, but the disagreeable curiosity he had felt about Herold defeated him.

"I'm sorry you wouldn't join us last night. Jo and I had no hand in the guest list or you'd have been invited ahead of time. Jo is a great admirer of yours."

"I've always been fond of her."

"The most attractive woman I've ever met," Herold said vehemently. "A remarkable beauty. Am I deluded, or do you suppose it could be so? I mean, why isn't every unmarried man in Mercer pounding on her door?"

"I think they all have at one time or another," Adam said, stiffening.

"Don't be alarmed. I'm not the out-of-town suitor investigating the object of my affections on her home ground. No, I know her too well to believe any evil of her even if I heard it. I hadn't counted on finding any such woman as Josephine," Herold went on. "And I shouldn't have. I can hardly afford it. You see, I'm supposed to rest for a year—do nothing, under a doctor's orders, and after that, be moderate."

These words prompted Adam to study his visitor. Herold's face was sensitive and intelligent with pointed nose and ears. His face and neck were tanned and hard-looking, but the lines around his eyes suggested either dissipation or ill-health.

"But Josephine is a wonderful girl. Tell me, Adam," Herold said, his eyes bright and alert, "what was she like as a child?"

"She was a smart attractive little girl. Very bright-minded but willful too, and as a teen-ager she was unusually conscientious. Pretty and thin, as she is now."

Herold laughed. "Oh, yes. Thin! Skeletal!" He saw that Adam was serious, and he stopped laughing. "The scales of kinship have formed on your eyes, Adam. If you think she is thin, have another look at her. Although she is not fat, she is hardly thin."

Adam smiled uncomfortably, and his face flushed. At the moment he could not visualize Josephine at all, and Herold's remark made him feel confused and at a disadvantage.

"I suppose I'm really too old for Josephine," Herold said sadly. "It's not that she makes me feel old. On the contrary she makes me feel young. That's what seems ominous. I believe you yourself are too young to know what I mean." He sat for a moment without speaking, and a muscle in his jaw twitched.

Over Herold's head Adam saw Mr. Chisholm's door open. Herold noticed the momentary flicker of Adam's attention and got up at once. "I'd better be going. I hope I haven't delayed your work irretrievably. I'm staying at Belle Wriston's, you know, in her guest house. Come over and join me for a drink. Any time really. I'm a night owl. You pick the time, Adam. You're the busy one."

"I'd like to, Cato. Glad you came in."

Watching Herold go, Adam realized that he liked him better now though not without misgivings, and he wondered if Herold had come to win his sympathy by representing himself as the victim of Josephine's magnetism.

Bob Reamer was watching Herold also. "Who in hell was that? Leslie Howard?"

"That's Cato Herold. He does look a little like Leslie Howard, Ream. He may turn out to be an even better actor."

Reamer gave him a puzzled glance, and Adam got up and walked past him to the door of Mr. Chisholm's office. Mr. Chisholm was washing down small white pills with water from a paper cup. Adam tapped on the open door, and Mr. Chisholm turned quickly. "Yes?"

"Mr. Chisholm, I'd like to talk with you for a minute."

"A minute's about all the time I have."

"Mr. Chisholm, I know I can trust you to keep this strictly secret." Adam pushed the door shut behind him. "That stock-buying I mentioned to you. It's The Taurus Company."

Mr. Chisholm nodded glumly. "I thought that might be it."

"You'd heard about it from someone else?"

"No, call it intuition. I haven't time to go into it."

"All I want is your approval for going ahead with buying the stock," Adam said.

"I don't approve. With listed stocks or over-the-counter stocks with active markets and published quotations, stock prices are a matter of public knowledge. And I should have no objection to your disposing of securities like those of The Taurus Company if some stockholder came to you and asked you to sell them. But you're doing this secretly, and no matter how much you pay for the Taurus stock, if it does well later, some persons are going to say that you, an employee of Duncan Chisholm and Company, tricked them into selling for your own profit. Not only are you a broker: every day you advise customers. It may appear later that you gave dishonest advice for personal gain. And if you say you're an agent for an unnamed client, some may even assume that I'm your client. No, I'm sorry, Adam." He reached for the doorknob.

"This is a chance for me to get some capital together," Adam said, stepping forward, and Mr. Chisholm looked at his wrist watch with annoyance. "You know how hard that is to do. It's a chance I can hardly pass up."

Mr. Chisholm turned a cold rigid face to Adam. "Does that mean you're giving notice?"

"No, but I ought to start moving right away on it, or the opportunity will pass. But I won't leave before you can get a replacement."

"Go ahead," said the other in a low voice. "If you have any doubt about my releasing you, you are released. You can clear your desk now. Good day." And he strode through the board room and outside.

Adam's expression gave him away, for as he walked toward his office, Reamer, looking at him with wide eyes, said: "What's the matter? Did he bawl you out or something?"

Adam did not answer. Maybe if I had waited until he was not in a hurry, if I hadn't insisted on having it out right then, this wouldn't have happened, he thought.

In two minutes he had arranged his books and papers on top of his desk. Although he was in a great hurry to get out, Adam typed a summary of the last conference with the pension fund trustees of a local company about its portfolio, put it in an envelope, and left it for Mr. Chisholm. Then he went outside to his car. I've been fired, he thought. No job.

~~~~~~

8

Outside the glare and damp heat felt more like August than April, and the metal parts of his car were almost too hot to touch. He loaded books on finance and other gear into his car and drove south along the main street. Although his forbidding expression had kept Reamer and the women in the office from asking any further questions, Adam felt self-conscious and angry about their looks of sympathetic dismay. The thought of Mr. Chisholm's former benevolence was more disagreeable than of his summary action just now. Adam hoped some day to go into business for himself, but this was too much freedom too quickly, and stirred up evil memories of the Salter Webbing Company.

Before he did anything else, Adam wanted to see what he was going to buy, and he drove toward Third Street and the railroad, where the mill was. He had looked up its history and found it closely tied to that of the town. Jeremiah Mercer had predicted in 1800 that here would be "the Southern Pittsburgh" because of "virtually inexhaustible" deposits of coal and iron, but by 1890 the coal and iron had been worked out, the big horseshoe works had been dying, and a hard depression had followed, during which the Square-M Wool Carding and Cotton Yarn Company had gone under. Jeremiah Mercer, "staunchly believing in the future of the town," had bought this company for ten cents on the dollar.

In 1905, James Monroe Mercer, upon succeeding his father, had renamed it The Taurus Company after the zodiacal sign under which he was born. He had floated a new issue of common stock, to which the Garths and other prominent families had subscribed, dropped the wool operation, and added a weave room and finishing plant for the production of toweling. When it was believed that Southern labor lacked the skill to make fine cotton goods, he had relabeled and transshipped his towels through Philadelphia. Between 1905 and 1940 he had increased the sales twenty-fold to nine million dollars annually.

Mr. Mercer had suffered a coronary thrombosis in 1940, after which he had become fearful and cautious, believing until 1945 that the war would last forever, and afterward dreading a bottomless depression. He had therefore hoarded the company's cash by paying out little in dividends and less for modernization and expansion. No employee of his had ever had a free hand, and growing older, he had become both feebler and more arbitrary. The Korean War had satisfied his feelings of disaster, and in August 1950, he had died at peace.

At some distance from the railroad Adam noticed a brick building surrounded by waist-high weeds, which he thought must be an abandoned warehouse. He drove around this building and came to a sign: THE TAURUS COMPANY. Beyond was the main building, a city-block long and four stories high, of brick the color of bloody gums and windows painted blue.

Adjoining the cotton warehouse was a small concrete-block outbuilding which contained cotton waste. As Adam sat there, he noticed with a feeling of unreality that the piles of waste were moving, and curiosity made him get out of his car and step inside the open door. The moving piles were swarms of rats eating seeds in the waste.

Everything that was wrong with the company came to him then—its second-rate management, its bad earnings prospects, the dilapidated state of the building, and very likely, he suspected the obsolescence of its equipment. A powerful irrational force had been operating on him—the glorification of everything about the Garths, which had made him accept Dr. Garth's judgment over his own. Glancing back at the building, he thought: this is what I should have seen before I lost my job. He had only Dr. Garth's word that he would buy the stock at seventy-five dollars a share— if he lived.

Adam drove to his apartment and there again studied the last annual report of The Taurus Company. It was hard to concentrate because he kept thinking that his own income had stopped whereas his expenses ran on. He had sold his stocks, and his dividends were halted. If he had held his stocks until today, they would have been worth four hundred dollars more, and the borrowed money was costing him twenty dollars a day.

Momentarily he regretted his old job at Selburn Warden and Stone. He could still get it back, but if he left Mercer, it would be with the idea of making a fortune and returning in triumph.

He inspected pages of his own neat figuring. Aside from machinery, the mill's apparent liquidating worth was roughly sixty dollars a share. So if he paid more than that and Dr. Garth died of a stroke, liquidation could ruin him. The Taurus Company's too strong to go out of business, he told himself. But that's what people had said about Liberty Mills.

The company's value depended also on two esoteric figures. One, Domestic Corporation Stock, at three hundred thousand dollars on the balance sheet, was Liberty Mills, on which liquidating dividends would soon be paid, and Sweetwater Pipe Company. The other was stock in a subsidiary, carried at fifty thousand dollars. Adam did not feel hopeful about these items, for evidently receipts from them, under Sundry Income, were only eight hundred dollars for the past year. He stared at these figures for several minutes. Then he telephoned Dr. Garth.

Dr. Garth sounded displeased at the news that Adam had left Duncan Chisholm. "That took some nerve, Adam. I hope you won't regret it."

"In a way I already regret it, but it was the only way to put this deal over."

"This means you can start seeing the stockholders now."

"I'm going to look over what I'm buying first. I wanted to ask you about the balance sheet. Liberty Mills and Sweetwater Pipe stock carried at three hundred thousand dollars. What is it really worth?"

"Substantially more. I don't know exactly how much."

"What is this subsidiary?"

"It's a real-estate holding company."

"What real estate? Not the mill village. That's listed separately."

Dr. Garth hesitated. "No, it's rural land the company bought when the city was considering some outrageous tax on corporations. When the mayor saw that we were serious about moving out, he dropped it."

"Fifty thousand dollars' worth of rural land?"

"Some of it was also an investment."

"What's the name of the subsidiary?"

"I don't recall. Some outlandish name Monroe Mercer selected."

"Would you get the details about it from the company?"

"No, it'll make Quigley suspicious."

"I think I'll look up the deed," Adam said. "When was it bought?"

"It was 1938 or 1939." Dr. Garth seemed short of breath and hardly even interested in discussing the subject, and Adam hung up with increased misgivings about Dr. Garth's health and faculties.

Adam spent all that day at the record rooms in the courthouse. He came across plenty of exotic corporate names. He felt especially sanguine about the Gorgon Land Company, but he could not connect it or any of a dozen others with The Taurus Company.

Early in the evening he telephoned Josephine and told her what Clyde Lavender had found out. "I went by the Magnolia Hotel, but this private detective had checked out, and his telephone in Birmingham doesn't answer. He must be a screwball, Peeping Tom or something."

She forced a laugh. "Sounds like it."

"He used to work here as a collection agent for a used-car company. James Sizemore. Ever heard that name?"

"Never. So let's forget it."

Her manner seemed cool, and he realized that she was not alone, and couldn't talk freely, and he quickly concluded the conversation.

He was waiting at the door of the probate record room when it opened the next morning.

Within ten minutes, from the reverse index of 1937 conveyances, a name jumped at him—The Scorpio Corporation. The address in the tax records was P.O. Box 1914—The Taurus Company's. The real estate turned out to be five acres of rural land, unimproved, and the tax stamps on the deed showed a value of five hundred dollars. That left $49,500 worth of real estate unaccounted for.

Nor could Dr. Garth explain the discrepancy. Was there another subsidiary? No. Was it in another county?

"It could be," said Dr. Garth impatiently, "but you're spending too much time on this. You need to be seeing stockholders."

"I'll get to that right away."

"It's not just the time. If you go around asking questions, it will alert Olin before you get to any stockholders."

"I'll make it quick. I'm going to have a look at the records in Clayton. I'll call you when I get back."

Clayton was the county seat of Wylie County, forty miles southwest of Mercer. Its main street was almost identical with Mercer's. J. C. Penney and Woolworth displayed the same merchandise in their windows, and the First National banks and Greyhound bus stations were on similar corners. Both courthouses were of red brick with indistinguishable ranting preachers and congregations on their lawns, and inside was the same public smell of germicides and troubled humanity.

There Adam found the rest of Scorpio's land. Township 13, Range 5, Sections 21, 22, 23, 26, 27, 28, and 33, plus Fractions A and B in Section 29. Adam traced the full sections on a topo map—forty-five hundred acres, green and rolling, without any improvements. Fractions A and B were just off the edge of the Clayton Quadrangle map.

When Adam left Clayton for the Scorpio land, it was an unusually still bright afternoon, but quickly the sky became overcast with a winter weight of clouds, and the wind rose. The farms he passed were returning to forest, and rotting farmhouses looked as though the land had been struck by a plague.

He wanted to see Fractions A and B. Fractions on a map usually indicated the existence of some natural barrier such as shoreline, and he wanted to see if this part of the Scorpio land held any improvements of value.

He turned at the best landmark on his map, an abandoned church, and within a mile from the highway, just about where his map ended, the dirt road became too rough for his car, and he slung his binoculars over his shoulder and started walking.

The road twisted and dipped into a swamp. He saw trees here which he had no idea grew in this part of the state—cycads and cypress, hemlocks, ironwoods larger than he had seen. Now and then above the shrill noise of insects and frogs he thought he heard voices, but it turned out to be the wind. A rank crawfish odor with just a kiss of sulfur in it came from wet ground.

Once he thought he saw a man watching him from behind a tree, but it turned out to be a tumor of knartion.

The ground sloped up, the roar of the wind grew so loud he could hear nothing else, and the woods became dwarfed and sparse. The leaves around him looked bleached with a fine powder, and a smell reached him like the smell of the ocean.

A sign stood in the middle of the road: KEEP OUT.

From beyond, the glare was so great that he did not see the rusty barbed wire and snagged his leg on it.

He came upon railroad tracks and followed them in. This siding must have cost a fortune, he was thinking, because the nearest rail line was miles away.

The tracks led him around a hummock to a cluster of buildings. These would be close to the center of Fraction A. This is the secret, he thought, this is why Dr. Garth wants The Taurus Company. High above him to the right was a line of machines and vehicles. Below was the river, broad and sluggish.

Adam walked toward the buildings, and beyond them was a crater a half mile across and a hundred feet deep, its sides wrinkled and mottled white and purple like bruised skin, a great withered sphincter. That ocean smell here was more like the stink of an alligator pit.

The crater, the shadowless day, the line of buildings gave him a feeling that he had been here before, but he decided as he breathed polluted air that it was rather a dismal feeling he would some day come again.

He was still so dazzled with the glare that he did not notice until he knocked on the door of the nearest building, that the wood had turned to a web of rot which flittered at his touch. He looked again at the line of machines above him. The front loader was rusty and ancient; the nearest trucks were of some extinct make.

Facing the river was a sign, as though the operators had expected traffic to rise from the greasy water, and craving an explanation, Adam walked down toward it.

He found there the bleached word: KIESELGUHR. Under it were smaller letters too decayed to read. "The whole place should be grown up in weeds," he said.

It had been a mining operation, perhaps for sand and gravel. The dust here was as fine as talcum powder, and he took samples and put them in an envelope. The dust made it hard to breathe, and gave him a feeling of lassitude and futility and a desire to get back to the shade.

The wind was too loud for him to hear it, but from the corner of his eye, he saw something move among the machines above him. He turned to see that an old automobile had left its place and was moving soundlessly toward him.

It came within a few feet of him, driverless, and a dozen yards past him the dust it made, as dense as smoke, as though it ignited the ground it passed over, concealed it.

When the dust cleared, Adam coughing violently, saw that it had lost a wheel and turned over at the riverbank.

The road on which Adam stood ran from the river over the hill, and he followed it up. Southward was the swamp he had come through. Before him lay a magnificent pine forest.

If the timber were nearly as good as it looked, here was a half million dollars not shown on the Taurus balance sheet. It was not anything to lose his head over, but this land could make the difference between his making money and being ruined. Now he could go after the stock with confidence and enthusiasm.

Could Dr. Garth have been unaware that The Taurus Company owned valuable land? No, Dr. Garth knew, and for some reason he wasn't talking about it.

He turned eastward again and started toward his car. There were fresh tire tracks from a side road, and at this intersection he found a sign dangling with rot and frosted with fine dust. BUTTER-MILK ROAD. Then he knew where he was. Below was the old ferry landing, across the river was Sweetwater County, and only a few miles away was the Garth house.

~~~~~~

9

At sunset as Adam followed the crooked highway back to Mercer, he reviewed the talk he had just finished with a Taurus stockholder in Clayton, Reuben Skinner. Skinner was a white-haired insurance man with a canine face and a hearty voice. Adam started by offering him thirty dollars each for his fifty shares of Taurus stock at once. Skinner insisted on telling the details of his swapping a building lot in Clayton to a neighbor, a former superintendent of The Taurus Company, for the stock.

Because Skinner continued talking, Adam believed that he was interested in selling, but the conversation strayed, from a chain saw this superintendent had borrowed and kept for two years, to business in Clayton and the mills there. Adam began to suspect that Skinner was an unusually talkative man who did not plan to do any more work that day and who had no intention of selling his stock. Adam grew restless. He tried to direct the conversation back to The Taurus Company, but Skinner escaped him. How about insurance? How well was Adam covered? It was like wrestling with fog. Adam got up. "Well, it's suppertime, Mr. Skinner. Here's my top price," said Adam. "Fifty dollars per share." Skinner replied in a sonorous voice: "Let me talk with my wife about it." And Adam fled.

He believed now that he had offered too little at the start. Dr. Garth had been right: he should have begun higher to jar Skinner's stock loose. He reviewed the stockholders' list, and a name kept pushing itself forward: Mercer Davenport, grandson of the town's founder and owner of two thousand shares. He hadn't been in Mercer for thirty years and his relatives here had lost touch with him. He was said to have homes in New York and Florida. He might be hard to reach in person, but he had enough stock to make the effort worth while.

It was a long way around from Kieselguhr through Clayton back to Mercer, and Adam got to the first traffic light outside Mercer at a quarter of seven. Mercer was several hundred feet higher than Clayton, and the nights were cool. It seemed to Adam that the air was cleaner in Mercer, the sky bluer.

When he reached his apartment building, he hardly noticed a dapper figure sitting in a canvas lawn chair in the gloom of the court. "Mr. Salter, could I have a word with you?" It was G. P. Moon, the last purchaser of Taurus stock.

Moon, a lean man in his forties, wore a dark blue suit set off by bright socks and a new hat with a gay striped band. Under the hat, Adam remembered, Moon's hair was gray and thick like wolf fur with no white or black in it. He wore gold-rimmed glasses and had a scholarly expression like a phrenologist. He was a lawyer and a hanger-on of Bascom Olin's, not the kind of lawyer Olin would get to handle corporation business, but Moon hoped to be, and in the meantime he was glad enough to get odd jobs which Olin gave him.

Moon had been born on a farm near Wylie Forge in the poorer, more mountainous part of Sweetwater County, where the principal industry was making moonshine whisky. It was said that before he became a lawyer, he had for a year been a touring hygiene lecturer on theater stages with a movie about white slavery or venereal disease called *Virgin for a Night*. The job as sanctifier of a salacious film seemed to have developed in him a winning quality of earnestness and gravity.

He had married a Reamer, and his only son was named Bascom in honor of his patron. It was said in Mercer: if you want to buy anything, see G. P. Moon, he knows where to buy it. You want to know something, Moon knows it.

"You got a minute?" said Moon.

Adam took a chair and waited. "These are nice apartments," said Moon, lounging back and smoking a cigarette. "If I had it to do over again, I'd rent an apartment. I wouldn't buy a house. You're doing the smart thing to stay right here, especially being a bachelor and all."

"Uh huh." Adam wondered if Moon had heard about his leaving Duncan Chisholm and had come to find out why. No, Moon wouldn't make a trip up here just for that. Adam said nothing but waited for the reason to come out.

"Mr. Salter, how would you like to buy some stock?"

"What stock?"

"In The Taurus Company."

Adam experienced an abrupt acceleration of his body processes, which jolted his heart and entrails. He felt as though hidden cameras and tape recorders had picked up everything he had said and done that day. It seemed that the man sitting before him had removed a mask to reveal Bascom Olin himself.

"What made you think I'd be interested?" Adam said in a husky voice.

Moon chuckled. "Well, everybody's bi'ness gets around in a town like Mercer. And see, I got a few shares of the stock myself."

"Want to sell? I'll give you twenty dollars a share for it. That's twice par value."

"I reckon I wouldn't want to sell my own stock. But I might be able to find some for you." He looked at Adam with an intense scholarly expression. "Maybe a thousand shares."

"Wait a minute. At twenty dollars that would be twenty thousand dollars. Do you think I've got that kind of money?"

"I thought maybe somebody you were buying for might have it."

"No, but I'd like to get maybe a hundred or so shares though."

"You just take a shine to The Taurus Company?"

"Well, I thought it might have some promise."

"It don't look so good to me," said Moon. "Paying no dividends for the past year, and from what I hear, them going in the hole this year too. Liberty Mills shutting down and all. You must know something the rest of us don't know." He paused and slouched back in expectant silence.

"You know the old saw: buy 'em when nobody wants 'em."

The silence continued. Adam knew he would have to do better than that. If he were evasive, Olin would suspect that Dr. Garth or some combination was behind Adam. Olin could put a dozen employees into the job of telephoning stockholders, saying: "Don't sell until you've talked with me."

"The reason I ast you was, I might pick up some stock myself if it looks good. And if you can't use but a hundred shares, there ought to be enough left over for me." Moon's voice sounded completely relaxed. "See what I had in mind was a swap of information."

"Can I trust you to keep it quiet?" Adam whispered.

"Sure," said Moon, also lowering his voice, "I want some of that stock too."

"They're going to cut the melon," said Adam hoarsely. "Two-for-one split."

Moon apparently had heard enough board-room chatter for this talk of a stock split to have a distinctly bullish ring. "So that's it," he said, half to himself.

"Where are you going to get this stock?"

Moon frowned and sucked on his cigarette. He dropped it and mashed it out with the toe of his sharp-pointed two-toned shoe. He seemed suddenly distant and preoccupied, but Adam could detect a well-controlled excitement. "I'm not sure I can get it. I'll get in touch with you."

"You aren't going to forget our deal, are you, Moon?"

Moon stood up. "No, I'll call you."

"Don't tell 'em they're going to split."

"Is the pig's tail pork?" Moon was already walking to his car with his springy slue-footed gait. "Like I said, I might like to get some myself, and I wouldn't want to send the stock sky-high."

Moon had believed him. Now he would go straight to Olin. Olin would know the rumor about the company's splitting its stock was nonsense even if he weren't on the board of directors. This rumor, and the ineffectual low price Adam had offered Moon, would confirm the opinion which Olin had, and Moon had gotten from Olin, that Adam was incompetent, certainly no threat to him, and he would feel there was no hurry about seeing stockholders.

On the other hand it was just possible that Moon had some money of his own and would buy Taurus stock on this rumor, thus making it difficult or impossible for Adam to get any. He couldn't count on Moon's being loyal to Olin or anyone else. Spiritually Moon was like a denizen of some tiny Balkan state artificially created by great powers who can afford no loyalty to anything at all. But he seemed to have something like loyalty to Olin, a certain satisfaction in being an enzyme by which the hunter digested the hunted, and Olin was the richest hunter in Sweetwater County.

Adam's nostrils were full of the smell of his own acid sweat, and his blood was charged not for cool thinking about corporate finance but for some violent exercise like a tavern brawl. He went inside and took a shower, but his muscles were still tight and tingling when he dried off and tried to think.

He sat in his shorts and sipped a cold can of beer. Again and again he went over what he had said to Moon, weighing the chances that it would work. As he cooled down and his muscles loosened, the residue of lies he had just told Moon seemed to form a greasy coating in his mouth.

Moon had come with his own lies, and that made the deception justifiable. And Moon's approach had been insultingly direct. And it's not just my own interest at stake, Adam thought, there's Dr. Garth's. So he had become Dr. Garth's G. P. Moon, doing errands for him and telling his lies, and he felt an urge to call Moon and tell him the truth.

But already this feeling of guilt was slipping away. There were other stockholders to see, especially Mr. Mercer Davenport.

~~~~~~

10

Adam spent the next seventy-two hours visiting stockholders. Late at night he thought about them, sifted the list and rehearsed his talk, and when he did get to sleep for a few hours, he dreamed about a hybrid of The Taurus Company and his father's webbing mill.

He had the same trouble with all the stockholders: they didn't have to sell, for times were prosperous, and the fact that he wanted to buy their stock made them greedy.

One stockholder was Miss Winnie McCaffery, whose house smelled like the eight cats she kept and treated as children. She ignored the fact of his mission; after he had explained with emphasis that she could not afford to take risks whereas he could, she said: "But Mr. Salter, would you *advise* me to sell?" He felt an exasperation then that he did not show. She had trusted him previously when he had sold her Woolworth or Consolidated Edison for their dependable dividends. He repeated that no one knew what would happen to The Taurus Company but dividends this year were unlikely and the company had become now entirely speculative stock. She was a long-faced irritable woman who watched her stocks, and if their market price fell two or three points, she was on the telephone demanding an explanation, but it was still true that he had been assured a profit and he would be making money by persuading her to sell. He refused to give her a summary opinion about selling her stock. It would have to be up to her. So she would go to someone else for advice. Chalk up another for Olin, he thought as he left her.

That day the sky was boiling up for rain. Any moment a wind

would rise and blow out the dust and pollen which sweetened and speckled the air like powder in an unventilated boudoir. He could feel it in the wetness of the air and see it in the shape of the clouds.

He was running out of local prospects, and again he made plans about Mercer Davenport. Through Dr. Garth Adam secured Davenport's address in suburban Connecticut, and Adam telephoned and got no answer.

Davenport had an aunt in town, Mrs. James Monroe Mercer herself, daughter-in-law of the town's founder, who with Robert E. Lee beard and frock coat stood in marble in a public park. Mrs. Mercer had come from a distinguished family: her grandfather had been a Confederate general, her sister had married an English earl, her eldest son had died a hero in the First World War. She was held in respect, even awe, as dowager duchess of Sweetwater County, and not without reason, for she was upright and generous. Her fortune was thought by some to be as great as Bascom Olin's. Certainly the estate of her late husband, for which Olin's bank was trustee, was formidable, containing among more valuable properties three thousand shares of Taurus stock. Adam saw her occasionally in the late afternoon, a figure in black in a long black car driven by a very black chauffeur, taking her daily ride. Dr. Garth had cautioned Adam not to try to buy her stock. He himself would talk to her later but he had no hope of getting any of it since Olin managed her estate.

But at Adam's request Dr. Garth called her about Mercer Davenport. She had not seen her nephew in years. She revealed this fact with a touch of asperity, as though this alienation served the ends of justice. Davenport's domestic troubles had been publicized in a metropolitan gossip column; this fact alone would have deeply displeased Mrs. Mercer. As far as she knew, he still spent his winters in Tarragona, Florida.

What kind of man was Davenport? The last time Dr. Garth had seen him, thirty years ago, he had just been a lanky college boy from an able family. He had inherited a comfortable fortune then, and if he had managed it well or let the right people manage it for him, he should be a multimillionaire now.

Adam telephoned Davenport's home in Tarragona, and on the fourth call a servant answered and said that Mr. Davenport would be out on a cruise until tomorrow. Adam left for Tarragona at four o'clock the next morning. Before breakfast he was out of the acid red clay of the highlands and into the rich pecan- and peach-growing land of South Georgia. He was in Florida by early afternoon, his hands glued to the wheel. He was tormented by the possibility that he was getting not closer to Taurus stock but farther from it. He had called on enough prospects for the price he was offering to reach Olin. He had a dismal presentiment that he would never see Davenport and would return to Mercer to find that Olin had bought all the stock which was for sale and Dr. Garth was too disgusted to speak to him.

The country was getting hotter, more expensive, newer as he moved down the Gulf Coast. It was off-season, and when he reached Tarragona at twilight, its glittering stores and restaurants had the air of a newly created world still waiting for human shapes to materialize and life to begin.

Adam spent four restless hours in this small rich town before anyone answered the door at Davenport's house.

He was a tall man of fifty. His gray hair and pale mustache looked like silver against his deep tan, and he had a long handsome face with small ears close to his head.

"This way, completely air-conditioned. Furnishings go with the house. The price is eighty-five thousand dollars."

Adam looked around. It was a typical Florida house with a lot of glass in it, low blond furniture, brightly colored draperies. Eighty-five thousand dollars was a very handsome price for it. "I didn't come about the house, Mr. Davenport. I'm from your home town. My name is Adam Salter. You may remember my mother, Rachel Garth."

"Why of course!" Davenport's face brightened. He mixed drinks while he asked about others in the Garth family. At mention of Dr. Garth, Davenport said: "Dr. Ivor Garth. That was a hard man. I see now how much you look like him. I ran into his daughter in New York this year. Tall lovely girl. A friend of mine, Cato Herold, was romancing her." Davenport paused, and he seemed about to say something further on this subject, but instead made an exasperated gesture toward the ceiling. "This house business is driving me crazy. These damned real-estate agents told me to ask for just forty-five thousand dollars for this house. Can you imagine? As I told them, I'm entitled to *some* profit." He handed Adam a drink and settled down abruptly. "Well, what can I do for you, Mr. Garth?"

"Salter. I want to buy your Taurus stock."

"Man, people have been trying to buy that stock for fifty years. I used to have a neighbor—Chip Bixby, director of Big Steel and other companies like that—said to me once, 'Mers, sell your little stuff and put all your money into blue chips. You can't watch those little unlisted companies.' You know what I told him? I said: 'Chip, my grandfather founded that company. And I'm not holding that stock just for the money. I don't want to sell and have that stock fall into weak hands.' Old Chip laughed and slapped me on the back and said: 'Mers, you're a damn fool.' " Davenport chuckled with mysterious pleasure at this anecdote. "Now *you* tell *me*, Mr. Garth, why should I sell?"

A key scraped in the front door lock, and Davenport arose eagerly. A young woman entered who for only a moment Adam thought might be Davenport's daughter. She had orange-red hair, was dressed in blouse and shorts. The principal impression she made was of blond beautiful legs. She was Miss Wing. She said in a flat loud voice: "You going to buy the house?"

"Mr. Garth hasn't come about the house, Bunny. In fact, if we can work something out to our mutual satisfaction, we may not have to sell the house." He presented it anxiously as a piece of good news to appease her.

She sat down and, staring at Adam, cried out: "Well, three big cheers for you!" Davenport, smiling indulgently, sat down beside her and patted her hand.

"Go on," he said to Adam.

"You asked why you should sell, Mr. Davenport. Here's why. The Taurus Company is in trouble. Like Liberty Mills, which folded this week." Adam glanced at Miss Wing and saw that her eyes were filmed with boredom. "The Taurus management is weak now, and if the present candidate is put in as general manager, it will be even worse."

Davenport said angrily, with a slight stammer: "Then why did you come all the way down here to buy it? Tell me that."

Adam was relieved at this question, for he had expected Davenport to ask if Dr. Garth, a director and insider, was the real purchaser. "Believe me I don't intend to keep it long."

"How much will you give me for my stock?"

"Fifty dollars a share," said Adam without hesitation.

"I won't consider a cent less than a hundred," said Davenport, tossing his head. "It's a stock with a splendid record—a seasoned stock."

"Maybe, but you should see the mill. It's pretty well seasoned too. I have here a certified check for eighty thousand dollars, and for the balance I'll give you my personal check for twenty thousand." Adam took the certified check from his pocket and dropped it on the coffee table in front of him.

Davenport glided forward to look at the check. "It's made out to me. What made you so sure I'd sell?"

"Because this is just too good an offer for a smart man to turn down."

Davenport's lower teeth chewed on his mustache, and his hand trembled with excitement. The man had had too much to drink for such a transaction even to be legal. Adam picked up the check carelessly and got up. "Why don't you sleep on it?"

"Wait. Have a drink." Davenport frowned with effort. "As you said, it's not possible for me to take an active part in The Taurus Company," he said gravely, stealing glances at Miss Wing, "and perhaps I should turn over this role to an interested man who can attend to the welfare of the company and the town which bears my grandfather's name and my own. *Perhaps.*" Miss Wing got up and wandered away. Staring at her backside, he raised his voice as though to recapture her attention with a golden phrase. "It's a responsibility I cannot, I shall not, shirk. On the other hand perhaps I should reassert an interest in the company—and guide its destinies. I'd hate to have hordes of jobless roaming the streets of Mercer, pillaging and looting, their wives and children starving because I had failed to see my duty and to do it."

Davenport twisted completely around and watched as Miss Wing disappeared into the back of the house. "Sweet little girl, but she doesn't know a damn thing about finance. God, I wish I could say the same about this wife I'm getting loose from right now." He turned back to Adam. "You know why this country has never fulfilled its promise? Because it desperately needs a large and thoughtful leisure class. I told Chip Bixby the other day: 'The brains of society are in and of its leisure class.' "

"That's a novel idea," said Adam, getting up. "When is the earliest I can call you in the morning?"

"Eleven," said Davenport, "or eleven-thirty."

Just before noon the next day Adam found Davenport and Miss Wing in the back yard. Davenport was giggling, gleeful, embracing Miss Wing. Miss Wing wore a sunsuit revealing lovely haunches, and her dark glasses made her face as expressionless as a corpse's. She was trying to escape Davenport's embrace with a squirming squatting motion. Adam backed up. Miss Wing saw him, said something to Davenport, who sobered at once, and smoothing his hair and mustache, turned and greeted Adam. He presented an envelope which contained a certificate for two thousand shares of Taurus stock. Adam had Davenport sign it over to him and gave him the checks. Adam then extended his hand, and Davenport responded with a flabby handshake.

"Give your family my best." Davenport seemed to want to say something more, and Adam waited. Davenport glanced over his shoulder at Miss Wing. "Don't ever leave Mercer. I wish to God I never had."

Adam returned to his car and examined the Taurus certificate, on which was an engraving of a woman like the Statue of Liberty but stripped to the waist.

Davenport had been about to retrench and sell this house until a stranger appeared and dazzled him with a certified check. Adam saw himself as a predator and Mercer Davenport as his natural prey, but because of the latter's air of affluence and his idleness, Adam had felt no qualms during the transaction.

If Dr. Garth lived to buy the stock, Adam would net about $40,000. It was not a fortune, but it could be the beginning of one. Now that this part was over, Adam felt that it had been too easy, too much a matter of luck.

But his misgivings were gone by the time he reached his motel. He was about to send Dr. Garth a victorious wire when his telephone rang.

"Adam? I've been trying to reach you all day," said Dr. Garth. "Don't buy Davenport's stock!"

"But, I *have* bought it!"

Dr. Garth groaned. "Any chance of getting him to call the sale off?"

"No, I'm sure he won't." Adam's throat was thick, and the telephone slippery in his hands. "What's happened?"

"Olin's bought the Cutter stock. The heirs welshed on their promise."

"What do we do now?"

"Just come on back to Mercer as soon as you can."

11

At twilight just north of Columbus, Georgia, Adam smelled rain
in the wind and saw lightning on the horizon. Clouds were growing
thicker and lower. Every point on his dashboard radio sputtered
with static.

He had put the stock certificate in his suitcase, but he had felt
compelled to stop and move it to the breast pocket of his jacket,
so he kept his jacket on in spite of the heat, and now the bulky
envelope seemed to burn his skin through the cloth. When stopping
at a traffic light, he examined the certificate to make sure that sweat
was not blurring Davenport's signature.

He was passing the big drive-in movie theater a few miles southeast of Mercer when the first drop of rain fell like a mouthful of
water on the windshield. The many-colored titans on the movie
screen seemed to grow more frantic as if hurrying to finish before
the storm.

Four or five drops spattered the windshield, then finding their
target, accelerated, and the downpour followed.

It was too late to go to the Garths, but before he went home, he
drove out the Buttermilk Road. A red-shaded lamp burning in the
house made a blur like a bloody fingerprint on his streaming windshield. He would have to wait until morning to see Dr. Garth.

He got soaked running from his car to his apartment door. Inside
he found a vase of red roses on the coffee table. There was no
card; they must be from Josephine. She had gotten the janitor to
let her in. Adam had no particular liking for flowers, but these
roses made him too happy to consider the fact that the gift did
not seem much like Josephine.

He was so worried about the Taurus stock he did not feel sleepy, and he remembered Herold's seemingly heartfelt invitation. And Josephine might be there. Adam realized that his presence might be unwelcome, but he found himself putting on dry clothes and getting ready to go out again.

Herold was staying with Mrs. Wriston, whose high stone house looked down on the lights of Mercer. The guest house Herold was occupying was below it, and so much like the larger house that the latter seemed to have given birth to it.

Adam rang the bell, and its chime was swallowed up in the music and rain. After a minute he rang again, then started away.

Herold's silhouette appeared in the lighted doorway.

"Who's that? Adam! Come in. I've heard all kinds of reports about you, that you'd moved to Florida and the like."

"That I'd been fired? Well, that's about half true."

The room which Adam entered was filled with a feminine smell of parties and lighted by a lamp which threw a soft beam like a tame walleyed moon. The carpet was deep and flesh-colored, and the dark brown wallpaper looked like linen. A big phonograph was spinning out music. "Sit down," said Herold with a smile. "This room expresses Belle's personality exactly, don't you think?"

"I've never met her. Just talked with her on the telephone." Adam took a deep armless chair. "That music sounds familiar. Mozart, isn't it?"

"Yes. *Eine Kleine Nachtmusik*. It doesn't sound as usual because it's played by a string quartet as originally written. There is a lost movement, another minuet and trio. I've often tried to imagine what it would sound like. What do you think? Once I spent several days at a piano trying to compose that minuet. Of course it seemed like a parody afterward and would have been even worse if played as a movement of the serenade."

"I took you at your word about being a night owl," said Adam.

"I was sorry afterward I didn't just say 'owl.' Isn't 'night owl' redundant like 'water fish' or 'play toy'?"

The record ended, and the changer softly flicked on the next record. "You know this? Brahms' first piano concerto?"

"Hey, you're sending in the varsity now."

"Yes, that's the way a piano concerto should begin. Brandy?"

Adam declined. He tapped a familiar volume lying on a table. "I see you have *The Cathexis of the Organon*."

Herold looked surprised. "You know the book?"

"No, but I'm conversant with Dr. Silberner's theories," Adam said, his accent becoming Viennese. "May I recommend for your attention his less popular but more profound monograph, *Vilifica-tion-Dreams and Affect-Energy*. Or *Die Wollust und Die Schreck-lichkeit* in ten volumes if you really want to go into the subject."

Herold looked amazed, then burst out laughing. He flipped open the book and said: "By Jove, he did write *Vilification-Dreams and Affect-Energy!* Somehow I didn't imagine you'd care for that sort of thing."

"I just saw this book at the Garths' and that title happened to stick in my mind."

"Silberner's book made trouble between Jo and her father. He found it and said it was filth. It's not filthy at all, of course, just the usual psychoanalytic subject matter. A lot about incest and the like and case histories. I love a lot of case histories." Herold talked rapidly, uneasily. "Jo'd been having some nightmares, and I thought this might help her to understand them."

"What kind of nightmares?"

"She won't talk about them much." He spoke in such a low voice that Adam had to lean forward to hear. "Oh, monsters, but she won't tell me what goes on. She can't explain her practical interest in the book to her father. There's too much constraint be-tween them to discuss anything so personal."

Adam wanted to pursue this subject, but he did not want to pry, and Herold showed increased reticence. Something's eating him, Adam thought. He was surprised that Josephine and Cato were ending their evenings so early. Perhaps that would explain Herold's mood; they had quarreled, and Herold was worrying about it.

"Do you think there's anything keeping Josephine stirred up? The nightmares are what make me ask."

Herold shook his head. He lit another cigarette, apparently un-aware that he had left another burning on the ash tray beside him.

"She told you about Sizemore?"

Herold looked puzzled, then said: "Oh, yes, that detective. He hasn't been around lately. Probably off molesting little girls some-where." Herold adjusted the phonograph nervously. "But tell me, Adam, what do you plan to do now?"

"Sell securities, I suppose."

"Is there something you'd rather do? Often one finds other professions than one's own attractive but impractical."

"Well, yes. You know Chesterton says that the most thrilling moment in a man's life is when he discovers he is not Robinson Crusoe. I've had that moment. It wasn't thrilling, but it was worth while."

"That's good," said Herold, "very good." He stood up again. "Will you excuse me for a moment?"

"I can't stay," said Adam.

"I'll be right back," said Herold. He walked quickly out through the corridor.

Adam sat there for perhaps five minutes until the record ended. There was a concluding rush of sound from the orchestra, and the machine switched off. In the sudden quiet that followed Adam thought he heard voices in a fretful rise of sound. He had no time to test it, for the sound stopped at once and Herold reappeared cool and smiling. "This second movement is a nice andante," he said.

There's a woman here, Adam said to himself. That's why it took so long for him to get to the door. That's why he was nervous. Surely not Josephine. A modern young woman wouldn't feel compromised at being found in bachelor quarters at eleven p.m.

Herold had talked in a low voice, so Adam had found himself keeping his voice down too, but it couldn't be to keep from disturbing neighbors. In the rain with the windows closed, a pistol shot inside would not have been overheard.

"I must go," said Adam, getting up. "I have a lot to do tomorrow."

"I see you are very conscientious about regular hours," Herold said with a humorous twinkle. "Very dutiful. You and your grandfather have more in common than your Old Testament name."

Adam smiled. "Dutifulness can make you dense. Sorry to have come in on you without warning."

There was a fleeting shadow over Cato's face. "No, come any time," he protested. "By the way I understand you're taking Blakely to the Chisholms' party tomorrow night. Why don't you two come with Jo and me?"

"Thanks, I don't know that I'm going to the party. The Chisholms invited me before I left the firm. Goodnight, Cato."

The rain had stopped, and the air was much cooler. Already Adam was beginning to doubt that what he had overheard was talking. Maybe it was rain or wind. He was tempted to wait and see who came out, but he couldn't bring himself to do that.

By his dashboard lights, he examined the stock certificate one more time before he drove home.

~~~~~~

Adam did take Blakely to the Chisholms' party, but they did not go with Herold. They were late because of Adam's engagement with Dr. Garth. At the last minute Dr. Garth had not felt like seeing him, so Adam had to be satisfied with a talk on the telephone. The Cutter shares now gave Olin possession or control of nearly half the Taurus stock. Dr. Garth was to meet with Olin to sound him out and ask him to compromise.

Adam entered the country club ballroom with Blakely, his eyes involuntarily hunting the larger Taurus stockholders. At least one had come: Blakely's father, General Julius Myerson—six feet four inches tall, president of Myerson Pipe and Foundry, director of a dozen sizable corporations, vestryman of St. John's Episcopal Church. Dr. Garth did not like parties of this kind and would not be there. But the others would be, including Bascom Olin. In spite of Dr. Garth's loss of the Cutter block, Adam had been expecting two thousand shares of Taurus stock to give him a taste of victory, but his mood was dimmed with misgivings. He had bought the stock with borrowed money, and his profit would be a middleman's at the expense of a now reluctant relative and a silly playboy. Right now he felt as though he had won at poker and had a stranger's I.O.U. for the money.

The party was a large informal dance with a small orchestra and as Blakely remarked, mostly for the older crowd. After they greeted the Chisholms, Blakely said to Adam: "I love Mr. Chisholm. Just looking at him I want to hug him. He's such a lonely man."

"Yes," said Adam, taking her in his arms, "but not so lonely as he'd like to be."

Blakely was delicately scented, smiling, excited by the party, and her hair looked soft and light like golden gas. "I guess they were all dead by the time you got back," she said.

"Who?"

"The roses." She was embarrassed, and he was too surprised to say anything for a moment though he had the feeling, why didn't I realize, of course, the flowers had to be from Blakely. "I shouldn't have brought them to you. Don't you worry: I didn't go inside your apartment. I didn't even *look* in. I gave them to your janitor to put in there. Men don't care anything about flowers, but I just wanted you to know . . ." Her voice trailed away.

"I meant to thank you, but there wasn't a card, and I was afraid—"

"Afraid they weren't from me? Which woman in your harem did you think had brought them?" She talked rapidly. "Don't mind me, I don't mean to sound sarcastic, I just did it on the spur of the moment, and I feel kind of silly about it now. Whoever heard of giving a man flowers anyway unless he's sick."

"Now, look, Blakely, it made me very happy to get those flowers. You aren't sorry about that, are you?"

This statement made her look at him with wide eyes and then relax against him, momentarily appeased. She was smooth and responsive, but dancing, she seemed even smaller than usual and made him feel oversized and awkward. "How was it in Florida?"

"Hot and sultry. How did you know that's where I'd been?"

"Josephine told me. Hands told me you'd left Mr. Chisholm, and I was afraid you'd gone to Florida to take another job."

"Who is Hands?"

"Mr. Bob Hands Octopus Reamer."

This explained the flowers: Reamer had told her he'd been fired, and the flowers were to cheer him up. "You've been going out with Reamer?"

"I don't call it going out. I call it fighting for my life."

Adam felt a tap on his shoulder, and there was Reamer asking for a dance, and as usual he kissed Blakely. He seemed to regard this act as a trade-mark of his: he kissed all women as a greeting. At parties Bob Reamer seemed to be everywhere, for no party was large enough or long enough to absorb all his energy.

Josephine was not in sight, and Adam asked Mrs. Chisholm to

dance. She was dark-haired, hard, and good-looking, and she seemed rather rigid in his arms after Blakely's softness. He hoped she could not tell he didn't like her much, but she was dangerously shrewd. "An admirer of yours has been singing your praises tonight," she said. "Cato Herold. He's a darling. I believe he knows everyone here already. He's wonderful with names." She fixed Adam with glittering eyes. "I'll tell you his exact words. 'I dropped in at Mr. Chisholm's office and talked with Adam Salter. Your husband is very lucky to have such a man working for him!' Maybe I shouldn't tell you this, but some time ago I overheard Duncan tell one of his partners—the one from Mobile—that you were worth three Bob Reamers." She was interrupted by General Myerson, who patted Adam's shoulder in a fatherly manner and whirled the hostess away.

Adam was still alone when the music stopped, and the orchestra began a fast rhythm which animated a few younger couples. Reamer led Blakely through it, reeling her out at arm's length and twirling her around while she watched her feet, frowning in concentration and talking to herself.

It was a good time of evening. The lights were flattering, the liquor was having its early mild effect on the crowd. "That girl of Dr. Garth's is really light on her feet," Adam heard someone say. There were Cato and Josephine, her red skirt twisting and blurring around her twinkling ankles. Herold was right, Adam thought, she's not thin.

Cato was directing her with skill, and she responded as though carefully rehearsed. Cato's face was serene and approving, but Josephine smiled with enjoyment, and the only time she made a wrong step she laughed aloud at herself. Except for that even in the most difficult turns they showed no strain. Her feet hardly seemed to touch the polished floor. There was in the way Herold danced now and then an exaggerated facility of his legs with a hint of humor and mockery.

Gradually others stopped dancing to watch. Adam was proud of her and a little sad, for she now seemed as inaccessible as the star of a play, and their grace made him aware of his own hairy musclebound legs, and his feet felt as inflexible as hoofs.

When the music stopped, Cato and Josephine looked at the surrounding faces in surprise, and flushed and smiling, left the floor amid applause. People looked at each other with pleased smiles. "Aren't they wonderful?" a middle-aged lady near Adam said. "I think they're about the sweetest-looking couple I ever saw."

Slow music started, and the floor became crowded again. At once Adam looked for Josephine. He spotted her passing from one man's arms to another and went toward her. Once more he lost sight of her, and he followed, turning his big shoulders sideways to squeeze through the crowd. He saw Josephine again, the shifting highlights of her dress following the rhythm of the dance. He felt self-conscious when he approached her as though stepping up on a stage.

Her partner bowed and withdrew. "I'm so glad you're home, Adam," she said smiling, extending her arms to him. She radiated heat and she was breathing deeply but far from winded. "I'm afraid I'm like a stove." She felt as light as Blakely, as light in his arms as she had looked in Herold's. "I didn't notice we were the only ones dancing there at the end. I hope people didn't think we were showing off."

"Where'd you learn to dance so well?"

"Cato taught me. He says it's the show-business side of his family coming out. Daddy would have died if he had seen us. He thinks that kind of dancing is vulgar. In fact he doesn't approve of any kind of dancing much." Her eyes were not far below the level of his own and with a little pressure he brought her cheek against his, and he felt against his chest the well-padded beat of her heart. Josephine's legs and feet unfailingly anticipated what he was going to do and communicated her enjoyment of the dance and even a trace of her lightness and grace. Her perfume was heavier than Blakely's, her lipstick a deeper red, and her hand was strong with long fingers. Her hair was called black, but it was shiny and full of color where its swirls and eddies caught the light.

He had to be direct; any minute someone would come to take his place. "Is something wrong, Josephine?"

"Why no," she said, drawing away and making a smile.

"That man hasn't been spying on you again, has he?"

"What man?" She laughed and put her cheek against his. "Oh, that detective. No, not since you chased him away."

"What's wrong, Josephine. Maybe I can help."

"Does it show?"

"Just a little. You've got the kind of face, that when you're sad, you don't just look tired the way most people do."

She said abruptly: "Adam, I may get an apartment in town."

"What about your father?"

She looked hard at him. "I guess I don't mean it. But I ought to get a job."

"What is it, Josephine?"

"Come, I'll tell you." He followed her through the crowd and got her a drink on the way outside.

There were a few men standing under the light at an outside bar talking in loud voices. Adam led her to a lawn settee in the shadowy bend of a hedge.

"This cool air feels good." She was already half through her drink. "Adam, I ought not to be unloading my troubles on you again."

"I asked for it."

He could hardly make out her expression in the semi-darkness, but he could see her white teeth and the whites of her eyes and her necklace like a circle of snow around her dark strong neck.

"Daddy doesn't want Cato to come to the house any more."

Adam was alarmed, for she sounded close to tears. "But why?"

"That's what makes me so mad." She sat forward on the bench, turning her upper body toward him. "He just *feels* that Cato is no good. He talks about Cato's not working even though I've explained again and again that he's following a doctor's orders. He talks about defective character, and that Cato's too old for me, and Cato's just thirteen years older than I am, and Daddy was seventeen years older than Mother."

Adam had asked for it, but as she talked this time, instead of being pleased at her confiding in him, her concern troubled and hurt him. "I'm surprised. Cato's a likable man."

"Daddy's so arbitrary. One thing he doesn't like is Cato's staying at Belle Wriston's, and Daddy doesn't approve of her. And he's not used to people with Cato's background. His accent, his manners, everything about him seem like a foreigner to Daddy. Daddy needs to go to a hospital for a thorough examination and I'm sure he won't leave town because Cato's here. He says he's a good judge of character, and he sees signs in Cato of moral rot."

"Is that the way he put it?"

"Yes." Her voice trembled with anger. "And I felt like telling him he was talking moral rot."

"Cato's too keen not to sense your father's disapproval."

"That's so true. For one thing Daddy won't call him by his first name. He's MR. Herold. But he doesn't know how much Daddy disapproves of him, and I'm going to have to warn him. Daddy might say something to him, and it will hurt his feelings terribly because he admires Daddy. He *likes* Daddy!"

"This may seem beside the point, Josephine, but I'll tell you a hard lesson I learned. I was very impatient with my father—he wasn't easy to deal with either—and because he'd always been around, I dealt with him on the assumption that he always would be. And one day he was gone."

She nodded. "You're right, I know."

Adam lighted her cigarette, and the wavering flame showed her drooping head and fine shadows in her face.

He was aware of questionable feelings which he had been resisting, a liking for the sentimental song the orchestra was playing because he already associated it with Josephine and this evening. She had been a rich man's child, a smart college girl, and she would always be to him what a pretty girl should be. She had become a woman whose salvation had already been worked out, and she had always made every condition which her pride demanded. Previously he had felt for her affection and admiration.

I'm in love with Josephine. The thought gave him a feeling of sudden withdrawal, and his love seemed not to have developed but to have been revealed to him like a prophecy of trouble. His own voice sounded strange to him then. "Let me talk with your father tomorrow and put in a good word for Cato. Casually of course."

"Adam, that would be wonderful. Daddy thinks so highly of you."

"Hey," called Bob Reamer, rapidly bearing down on them. "You two are mighty serious over here. Come on, Josephine, let's dance before this mambo is over."

"Blakely will be wondering where you are, Adam," Josephine said, getting up.

Reamer grasped Josephine's arm, and Adam felt a twinge of jealousy at the sight of his touching her.

He was about to follow them in when a short powerful figure coming from inside pushed through the door ahead of him. For a moment Adam did not recognize him in the dim light. Then he saw by the big jaw and the hook nose that it was Bascom Olin. His eyes were set deep in Corsican darkness. He turned those black-ringed eyes on Adam. "Good evening, Mr. Olin," Adam said, and thought he saw a glint of amusement and a faint lip-stretching smile. It was not a smile of greeting.

Ellis, the mill's superintendent, and Quigley, its president, were standing at the bar, and against them Olin looked like a big thumb against two pale fingers. The sight of those three—a majority of the Taurus directors—gave Adam a jolt. He passed through the doorway and turned in time to hear Olin say in his grinding bass voice: "Speak up. What is this it's so important for me to know?" Quigley whispered his answer.

Adam went inside with the feeling that the next time he saw Bascom Olin, neither would be smiling.

∾∾∾∾∾∾∾∾∾∾∾∾∾∾∾∾∾∾∾∾∾∾∾∾∾∾∾∾∾∾∾∾∾

13

When Adam arrived at the Garths' the next afternoon, Josephine called from the patio to come inside. She met him in the dining room where the air seemed mottled after the brilliant afternoon sky. "I tried to telephone you. Daddy's out. There's a funeral of one of his old friends this afternoon. I rang and rang."

"I missed you at church this morning."

"I sinned today. I played tennis with Cato this morning."

The bright imprint of the sun faded from his eyes, and she was gradually revealed in the wan cool light which filled the Garth house. She was dressed in a white blouse and dark skirt and was reflected by mirrors and the curved glass fronts of cabinets. All day he had been hoping to see her, and her beauty seemed so great that even if he had not known her and passed her on a city sidewalk, the sight would have made him happy.

"Where's Cato?" he said.

"Playing golf. It's a good day for it, I guess. I've felt guilty all day about making you listen to all that dreary talk last night."

"I was just sorry we were interrupted." She seemed so happy and untroubled that he asked: "Has anything changed between your father and Cato?"

"We haven't talked about it today. Come out on the patio."

"I hear some Yankees are restoring the Chobot house. Let's drive down there and see what they're doing. I'll talk with your father later."

"I'd love to." At the front door she said: "Let's walk over there instead. I really need the exercise."

They went out the back door into cool air, which was just right to bring out the best smells of spring. "I guess I haven't been out there in fifteen years," he said. The big scuppernong arbor still contained its dark shade, and in spite of the season a winelike smell hovered over it. "Spring's later here than in town." He had felt more and more doubtful about speaking to her father about Herold. He could not come on a pretext of talking about the mill, for Dr. Garth would not discuss business on Sunday.

He followed her through the blooming garden and out the back gate.

The path they took led into a pine forest. She walked with a light step on sandaled feet and with such vigor that he decided she really wanted exercise. Following, he could admire her figure at leisure, her small waist, the curves of her back, her well-shaped legs.

The woods thinned, and breathing hard, they came to a high outcropping of gray rock. Josephine sat on a boulder, and he stood behind her. Below them green pastures rolled southward to the Buttermilk Road. It seemed beneath them as if they were flying. The air was so clear that far-off things appeared unnaturally distinct, and the cattle grazing below looked still and miniature like figurines. This land was part of the old Garth plantation which Dr. Garth had sold years ago. Far to the east beyond the river Adam saw the white and purple of Kieselguhr.

"I thought we'd see the Chobot house from here," Adam said.

"It's over the ridge. What happened to old Miss Chobot? I never could get anything from Daddy about her when she died."

"She had once been a famous beauty, but she lost her mind, and locked herself in the house for forty years." But Adam knew more: at her death the smell had alarmed a peddler, and the authorities who entered the house found it unbelievably filthy.

"Tell me, Adam, what do you really think of Cato?"

I should have known she'd been thinking of him all along, Adam thought in keen disappointment. "The first day I was put off by his being so fluent," he said, "but now I like him. And so does everyone else, I hear, except your father."

"When I met him," she said, "I was a little afraid of him because so many clever intellectual men turn out to be egomaniacs, but he's not. He's really just as kind and gentle as he seems to be."

"Then his charm should wear very well."

"There's no question about his being charming," she said a little sadly. "But do you think he has the qualities that don't always go with charm?"

"What qualities?"

"I mean, Cato has a million friends. And he should because a lot of them owe him money and abuse his hospitality, and he doesn't give it a thought. But they're not all parasites. A lot of them are people more like you, and they'd do anything for him."

"I can easily believe it."

With her brown bare arms folded over her bosom she was gazing out at the mountains across the valley and biting her lip. "What I mean is that often a man who gets along so well with everyone doesn't have—doesn't have—well—strength of character."

The look in her eyes then was surprisingly cool and critical. It made him wonder—and hope.

"Let's go on," she said.

The shifting wind at the top of the ridge sounded like the far-off roar of a football crowd. The trees here were small and gnarled as though the wind had tried to twist music out of them. Northward the ground curved and fell off steeply from their feet into a narrow valley. The sound of a waterfall came from far below, and they saw a big bird floating over the center of the valley. "I don't remember any of this," Adam said, "and I thought I knew every foot of this land."

They had to climb down among the trunks of fine elderly trees, between and over rocks, reaching for handholds. His muscles were warmed up enough so that moving was a pleasure. He went ahead of her, offering his hand until he decided that she did not want to be helped. The sound of the water growing louder made him feel that the whole valley was alive. "Listen," she said, breathing hard, and the cry of a nighthawk came from the shade beneath them. "I used to ride along the ridge a lot, but this drop was too steep for the horses."

They reached level ground and came on an open field, parklike and European in smoothness, through the center of which ran the stream lined with willows, and all along the valley rivulets poured into it. They found the stream was much too broad to jump. "Oh, oh," she said. "The Chobot house is just over that next ridge but I'd forgotten how much rain we'd had." They walked along the stream, but it grew much wider, and they slowed down and finally stopped. Josephine looked it over and turned to him sud-

76

denly. "I don't have any right to be so happy, nothing's changed, but I can't help it."

"I feel the same way." That afternoon his feeling for her had grown more intense, but it was not only a joy but a burden. He felt that it would help if she knew he loved her. He had thought of nothing else all day, and it was hard to believe she didn't suspect it.

She picked a wild flower and twirled it between her finger tips. "It's late. We'd better go back before it gets dark."

"Wait," he said. The scene seemed so familiar that he felt he would remember something important if he could see it from the right point. "Let's walk up the valley a little way."

Moving upstream he talked about how it was surprising that this rich ground wasn't overgrown with brambles. It grew softer and marshy. "Maybe we ought to get on higher ground," he said.

They climbed up the slope again, and when they stopped to rest, she leaned against a beech tree, breathing hard from the climb. Her black hair rested on the silver-gray tree trunk, and there was a sprinkling of perspiration on her forehead just below the hair. Adam drew close to her, leaning against the tree with one hand above her head. Seeing her flushed face and smelling the perfume she had worn last night made him think of the way her body had felt in his arms when they were dancing. He wanted to tell her he loved her, but he could not bring himself to say it. His instincts told him that this was the wrong time. She was looking over the valley and when she realized he was looking at her, her eyes met his gaze, and she smiled brightly. "You have beautiful teeth," he said. His heart beat violently, and he had to swallow and catch his breath in the middle of the sentence.

"Thank you."

He wanted to touch her, it seemed the only thing that would satisfy him. "Josephine," he said. She looked at him expectantly. He shook his head, swallowing, his heart chopping, and moistened his lips. Her gaze sank until she was looking at the ground, and when he shifted his footing suddenly, her eyes moved quickly up to his face with a flicker of uneasiness.

He slid his hand down the tree trunk until it touched her hair. She started and said faintly: "Adam, we'd better—"

He moved against her. She seemed to try to flatten herself into the tree and at the same time slip around it. One of his hands caught her supple waist—the ball of his thumb against her belt buckle, his palm slightly over her hip, his finger tips resting on her spine.

Her eyes widened in amazement; she parted her lips to speak, inhaled sharply, and pulled at his wrist with both hands. He knew with a frost on his heart that she had not suspected what he felt and had invited nothing.

He took her neck and head in his other hand and tried to hold her mouth to his, but they only touched roughly for an instant. She turned her head away, twisted backward against his grip, and her resistance excited him and made him angry and desperate. He had to force some consent from her, or he was ruined. For a moment they struggled in silence, hands slippery with perspiration, her teeth clenched, back arched, face pink and furious. Her blouse pulled out of her skirt, and his hand touched the slick silky cloth underneath, and he felt a sharp collision of knees and feet.

She went limp, then wrenched away from him with all her weight, breaking his grip, and fell hard to the ground.

"Are you hurt?" He reached down to help her up. Her skirt had slipped half way up her thighs.

She got up, avoiding his hands, and immediately turned and walked quickly up the hill, brushing leaves and dirt from her hair. The fall had smeared her white blouse and the seat of her skirt with mud.

"Josephine!" he called, going after her.

She would not look around. He walked after her as fast as he could, following the motion that her hips gave the skirt and the flashing of her legs. His grip had been hard enough to leave bruises, and the thought of hurting her made him sweat with panic. Their struggle had lasted a minute—no more—and ended because she was too strong to hold. He could have overpowered her but not without a fight.

He called her once more, but the wind on the ridge which cooled his sweat blew the sound away. He could not catch up with her, for as soon as he drew close, she ran to keep ahead of him, and he would not compound the outrage by running her down. The walk from the house to the valley floor had taken an hour. Now they were retracing it in half that time, measured by the angry sidewise flicking of her skirt ahead of him.

The pines grew denser near the house, and she faded into the shadows there. That was when he stopped hoping she would relent, and with a rusty bloody taste in his mouth he started running.

He burst out of the trees and scanned the garden and the back of the house. Josephine was gone. He looked for her in the down-stairs rooms and terrace, which were charged with a reproachful stillness and order. As he made a circle through the house, it occurred to him that he should leave her alone now out of fairness, but that thought was not strong enough to break his stride, and he bounded up the curving stairway, calling: "Josephine!"

There was no answer. The upstairs hallway was dim, lighted only by the gray square of twilight in the front hall window. He went to the southwest room and knocked on the door. He felt for the knob with a shaky hand, his arm muscles quivering with stress and his heart spurting. The door was locked. "Josephine, I want to talk with you!" he shouted. He put his ear against the door and heard no sound. In those few seconds since he had stopped moving, he noticed that he had a terrific headache.

He heard a noise outside, and it took a moment to identify it as the shutting of a car door. He turned to the front window and looked down on the long black top of Dr. Garth's car, framed between the central columns.

Adam reached the stairs and saw red tracks on every other stair coming up to meet him. He looked at his shoes in dismay. They were rimmed with crusts of drying mud. Descending, he tucked in his shirt, which was so wet it stuck to his back, and tightened his tie. He could not remember where he had left his jacket.

He was near the bottom when the front door opened, and Dr. Garth stepped inside. His weaponlike head and neck projected from a suit which looked black against the white woodwork. He was removing his hat, and it stopped in midair as he caught sight of Adam. He continued looked fixedly as his hat slowly sank to his side.

"How do you do, sir," Adam said hoarsely. "Josephine and I have just taken a walk."

"So I see," said Dr. Garth, looking from Adam to the tracks on the carpet.

"I'm afraid I brought in some mud. I'll get a broom and get it up."

"You'll only spread it. Rutherford will take care of it in the morning." His look, full of curiosity and displeasure, was of a kind Dr. Garth had never directed at Adam before. "Where is Josephine?"

"She's upstairs." Adam advanced slowly, expecting Dr. Garth to demand an explanation, but after a long few seconds, the older man said formally: "Won't you come into the parlor and sit down?"

"No, sir, I have to go." Adam muttered a goodbye and walked past Dr. Garth. He did not look back before he was outside, but he had the impression from the creaking of floor boards and displacement of air that Dr. Garth was moving toward the stairs.

About the time Adam reached the Buttermilk Road it occurred to him that he was leaving Josephine to think of an explanation and perhaps to face her father's wrath. No, she had nothing to fear from her father. In any case he couldn't have carried on coherent speech with Dr. Garth and would have given himself away further by trying, for his head ached so that he could hardly see.

He began a battle for his self-esteem at once, trying to reshape the attack so that she had invited it, and he had been less violent, but thinking about it made him feel worse. He realized why Herold had not been with her. Herold had unquestionably invited her to go with him, she had wanted to go, but when she couldn't reach Adam by telephone, she had stayed out of politeness to receive him. The question of how she felt was too painful to dwell on: just how disappointed, angry, disgusted.

He tried to distract himself with details. Why had she left no tracks? She must have taken off her shoes at the back door or wiped her feet. Where was his jacket? He couldn't even remember when he last had it on.

I've never done anything like that before, he thought. That's not like Adam Salter, Eagle Scout. Randolph Scott wouldn't have done it. But he couldn't kid himself out of it.

As soon as he got to his apartment, the headache and the memory of what he had done made him shut his eyes and squint. The darkness drained away, and he could see Josephine's rich black hair against the silver beech bark. She had expected him to go on talking then, and that expectancy and the opportunity he had read as consent had been merely friendliness and trust. It was the only kind of intimacy he could have with her, and that was what he had betrayed and spoiled for good.

When he finally got to sleep about four o'clock the following morning, he dreamed that by a wan light he followed Josephine down the Buttermilk Road. The river was gone, and he walked all the way to Kieselguhr, which now held a tarn of black septic water. He woke from it with the belief that Josephine was in his room. The conviction was so strong that he turned on his bedside light only to lie back with burning eyes, wondering how he would ever face her or Dr. Garth again, and gradually he drifted off to a crowded twitching sleep.

~~~~~~

14

His mind clouded with sleep, Adam awoke with a vague feeling of evil. Then yesterday came back to him in vividness and detail. It was now ten minutes past seven. He had slept only three hours and those badly. Kneading his sore neck, he started a pot of coffee. Seeing the hour confirmed on the stove-clock dial depressed him because he had visited all the Taurus stockholders and for the first time since leaving Duncan Chisholm he had no schedule to follow.

He noticed his muddy shoes of yesterday, and under the mud he discovered that the leather was badly scuffed and scratched. Of course he had worn his best shoes to the Garths', and he did not now have the money to replace them.

He took an uncomfortably cold shower, and afterward as he drank his coffee, he again relived and analyzed the incident with Josephine. He had hoped it would appear in a better light today, but instead his action now seemed irrevocable. It also seemed astonishing. He could not conceive of Herold's making such a mistake. Lately Adam had managed to dismiss the sight of the kiss in the convertible, but now the memory chilled him to the bone.

He was calm enough to realize that he, Adam Salter, church-going though lukewarm, and a virgin though nearly thirty, even-tempered, dependable, ambitious and ready to sacrifice for his ambition, fit and hard from gymnastics and weight-lifting at the YMCA, had shown a symptom of something fundamentally wrong with his life and that he should not ignore it. He was still in his bathrobe, drinking his third cup of coffee and turning over this dim idea, when the telephone rang. "Adam?" It was Dr. Garth. "I want to see you at once."

"Yes, sir." Adam's heart pounded as though he had been transported to the stairway where Dr. Garth had found him the afternoon before. It was not a request but an order, and an emergency, Adam thought, for Dr. Garth to telephone him so early, but he looked at his watch and found that it was nine-thirty.

He was not hungry, and his instinct was to hurry to the Garths' without breakfast, but he had not liked Dr. Garth's commanding tone on the telephone, and he needed time to think. He knew that Dr. Garth could not have persuaded Josephine to tell him what happened, but he might want Adam for a cross-examination.

Adam shaved carefully, put on a freshly pressed suit, and contrary to his custom went to a restaurant for breakfast. There he thought of what Dr. Garth would ask and what he would answer. It was a gift of his even under great strain to be able to cool himself off and usually to perform well. Though he did not feel up to seeing Josephine, he prepared words of apology and explanation.

There had been times when the Buttermilk Road had passed under him like a rainbow, but today it was like a cable pulling him in. Rutherford, formal but betrayed by nervous brown eyes, admitted him and said Dr. Garth was waiting in his study. There were no signs of yesterday's tracks on the carpets.

In the parlor Adam stopped at sight of Cato, curled catlike in a chair with his shoes off, smoking and staring at the wall. He moved only his head and looked at Adam from pouchy eyes. "Mawnin, cunnel."

"How are you this morning?" said Adam stiffly.

Herold's voice was a whisper. "Dreadfully listless. Trying to be quiet and inconspicuous so as to draw no lightning. If you're looking for Jo, they're in the garden. Amid the murmur of innumerable bees. Surveying sites of ye old brick kiln and ye old immemorial slave quarters and outdoor kitchen."

"Dr. Garth too?"

Cato rolled his eyes. "I think he's in his sanctum."

Adam walked on toward the study. The fact that Herold was there and in a posture of being very much at home suggested that his situation had been repaired, which seemed easy enough, overshadowed as it was by his own blunder of yesterday.

"Adam," Herold called to him, and Adam retraced his steps to Herold's chair. "Something's worrying Jo. Something new that happened yesterday, I gather. She didn't tell you, did she?"

"No. What kind of thing?"

"That's what I've been trying to imagine. As though she'd seen a bloody automobile accident or a public execution. But something personal." Herold was scrutinizing Adam's face. "She seemed shocked and withdrawn last night. I've seen her that way after a particularly horrible nightmare."

"How about today?"

"Oh, today she knows she has reason to be upset."

Adam heard the click of a door latch and looked around. The study door was opening, and the massive figure of Dr. Garth was revealed. His face was dark, his eyebrows meeting and rolling over his eyes. Without saying anything, he walked back to his desk, expelling his breath impatiently.

Adam crossed the library and entered the study.

"Shut the door, please," said Dr. Garth, and Adam did so and sat down. Through the north windows Adam could hear women's voices, but he could not see the speakers.

"I'm going to New Orleans to a hospital for some tests, and you and I need to get a few things understood before I go. Saturday Olin said his plans weren't settled, but he insisted his son would be an asset to the company. He said we could work something out. Myerson called this morning to say that Olin's found out about your getting Davenport's stock. How I don't know." Dr. Garth's face became grim. "When G. P. Moon told him the story of yours about splitting the stock, I hear that Olin rocked with laughter and said: 'I used to think Salter was a fool. Now I know he's a fool.' I suppose that's what you intended. He seems to have heard the truth Saturday night." It was clear that Dr. Garth disapproved of this deception.

"Does Olin know I'm buying for you?"

"I haven't any idea. Right now he's too mad to care. He feels you made him look ridiculous, and now he's stirred up enough to bid up the price of the stock considerably. Do you think any of the stockholders would sell stock at higher prices?"

"Yes, sir."

"It's too late to go after more of it. We can't outbid Olin. I have it on pretty good authority that he has at present a million dollars in cash. However, I don't know yet whether this concerns you or not. You can get out of the line of fire if you like. I can buy the stock from you this week or next. It will cost you a lot more in taxes, however."

"I want to stay in. What do you plan to do?"

"Talk with a few of the larger stockholders who aren't already committed to Olin and try to get them to see it my way. Chisholm, Rice Alexander, P. D. Emery—men like that. Alexander isn't general counsel for the mill, but he ought to be. Tell me what you want in this."

"I want to do whatever's necessary to protect my investment."

"Then you're going to have your hands full. Olin has a majority on the board of directors, and proxies are solicited in favor of management for the meeting in August. Stockholders are in the habit of just signing their proxies over to Quigley and mailing them in."

"That's a habit we need to interfere with, and we're going to have to make our play no matter how mad it makes Olin or anyone else."

"What are you thinking of?"

"Let the stockholders know the company's losing money. Also let them know that the company owns five hundred thousand dollars' worth of timberlands."

"Five hundred thousand? Nonsense."

"I'd think one of the first steps would be to get a lawyer."

Dr. Garth waved the suggestion away. "No, I want to keep it out of the courts."

"A lawyer might keep it out of court, which is where most proxy fights end up."

"Listen. This is no proxy fight and in your zeal don't undertake to destroy the enemy. We couldn't do that even if Olin were not rich. For practical purposes we can't even regard him as an enemy, only a rival." He paused to give Adam time to digest this.

"What about trying Calvin Davidson along with the three men you mentioned?"

Dr. Garth snorted. "That *would* be a waste of time."

"Why?"

"Because he works for Olin."

"Olin owns the Sweetwater Pipe Company?"

"He controls it."

"It's beginning to look as if Olin owns everything in town. How about this: instead of trying to line up those three, Mr. Chisholm and the others, against Olin, propose that the board be increased to eight and just ask them to be candidates for it. They're honest, well-heeled, well-educated men. They should certainly act for the good of the company. If Olin obstructs their election, it should convince them that their interests as stockholders are not being served."

Dr. Garth reflected on this. "You have a point. It would break Olin's majority on the board if only one were elected." He studied his desk calendar. "I'll be in New Orleans for most of the week."

"Sir, I think it ought to be done as soon as possible, because if that plan doesn't work, we'll need to have something else rolling."

Dr. Garth nodded his head not in agreement but to dismiss the subject and end their conversation. Adam arose and said: "Would you mind telephoning me before you leave, so I can be taking some other action if they refuse? For one thing we probably ought to entertain some of the key stockholders."

"Entertain them? How? Fill them with liquor?"

"If they drink, yes. The idea would be to get them relaxed so we could present our point of view."

"I'll have none of this fawning on stockholders, or any other Wall Street shenanigans. I'll call you when I have some news." As Adam reached the door, Dr. Garth said: "Who was that you were talking to in the parlor?"

"That was Cato Herold." Adam saw at once that this was an opportunity to speak in Herold's favor as he had promised. "He's a very fine fellow by the way." He found the words hard to speak.

Dr. Garth responded with a bitter laugh, and the statement: "Yes, I understand that he's the toast of the country club."

"I think there's more to him than that."

"He is an idler; he is thirty-seven years old and has no profession, though Josephine tells me he has held various jobs such as being a dancing master and a model for men's clothes. And I think he is not sincere."

"He seems sincere to me. In fact, more honest than most people."

Dr. Garth shook his head. "That man is a dissipator. I know the signs, which are all over him. A dissipator of money, of health, of energy, of order. I am a physician, I am seventy years old, and I have seen many like him through the whole course of their lives. He is a parasite. His kind destroys everything he gets hold of. Josephine is a young woman of superior qualities. When her mother was dying, Josephine was remarkable—as a comfort to me and as a nurse to her mother. I want the man she marries to confirm in her these qualities and not whatever weaknesses she may have."

"Herold seems to have some fine qualities too," Adam began, but Dr. Garth interrupted him.

"She has taken an interest in no man I have disapproved of so much—with the possible exception of young Olin." He spat out the words.

"Jack Olin? When was this?"

"When she was eighteen. He was much too old for her, too loose, and generally unsuitable."

"Herold isn't the Olin type at all."

"When you and Josephine are older, you will see that I am right about Herold." What he had just said seemed to take away all his interest in Adam's opinions. "You may quote me to Josephine or to Mr. Herold. They know what I think. But to no one else." And with this not very flattering injunction in his ears, Adam left the room.

As he closed the study door, Adam heard a woman's voice coming from the front of the house. It was a thick voice, a beautiful voice, and did not seem entirely unfamiliar. A Yankee, Adam thought, specifically a New Yorker with an accent like Herold's. Through the dim breadth of the two rooms he saw her light-colored hair and slender outline clearly against a front window.

Adam did not feel like making himself agreeable to a stranger, but he had to see Josephine. The voice rose out to gather him in: "This must be Josephine's brother."

"Leah, this is Adam Salter, Jo's cousin," said Herold, getting up. "And this is Leah Fraden."

Leah advanced not only to offer her hand, but to inspect him with eyes as bright as though she had fever. Her features were delicate and her forehead high. Her fair skin was youthful, but her figure was even more striking; it was, in a knitted dress, slender and small-waisted, the figure of a sixteen-year-old girl. She looked with an intense gaze, then gestured with thin fingers toward the ancestral portraits: "Yes, and quite a resemblance to them." She compared Adam with his ancestors. "Poor dears! It's such a disadvantage to be dead." She added: "Now I remember. You're the stockbroker."

"I used to be. Right now I'm out of a job."

"Like Cato and me," she said. "And Josephine." She sat down

and crossed her legs, which were beautiful and slender. "Oh, here she is."

Josephine entered and started at the sight of Adam and greeted him in a low voice. She wore a dark dress with a high white collar, which looked deliberately prim, and loose enough to disguise her figure. She crossed the room and took a chair in the far corner, so that he had to twist around to look at her. Adam had been in doubt about Leah's age until Josephine came in, and the contrast made him decide she was older than she looked at first glance—probably in her middle thirties.

The silence which fell on the room was so noticeable that Adam looked inquiringly at the others. Herold, for once subdued, was studying the medallion over the chandelier. Leah returned Adam's glance with a smile.

"Josephine has just shown me the garden," she said. "Everything blooms so early in the South. I'm visiting Belle Writson, Mr. Salter. Her house doesn't seem authentic like this one—not official old Southern." Yes, thought Adam, this woman's personality fitted · with the picture of the rather Bohemian company Mrs. Wriston was said to attract. "Belle told me not to leave Mercer until I'd seen the Garth house. Look at the painting of the Indians there. They have such delicious shiny muscles. Look at their buttocks. And what about the other oil over there? The one that's sort of a brownish black?"

Josephine twisted around in her chair. "Some Dutchman. Maes, I believe his name is. My grandfather bought those paintings. He didn't like American primitives and gave away or sold them."

Leah got up and examined various objects in the room. She looked up at the chandelier, then turned on the light switch at the door. The light spread in many colored dusty rays and lighted their faces. Leah reached up and with pointed fingers touched the prisms, and they tinkled glassily.

She went to a well-arranged vase of roses on the piano and smelled them critically, narrowing but not shutting her eyes. From there she moved to the fireplace. The attention this visitor gave everything was making Josephine intensely nervous. When Leah touched the marble of the fireplace, Josephine cried out: "It's aw- fully hard to keep a house like this clean!"

Leah turned and looked at Josephine from under drooping lids. She examined everything, the tables, the twenty-four-inch pine floor boards, the woodwork, with the sharp interest of a connoisseur who is also a dealer. Then with the air of having finished her inspection, she turned to give not the resounding eulogy Adam was expecting but this statement in a very soft voice: "I'd like to see it all, Josephine. The upstairs too. And your father. Belle said I ought to see your father." Josephine stirred, and Leah said: "Not right now, but before I go." Leah closed her eyes and inhaled deeply. "And the smell—that's something that can't be reproduced. You can't buy that." There was irony in her tone, some private joke on which she seemed to be dwelling and which Adam did not understand.

"It's really a mellow wonderful house," Herold said insistently. "Isn't it, Leah?"

She did not reply.

Adam had remained in spite of his restlessness, hoping that he would have a moment to speak with Josephine alone. If he could make her listen to an apology, he could exact some sign of forgiveness. As minutes passed, he lost hope; the company was going to stay all morning. He arose. "Will you be in town for a while, Miss Fraden?"

"I'm not sure yet. I have a good many things to do and it just depends on how long it takes me to do them." She smiled at Josephine and Cato.

Adam said goodbye and was at the front door when he heard Josephine call his name. His heart leaped. He waited, and she came into the hall. "You left this yesterday," she said. She brought the jacket of his suit and held it out to him at arm's length. Her face was pale and strained.

"Thanks. I couldn't remember where I'd left it."

"On the chair in the back hall by the stairs."

"I don't even remember taking it off." She was about to leave him. "Josephine, I'm sorry," he said, his voice low. "And I want to explain."

"Don't explain." Her voice was cold. "I was surprised yesterday, or I wouldn't have made such a fuss."

"I would have settled for a fuss, but you wouldn't even talk to me."

"Let's forget it." She would not look at him. "I certainly don't want to talk about it now."

"But you're not forgetting it!" he said, realizing his tone was growing angry and defeating his purpose.

"I've been trying to." Her manner seemed softer, yet he knew his relationship with her was changed for good. The sight of her—her melancholy eyes, her beauty, and the dignity which he had disturbed yesterday—wrung his heart. "I'd better get back to my company," she said, half turning. "Oh, yes. Blakely's been trying to telephone you. She wants you to call her." Whether she intended it or not, this message sounded like a rebuke.

Again he felt an urge to lay violent hands on her to hold her. "Josephine, listen to me!" He took a step toward her, and she backed away. "Could I see you this afternoon?"

"Daddy's leaving today," she said, looking in the direction of her guests, "and I need to spend the afternoon with him."

"How about right after he leaves?"

"I'm afraid not. I have an engagement."

"Then you name the time."

"I'm sorry, Adam, I'll be staying with the Myersons while Daddy's away, and I'm expecting to be awfully busy for the next few days."

"I see. Goodbye, Josephine."

Adam walked to his car. His anger faded, and he now felt anxious and sad. The conviction was growing in his mind that Josephine and her father looked on him as a poor relation, which he was. He could think of evidence to the contrary, but he was not one of the family, for here he was not allowed to make a mistake. He felt if he mishandled the Taurus deal, the door behind him would close for good. Yet he had a feeling of gratitude that he had the challenge of that problem, and he was itching to be turned loose on it.

15

Adam spent most of that Monday waiting in his apartment for Dr. Garth's telephone call. In these hours of enforced idleness he imagined the dark shapes his future might assume. He tried writing Josephine a letter declaring his love, but the result was clumsy, and he tore the letter into such small pieces that not a word was intact. He was becoming aware that Josephine, being a woman and no fool, must have guessed the nature of this explanation he was so anxious to give her, and that she was so much in love with Herold that she had no desire to hear it. Adam had regarded his feeling as being sizable enough at least to be interesting, even flattering, and the awareness that it did not interest her shriveled his heart. Now he had a feeling of hardness close to an inclination to inflict pain, a feeling he did not resist so he would not be hurt easily.

Dr. Garth's revelation about Josephine and Jack Olin strangely depressed him. It occurred to him that Dr. Garth's real reason for opposing Jack Olin might be personal, that they had clashed over Josephine and Dr. Garth would not forget it.

Dr. Garth too had recently retired from medical practice. Doctors did not willingly take this step, and Dr. Garth had perhaps felt bereft of power and wished to compensate for it in another direction. Certainly his own use of Adam extended his power. A promise had gotten the use of all of Adam's time and a hundred thousand dollars.

Dr. Garth was still thinking of his own moves as changing things in a decent way without going outside the Rotary Club, but Olin would know, as would Alexander, Chisholm, and Emery, that when he talked about electing new directors, he was trying to shift control out of Olin's hands.

That day Adam got the test results of the sample he had picked up at Kieselguhr. It was mostly silica with some alumina, iron, and alkali. The chemist said there was nothing uncommon or interesting about it. He knew the area. The word kieselguhr, he said, meant diatomaceous earth, formed from algae skeletons. While mining for brick clay, an early settler, Amos Chobot, had found a little kieselguhr there. In the 1920s, kaolin had been discovered at Kieselguhr, and the big mules of Wylie County had invested millions to mine it. But the deposits had turned out to be shallow, the millions lost, and Kieselguhr had become a local byword for failure.

The weather made Adam restless. The barometer was dropping again, the clouds were dark and swollen, and the wind blew from the southeast. As Dr. Garth's train time approached, Adam paced his apartment and looked at his watch at intervals of less than a minute. The train was to leave at five-twenty, and when a quarter of five came, Adam was sure that Dr. Garth was not going to call him. He dialed the Garth's number and got no answer.

Adam drove to the railway station. Rain and heavy late-afternoon traffic delayed him, and when he reached the station, the train, its wet metal sides gleaming like silver, was already moving. Josephine was walking slowly along the platform, and Adam suppressed his instant response of excitement at sight of her. She looked worried and sad. Adam drove up beside her and said, "Did your father leave any message for me, Josephine?"

"No, he didn't, Adam."

"Thanks." He backed away, turned with a screeching of tires, and drove away. Dr. Garth had not seen fit to tell him what had happened, and his hands were tied until Dr. Garth reached New Orleans in the morning. He did not really have much hope about Mr. Chisholm since Olin was his best customer. However Adam felt hopeful about Rice Alexander and fairly certain that P. D. Emery, president of a rival bank, would accept. If either were elected, the board of directors would at least be deadlocked. But he had to assume that Dr. Garth had failed, and he worked on a program to present to small stockholders. That night he sent a telegram to Dr. Garth at the hospital in New Orleans asking him to telephone.

Dr. Garth's call came early the following morning. In response to Adam's question, he said: "They all said no."

"Mr. Emery too?"

"He seemed willing at first, but he called me back and said he'd decided against it."

"They didn't say why?"

"They didn't have to. Rice Alexander's law firm is retained by several companies dominated by Olin, and it's obvious that Emery just doesn't want to antagonize Olin. He said it was contrary to his policy to get into a dispute in which he might make enemies for the bank."

"I'm sorry to have bothered you with this, but as you know, I couldn't do anything until I knew how you'd made out."

"I'll be back Saturday. Don't do anything until then." That was his final protest, and Adam realized that Dr. Garth did not want to argue or even to think about these problems.

Dr. Garth had not told him about this defeat because he wanted Adam to do nothing, even though the next few days might be all important. This was not like Dr. Garth. Adam was dismayed at his attitude but even more dismayed that Olin had such power in Mercer that not even a business rival like P. D. Emery would risk displeasing him.

From that time Adam worked in a cold fever on the small stockholders' committee to which Dr. Garth had objected. Adam found it necessary to do everything with immoderate force to keep from brooding, and when he passed an hour or two without worrying about Josephine, he congratulated himself on managing to do without her.

The uncommitted stockholders owned 13 per cent of the stock. Adam divided them into three groups. The first consisted of P. D. Emery, Rice Alexander, and Duncan Chisholm. The next block, of a thousand shares, belonged to Mrs. Belle Wriston. The third was an amalgam of some two dozen small stockholders like Miss Winnie McCaffery. Clearly the same arguments would not appeal to all three groups, and he needed almost all of their proxies. The smallest stockholders would want dividends at once. Emery, Alexander, and Chisholm would be more critical, more interested in getting the company on a sound long-term basis. Just what would satisfy Mrs. Wriston Adam did not know, for she had refused to see him when he telephoned about buying her stock.

Adam turned then to The Taurus Company and there called on Mr. Hubert Quigley, the president, a pale, worried-looking man who smelled of lavender water, and whose reception of Adam, after keeping him waiting for forty-five minutes was hostile and constrained. So was that of the superintendent, George Ellis, a plump and ordinarily amiable man. When Adam asked to examine the company records, Quigley said: "I've got some charts here that should answer your questions." The charts were works of art in colored ink, but they revealed practically nothing, and Adam complimented him on their elegance and again asked to see the books.

Quigley frowned and cleared his throat. "I'm afraid that won't be convenient now."

Of course Adam needed an accountant's help with the books. What he really wanted was to get inside the mill, and he was turned over to Jimmy Nabors, red-haired and freckled, twenty-two years old, out of college that January.

Much of the operation was new to Adam, for the Salter Webbing Company had done nothing but weaving.

The machines they moved among were thunderous reefs of black iron, edged with rust and shadows. Gross as they were, their operations were delicate and feminine—essentially cleaning and smoothing out cotton fibers, then twisting and interlocking them in a fabric. They were tended by skinny mountain men, for the cotton mill unlike the foundry did not build weight-lifter's muscles.

One machine Adam had no trouble in distinguishing afterward was the slubber, which slung out a loose white rope of cotton. Passing between rows of these machines, he tripped, and a whirling flyer struck his elbow and numbed his arm. Jimmy apologized for the can full of nuts and bolts which had tripped him. All along, Adam, rubbing his aching elbow, looked for a soft place to dig in his nails.

The weave room was the first such place he found. The heat and terrific screeching clatter affected him like old poison. Several workers and looms were idle, and Adam asked why. "You remember that slasher they were cleaning out?" Jimmy said. "They got bad starch in it, and there's not enough warp yarn until it's running. Those old slashers are too slow anyway."

They moved on slowly over trembling sagging floor boards. "Are those looms waiting for the warp yarn too?" Adam shouted, indicating a block of twenty idle looms. Jimmy explained that the weaver who ran that block was sick, and those looms were so old and ornery that no one else could make them run.

When the tour was finished, Adam asked Jimmy what was the

most modern department of the mill. "Mr. Mercer put in new drawing and spinning back about 1939," Jimmy told him.

"What do you need in the way of equipment?"

Jimmy laughed and gestured to indicate the whole mill.

They were on their way out through the opening room when it was Adam's misfortune to see a man with his back to them turn suddenly, his wide scream soundless in the roar of the machines, and blood spurted from the tips of his fingers. Other workers surrounded him at once, and a minute later an overseer had him on the way to the hospital.

The injured man had tried to make an adjustment or get some foreign object out of the picker, and the first joints of three fingers had been shredded between feed rolls and the whirling points of the picker beaters. "We just can't get them to stop the machine before they put their hands in," Jimmy said, his face white. "If it was up to me, I'd put a safety bar on each picker lid so you'd have to stop the thing before you could get into it."

As Adam walked through the front office on his way out, a short handsome man overtook him and introduced himself. He was Lloyd Bowers, purchasing agent; he had known Adam's family for years. He had a blue jaw, and thick short black hair mixed with gray. His eyebrows sloped upward to form a chevron. Adam explained that he had bought some stock in the company and wanted to have a look at his investment. "If there's *anything* I can do for you," Bower said in a soft kind voice, "just let me know."

Adam went outside with a nose full of lint, his throat sore from shouting questions, and his ears still ringing.

He could take no action with the stockholders until Dr. Garth returned Saturday. In the meantime he wanted to be in a better position to understand what he saw at The Taurus Company, and that week Adam visited all of the other textile mills in Mercer. It turned out that business was not so bad as Quigley said it was. Some mills were working three shifts six days a week, and all seemed to be prospering. There were differences that struck Adam at once: their housekeeping was better, the executives seemed more vigorous, the employees were busier.

Of all Taurus products local merchants carried only the four-dollar towel—rich and soft, made of silky Egyptian cotton. It was a product to be proud of, but the Taurus cheaper retail line had withered away.

Now Adam was chafing to go at the stockholders, and early Saturday, he called the Garth house. There was no answer, so he asked for Josephine at the Myersons'. "Daddy's sick," she told him. "He came down with flu Thursday. He won't be home for another week."

"How can I reach him? I need to talk with him."

"About business? I don't think you should, Adam."

"It's urgent."

"That's why you shouldn't talk with him about it now."

Adam thought this over. "You have a point." And as eager as he was to go at the stockholders, he could use some time visiting towel mills out of town to have a further basis for comparison.

"You forgot to call Blakely, didn't you, Adam? Remember, I told you Monday? She's right here."

His businesslike tone alarmed Blakely, and she spoke breathlessly as though getting out the whole invitation before he could hang up. "I want to know if you can come out to the cabin Monday night. Cato and Josephine will be there, and we'll cook steaks." Adam explained that he was going to be out of town on business, and she said she would ask him again when he came back.

He spent the next week on the road going from one towel mill to another, asking questions, and sometimes he tried to draw out an executive on the subject of the Taurus's reputation, but he could only get bits, fragments, dim impressions. He did pick up one very important fact: that the major towel companies were under injunction by the Department of Justice not to acquire any more companies in the field, so very likely The Taurus Company could not be sold to another manufacturer.

The best mills were the easiest to get into. The capable managers were proud of their work and willing to talk about it. One towel maker, the State Line Manufacturing Company, had a brand-new one-story building on a green lawn that looked like a college campus. The mill had just gotten a hundred new shuttleless looms to make piece goods, and Adam looked at the quiet gleaming weave room with awe. There were very few human beings in view; whereas The Taurus Company had a weaver running twenty looms, here one man ran a hundred.

That night Adam again telephoned Josephine at the Myersons'. Dr. Garth was still sick with flu at the hospital. Blakely renewed her invitation, this time making it for the following Friday, and Adam accepted.

Tossing in his hotel bed, Adam tried to decide what to do about the mill. He did less thinking now than brooding about a picture in his mind, which kept him awake and stayed on in dreams and drove him from bed early in the morning. It was the Taurus weave room, its thunder and mist breaking over him. But the abyss did not open completely until Monday morning when he actually saw it again, and with Jimmy Nabors at his elbow, had this dismal image in his mind sharpened. The place was a true reflection of the clutter of Hubert Quigley's mind.

This is where I've got every cent I own invested, Adam said to himself. This is another Salter Webbing mill. Another Kieselguhr.

This time he knew better what questions to ask, but apparently Jimmy had been warned, for he gave answers in too low a voice to be heard in the mill, and outside he was evasive. When Adam pinned him down, Jimmy said he'd better ask Mr. Quigley about it. Apparently all the employees had been alerted. Even Lloyd Bowers, the friendly purchasing agent, was too busy to look up when Adam passed.

After the proper delay, Quigley received him, even more coldly this morning, for he had just gotten Adam's letter asking to examine the books. "You may inspect them one week from tomorrow," Quigley said stiffly.

"Mr. Quigley, have you given any thought to diversification? Elsewhere I see terry cloth beach blankets and dish towels, synthetic fiber decoration, printed designs on beach towels—"

"Prints look cheap, Japanese. So does that metallic gold thread. It's just a fad. Look here, Salter, we're doing all right—"

"I'd heard the company was losing money."

"We'll be in the black by the fourth quarter. Let me show you—" Quigley again brought out his many colored charts.

"I'm not insisting that the particular products I mentioned would be for us. But I wonder if we're putting enough emphasis on styling. I hear yellow, pink, and brown are very popular, and here we seem to specialize in white towels."

Quigley's lip curled. "We make a quality towel, not fifty-nine-cent junk. Our customers want a white towel because they can afford to put a colored monogram on it. White is more absorbent, a better towel. We make some colored towels for our less expensive line. But we're a high-wage town here. We just can't make money on ten-cent-store goods."

"Couldn't high labor costs be offset by more modern equipment? I'm thinking particularly of the weave room."

"Of course I've considered that. I have not believed in the past, nor do I believe now, that it would pay at this juncture. We have a piecework incentive plan with job loads written into a three-year union contract. We can't afford to pay for labor *and* new looms."

"We could change the basis of that piecework plan."

"We could, could we?" Quigley laughed scornfully. "There'd be a strike, and we certainly can't afford a strike."

"You've got good workers here. They'd allow changes to save the company." He ignored Quigley's skeptical grimace. "When does the contract with the union expire?"

"In September."

"Do you plan to renew it as now written?"

"Any plan for the labor contract is presently classified 'SECRET.' Now, if you'll excuse me, Mr. Salter, I'm quite busy. Good day."

Your decision, hell! thought Adam. What am I *talking* to him for? New equipment with the present management would be a waste of money. Here was where the vein was open and the company was bleeding to death.

The labor contract was what made Adam decide not to wait for Dr. Garth. His program was incomplete, but Olin needed only two hundred more shares for absolute control; then the contract would be renewed and the company doomed. So that day Adam began visiting small stockholders. It was not yet an open declaration of war for control of the company but a mildly worded five-point petition asking for the sale of the Taurus timberlands to pay for new equipment, a complete annual financial statement instead of the meaningless figures of capital and surplus which the company had been sending to stockholders, a modest cash dividend, cumulative voting for directors, and Adam Salter as a director of the company.

Instead of disparaging the company's management, he stressed possibilities, remedies, values—especially the valuable real estate —for he did not want to frighten the stockholders into selling to Olin. Adam did not wholeheartedly favor a cash dividend now, and he knew Dr. Garth would oppose it, but as he had expected, the small stockholders greeted the suggestion enthusiastically. A Birmingham stockbroker, who did not name the party he represented, had already visited most of these stockholders in an effort to buy them out, and the existence of the real estate seemed to explain why their stock was suddenly in demand. Olin's agent was offering fifteen dollars a share more than Adam had offered, and this gave the stockholders a buoyant sensation of rising prices. Adam did not in his arguments mention Bascom Olin, nor did he intimate that he had an ally on the board of directors.

Adam made a point of seeking out G. P. Moon. He did not expect Moon to sign the petition, but Moon talked constantly and went everywhere, and Adam wanted the concealed assets to get around Mercer. Moon looked wary, but frowning and pursing his lips, he listened to Adam and replied that he would think it over.

The first of the more sophisticated stockholders Adam approached was P. D. Emery. Mr. Emery, a chill-faced liver-spotted banker, listened to Adam and said: "Now let's see. You say you can replace these three slashers the mill has now with one new slasher, which would cost fifty thousand dollars. Now how much will that save in a year?" Adam said he would save in direct labor at least three men on two shifts, or fifteen thousand a year. And he guessed it would pay for itself in a couple of years through greater loom efficiency, less waste, and fewer weaving seconds.

"You *guess!*" Mr. Emery did not raise his voice, but Adam had the sensation that he was shouting. "What kind of figures have you given me? A bunch of guesses. You favor diversification? Do you know how much it costs to put a new design on a dobby loom? Ten dollars or fifty dollars or a hundred dollars? You say the company needs to modernize. How soon would long-draft spinning pay for itself? In two years, or six years, or never?" He threw down his gold pencil. "I worked for the Liberty Mills for six years, and I'm now on the executive committee of the board of directors. Don't think we weren't looking for every way in the world to cut costs. And we had a lot more to go on than guesses."

"I don't know exactly what the company's costs are," Adam said, "and neither does the management. That's another thing they need—standard costs. But if you doubt that new equipment is needed, Mr. Emery, go down to the mill yourself, and look around."

"I suspect that's about what you've done too. All my life people have come in here that want to spend money. That's their solution for every problem. A lot of them sounded as smooth as silk, but when they got hold of the money they wanted they frittered it away. Call me again, Mr. Salter, when you can give me something besides guesses."

Adam got up, feeling battered, and said he could come back after he had seen the company's books. No doubt about it, he had gone off half-cocked, and had had the bad luck to run into someone who knew the textile business. He decided to get detailed cost figures before calling on Duncan Chisholm and Rice Alexander.

By Friday Adam had twelve signatures on his petition. Small Stockholders' Committee was no misnomer. He hadn't the signature of a single face card. His supporters were people like Miss Winnie McCaffery, the lady of the cats, who owned two hundred shares, and Mrs. W. T. Sloan, aged eighty-two, who owned twenty-five shares, and altogether, they held less than three per cent of the stock.

At noon on Friday Duncan Chisholm telephoned Adam's apartment and asked him to come to his office before two o'clock.

At one-thirty, Adam looked around eagerly as he passed through the board room. Nothing had changed except that he no longer worked there. The Dow-Jones Industrial Average was within a point of where it had been when he left. He had a fleeting but keen sensation that he had been out of his head to leave his job.

Mr. Chisholm was waiting in his office, and began in his clipped crisp way: "Adam, I asked you to come in for two reasons. First, Mr. Olin has asked me to offer you eighty-five dollars a share for your Taurus stock."

"I'd think he'd want my stock more than that, Mr. Chisholm."

"He also offered to pay you a premium of fifteen dollars a share over whatever price you paid."

"No thanks."

"Think it over, Adam. It's a sure profit though not for me. I'm doing this for nothing—as a favor to both of you."

Adam glanced at his watch. Mr. Chisholm had picked this time because Olin usually came in around two o'clock, and he must have asked Mr. Chisholm to report to him then.

"I have something else to offer you, Adam. That's advice." Mr. Chisholm seemed to be choosing his words carefully. "All young men who are worth anything try to move too fast—as you are doing. I traded in the stock market until I recognized that I had to be as patient as a farmer, to sow at one season and harvest at another." Mr. Chisholm's thin worried face declared his sincerity. "I've heard you say how much you liked Mercer and how you plan to stay here. If you are not careful, you may get yourself quarantined so that no one can afford to hire you or do business with you. Rumor has it that you have some powerful allies from out of town. Let me urge you to let your backers do what you are trying to do in another way. If you have no such allies, what can you achieve with less than 10 per cent of Taurus stock and this feeble stockholders' committee?"

"I'm dissatisfied with the management."

"Mr. Quigley retires next year. Then there will be a change."

"It's the change I'm afraid of. I hear Jack Olin is being pushed as the next president of the company."

"I know nothing about that, but I think the company could do a lot worse. He strikes some people as being a little haughty, so they'd like to believe he's incompetent, but I've seen signs of real ability in him. For one thing he's done well with his investments."

"He must have consulted a very able stockbroker," Adam said, smiling, but Mr. Chisholm's words made him anxious.

"I advised Jack, but he made the decisions, and he certainly didn't do everything I advised. He's independent, and the man on the street resents that. I've always assumed you'd be one to copper his bets."

"Mr. Chisholm, if I can prove Jack Olin is not capable of doing that job, would you oppose his being given it?"

"I will *support* the candidacy of the best available man for the job. I urge you to do likewise. And let me remind you that the raiders who win proxy fights against well-entrenched management are loaded with money, and even with money it's exceedingly hard to accomplish."

"Here's another point. You know how Bascom Olin treats the smaller stockholders in the companies he controls. Whether or not I'm helping my own status here as the rich man's friend, isn't the small stockholder in The Taurus Company due more consideration than he's getting? Doesn't he have a right to know what the company is earning, and to receive a reasonable amount of that money in dividends?"

"Yes, but that's a more general problem for any fair-minded

director. The small stockholder wants dividends. Not that there is any question of the company's paying dividends now since it's losing money. The man like Bascom Olin in a high tax bracket wants the money plowed back. Their interests are opposed. My taxes are high, too, but in those companies of which I'm a director I've tried to treat all stockholders fairly."

"So I've heard. But I'm talking about Olin. What can the small Taurus stockholder do? There's no public market for his stock, so usually he can't sell it at all except to some insider and then for a fraction of its value. Before I started this campaign, he had no chance of disposing of his stock at any decent price. Now he does because Olin's bidding against me. That's why I don't understand your position in trying to quiet me down."

"I'm only pointing out that you are working yourself into an inextricable situation," Mr. Chisholm said coldly, getting up. "If you should change your mind about selling, let me know."

"Would selling my stock to Mr. Olin make peace between us?"

"I think it would."

Pretending to consider the proposition, Adam looked at Mr. Chisholm's lean face. He was a man Adam respected and whose respect he wanted, but he was aware that he could not have Mr. Chisholm's approval and follow his own ambitions. "Come to think of it, I guess Mr. Olin's about the last person I'd sell my stock to. Tell him that, will you?" Mr. Chisholm nodded, raising his eyebrows, and said nothing more.

As Adam passed through the board room, he saw Bascom Olin's Homburg and back, for he was facing the other way looking at the prices on the Translux. There sits a man with a million in cash, Adam thought, and he's here early.

Adam went outside and glanced at his watch. He wanted to give Mr. Chisholm just enough time to relay his answer, which should get Olin's temper up.

Mr. Chisholm's opinion of Jack Olin had jolted him, for he had thought disapproval of that young man was universal. He reviewed what he knew of Jack Olin. Perhaps his own ideas had been too greatly influenced by Dr. Garth and by his own impression of Jack as a playboy and idler.

Jack came from an able family. Bascom Olin's father, a man known for illiteracy and coarseness, had accumulated a quarter of a million dollars by shrewd trading. The family fortune was now estimated at fifty times that and more. Bascom Olin was a hard worker, and like Dr. Garth he had the money and nerve to buy when others had neither, but while Dr. Garth had spent most of his time practicing medicine, Olin had bent all his efforts toward calling the turns—or more accurately, riding the trends. In spite of Olin's nimble financial twisting and turning, Adam doubted that he could have built up a first-rate industrial company like The Taurus Company of the 1930s. He didn't have to. He had the money to hire men who could or to buy companies which were already sure things.

Adam had often wondered what a man of Bascom Olin's temperament was doing in the gregarious atmosphere of the board room. Some said he was too stingy to keep a ticker in his office. Others said he came in to poll the board room crowd and sell what they were buying.

The Olins had behind them a tradition of successful narrowness and shortsightedness, of false pride that paid off. They were unique in Mercer in having had money for several generations without getting any real education or good manners or public spirit.

Jack seemed to be an exception. Any newspaper article about him stated that he had been educated at Exeter and Yale—which gave the impression that he had started the game with a pair of aces back to back, but he had flunked out of Yale after six months. He had married a rich aristocratic young woman, whose lovely face could be seen in newspaper photographs in connection with various charitable causes. Jack had done well in the army. It was clear that he had never met anything that could change him. Now at thirty-one he was ready to come home and start taking over. Adam would have to deal with him for the rest of his life. And Dr. Garth might die in the hospital.

Another question puzzled Adam. Why should Olin pick a lame horse like The Taurus Company for his son to ride? Olin controlled at least ten thriving companies, and hidden assets or not, the next president of The Taurus Company was going to have a long row to hoe getting the company into the black again.

But The Taurus Company had apparently attracted Olin for years, and he had been moving in on it since Monroe Mercer's death. Through his bank's trust department, he had prodded the latter's estate to sell over half of its sixteen thousand shares, which he and his underlings had bought. After a few years much of this stock had come into Olin's hands, and now he had ten thousand shares in his own name. Adam had assumed that he must be making a place for an idle son. At the same time he might see such great values in The Taurus Company that he wanted to make Jack president as another move toward absolute control of the company with the usual strangulation of smaller stockholders.

No, Jack might be very successful at getting what he wanted, but he would not strain himself to save The Taurus Company, and Adam was determined that Jack Olin should not be its president. He looked at his watch. Now was the time. He went back and pushed open the black-painted glass door and went inside.

Olin was just coming out of Mr. Chisholm's office. He was scowling angrily as Adam hoped he would be. A feeling of cold tension throughout his torso, Adam went to him and said: "I'd like to talk with you for a moment, Mr. Olin."

"Changed your mind?"

"No, sir. I want to buy your Taurus stock," said Adam, raising his voice. All the board room hats and faces turned, and all eyes were fixed on Adam and Bascom Olin.

"I deal only with principals," said Olin, moving to pass Adam.

Adam blocked his way. "I *am* a principal, and I'll give you ninety dollars a share for your stock."

"Not interested," said Olin, once more trying to get past.

"You name a price."

Olin's eyes flashed. "I know damn well you haven't got the money to buy my stock!"

"I've just recently bought two thousand shares, Mr. Olin, and I'd like to buy a few thousand more."

"Get out of my way," said Olin. Adam stepped aside, and Olin strode past him.

"If you change your mind, let me know!" Adam called to him. Olin did not look back and slammed the door hard.

Quickly Adam looked around the room at the wide eyes of the board room crowd, including Reamer's in open credulity, staring after him, and heard then the murmur of excited talk rising against the chattering ticker. His gaze swept over to Mr. Chisholm, thin and erect in his doorway. Mr. Chisholm looked gravely at Adam and shook his head.

~~~~~~

16

The Myersons' summer cottage overlooked the cove of a big lake made by a power dam fifteen miles above Kieselguhr. Adam reached it late that afternoon by a serpentine road following the shoreline of the lake. He had a feeling of pressure, almost a hangover, when he did something not in his style, and he felt as with the deception of G. P. Moon that his footwork that afternoon had been too fancy to become him. He had been completely self-controlled then with a brashness which seemed a present from his glands. His body processes were still charged from the encounter, and this doubled the bile he tasted at the prospect of meeting Josephine with Herold.

Through the drizzle which fell slanting across big pine trunks, he saw the Myersons' cottage and Herold's convertible in deep shade. It was much colder here than in town. The reflecton of trees made a brim of green around the rain-speckled lake, and the shadows on the far shore were already as black as the mouths of caves.

Adam knocked and entered the big room where a fire was burning in a fireplace with damp wood snapping. Despite its civilized rusticity, the cabin had the male air of a fishing camp where men got away from their wives, and against it Blakely had made a small protest with vases of flowers and mountain laurel. Adam, moving into the room, was aware of the changing smells from the rain-soaked forest outside to the fire and the slightly musty smell of a cabin closed up all winter.

Blakely, wearing an apron over her sweater and skirt, came from the kitchen. "Hello, Adam." She seemed cheerful and shy. "It would rain."

He was relieved, for her eyes were full of undisturbed confidence. She certainly trusted him not to misbehave with her best friend. "Fire looks good," he said.

"What would you like to drink?"

Coffee, he felt like saying, and argument, for he was so tired and keyed up that his nerves were feeding on themselves, but he took beer. He sat on a kitchen stool and drank from the frosty can. At first his system fought the relaxing effect of the beer and the warm kitchen, but soon the cold fluid seemed to wash out the dusty corners of his stomach. He sat back and watched Blakely cut up vegetables for a green salad.

"Steaks look nice and thick," he said.

"They've been marinating for two days. With the rain I guess I'll have to cook them inside."

"Where are Josephine and Cato?"

"Out on the porch. Cato's telling Josephine dirty stories. Go on out there. I'll be through with this salad in a minute."

"I'll say hello. You look good in that apron, by the way." And happy in it, too, he thought. He took his half-finished beer out on the screened porch. Cato was lying on a glider there, his glass balanced on his chest, and Josephine was sitting in a chair at its head.

"We didn't hear you come," said Cato. "The sound of your coming must have been obscured by thunder."

"Or the squirrels running on the roof," said Josephine. She smiled without constraint, and Adam found himself responding to the magnetism of her beauty as before, and it goaded him into an angry inner laugh at himself.

"Sit down here," said Herold, swinging his legs to the floor to make room for Adam on the glider. "Those chairs over there are wet."

Adam walked to the screen. Tall pines made a carpet of needles on the slope down to the water's edge. The lake and far shore grew misty and melted into each other. A fine blowing rain penetrated the screen and chilled his face. Adam turned back and faced them. "How is your father?" he asked Josephine.

"I talked with him today, and apparently nothing's conclusive yet."

Cato wore a plaid wool shirt and white flannel trousers so old they were slightly yellow—a costume just right for the occasion,

Adam decided. He wore a business suit, for he owned no sport clothes. Josephine and Cato were leaning toward each other, drawn, Adam knew, by understandings which excluded him. "I have the feeling I interrupted you, Cato."

"I was about to tell Jo another very old very dirty story. Zeus fell in love with a maiden named Leda and became incarnated in the form of a duck. Yes, that was it, an ugly young duck. This duckling, not remembering he was Zeus, obviously wasn't old enough or grand enough to do anything about an Olympian passion and had to content itself with sordid fantasies until one night he woke up to find himself a swan. He sought out Leda by starlight. Putting the loftiest interpretation upon it, it is easy enough to see how it happened—they were both bipeds, both lily white—in the dark it was hard to distinguish—one thing led to another. Then as dawn, the rosy-fingered, crept over their bower, imagine their horror as by slow degrees they saw they were not of the same species, nor of the same order, not even the same phylum. But they had to stay together for the egg's sake."

"Oh, Cato," said Josephine, laughing. "What a perfectly dreadful story!"

Cato looked at her morosely as if disappointed that his story had not turned out better. "Yes, remind me not to tell it to your father."

A lapse in the conversation followed full of the noise of dripping woods, and the light seemed to fail visibly. Both Cato and Josephine were woolgathering. Did Cato know about Adam's blunder of that Sunday afternoon?

If so, he was not taking it seriously, and Adam realized that his feeling of guilt might be excessive as was Josephine's anger. A man had made a very awkward pass at a woman and had offended her. This should not ruin anyone's life.

He would patch it up even if it took years. Josephine was worth the effort. As he relaxed, with this feeling of patience, he realized that the trouble with them was something else. He had interrupted some serious talk, he knew, and not about ducks and not about himself.

"Isn't it sweet of Blakely to have us," said Josephine. "She's quite a good cook."

"You're a good cook too," Cato said.

"I can cook a few things. The things everybody can cook."

"The ones I've tasted seemed very fancy."

"The fancy dishes are the ones everybody can cook."

"Nonsense. But your modesty becomes you, dear girl," Cato said, patting her knee. "My compliments to the chef."

Josephine flinched and buttoned her sweater, saying: "It gets cold so suddenly."

"I'll see how Blakely is doing," Adam said and went into the kitchen.

Blakely looked up eagerly. "I like that tie. Is it new?"

"About three years old." She was redoubling her efforts to please him, and this afternoon he valued her attitude a great deal. "Josephine and Cato seem a bit tense. Do you know what's the matter?"

Blakely whirled, her eyes flashing. "It's that woman! She's been with them all the time and worn them out. Thank heaven she left this morning."

"You don't mean Mrs. Wriston?"

"No, that Leah." Blakely turned her small angry face toward him. "She despises this town, she despises us!"

"Then what is she doing here?"

"I think she's trying to take Cato away from Josephine!"

"Is that what Josephine thinks?"

"Josephine won't talk about her. As if Josephine didn't have enough on her mind without that woman deviling her! I like Dr. Garth, but now that he's sick he's imposing on her too and wearing her out and just about to drive her out of her mind. Josephine doesn't complain, but I can see it. Now this Leah has to make trouble. She gives me the creeps!"

Adam had suspended judgment about Leah Monday morning out of immediate preoccupation and habit. Perhaps Leah and Blakely just didn't get along. Leah would resent Blakely's freshness and youth and Blakely the other's Herold-like cleverness. And Leah was like Herold—in accent and manner; they had the imprint of the same kind of life. Yet Cato was decent where in a subtle way she was immodest.

The strain in the situation must come from Leah's having some hold on Cato or Josephine. Otherwise she could not have imposed on them. Josephine might have allowed it for a single morning out of politeness, but no longer. Adam got up to have a look at Herold.

"Speaking of people being tense," said Blakely, stopping him, "maybe I shouldn't say this, but you have something on your mind too, don't you?"

"Just business. I've been trying to get a deal going."

"Is there anything I can do?" she said. He looked puzzled, and she added: "I've got a lot of influence with Daddy-o."

"Thanks, Blakely, I don't think so."

Josephine came into the kitchen and said: "Let me help."

"I have everything about ready. You entertain the men."

"No, I want to help. Are you going to have dinner in front of the fire? I'll set the table."

"Are you all ready to eat?" said Blakely. "When should I start the steaks?"

"Now," said Josephine. "Whenever you're ready. Never ask Cato if he's ready to eat. He never is."

Adam caught Josephine's eye, but she just looked away with a quick distant smile.

"Adam," said Blakely behind him. "Would you and Cato put the big table over nearer the fire?"

As they moved the table, Cato said: "So this is Blackberry Winter. Take it away. One can see one's breath on the porch."

"You'd better enjoy it because when this is over, it will be very hot again."

Cato took his drink to a window seat in the far corner of the room, and Adam joined him. "I saw you downtown today, Adam. You were walking fast and you had an expression of savage determination. I trembled to think of how you would smite the wicked who were obstructing you."

"I didn't see you."

"I was across the street from you. You seemed rather troubled, Adam. And do now."

Adam looked around and saw Cato regarding him with sympathetic interest. "Blakely just made the same observation. I've got a business deal that has to be done on the quiet and in a hurry."

Cato raised his glass. "Let me wish you every success."

"That lady who was with you Monday morning? Who is she?"

"Leah? She's a friend of Belle's. Excuse me, let me see if I can help—"

"What kin is she to you?"

Cato looked at Adam in astonishment. "Kin!"

"Is she your sister?"

Slowly Cato sank back on the window seat. "I hadn't realized the resemblance was so strong."

"It's not just the resemblance. The way you acted, too."

"I see. I suppose it was rather transparent. Don't tell anyone, not even Blakely. You must have guessed why I'm keeping it a secret."

"No."

"To protect Jo." Cato sighed. "Leah has a serious flaw. I'd rather not tell you what it is."

"She seems very obliging to put up with being incognito and adopting another name."

"That was my condition for letting her come. Fraden is her middle name. Is not telling you more unfair?"

"By no means."

"Adam, if you don't look out, you're going to be a pillar of the community. Don't misunderstand. I envy that quality."

"What quality?"

"Temperance. You are curious but not to excess."

"You're kicking my leg, boy."

Herold looked glum. "I'm perfectly serious. Someday I'll explain to you why I lack that quality."

"Why not tell me now."

"I'll need a drink for that." He lowered his voice when Josephine came from the kitchen. She spread a bright checked cloth over the table they had moved. Josephine seemed totally occupied with the simple task of smoothing the cloth and putting cutlery on it. The firelight colored her face and calves with reds and yellows and modeled and rounded her body.

"You're lucky to have your background," said Cato between sips of Scotch. "Mercer, I mean."

"What's so special about Mercer?"

"That's just it. My background, I see now, is the special one."

Herold stopped to listen when Blakely came in and said, laughing: "Josephine, honey, I said the big plates, and not those knives. We'll need the knives with the serrated edges."

Josephine smiled and nodded. "I'll do better."

Blakely embraced her. "I'm so glad you make mistakes sometimes, Josephine," she said, squealing. "It makes me feel so *good!*"

Adam turned to Cato. "Is the problem of Leah what's worrying Josephine now?"

"Yes, that and her father. What a father he is! The tyrant should have had a dozen children instead of one to absorb his authority. My case was different. There was a shortage of men in my child-

110

hood. My father died when I was six. I—we—were raised by two neurotic women, my mother and my maternal grandmother. He seemed to sense that he was going to die young and left a good bit in writing—advice, encouragement in steamer letters, so to speak. In fact he had prepared so well for his death I've suspected that he gave up his life rather willingly. I spent most of my childhood on the move in Europe. My mother expected me from the time of my father's death to act like an adult—an unusually prudent and understanding adult at that. I cannot remember a time when she didn't tell me, 'You're the head of the family now.' She talked endlessly about problems of her own, including problems of the heart, which children are usually spared."

Cato gestured with his glass. "Look at Jo there. You see in her face all the qualities which my mother and grandmother, and Leah too, lacked—honesty, loyalty, generosity, and you might go so far as to add kindness. There is the only form in which I can believe in those virtues. You can understand why Jo seems a last chance for me. I've waked up at three o'clock in the morning and from then till dawn engaged in what I call 'pit-gazing.' And the blackest of all the black fears I have then is that I may lose her."

She was at that moment righting her mistakes in table-setting, her face set in the same seriousness, looking very smooth against the rough stone of the chimney behind her. Buttoned, her sweater seemed a little tight, emphasizing her shoulders as well as her bosom. Physically she gave an impression of strength though her mistakes in table-setting just now seemed to Adam a winning evidence of weakness. He turned as Herold resumed his talk.

"My money was well protected but I was not. I was misused by a homosexual schoolmaster and by an almost equally perverted governess before I was twelve. I had an affair with a friend of my mother's before I was out of prep school." He laughed. "Affair! I was fourteen, she was twenty-five."

Behind him Adam could hear the girls' footsteps coming and going, Blakely sharp and quick, Josephine's longer and softer, sometimes fading away entirely on the rug.

"So to me Mercer seems very wholesome. There must be plenty of vice here, but the pressure of public opinion is against it. I remember at the age of fifteen polling some friends about what adultery was. We finally agreed that it was seduction of a woman without her husband's consent. The sexual business is not the part

I consider most corrupting. What really worked against me was that I never belonged anywhere. Here you can have ambitions, without appearing ridiculous, of becoming president of the Rotary Club or a vestryman in the Episcopal Church." He had been speaking with some vehemence and excitement, and when he stopped abruptly, Adam sat in silence for a moment.

"Well, you know what old John B. said. The road to hell goes from the gates of Heaven as well as from the City of Destruction."

Instead of flinching in embarrassment at this unwieldy quotation, Cato's eyes twinkled, and he said: "Bunyan! How refreshingly old hat!"

Adam was sure that this self-revelation was not a hard-luck story to win sympathy or pity which Herold told just anybody during the sixth highball. The account of his childhood suggested that Leah's flaw was moral, probably sexual. Yet Herold had been defending himself, not Leah. Against what imagined accusation? "It seems to me you've come through all that unscathed," said Adam. "I suppose what you're suggesting is that your sister was the one who suffered from your unstable family life."

"I did not come through unscathed."

"Then Leah was the one at your place that Friday night."

"Who did you think? Certainly not Belle!"

"I didn't know then that Leah was in town. I was about to decide I was hearing things. What did you do with Leah during the Chisholm's party?"

"That was a piece of luck. She had a sick headache that night."

The steaks sizzled, and the tempo of Blakely's walk increased. "Dinner is served, gentlemen," she called out, and Adam and Cato arose.

Adam was not satisfied. He had a feeling that Cato's story was defective. Four of us know about Leah now—Cato, Josephine, Belle Wriston, and I, and of course Leah. That's too many people to keep a secret. He thought of Mrs. Wriston—a woman with perhaps other secrets—and his curiosity was becoming intemperate. His idea of what he expected to learn from her was still too vague to put into words, but he thought he needed to have a look at Mrs. Wriston.

~~~~~~

17

Down in the valley the streets of the older part of Mercer were geometrically straight, but on the mountainsides to the east and south the streets curved for reasons of fashion and to fit the slopes. The most expensive houses now were high, flashing at night like the dress circle of an opera house. Mrs. Wriston's Gothic house, on the other hand, suggested a winged gargoyle projecting from a cathedral roof about to spread its wings and fly over the town.

A half century ago Mrs. Wriston's grandfather had been awarded ten thousand dollars in a damage suit against a railroad—a very large judgment for those days—and against the best financial advice had put it all into Procter and Gamble common stock. It was the only sign of financial acumen or even intelligence that the man had ever shown or needed to show, and all that his heirs had to do was hold onto the stock, which they had done in lieu of work. This family tradition had been behind Mrs. Wriston's refusal to talk with Adam about selling her thousand shares of Taurus stock when he called her ten days earlier. This Saturday however she surprised him by agreeing at once to see him.

Belle Wriston's childless marriage had ended with the death of her marvelously inert husband ten years ago. Adam had assembled a picture of Mrs. Wriston from Blakeley's disconnected stories, such as her having had as a secretary a local high-school boy some years before. She was the kind of woman who had friendships like love affairs, for she seemed to demand some performance which no mere friend could supply. She had a history of seeing new friends constantly for a few weeks, bombarding them with presents and entertaining them, calling them several times a day, wearing them and herself out, then quarreling over some trifle and parting for good. She had been through most of the susceptible material in Mercer, so she adopted and sponsored newcomers and eventually discarded them. She spent a lot of time in New York, and what she did there the ladies of Mercer would have liked very much to know.

Mrs. Wriston received Adam in a lushly furnished interior and a cloud of strong scent. Her huge eyes were like those of a nocturnal animal such as a lemur. Her black hair was piled on top of her head in a ponderous mass, and her face came down to a small heart-shaped mouth and a pointed chin. She wore a golden jacket with a tight belt, black toreador pants, and golden embroidered slippers. Her figure with large, magically pointed breasts and a tiny waist swelled this costume voluptuously. Adam had heard that she was close to fifty, and at an age when farm women of Sweetwater County were often toothless great-grandmothers, she looked weirdly young, not well-preserved but the product of black rejuvenation like a vampire. If you had strong nerves, you could recognize that she was beautiful.

Adam followed her through a room of bright red, blue, and orange. "You have an interesting house, Mrs. Wriston."

"Yes, I decorated it myself."

A picture window squared and sealed out the town, now twinkling like a jeweler's showcase. Just below, two high stone walls lay like legs around the guest house where Cato was staying.

Mrs. Wriston with the slow smooth gait of a woman who had plenty of time on her hands glided to a fertile crescent of a sofa. "You're a Garth," she said. "I'd have seen it even if I hadn't known anyway. Oh, I know the Garth face. Well, where's your petition?"

He handed it to her and sat down opposite. She glanced over the sheet without reading it, then looked at him from head to foot, meanwhile holding the corner of the petition between her lips. Adam took this occasion to tell her about the Taurus real estate.

"Now what's going on here?" she said. "Are your uncle and Bascom Olin fighting about who's going to run the company?"

"If you mean Dr. Garth, he's a first cousin once removed. Though I'm sure he would approve most of the points in it, Dr. Garth doesn't know about this petition."

"He doesn't! Why not? Everyone else in town does."

"Dr. Garth is in the hospital in New Orleans."

114

"I see. And you want to be a director? Well, I wish they'd start paying something again. People think I'm rich, but I'm not all that rich. It's certain I'll never see that money if it's not paid me in dividends."

So that's the key here, he thought. He was gratified to find out so quickly. The woman may be queer, but she's no fool. "Yes, as you'll see by the petition there, I favor giving stockholders some of the gain from the Liberty Mills liquidation, and when the company is in the black, paying out 60 per cent of earnings in dividends—"

"I hear you sassed Bascom Olin down at Chisholm's place yesterday."

"No, I just offered to buy his stock." Adam tried again. "Although the company needs capital for modernization, I believe it can afford to make a cash disbursement of perhaps two dollars a share—"

"How about a drink?" She folded the petition which now had a smear of lipstick in one corner. "I've been wanting to have a look at you. Cato's taken a shine to you. I had a party in my hotel suite in New York, and that's where Cato met Josephine Garth. That doesn't mean I could help her falling for him any more than she could. I'll bet old Dr. Garth would like to cut my throat for introducing them." She leaned toward Adam as though trying to swallow him with her eyes. "You know Dr. Garth. What does he think of Cato? Hates him, doesn't he?"

That was the catch, Adam thought. She was easy to see this time because she wanted information. "Well, Cato grows on people."

"Dr. Garth thinks Cato's not good enough for his daughter, but Cato's too good for her. He doesn't have any meanness in him toward anybody. Cato never was a brat. When he was ten years old, he was as charming and polite as he is now. His mother was a good bit older than I was, but she was one of my best friends. She didn't know how to raise Cato. I told her, 'Here, if you're going to ruin him, give him to me.' Cato's grandfather, John Cato Lanier, was a great actor, but that was all. A lot of theater and café society and good looks but no quality on that side of the family. Now Cato's father was a rich man from an old-line family and a gentleman. You never see that kind now. Everybody around here's too much in a hurry to make back the money they say their granddaddies had before the Civil War ruined them. Southerners like down in the Black Belt tell you they aren't like Yankees—they think we're Yankees—and don't care anything about money. They're lying. It's just too hot down there to work for it. But Cato's father was not that way. He just wasn't mean enough. Not mean enough to live."

"I don't understand you."

She patted her voluminous black hair. "Not like you. He didn't like to butt heads. Didn't count his change. You count your change, don't you?"

"Yes, don't you?"

"Sure I do. But Cato doesn't and neither did his father. I knew the minute I saw you you were a tough boy."

"Yes, Cato's interesting, and so is Leah. I met her at the Garths'."

Mrs. Wriston stared at him with night-seeing eyes. Adam searched them with his gaze, but instead of finding their vastness revealing, he was lost in darkness.

"Uh-huh," she said, suddenly displeased. She picked up the petition and slapped it on her thigh. "Well, thanks for coming over." She got up and crowded him toward the door. "Leave this here for a day or so, and I'll think it over."

"If you don't mind, Mrs. Wriston, I'll send you a copy. I'll need that one with the signatures." As they stood only a foot or so apart under a dim overhead light at the front door, he looked closely at her face for the hairline scars of plastic surgery. There was no sign of them. His parting impression was of eyes, drowning pools with suction in them.

He had mishandled Mrs. Wriston, and she might never sign his petition though he was not through trying. He had another copy of it in his breast pocket, which he had not left with her because he wanted an excuse for coming back. He felt that he had not wasted his time. He reviewed what Herold had said yesterday and what Mrs. Wriston had just said, and he tried to identify the blanks in their stories. So much was left out. Yesterday Herold's confessions had temporarily disarmed him. Now he had some indigestible impressions to make him suspicious again.

One blank in these tales of Herold's childhood and family was Leah. Did this failure to mention her mean she had been "away"—in a mental hospital?

Doubtless Mrs. Wriston had decided that Dr. Garth had sent him on Taurus business, and when he inquired about Leah, she concluded that he had also come on Cato Herold business. She had a point, for Dr. Garth would be a man to have Herold investigated, and in turn that brought up James Sizemore, the private detective, who could have been waiting for Herold. Sizemore's procedure did not fit this theory even allowing for the greatest ineptitude, but someone had hired him.

Adam still had a half-dozen stockholders to visit. After he saw them, Sizemore's office in Birmingham would be his next stop.

18

When Adam called James Sizemore's office in Birmingham early Monday morning, the operator reported that his telephone had been disconnected. So Adam asked Clyde Lavender to inquire about Sizemore through the Birmingham police.

Clyde had the answer for him in half an hour. The police had revoked Sizemore's city license as a private detective and closed his office. Several clients had complained about him. One was a manufacturer who had hired him to find the thief responsible for inventory losses. Now he was accusing Sizemore of collusion with the thief and suing for his bond. Sizemore had moved to the town of Clayton and opened a photography studio there. "He wasn't getting any detective bi'ness to speak of anyway," said Clyde. "That is, *good* bi'ness. A woman want to get a cut-rate job on catching her husband with some slut in a two-dollar motel room, Sizemore was the man to get. But there wasn't enough of that, a divorce being as easy to get as it is in this state now."

Adam was about to call Sizemore when his telephone rang; the Birmingham operator preceded a pleasant unfamiliar voice: "This is Dean H. Byroade, Mr. Salter. The Taurus Company has asked me to help out, and I understand you have some improvements to suggest about company operations. Would you have lunch with me today to talk them over? Oh, excuse me, my secretary is signaling to me that I have a luncheon engagement. Would coffee at the Mercer Café be convenient? How about three o'clock?" Adam agreed, and Byroade thanked him and promised not to keep him long.

Adam arranged a four-thirty appointment with Sizemore in

Clayton, and early in the afternoon, after a conference with the accountant who was going to inspect The Taurus Company's books for him tomorrow, he called a college classmate, a Birmingham lawyer, to inquire about Dean Byroade. The friend said that Byroade had been a successful Wall Street lawyer, had married a Birmingham heiress, and had come there to open a law firm and manage her properties. What kind of lawyer? "This kind: no matter how big his fee is, you can't help feeling he's doing you a favor by taking the case." Adam took the remaining few minutes before meeting Byroade to look him up in *Who's Who*. Byroade, it seemed, was also author of *Strategy in Corporate Proxy Contests*.

As Adam walked toward the Mercer Café, he imagined the conference. At first he pictured sitting in the crowded restaurant, but Byroade would probably prefer the private Banquet Room. Instead of trying to buy his stock Byroade intended to talk him out of making more trouble and perhaps to threaten by a judicious weighing of consequences to the career of Adam Salter. As the charm of Byroade's voice became dimmer, Adam began to expect a roomful of Olin men, perhaps Olin himself, and a stenographer taking down everything he said.

Byroade had warned him that the agenda would be Adam's own program for The Taurus Company. If he, Adam, withheld his ideas, any transcript would be damaging. If he gave his program in detail, he would forearm Olin, and perhaps the Olins would even steal some of his ideas.

When Adam stepped inside the restaurant, the manager told him that Mr. Byroade was waiting in the Banquet Room.

Adam braced himself for a lion's den, but in the long cold room there was only one man—handsome, well-tanned, gray-haired, with sooty black eyebrows. Smiling, he greeted Adam warmly. In spite of his voice on the telephone, Adam had been expecting a Bascom Olin type, but Mr. Byroade was more like Duncan Chisholm though less aloof, warmer in manner, more high-powered.

While the coffee was being served, Byroade looked attentively at Adam and said: "I stopped to ask my old friend, Duncan Chisholm, about you. He seems to think highly of you. Let me say in passing that I'm very glad young men of the kind Dunc says you are do come back to their home towns instead of hiring out to the highest bidder in New York. Eventually Dunc could have written his own ticket on Wall Street, but he came back here. I tried the other way, and it feels mighty good to get back to the deep South."

"I like it."

Adam's wariness and reticence did not seem to affect Mr. Byroade. He smiled and said: "I'm not the new general counsel of The Taurus Company, by the way. I'm just helping out. I hear you have some reforms to suggest. What kind of thing do you have in mind?"

"How much detail do you want?"

"Just whatever you think is important."

Adam hesitated. Byroade's presence weakened his suspicions, and to be niggardly with his ideas now seemed foolish. "It's almost a classic example from an industrial management textbook of how not to run a mill," Adam said. "The key problem is antiquated machinery. The mill has to have new slashers and looms. But for them to do any good, the job loads have to be increased. Very unrealistic job descriptions are written into a three-year union contract, which expires in September. That's why I'm in such a hurry. If the present contract is renewed, it's going to hamstring management for three more years, and Quigley hasn't the guts to fight for a sound contract. As a matter of fact, talk with him about making *any* changes. Shuttleless looms? No, makes a bad selvage. No dobby applications. Big card cans? No, pinches the sliver, causes breakbacks. Plastic shuttles? No, too much wear on pickers. In other words, if anyone anywhere has ever found a single drawback to some improvement, he won't consider it."

As Adam talked, Byroade sipped his coffee and listened closely, and there was praise in his gray eyes when Adam made a good point. "The Taurus Company has two strong lines," Adam said, "its linen supply and its four-dollar towel. But even the four-dollar towel, that used to be the Cadillac of the towel trade, is getting to be more like the Packard. Quigley's neglecting the whole field of the inexpensive towel sold retail, and that's where the future is going to have to be." Under the stimulation of Mr. Byroade's attention, Adam gave some detailed examples of products for which he felt particular enthusiasm, such as beach blankets with novelty designs. "I don't see how he could miss with the increase of leisure time and back-yard swimming pools."

Byroade nodded. "And you tried to tell Mr. Quigley all this. I see why you felt that you were wasting your breath."

"It's not just Quigley. You know P. D. Emery? He's president of the Mercer Bank and Trust. I went to see him about this, and he mauled me pretty well. His test apparently is will new machinery pay for itself in two years. Of course you've got to get your money back fast on new equipment. But take the cloth room at the mill. It's half glare, half shadow. The power company estimates it will cost about five thousand dollars to put in fluorescent lights. How many employees will that eliminate? None. It won't save any money on current either. So you can't prove with numbers that new lighting would ever pay for itself. But it would mean greater efficiency and better morale because of less eyestrain and fatigue, and higher quality because in addition to sewing and cutting, they're inspecting cloth in there, and they've got to see it to inspect it. I believe you have to consider something besides the pay-out period. But apparently Mr. Emery and his school disagree."

"I suppose they've found, as I have," said Byroade, "that some managers tend to throw away money on frills, and it's the duty of directors to prevent this. Not that adequate lighting is a frill, of course. Mr. Salter, may I pass these ideas on to Mr. Olin? I don't know just how well aware he is that some drastic changes may be needed."

"If you think it would do any good, go ahead."

"Let me ask this. Instead of my relaying your ideas to Mr. Olin, why not present them directly to the entire board. Dunc says the company has three strong directors—Mr. Olin, General Myerson, and Dr. Garth, and they should be interested."

"I don't think Mr. Olin will have any of that."

"Oh, I think so," said Byroade with a friendly smile. "He's got money in the company too, you know."

"Suits me."

"Good. Now may I arrange a date in the next two or three weeks for you to speak to the board? I think you'll find it is more effective than trying to work through stockholders—or Mr. Quigley. I'm afraid too much publicizing of these problems tends to weaken their confidence in the board and in the long run hurt the company. Don't you think so?"

Adam was on the point of agreeing and caught himself. "Don't you think the stockholders have a right to know what goes on?"

"Yes, but I also believe the board of directors must have the authority as legally it has the responsibility." He gave Adam a chance to comment, then looked at his watch. "I'm afraid I've taken most of an hour." Adam was surprised; the time had passed quickly.

At the sidewalk Byroade said: "Mr. Salter, I feel a lot better having talked with you. Frequently when a company is having a bad year, some professional troublemakers spring up who're pretty irresponsible. You'll find your decision to go through the board of directors is right—certainly the most efficient means of gaining your ends. The way Quigley's running it I don't think the information you'd get out of the company would do much good." He paused, and his keen glance played over Adam's face. "By the way, Dunc says you aren't working for him now. I'm involved in promoting a good many companies, and we seem to have plenty of everything except young executive talent. Could I interest you in coming over for a talk about an opening with vast opportunity? I can promise you that executive compensation is one thing I don't believe in economizing on." Adam thanked him, and Byroade said he would keep in touch. They shook hands and parted, Adam going to his car, and Byroade walking toward the Merchants' National Bank.

Adam was halfway to Clayton before reality began to return to him. Byroade had stirred such a desire to please in him that for one happy hour it had seemed that they were on the same side. Adam felt that he had been deceived, that his ideas had been stolen, but actually Byroade had been frank enough. He had admitted working for Olin, that he had investigated Adam, that he was not in favor of allowing any power to the small stockholders.

He didn't come to pick my brains, Adam said to himself. Those ideas had been commonplace. Any management engineer who knew the textile business could have done as well after one day at the mill. Byroade had wanted to have a look at the enemy, slow him up, sidetrack him. Previously Olin had underestimated his opponent, and this error had given Adam a little time. Now if Olin followed Byroade's advice, he would be better prepared for the next move. Byroade is as able as I am, Adam thought, but with twenty-five years more experience.

He also realized that he had practically agreed to do nothing until he had addressed the board, and this would buy time for

122

Olin. Byroade had been working him toward a commitment but was in no position to commit Olin.

The fact that Byroade had investigated him made the activities of the detective, Sizemore, a little more comprehensible though Adam did not yet see Olin's object.

Sizemore's studio was between the Wylie Loan Company and Trixie's Beauty Shoppe in the dim arcade of a five-story building in Clayton. On the door were the letters: JAMES SIZEMORE, ART PICTURES.

Sizemore himself was a big man in a cheap new gray flannel suit and a pink shirt. On his desk was an enormous brilliantly tinted photograph of himself beside a teen-age girl with thick lips, no doubt his daughter.

Sizemore had the smell of bad luck about him, and so did his office—a windowless room with two peculiar angles on the far side as though it were a scrap sawed off a larger unit to make a space unrentable to anyone but its present tenant.

He seemed to be a man who had tried sobriety and drunkenness, honesty and thievery, and nothing had worked. He had tried to make money from the corruption of others and was now trying to cash in on his own—and on mine, Adam thought. No, Dr. Garth had not hired him to check up on Herold. One look at Sizemore would have been enough for Dr. Garth, who aside from moral objections would not have dealt with a man so plainly meant to fail.

Adam could not tell whether Sizemore recognized him. The man was looking at him suspiciously from eyes he could not seem to open very wide, but suspicion was part of his nature and his job.

"I'm interested in getting some information about someone, Mr. Sizemore. Do you do this kind of work?"

"I do all kinds of work."

"What do you charge?"

"Fifteen dollars a day plus expenses. Ten cents a mile for traveling." Their common interest in how much money would change hands seemed a relief to Sizemore. "That's a rock-bottom price. Most investigators charge twenty-five a day plus for shadowing."

"Let me tell you what my problem is, Mr. Sizemore. There is a person—I suspect a local banker—who was very much interested in a certain physician and his daughter in Mercer. Just recently he was so interested he hired a private detective from Birmingham to watch them and their associates. What I want to know is who hired that detective, what for, and what he found out."

Sizemore's face with drooping lids had been motionless while Adam talked. "How long did you figure it would take me?"

"It would equal a two-day job. No traveling." He had used this roundabout vagueness to save the man's pride but he did not want to risk being misunderstood. "Thirty dollars," Adam said.

"It wouldn't be ethics to give out information like that, but what right has a person got to ethics that hasn't got any ethics themself?"

Ethics. Now what did this word mean to Sizemore? Then it came to Adam. "You mean he hasn't paid you?"

"That's right. And it's a lot more than any thirty dollars." He sat reflecting, his mouth shrinking until it was no larger than the birth-stone in his ring. "Give me an hour to work on it."

Adam had a cup of coffee at the Arcade Drug Store and tried to decide what Sizemore wanted the hour for. Often for reasons he couldn't understand Adam had been taken for a police officer or an FBI agent, and perhaps Sizemore, thinking this might be a trap, wanted to check on him before he took his money.

Adam could not imagine Olin's interest in having this man watch Josephine, and he doubted that Olin would hire the man, but G. P. Moon might to get something done for the boss in his own way. Or Dr. Garth might be concealing something, and G. P. Moon might see some angle in it for himself—some blackmail.

An hour passed, and at Sizemore's door, it struck Adam that Sizemore had needed to try to collect his money. Sizemore was sitting at his desk. "I'm sorry, Brother Salter, but I just haven't been able to run it down for you. Another case I'm on came up, and I haven't had a chanst to go through my files. If you could give me another hour or so—"

"I'm afraid not."

"If you'll give me your phone number, I'll get in touch with you within the next twenty-four to forty-eight hours."

"It's a sure thirty bucks. What I want to know is going to come out soon anyway." Sizemore looked unhappy at the thought. "You can reach me here," Adam said, writing his telephone number on a scrap of paper. He gave Sizemore the paper and went outside. He was glad to be going back to Mercer where the sky was bluer and the girls were prettier.

~~~~~~

19

Adam had a late lunch at the Post Office Café an hour before he was to meet his accountant at the mill, and while he ate, he wrote out a list of particulars he wanted—the backlog of orders, age of receivables, excessive expense accounts or other perquisites, recent transfer of stock, and most of all about costs of production. As he was paying for his lunch, the *Mercer Times* was put on the rack, and from the front page he was met with the dark handsome face of Mr. Jack Olin. Mr. Olin, the caption explained, had just been employed as vice-president of The Taurus Company.

Even the newspaper photograph suggested a quality of intolerance, a short temper like his father's, the kind of temper which made people avoid straining his patience. Even as a schoolboy he had been strangely formidable to adults and not just because his father was rich.

It was a smart move, Adam reflected, with Dr. Garth sick and away.

Outside Adam glanced up at the glittering front of Olin's bank. There was a big window in Bascom Olin's office on the second floor which faced the intersection. From this overbearing site Olin could survey the street, and Adam, unable to look toward the window without looking into the sun, had the feeling that Olin was watching him now.

The picture of Jack Olin recurred again and again from the wire newspaper racks along the sidewalk, and his triumph seemed to reverberate in the air. Adam was tempted to call on Dr. Garth for a protest as a director who had not been consulted, but he restrained himself. Dr. Garth shouldn't have an emergency thrown at him when he was ill.

General Myerson was the only man in a position to help, and Adam went to a telephone booth to call him. As soon as he gave his name to the switchboard girl at the Myerson Pipe and Foundry Company, he struck a barrier the existence of which he had forgotten because of his easy relationship with General Myerson through his daughter. General Myerson was in conference now. What firm do you represent? Is there anyone else who can help you? Is there any message? Would you leave your number, sir, and General Myerson will call you. Adam left his name and apartment telephone number, realizing he had been strained out in the net for unwanted salesmen, fund-raisers, job-seekers.

Adam walked toward his car. It seemed that he had spent weeks on this project and accomplished very little. He had signatures representing about 3 per cent of the stock if he got Mrs. Wriston's backing, and counting hers—prematurely, for on his second visit she had been as erratic and noncommittal as before—Olin still lacked only 251 shares for absolute control.

"Hidy." It was G. P. Moon, lean and wolfish against a shady corner. He did not have his usual smile. "Mr. Salter, how about stopping in the café here and having a cup of coffee with me?"

They went inside and took a booth in a far corner.

"I guess you saw that about Jack Olin coming to work for the mill. Ehbody saying the company must really be onto something good. A fellow told me the mill had contracts for all the uniforms of the whole Air Force. Another fellow told me the mill owned a lake in Louisiana that had as much oil under it as half of Texas. No wonder they're going to split that stock."

Adam looked up quickly to see a twinkle in Moon's eye. "I guess with these contracts and oil lands and all, whoever was going to sell us that stock must have changed his mind."

Moon laughed aloud. "Yeah, I guess we fed each other some tall lies. Difference was, you didn't believe mine, but I believed yours."

"I felt kind of bad about it, G. P."

"Oh, no hard feelings. Olin and I had you figured wrong. That is, I made the mistake of letting him do my figuring for me." As devious as he knew Moon's temperament was, this camaraderie made Adam curious. Moon seemed to perceive this, and said: "One thing about being a lawyer, you learn to deal with people who're trying to outsmart you without getting mad. You don't take it personal. It's bi'ness." He sipped his coffee. "You faked him again when you offered to buy his stock. This is how I'm different from Olin. You wouldn't have fooled me twice. Of course if you'd given him time to think it over, he would have known you were bluffing. You knew he had that wire edge, so you didn't give him time. I'll have to hand it to you."

"Thanks."

"I guess you wonder why I'm jawing with you. I want to make a deal with you. I'll help you if you'll help me."

"I don't get you, G. P."

"I mean you believe in that, don't you? If somebody does something for you, you believe in returning the favor."

"Yes, I do."

"You got that petition with you?"

Adam took the folded paper from his breast pocket and handed it over. Moon wiped the water rings from the table top with a paper napkin and flattened the petition on it. He pointed to the red lip-print left by Mrs. Wriston and said: "Whose John Henry is that?" He took out his fountain pen with a flourish and signed his name in enormous green letters. Adam turned the petition around and stared at the signature. "What's in that fountain pen, Moon, disappearing ink?"

Moon laughed a pleasant laugh. "You know my cousin, Reuben Skinner, over in Clayton? He called me just as soon as you left his office that day I came to see you. That's how come I knew so fast what you were doing. Anyway, Skinner wants to sign too."

"Listen, G. P. You know this pledges your proxy too, and there's no way of keeping that from Olin."

"I'm leaving Olin. You don't believe me, do you? One reason is Jack Olin. As long as he was out of town, it wasn't perfect, but I could stand it. I don't care for the old man much, but I can't take his boy at all."

"You seem to know him pretty well. What's he like?"

"He's this kind of fellow. If you were standing there hidying with him, and he saw a black widow spider crawl up your vest and about to go down your shirt, he might see fit to mention it and he might not. But he's shrewd like his old man. That was his idea about coming on and taking this job before everything was settled. He's got a hot temper like his old man too, but he can stay mad longer. And he's handy with his fists. Now you take yourself—you want to be head of a big company. That's your ambition. He don't care nothing about bi'ness. His ambition is for somebody to swing on him so he can beat hell out of them without having to pay damages. He keeps in shape for that. And *I mean he's good*."

"Well, as you know, I don't care for either one of them, but I still can't figure you out." Adam tapped the big green signature. "You know this is a declaration of war. Olin won't forget it."

"I know that a lot better than you do, and that's the way I want it. The night I saw you I went up to that fine house of his—some say it's fine, I don't like that yellow brick, looks like the color of a Chinaman's snot to me. He wanted me to see you in a hurry, and when I came in, Olin was eating dinner alone. I stood there and answered questions for twenty minutes like a nigger while he sat there and stuffed himself. He didn't even ast me to sit down. Where I come from, even a sharecropper that can't write his name has got better manners than that." His mouth stretched downward with resentment. "And that's not the worst thing either."

"G. P., I think it's to your interest as a stockholder to vote with me, but I don't have Olin's kind of money, and I can't do his kind of favors."

"Not now maybe, but even if I never did get any business from you, I want it this way. See, I'm going to run for mayor."

"I can't bankroll you for that, and under the circumstances Olin will be sure to back your opponent."

Moon laughed. "I run for city commission two years ago. I was the Olin candidate. He told me to run. Then he went out and told the people that work for him to vote for me. So did his men, like Calvin Davidson. I finished third in a field of five. I learned then I wasn't quite as popular a fellow as I thought I was. But mainly I learned that Olin is poison in Sweetwater County politics. You know what they call him behind his back—Bastard Olin. There's fifty thousand people in this county that's had a mortgage foreclosed on them or somebody kin to 'em by the Merchants' National Bank. No, I couldn't ask anything better than for Olin to try to beat me in the next election. See, he can tell his men he'll fire them if they don't vote his way, and he can even buy votes, but they don't stay told and they don't stay bought. Once you get into that booth and that curtain closes behind you, nobody knows how you vote but yourself and God Almighty."

"So this is your first step to get loose from Olin?"

"See, Adam, I've learned something. I used to think if I ran with the rich boys, it would make me rich too, but Olin's too tight for that. Dr. Garth may be different. You being his cousin, you ought to know."

"I'm not rich yet. Let me get this straight. You want to let the public know you're not working for Olin any more. But you don't think I'm going to win. Well, something must be worrying the Olins or they wouldn't have hired that heavy artillery from Birmingham."

"Byroade? They're taking no chances." Moon obviously resented Byroade. "No, you got a chance to win. Not a good chance. You sure made the price of the stock go up. I'll say that for you. Olin's bought a little stock and paid a hell of a lot for it, and he got it from bearing down on people that are beholden to him. He had those proxies anyway, seeing that you don't have no secret ballot on this kind of election. Anyway those in the company know that if you get in there as president you'll sweep 'em right out."

"It's director that I'm running for, not president," said Adam, showing him the petition.

"I know that would come first."

"Moon, you think I want to run the mill myself? No indeed."

"You mean to tell me you gave up your job down there at the bucket shop and you've been spending all this time on this deal and you intend to let somebody else run the mill?" Moon grimaced in disbelief.

"That's right."

Moon smiled. He was still skeptical but too smooth to argue. "I was kinda hoping for some law bi'ness from the company if you got in." He took a huge gold watch from his pocket and said: "I got to go to the office. Skinner will be in town this week, and he'll sign too. See you later."

Adam watched him go. Moon and his cousin had only two hundred shares between them, but Moon seemed such a weathervane to him, so totally adaptable, that this alliance gave him more hope in a way than if a better man with more stock had joined him.

He had been entirely frank with Moon. He had not been planning to run the company himself. The company was dying now, worth more dead than alive to the stockholders, but it could be saved. After August it would be too late. But the company still had a good name, it had a lot of cash and the timberlands east of Kieselguhr could be turned to cash.

Although Adam liked stock brokerage, its potential in Mercer was limited; moreover he often felt a desire for a business with a more tangible product so that he would not always be a middleman. If he went into a well-managed company, it would take years for his personality to make a mark on it. But The Taurus Company would feel his presence the first day. The organization he would put together to save the company shaped itself in his mind. He would fire Quigley and Ellis, shut the mill down for a few weeks, paint and clean up, modernize, retrain the men, and increase job loads. He could sell Dr. Garth only enough stock to pay off his note. Adam sat there, clenching his fist with excitement. He knew Dr. Garth wouldn't like the idea, but he wanted The Taurus Company himself.

Belton, the accountant, a middle-aged man just over five feet tall, with a small calculator on the chair beside him and a worried look on his face, sat in the ice-cold waiting room at the mill. "They told me to go home," he said in a forlorn voice.

Adam turned to the receptionist. "It's all arranged with Mr. Quigley."

The woman looked into her lap. "I'm sorry."

"Where is Quigley?"

"Mr. Quigley is in conference."

Adam strode around the desk, and the receptionist stood up to protest. He stepped around her and walked to Quigley's office. The door was locked. He turned the knob of Ellis's door across the hall. The door opened, and Ellis looked up in dismay. "I've come to see the records, Mr. Ellis," Adam said.

Ellis swallowed and shook his round mild face. "It just can't be done today. Look, Mr. Salter, we've got more work this week than a show dog can jump over and—"

Adam called out down the hall. "Mr. Belton, will you come in here, please." When Belton, very uneasy, stepped into the room, Adam said: "Mr. Belton is my witness. Mr. Ellis, you are superintendent of the company. You are aware that as a stockholder I have a statutory and common-law right to see the books and records. You also realize that as an officer of the company you make yourself liable for damages by refusing. Knowing these facts, do I understand that you refuse?"

"Wait a minute," said Ellis hoarsely, his bald head beaded with sweat. "Let me find out what the story on this is."

He went past Adam and crossed the hall to Quigley's door and knocked. Adam followed and signaled Belton after him. "Hubert?" Ellis called through the door. "He's here. I need to talk with you." The bolt turned, and the door opened. Quigley stood aside and revealed at the center of the plush office Jack Olin in Quigley's chair, his feet on the mahogany desk.

"I didn't know what to tell him," Ellis said.

"Mr. Quigley," Adam said, trying to keep his temper. "You gave me your word I could see the books today."

Quigley looked helplessly at Jack Olin, who seemed immune to the pressure from Adam that was making the other two sweat. He did not even turn his Arab gaze in Adam's direction when he said: "According to the bylaws nobody can see the books without approval of a majority of the directors."

"I looked up the charter. I didn't see any such article."

"Then you must be *blind.*" Jack Olin said, inspecting his fingernails.

"The stockholders amended the charter," Quigley said. "I believe it was 1951—"

Adam looked closely at Jack. The last time they had met he had lacked the interest he now had as a former suitor of Josephine's and heir apparent to The Taurus Company. Jack had big wrists and ankles. Money seemed to have hardened his body instead of softening it; rich man's games had left his face as weather-beaten as a sailor's. His big hands, coated with blue-black hair, moved slowly and gave the impression of a man presently at leisure whose occupation was extremely dangerous.

"I don't believe any such bylaw will hold up in court," Adam said, trying to hold his voice steady. "Mr. Quigley, you know I'm a stockholder, and that withholding the books is a violation of state law. Do I understand that you refuse me access to them?"

"That's *right,*" said Olin before Quigley could answer.

"I don't think, Mr. Jack—" Quigley began.

Ignoring Quigley, Jack Olin took his feet off the desk and looked at Adam for the first time. "There's only one way to find out what will hold up in court? Want to try it?"

"You bet I do," said Adam. He turned to Belton. "Let's go." Both Quigley and Ellis made restraining gestures.

Outside Belton said: "Look, Mr. Salter, I didn't expect to get mixed up in any lawsuit—"

131

"They're the ones who're mixed up in a lawsuit," Adam said. "All I want from you right now is an affidavit."

They stopped at the first public telephone, and with Belton waiting unhappily, Adam called Rice Alexander. He had hardly finished relating the situation before Mr. Alexander firmly turned down the case. What next? Adam thought. Go through the Sweetwater County Bar Association list and hope to find a lawyer who isn't working for Olin or hoping to? There were some independent lawyers, but he hadn't been in town long enough to know who they were. There was G. P. Moon. Moon's clients had been mostly plaintiffs in personal injury suits and the like so he probably didn't know much corporation law, but he was available. So Adam called Moon.

"How much will it cost, G. P.?"

"I won't charge you a fee. I'll have to do a little *re*search on this."

"I've already done a little *re*search on this and you petition the circuit court for a writ of mandamus directing the officers of the company to let me see the records. And I need it right away.

"Keep a cool stool, boy. Just come on up to the office and bring Belton with you."

"How does it sound, G. P.?"

"This is just to slow you up."

"And what is all this about Jack Olin's having a hot temper? He's as cold as a snake."

"That's just control, boy. Inside I'll bet you two to one he was burning like a furnace."

"He sure seems to be taking hold."

"Him or Dean H. Byroade. You got anything to hide?" Moon didn't give Adam time to answer. "Well, if you do, they'll find it out and use it on you. If you don't, sometimes they develop something. You're a pretty upright fellow. Maybe they'd have to hit at somebody close to you."

"There's nobody that close to me now, G. P."

Before the courthouse closed that afternoon, Moon had taken statements from Adam and Belton, filed a petition, and the hearing in circuit court had been set for one week hence.

Of course whether anyone wanted it, a proxy fight had started. A half-dozen jobs needed to be done at once, such as getting proxy forms printed so Adam could start soliciting votes, but here again he would have to wait for Dr. Garth.

~~~~~~

20

Adam had just finished dinner at a downtown restaurant and was walking toward the post office. He had had an engagement that evening with a cotton broker to discuss the mill's cotton-buying program, but the man had called it off. Adam had taken his note-book and some textile magazines to the restaurant, but he was so saturated with the subject that his mind refused everything he tried to put into it.

The sign of the Mercer Bank and Trust Company across the street winked 7:20, then 68 degrees. He had finished eating earlier than he had intended, and now he did not feel like being alone. Spring penetrated even these treeless downtown streets, and the soft sweet air against his face made him unspeakably sad. It was a bad evening for a man with no hobbies, no job, and no family.

Only a circular awaited him in his post-office box, and he discarded that and paused on the steps outside.

For a few seconds nothing moved as far as he could see. He seemed to be in a backwash when everyone had somewhere else to be but him. Then some headlights appeared far down the street. The mercury lamps were just coming on in the twilight, and the convertible which had looked maroon at a distance became purple under their discoloring glow.

It was Herold's convertible, the top down. Beside him sat Josephine. Her head was drooping, her hair rippling in the wind, her lips moving soundlessly. For once Adam had not even been hoping to see her. She wore a cotton dress with a sailor collar, and in spite of the mature turns her body gave the dress, she had a look of youthful vulnerability. The wanton light made her pale, and even at this distance she looked miserable.

Adam waved, and though her gaze seemed to pass over him, she did not greet him. A moment later the car turned and disappeared. Adam stared after them, his restlessness now almost intolerable.

Why was she so troubled? The more he thought of Sizemore, the more it seemed that the questions of Josephine's preoccupation and Sizemore's errand might answer each other.

Since Sizemore had lived in Mercer, Adam had assumed that someone who had known him here had hired him—someone like G. P. Moon. He was now in a position to ask Moon for some straight answers, and he called him. Moon remembered Sizemore all right.

"Would Olin have hired him?"

"Olin wouldn't touch him. The kind of feller that'd hire Sizemore would be somebody had picked his name out of a telephone book."

Adam tried to force together what he had learned, and he found that evidence pointed toward the venereal area in which Sizemore seemed to specialize, and this made him think of Belle Wriston and in turn of Mr. Cato Herold.

The ones here who knew him were Josephine and Belle Wriston, and neither of them would suit his purpose. Mercer Davenport had known Herold too, and Adam telephoned him. Once more he waited impatiently for the operator to locate Davenport. It seemed to Adam that he was spending the best years of his life on the telephone.

"Mercer Davenport here."

"Mr. Davenport, when I saw you in Tarragona, you said you knew a man named Cato Herold. Do you happen to know his sister?"

"His sister? No."

"Do you know anything *about* her?"

"I thought Cato was an only child," said Davenport, irritated. "Look here, Salter, why don't you ask Belle Wriston about all this? She knows the family. In fact I met Herold through her."

"Just let me ask you one more question: have you never met nor heard of a woman named Leah Fraden Herold?"

"Of course," said Davenport, "but Leah's not Cato's sister. She's his ex-wife."

So that's the flaw, Adam thought, remembering Herold's words. It was a strange and mistaken decision for Herold not to admit from the start that he had been married. I should have been able to figure that out and would have if I could have thought of sufficient reason for concealing it. Divorce seemed scandalous in Mercer only among the older and more conservative, and it was not so damaging to be worth running such risks to conceal.

For a minute or so he wondered how to tell Josephine or whether he should tell Josephine. But he realized that she could not help knowing.

~~~~~~

21

Adam reached General Myerson by telephone later that evening and said that he wanted to discuss a private matter with which the general was already acquainted. It was agreed that since Adam was going to the Myerson's the next night for Blakely, he would come a few minutes early to talk with the general.

Mrs. Myerson answered the door. She was small and still pretty and looked like Blakely. She seemed to give an impression of confusion deliberately as though being definite were rude. Clarity and efficiency were for Yankee women. She sometimes had to inventory the whole family before she could think of the appropriate name. "Janie . . . Alice . . . oh, you know, I mean Blakely." She had to say something spectacular to draw even a routine protest from her daughters. Her daughter, Jane, was away at Sweetbriar, and in contrasting her daughters, she had once said to Adam: "Sugar Baby is my intellectual daughter." Blakely had cried out: "Mother! Adam thinks I'm the most unintellectual person he ever did see. And he's right."

Adam was fond of Mrs. Myerson. She was too sweet for some tastes, perhaps, but sweet to everyone.

"Blakely's dressing," she told Adam. "But here's Julius."

Brigadier-General Julius Myerson then appeared. He was lean, perpetually tanned, taller than Adam. Though nearly sixty, he had a full head of black hair. Cordially he shook Adam's hand and showed him into a sitting room toward the back of the house. There was a tray already set out there with a silver ice bucket and a bottle of twenty-year-old Scotch.

When the drinks were ready, they settled back in their chairs, and General Myerson stopped the small talk and looked at Adam expectantly.

"Sir, I'm sorry to come to you with this, but since Dr. Garth is ill, I felt I shouldn't alarm him and I thought I ought to look after his interests. I'm talking about what's happened at the mill this week: Jack Olin's being hired in a top position without consulting the directors. I thought that if some protest were registered at once, perhaps Mr. Olin might be persuaded to give this up."

Even as he talked Adam saw for an instant an expression of amazement on General Myerson's face. Then the face revealed nothing, and when Adam finished, he had a dismal feeling that bringing this matter up made him look like a presumptuous upstart. Could it be that Dr. Garth never has mentioned this to the general? Bascom Olin lived less than a block from here, and however he and General Myerson might differ on business matters, they were neighbors, perhaps cronies. Adam swallowed hard and groped for something to put a stop to this silence.

General Myerson sat still, looking at the ceiling, then set his drink down with great care. "I don't feel free to discuss it at this time. In any case action will depend on the directors, and a meeting will have to wait until Dr. Garth gets back." He arose, and Adam did likewise. "Excuse me. Blakely will join you in a moment." He did not look directly at Adam, but from the profile Adam thought he saw a peculiar sour smile on the general's lips.

Adam heard him walk to the stairway, where there was an exchange in low tones, after which the general went upstairs.

General Myerson's reply at first seemed to imply a tacit alliance, but testing it in his mind, Adam realized that it was totally noncommittal. He reviewed his own words to see if any of them might have been offensive.

Mrs. Myerson, from the hallway, gave Adam a bright smile, reassured him about Blakely's being ready in a minute, and also went upstairs.

She returned at once. Adam was offered another drink, again told that Blakely was almost ready, and Mrs. Myerson engaged him in very light conversation. She seemed a little more nervous than usual but hospitable enough. She mentioned that Josephine had already gone to an early cocktail party and would be late to the one to which Adam and Blakely were going.

Twenty minutes later Blakely appeared in a bright new dress, hair shining, her small face glum, and during the ride to the Ben Knowlands' party, she said almost nothing.

The hostess, Vera Knowland, a close friend of Blakely's, answered the door. Her husband came forward to greet them also. Both regarded Adam with horrified smiles. Not Blakely, just him. What's wrong? Adam thought, looking around. The room was noisy and full of people. Knowland asked what they wanted to drink and went to fetch highballs from the bar.

This was a married crowd, so instead of being paired off, the women in their circle to his left talked about babies, clothes, and servants, and the men gathered around the bar exchanging jokes and talking about business and sports. Adam saw with a glance that they were among the more prosperous young business and professional men of Mercer. He knew them all by name. A few he picked out as shameless snobs and social climbers, and others were known as wife-swappers, but he could not decide at first what they all had in common except that they were very social and that he had not been attracted to them.

Adam was standing with Blakely between the two groups. "Let's sit down," he said. "Blakely, have you noticed anything odd—"

"There's Charlotte Carpenter," Blakely said. "Excuse me, I want to speak to her."

Knowland presented Adam with his ginger ale and left him. The Knowlands were apparently decorators of the household magazine school, which favored cutting the legs off old varnished dining-room tables and painting them bright colors to use as coffee tables and such. Adam stood sipping his drink for several minutes. Blakely had taken a seat among the women and seemed to have no intention of returning.

Near Blakely Adam noticed a blond and pregnant woman so beautiful that he kept looking back at her and wondering who she was and why he had not seen her before. Her identity did not occur to him until, moving to join the men at the bar, he heard a familiar voice come from the circle of backs. It was Jack Olin's. The regal young woman would be his wife, Dorothy. Adam moved to get a better look at Olin. He could make himself charming when he wanted to, and he was doing so now, turning his very white smile from one speaker to another.

Of course Olin's presence explained the Knowlands' distress at his arrival. They had invited Adam to this party before they knew how he figured in the Taurus trouble.

I'm not going to stand around alone, Adam decided, and he went on to join the men. As he approached, Jack Olin and three others turned and went the other way to a porch. The crowd was half gone by the time Adam reached the bar. Those who remained greeted him politely but with reserve, and Adam was becoming aware that this was Jack Olin's crowd. The group had nothing against him, but they owed him nothing, and none could afford to risk being thought on his side. Certainly the host, who was busy at the far side of the room, could not after his blunder of inviting Adam. Well, at least I know how things are. But how about Blakely? Surely she was not afraid of the Olins.

The remaining men did not leave him rudely or abruptly but one by one with a concluding remark or excuse: "I'd better stop fooling around and go ahead and take this drink to my wife" or something like that. In five minutes Adam was alone at the bar with the colored bartender, who took the opportunity to go back to the kitchen for more ice and setups.

Certainly he was not going to push in with the men again, and he would probably make the women just as uncomfortable. They would not have dinner for another hour. He couldn't sit down with a magazine nor could he leave. It would be convenient if Blakely would come back to him, but until then all he could do was look conspicuous.

The doorbell rang, and there were Josephine and Cato. Their arrival stirred as much interest as his own but of a favorable kind. They were the length of the room away, and Adam raised his glass and nodded in greeting. They did not seem to see him, and he turned back to the bar. He was sorry she had come, for he did not want her to see him as an outcast, and he did not want to risk testing her.

A minute or so later he felt light fingers on his arm, and he turned to see Josephine smiling at him. She slipped her hand into the crook of his arm, and he felt a hot flow of gratitude in his heart, more gratitude than he would care for anyone to know about. Still an unhappy thought persisted that she just didn't yet know what the situation was. "You'd better keep away," he said, "you'll get leprosy."

"I'm immune."

He felt a hand on his other shoulder, and there was Cato. "Do you mind if a couple of bores attach themselves to you for the evening?" said Cato. He picked up Adam's glass and sniffed it. "No, I can tell, you're too drunk to care." Adam laughed with relief.

Cato turned and, resting his elbows on the bar, looked at the room. "You can smell money tonight, can't you? You can even hear it. Money talks everywhere, but Olin money doesn't just talk, it screams, it twitters, it howls, and sometimes late at night when everything is very quiet, you can hear it giggling itself to sleep."

If Adam doubted that they understood the situation after that, he had only to overhear Josephine a few minutes later whisper to Cato: "What could be the matter with Blakely? To let him just stand around alone." Adam was wondering himself.

Adam was in church the next morning, subject to that peculiar lethargy he usually felt there, induced, he thought, by the presence of awesome responsibilities he knew he was neglecting, when a thought occurred to him: that Blakely had expected him to ask the general for her hand. At first the idea seemed laughable. Did she think he was so old-fashioned as to approach her father before he raised the issue with her?

He was a penniless nobody, and the general would not want him for a son-in-law, but if that's what his little girl wanted, he would go along with it. And the general had certainly seemed ready to discuss something besides The Taurus Company.

In spite of trying to concentrate on the sermon, Adam kept thinking of Blakely. She had attracted him greatly before Josephine came back to Mercer. Now he loved Josephine, but he also felt that marrying Blakely would be accepting second best even in a worldly sense. The Myersons probably had as much money as Dr. Garth, they were certainly more active socially, and he suspected that General Myerson would be a more reasonable father-in-law. But Josephine, besides the particular magic she had for him, was a Garth.

~~~~~~

22

The telephone ringing near his head awakened Adam, and with feelings of emergency and alarm he picked the instrument out of the dark. "Adam, this is Josephine. Could I talk with you now? Do you have company?"

"No, I'm alone. What's happened?" It seemed too much like a wish-answering dream to be real, and he was still not well awake, his blood swamped with sleep. Then he saw that by the luminous clock dial it was only eleven p.m. "Where are you, Josephine?"

"I'm at a corner telephone booth. I'll come up just for a minute."

He dressed as quickly as sleep-weakened fingers would move and was tying his shoes when she arrived. "Oh, Adam," Josephine said, aghast. "I woke you up!"

"No, no." He took her arm and conducted her, resisting, into the room. She wore a white spring coat with a brilliant yellow scarf, and the gardenia pinned to her coat, its petals just darkening, shed a rich sweet smell. "I did though. I really am sorry, Adam. It's not proper for me to come here anyway. It's forward."

"Let me take your coat," he said. She pulled the scarf, which came out of her collar to make a puddle of gold on the coffee table, and unbuttoned her coat. "No, I'll keep it on. I won't stay but a minute." She sat on the edge of a chair, her knees primly together. "You're so neat, Adam," she said, looking around. "So orderly."

"Not much here to get disorderly." He had never had any women visitors before, and he wished he had a rug on the floor, and curtains to cover the naked glass. He felt some embarrassment too at his book shelves with titles like *Ten Steps to Greater Mental Efficiency* and *How To Make a Million Before Forty*. He jerked the blind cords, and the blinds dropped with a clatter which made her jump.

"I came because Belle Wriston's heard something you ought to know. Someone is telling around that you're an agent for a big competitor that wants to control The Taurus Company. She asked all about Daddy's part in it, and of course I didn't know anything."

Now he saw more disadvantages in suppressing his connection with Dr. Garth. "It's late. I'll have to see Mrs. Wriston tomorrow."

"Who in the world *would* say such a thing?"

"Maybe Jack Olin. I hear you used to know him well. Would he?"

"He might."

"What's Jack like?"

"Well, that's why I broke off with him. I found out. Years ago when I was a college freshman, Jack took me to a dance. Naturally I was thrilled to death. A boy I used to go with named Ronnie Williams was there. Ronnie had been a high school football star. He was tremendous and all muscle. Jack was a lot older than this crowd, and Ronnie didn't know him. Ronnie'd been drinking, and he was cocky and belligerent. I didn't see what led up to it, but Jack and Ronnie went outside. Jack came back in five minutes without a scratch on him. He'd knocked out all of Ronnie's front teeth. That night when Jack was taking me home, a white rubber thing fell out of his coat on the car seat. It was a crescent-shaped mouthpiece he carried with him to keep from having his teeth broken. So he was ready for trouble. And he tried not to show it, but he was just delighted that he had hurt that boy so badly. I didn't realize until then I didn't really like Jack at all."

"That fits what I've heard."

"Why would the Olins want that terrible run-down mill? It depresses me just to look at it."

"That's just when a fight does start over control of a company. As long as it's making money, the management rides high, just as folks at home make heroes out of generals when they're winning the war. Of course the company has a lot of cash and real estate too."

"Well, I really don't care about it except that I hate for Daddy to take on a new problem now."

"It's really an old problem. The company has been badly managed ever since Bascom Olin's had control of the board of directors. Your father tried to get something done about it, but he and General Myerson are outnumbered. The Olins are doing everything they can to discredit me with rumors like the one you heard tonight. It was good of you to leave Cato to tell me this, Josephine."

"No, Cato and I had an argument. I think of myself as a good-tempered person, but sometimes I'm just awful. I was so mean to poor Cato tonight, though God knows he deserved it. I've been pretty hard on you too."

"Forget it. You had provocation."

"That was another reason I wanted to see you. I wanted to thank you for talking with Daddy about Cato. I didn't know until Daddy mentioned it today on the telephone. I especially appreciate it after I acted so childish about that Sunday afternoon. That mess was partly my fault. I knew it was an impulse of yours, and I was encouraging it by letting us be alone together for so long."

"No, you weren't encouraging it." He hesitated, then warmed by the change in her and forgetting his bitter resolutions about protecting himself, he went on. "And it wasn't an impulse. I thought you might have figured that out. I'm in love with you, Josephine. That's what I've been trying to tell you."

"Really?" She seemed embarrassed. "I'm just not right for you. The girl who ought to have you is one who can give you her whole-hearted devotion. You deserve it."

"Somebody like Blakely?"

"I guess you know she's gone on you, and that she was expecting something pretty tremendous last night. She's a wonderful girl, Adam."

"I agree."

Josephine stood up. "I ought to go." In his haste to keep her, Adam grasped her arm roughly, released her at once for fear he would frighten her. She smiled and sat down.

"Josephine, I won't keep worrying you with this, but I want to help. I can see you're under a strain. I don't know all the reasons, but enough. I mean, that Leah's not Cato's sister."

She looked up quickly. Then her face fell. "Cato felt guilty about letting you believe that. How'd you find out?"

"I asked Mercer Davenport. Josephine, I think it was an error not to admit from the start that Cato's a divorced person."

She nervously turned her watch on her wrist. "They're not divorced," she said, avoiding his gaze.

"They're still married?" His brain could not quite take it in, but his blood seemed to, for it rushed coldly from his skin. "That makes things clearer. Like the private detective."

"You're shocked, aren't you?"

"Not so much shocked as alarmed. Don't you realize that people are going to put the wrong interpretation on this?"

She talked rapidly: "Belle didn't tell me that Cato was married when she introduced us at that party. Naturally I thought he was interesting; New York's a big city, but I hadn't met many men who were attractive and unattached, but as much as he attracted me, I wouldn't have seen him again if I'd known he was married. Why Belle didn't tell me, I don't know, because she certainly would like to have him all to herself. Finally Cato told me. He waited just long enough for me to fall in love with him." She paused to reflect. "I can't blame him. It's getting harder for me to blame anyone for anything. I must be losing my moral sense."

"Why aren't they divorced? I assume that the marriage is in name only."

"Leah won't let him go. She doesn't want him, but she doesn't want anyone else to have him either. Still I know I'm in the wrong. When I came home, it wasn't just to be with Daddy. I was breaking off with Cato. When he came to Mercer, he said he was establishing his residence here. A divorce was in the mill, it would only take a week or so. Everybody knows how lax the divorce laws are here, and I believed him. The night of the Chisholms' dance, he told me he hadn't been able to reach his lawyer that day, but he had every reason to believe that his decree had come through. Otherwise I'd never have let you speak in his favor to Daddy. Tonight, Cato finally admitted that he could get a divorce in a day or so all right but only with Leah's consent. And I blew up."

"You did right to blow up."

"He's sweet, gentle, always fun. But he expects me to be the strong one, and I'm not that strong." She got up again. "This hasn't helped. Sometimes when you talk instead of keeping it pent up, you feel a lot better, but I feel so sad."

"I'm a lot more worried about Leah than either of you seems to be, Josephine. She must have hired this detective, Sizemore, and divorce is his line."

"She doesn't want a divorce. She just had me watched so she would know when Cato came down here and she could descend on us."

"Why did she come here, Josephine?"

"You think everyone is as practical and purposeful as you are. I don't think she came here for anything in particular. She's just here to devil him because she has nothing else to do. She doesn't want Cato back, but she won't give him up either."

"If she doesn't want to lose Cato, she must be here to bust you two up. She's going to get acquainted here, then spread the word that she and Cato are married, to cause a scandal and put pressure on you to turn him loose."

"Cato's sure she won't do anything that drastic."

"Do you think she'll be able to *resist* doing it?"

"She'd better. Anyway she's gone now."

"Has she never taken you aside to ask for anything or threaten you?"

"She's taken me aside, but she was so subtle I couldn't make out what she wanted."

"So the only pressure she's put on you is just being in town?"

"Yes." Josephine got up. "I have to go, Adam. I feel bad about waking you up." She moved toward the door.

"When can I see you?" he said, drawing near her. "Tomorrow?"

"All right."

"Let's see. I'm going to Connor's Chapel to visit a mill down there. I guess I'd better see Mrs. Wriston first. I'll call you when I get back. Have dinner with me. We'll go to Mammy's Log Cabin."

Her face brightened, but she caught herself and her smile faded. "That would hurt some feelings, Adam. Let me think about it."

"Go on and admit it, Josephine. The real reason you left New York was you were tired of Cato. You missed him at first, but as soon as he'd been here a day or so, you'd had enough of him."

"You're guessing wildly!"

"True. But I think I'm pretty close. You've been falling out of love with him for some time. He's charming and attentive, so you've continued to see him. But mostly he's a habit with you. A bad habit."

She turned the knob and opened the door. He pushed the door

shut, slid one arm behind her neck and the other around her waist. She did not resist but kept her head lowered. He had promised himself he wouldn't do this. He tried to kiss her, but she shook her head. "It's too soon," she said, catching her breath. He released her. "We've known each other a long time, but we don't really know each other well." She looked up at him and smiled. "But you must be getting under my skin. I've dreamed about you twice this week."

"Bad dreams?"

She made no answer but reached for the knob, and they went into the cool air outside. The full moon was keeping a mockingbird awake, and it seemed to be able to sing all night without repeating any part of its song. "I'll ride over to the Myersons with you and walk back," he said. "It's not far."

"No indeed. I'm not going to have Blakely see me go out with one man and come in with another. Especially not with you. I believe she thought I was flirting with you at the party last night."

He watched her drive away and walked slowly back inside. She had left her yellow scarf on the table in his living room. He picked it up and found that it was lightly scented with her perfume. He had let her get away too easily tonight, and he planned not to make the same mistake tomorrow.

~~~~~~

23

Adam returned from Connor's Chapel the next day just before sunset. He thought he had left a light burning in the bedroom because of the glow which came through the partly open door, but the light was strange in color and direction.

He found Josephine's scarf on a chair, and a late sunbeam fell on it from a window. The brilliant reflected light turned the stuccoed walls the color of gold. The happiness which he felt about Josephine and had delayed all day on purpose burst on him. He picked up the scarf, and its perfume helped him see her clearly in his mind's eye.

Yet he was also fearful of losing Josephine, and now he knew why he had withstood his feelings of happiness. What she had said last night gave very little to go on; today she might again be in love with Herold.

He had dwelt in his spare moments that day on Leah and the power she held, but that seemed soluble to him now. He himself was the solution, for he would replace Herold.

He telephoned Josephine at the Myersons', and the maid said she had gone home. When he called there, Josephine answered, and his voice seemed to please her. "I've been trying to reach you," she said. "How did you make out with Belle?"

"I didn't convince her. She wants to talk with your father."

"That's what I was calling you about. Daddy's home, and since this is his first evening, I told him I'd have dinner with him here."

"He'll go to bed early, won't he? How about later on?"

"I shouldn't, Adam."

"I've been looking forward to seeing you all day."

"But I feel so guilty about Cato. And Blakely." She hesitated. "All right. I'm sure Daddy will be in bed by nine."

The disappointment about this delay was swept away by almost intolerable excitement. For once he felt the need of strong drink to take the edge off his nerves, but he settled for a cold beer. As he drank it, he tried to deal with the tantalizing uncertainties of how Josephine felt about him. Beer filled the nervous emptiness where his appetite should have been, but he went to town for dinner, for he could not make himself sit still in his apartment.

It was only seven-forty when he finished dinner, and he still had over an hour to kill. He drove around town and soon found himself crossing the railroad and driving up to the Taurus fence.

He had gotten nowhere with Mrs. Wriston. She would not tell him who had accused him. He had said that it made no difference who actually told her, the Olins had started it. She wouldn't comment on that.

It was a good thing Dr. Garth was back. Adam realized that Dr. Garth could do a lot which his own energy and resourcefulness could not do. He could deal with the general as an equal, and Mrs. Wriston would take him at his word.

That morning Mr. Harlow Stubbs, general counsel of The Taurus Company, had come to see Adam and wasted nearly two hours with slow talk. If Adam would call off his lawsuit and submit a list of particulars to be extracted from the company books, an independent firm of accountants would get the figures for him. Adam had refused. It might take weeks. Also, Adam was hoping to stumble on something in the company's books. Stubbs' visit had made him so late that the mill's cloth-room operation had shut down when he reached Connor's Chapel.

Adam's presence seemed to disturb the night watchman at the gatehouse, for he put down his magazine and stood up. Adam got out and introduced himself to the old man, who shook hands with him shyly.

It didn't take much coaxing from Adam to get him to tell his story. He had come down from a mountain farm and been hired as a weaver soon after Monroe Mercer had become president at the mill. He had hated living in town, and after a few months here, he had taken his family back to the farm. That one trip had been enough. He had missed the weekly pay envelope, the nearest school had been twenty miles away, and he and his family had been lonesome for the first time in their lives. He had made one crop of twelve bales of cotton off the whole farm and then came back to Mercer to stay for good. Mr. Mercer had said when he walked in: "I knew you'd be back." Adam recognized this as the story of hundreds of the millworkers here. "They don't make 'em like Mr. Mercer any more," said the watchman. When Adam pressed him about the difference between Mercer and the present management, the man mentioned that Mr. Mercer knew when his wife had a baby, and when his son was killed in the war, Mr. Mercer came to the funeral. Mr. Mercer and Dr. Garth personally contributed half the cost of building their neighborhood church. "Mr. Quigley, he don't even know my name." With that, the old man seemed to think he had said too much and abruptly started on his rounds again.

The moon was just coming up, and the black pavement of the Buttermilk Road was laced with silver as Adam drove over the mountain. The lights of the Garth house flashed and beckoned through the trees. He drove quietly up the smooth pavement, and the rear of Herold's convertible appeared in his headlights.

He knocked on the glass and at once heard hurried footsteps in the hall and saw a moving figure dimly through the curtained side-lights. Josephine opened the door, and before he could speak, her expression warned him. "Daddy's gone to bed, thank God."

He followed her into the parlor where only one lamp made a sphere of light in the big shadowy room. Beside the light was Leah, her thin gauzy dress floating like bleached seaweed. She absorbed the light and diffused it through the room with a discoloring glow. "Good evening, Mr. Salter," she said. She turned to Josephine. "Is he a witness for you?"

"He didn't come for that, but as far as I'm concerned, he can hear whatever you have to say."

Leah raised her eyebrows and shrugged her shoulders. "I was just telling Josephine about Cato's Erotic Year. Yes, like the fiscal year of a business. I have observed it now for such a long time and have found that his erotic periods last about one hundred calendar days on the average, often beginning in the spring and usually ending with a period of alcoholic indulgence, contrition, and his coming back to me. The average time he is with me is about hundred and fifty calendar days before he finds another affair necessary to his ego. The trend has been, as he grows older, for the cycle to

149

become longer. The affair before the present one lasted one hundred and seventy-three days, and he was with me just under six months. I suppose he is slower about pursuit, due to a diminution of his glandular powers, and so conquest and resultant surfeit takes longer. Do you suppose that could be the explanation?"

Adam stood rigid with astonishment. He expected a protest from Josephine, but she was silent, her eyes wide and her mouth firm.

"The reason I review this is that my husband's infatuation with Josephine has taken longer than the trend would lead me to expect. It is now two hundred days old. This affair seems to retain its sweetness for a long time. So I thought I ought to investigate the source of his enamorata's charm. When I saw Josephine in New York, all I had been able to see was a big strong girl of the kind Cato can't seem to resist. Yes, he loves strong-willed women for obvious temperamental reasons, and physically she is the maternal figure his mother never was. He needs a bountiful bosom and a capacious womb to satisfy his infantile cravings, but many of his women in the past have had those attributes. Look at Belle Wriston. Even in middle age she is typical. So what was the secret of your appeal? Mr. Sizemore gave me some idea, but Dun and Bradstreet would have helped me more. This time his voluptuous brunette is an heiress. But I was still mystified. Rich mistresses are plentiful for the charming Mr. Herold, particularly since he has no quarrel with middle age, but there are plenty of young ones too. It took a long time to get it out of him. You see, Josephine, you came at the right *time*. He is running out of money. Once he had a substantial income, but that never has been enough. It has been in the wrong things, too much in bonds and ten-cent stores and badly managed real estate, and of course Cato has been too busy to worry about it. So the income has diminished, and he has simply cashed one of those bonds when he needed money. The more he went into capital, the more his income dropped and the faster he had to sell things. So now, Josephine, you understand why your appeal is not waning."

She had been watching Josephine closely for the effect of her words. Now she moved forward with self-conscious grace and fixed Adam with her eyes, which were murky and green like jade. "Do I see some disapproval of this analysis of my husband's infidelity in your puritan countenance, Mr. Salter?"

"It's so dark in here I'm surprised you can see anything at all," said Adam. He did not like having her in this house. She seemed to blight even the lamplight. He could not tell how she really felt: this irony and superciliousness might be a disguise for a wife who was hurt, mistreated, but persisted in loving her husband. Her lack of candor was not what exasperated him. It was the fact that her talk, despite its nervous forward movement, seemed to lack purpose and to rise in an uncontrollable overflow.

"I will admit I was amazed that you tried to bribe Mr. Sizemore," she said. "I thought you were above trying to degrade other people with money."

"I didn't like it," said Adam, his face growing warm, "but it consoled me to think that I helped him get money due him which otherwise he could not have collected."

Immediately Leah stopped swaying and looked at him very hard. It was a face and expression which he had seen too rarely to interpret confidently, but he thought: she hates me, and after a moment's reflection: she hates men.

"You may be interested to know that your inquiries are what brought me back to Mercer so soon. It occurred to me after I had thought about it, that this time the affair might be different. And seeing such a brawny young man working against me, it was a good thing I came back to protect my interests."

"I am not working against you knowingly," said Adam. "For one thing I don't even know what your interests are."

"How old are you?" she asked him.

"Nearly thirty."

"You look older than you are, as the muscular type often does, just as Cato looks younger. I'm glad I came back." She said this in a mocking way, but he felt that she had reserved special hostility for him. "But if you don't know what I want here, your energy exceeds your sense."

He felt his anger rising and some hot words with it, but caught himself. "Perhaps, so why don't you tell me."

"I want to talk with Josephine alone. I think she will more readily understand me, for we have so much in common. I'm sure in agreeing to have you here, she didn't know all I was going to say."

Adam caught a look which passed between the two women, but he was surprised when Josephine said: "Maybe I had better talk with her alone, Adam."

Josephine walked to the door with him, and he said: "I don't want to go. I've got a feeling she's just waiting for you to turn your head so she can set the house on fire."

"I can handle her."

"Be careful. Don't let her make you mad. That's what she's trying to do."

"I'm just going to listen."

"Josephine, you've *got* to let Cato go. Go back in there and tell her she can have him."

"I can't do that to him—not that way. I'm not going to have her run back to him and crow."

"It's not for me. I could wait for years if I had to, but she won't wait."

"She doesn't really want him. I'll see what she does want."

Her manner reassured him. Josephine can handle it, he thought. Adam took her in his arms, and she clasped her hands over his back and squeezed with a movement which suggested some agitation other than love and so tightly that her knuckles pressed painfully against his spine. He kissed her on the cheek and said: "Telephone me when she leaves."

Outside the moonlight was so bright he could read the license numbers on Herold's car.

It did not seem very important to him whether Leah's view of Herold's behavior was correct or not. But whatever the reasons, Herold had done Josephine a great injury by coming here and drawing Leah after him.

Still, Adam couldn't see what Leah wanted. As much as she seemed to enjoy talking and humiliating Josephine, Adam doubted that she was here just for that. There was an authority he could consult: her husband. With that in mind, he started his car. He could still feel the place between his shoulders where Josephine's hands had pressed.

He made the circle and rolled down the driveway. The moonlit columns appeared in his mirror, and he thought of the big man sleeping beyond them and how this trouble would affect him. It would kill him, Adam thought. It really would.

Adam found Cato sitting on the porch with Mrs. Wriston. The glittering town lay beneath them. They were drinking brandy, and after declining it and offering apologies to Mrs. Wriston, Adam asked if he could talk with Cato for a few minutes. That Herold was not quite sober was shown Adam by Mrs. Wriston's understanding and Herold's failing to understand that Adam meant a private conversation, and seeing that Cato gave no sign of complying besides an attentive posture, Mrs. Wriston said she was going inside for a wrap. Then Herold saw what Adam intended and said they would go to the guest house to talk.

There was an outside stairway which led down the back of the house in to a bright garden and then made a turn downward again into the parking area and driveway. Herold, carrying his glass, slowly led the way.

In the guest house Cato turned to him expectantly. His attentive and, above all, friendly face was also serious, because he was expecting Adam to talk seriously but trusting him not to bring up anything unpleasant. Adam had been harboring some sharp words, but he thought better of them. What he really wanted to know, after all, was what to expect of Leah. So he began more softly. "I've just come from the Garths'."

"You saw Leah? I was afraid she might go there." The only effects of alcohol now detectable were the heightened ruddiness of Cato's face and the smell of brandy. Without knowing and without wanting to know anything about fashionable spirits Adam had no doubt that this was an expensive brandy, and it gave him a small feeling of irritation because of its connotations of idleness and self-indulgence. "I judge from your expression that she told you," said Cato.

"That Leah's your wife? Look, I'm really alarmed about this. I don't know her well enough to know whether she intends to use the dynamite she has, but—"

"I know her much too well, and I don't think she will use it."

"Then what does she want in Mercer?"

"She wants to make me suffer. It's her way of making the world pay because she's thirty-five years old, because our marriage is a failure." Cato was warming to his subject. "Let me show you something." Cato got out a leather folder which contained a photograph of himself in a cutaway and Leah in a wedding gown. They both had a silvery radiance about them, and Leah's beauty was disconcerting.

"You both looked sixteen."

"I was twenty-three, she was twenty-one. She really was like a flower, wasn't she?" said Cato. "And the picture doesn't do her justice. Even on that day, our wedding day, I saw some qualities which disturbed me, but which were disguised in part by her youth. She was an obsession with me. I couldn't keep from marrying her."

"Cato, look. This thing can do a tremendous amount of harm—"

"I believe she could have had any man she wanted. So despite my misgivings, how could I spurn her?"

Adam glanced once more at the photograph. "Her figure has hardly changed." But there was no question that she had lost her freshness in fourteen years. Even then, before they had a bad marriage in common, they looked alike.

"I had some idea of the worst very soon. She never would want children, for one thing. But it took my mother's death for me to realize that at heart she was cold, cold, cold." Cato shuddered. "Shallow or not, my mother loved me, but to Leah her death was just a colossal inconvenience. That was when we quarreled, and I left her. Quarrel is too warm a word for it. What developed was a cold hateful breach."

"Tonight she indicated that your marriage had been off and on," said Adam. "Her version was that you were the typical philanderer who came back to her after each dalliance."

Cato expelled a bitter laugh. "I have tried again and again, usually at her beseeching, to get along with her. It's a measure of my capacity for self-deception. Each time, year after year, I have hoped that she had changed for the better—or merely changed. After I've been with her a few months, I have left her to keep from going out of my mind. And now she simply will not believe I'm through with her."

"She wants you back, doesn't she?"

"She expects me back, and she wants something—not the real me."

"Aside from metaphysical considerations," Adam said with some vexation, "since she can't have the real you, will she accept your physical plant in lieu of it?"

Cato looked surprised and injured at Adam's tone. "I'm not fencing with you. You don't appreciate my predicament. She would only take me back to try to ruin me." He waited a moment and said: "You don't believe me? You heard her discuss me tonight. Did she give the impression of being a woman who was hurt, who was in love with her husband, or even cared a little for him?"

"Naturally she didn't. She was talking to two people she considered hostile to her." Adam stood up abruptly. "She says you have had other women—'mistresses' was the word she used—and that you are interested now in Josephine's money."

"I hoped you of all people would see through her and understand me. 'See through' is not really the right phrase. That hard surface is all there is to her. As for the question of money, that was just another way Leah was attacking me and upsetting Jo."

"Then you're not just trifling with Josephine?"

"I think I've taken you into my confidence enough for you not to have to ask that question," Cato said. "You know how I feel about Jo."

"If you love her, don't you care what harm Leah can do simply by revealing her identity here? Don't you realize what towns the size of Mercer are like?"

"I certainly don't want her here and didn't ask her here."

"But she came because you were here."

Cato's eyes narrowed. "You're implying that I should go away?"

"Until you're divorced. That might save Josephine."

Cato's manner was suddenly dry and cold. "Since we are speaking so frankly about personal matters, I should like to inquire about your interests in this matter. Are you truly detached in giving me this advice—just a cousin and friend of the family? Or have I seen signs that you might have something else at stake?"

"Yes, I'm in love with Josephine, and if I had been in your place, I would never have come here until I was free of Leah."

"Free of her! I'll never be free of her!" Cato made an angry gesture. "Your saying that only shows that we don't mean the same thing by love. That you don't need Jo as I do."

"That's just—" Adam realized that he was shouting. He would get nowhere with Herold on this point. All he could expect was a small advantage from the evening. "Have you told Leah what you just told me, that Josephine, is 'different' so far as your plans are concerned?"

"She didn't believe me."

"Then leave it that way for a while. Don't make her desperate. Don't give her a final no. If you'll think it over, you'll realize that everything you've told me tonight about her supports my point: she won't be able to resist trying to ruin Josephine before she leaves." Adam went to the door. He knew that his bluntness had offended Cato, but he felt too impatient with him to smooth it over.

"Watch her," said Cato, "and watch yourself. She has a way of bringing out the worst in those around her. Since Leah came, I have seen changes in Belle. She's become queerer, more lustful, more miserly." He paused. "I can't blame my temperament on Leah, but she did seem to stimulate abnormal growth in my weaknesses, such as indolence and irresponsibility—and thirst."

"And which of my worst qualities do you expect her to bring out?"

Cato shook his head. "If you are not too deeply involved in this, you may not be susceptible."

"But you know I am involved."

"Then she may make you cruel."

"And Josephine?"

Cato groaned. "I've been hoping all along that Jo will be immune."

~~~~~~~~~~~~~~~~~~~~~~~~~~~~~~~~~~~~~~

25

Adam drove back to his apartment and sat on his bed to wait for
Josephine's call, but he could not make himself stay still and immediately got up and paced around the room. He felt that he
had alienated Cato without learning anything. However he had
learned that Cato accepted Leah as something permanent and uncontrollable in his life and planned to do nothing to get rid of her.

It was past eleven. The town was still enough for the forlorn
sounds of freights to carry distinctly to him, and they seemed very
close. The air was cooling rapidly as it usually did toward midnight. Adam, during his watch-checking and pacing, noticed something bulky in his pocket and pulled it out. It was Josephine's
yellow scarf, which Leah's presence had made him forget.

At eleven-fifty he decided he would give her five more minutes.
Leah could not possibly have this much to say to Josephine.

The five minutes passed, and itching with impatience, Adam
got in his car and drove out the Buttermilk Road at high speed.
When he emerged from the trees at the lower end of the Garth's
driveway, he thought he saw a light, but it turned out to be the
moon reflected in a window. Drawing nearer, he found that
Herold's convertible was gone. He stopped his motor and listened.
There was the shrill calling of tree frogs and crickets but nothing
human on the air. Anxious and mystified, he returned to his apartment.

As early in the morning as he felt he could, he telephoned
Josephine. Rutherford answered and said she hadn't come down
yet. Adam gave his name and asked that she call him.

Josephine had not responded at ten o'clock, and Adam telephoned her again. When she came to the telephone, she spoke so

low he could hardly hear her. She was busy today. She was supposed to go to a luncheon. Could he see her afterward? She didn't know what time it would be over, and Blakely had said something about a bridge game after the luncheon. "Josephine, what in the world? You were going to call me last night as soon as Leah had gone, remember?"

"It was late when she left. I didn't want to wake you."

"I know it was late, and I was staying up for your call. What's happened?"

"Nothing yet. I've got to go now. Daddy's waiting."

He did not know what to make of this burst of frivolous activity when such a serious matter was in the balance. Why hadn't she called? Leah must have put some sinister interpretation on his actions and turned Josephine against him.

Although he was in a hurry to see Dr. Garth, he wanted to go late enough to allow Josephine time to get home; he telephoned Dr. Garth, and after inquiries about his health, to which he got noncommittal grunting replies, arranged an appointment for four that afternoon.

Dr. Garth received him in the study. He sat at an open window cleaning a big revolver. Adam renewed his inquiries about the other man's health and received the same uninformative response. Dr. Garth looked about the same, a little thinner in the neck, and his voice sounded less vigorous—what you expected after a case of flu.

Adam had spent most of the day at the courthouse law library reading cases involving inspection of corporate records, and he was so full of the subject of The Taurus Company he had even been able to forget about Josephine's problem for that time. The sight of the grim face before him stirred a foreboding: Dr. Garth would disapprove of most of what he had done. Stalling, Adam asked about the gun. This was an old Colt .45 which Dr. Garth had gotten rechambered and rebarreled to use .32 caliber ammunition. "I always keep the Colt loaded down here and a Smith and Wesson .44 Magnum by my bed. This far out of town you have to be your own police force." The smell of the oil he was using was strong in the room.

"Sir, they've made Jack Olin vice-president of The Taurus Company in your absence," Adam said, expecting a storm.

"So I hear. What else happened at the mill?"

Adam began with the stockholders' petition. While Adam talked,

Dr. Garth was polishing the revolver and glancing out the open window, his big nose and chin sharply outlined against the daylight. At the mention of G. P. Moon an expression of distaste passed over his face. As Adam took up the moves the Olins had made, particularly the hiring of Dean H. Byroade, he felt each item claw at him for action. When Adam finished, Dr. Garth seemed to withhold comment in expectation of hearing more, and Adam, his throat dry from talking, tried to think of what he had left out. He extended the stockholders' petition. "Besides my own, this represents one thousand one hundred and fifty-three shares in our favor."

"Put it on my desk, please," said Dr. Garth, not looking up from his gun. That did not seem much attention, considering the work which had gone into that petition. "Myerson tells me you went to him. You shouldn't have done that."

"So I've decided."

"On whose advice are you taking this to court?"

"It was my idea. G. P. Moon's doing the legal work for us."

"G. P. Moon is doing nothing for me. How did you manage to win over the least desirable of all Olin's allies?"

Adam resisted taking offense. "I needed a lawyer, and Rice Alexander turned me down."

"That should have made you question the wisdom of suing."

"Well, sir, now that you're back, what course do *you* recommend?"

"I'm not going to court, particularly with Moon for a lawyer."

"We need his proxies. I'll admit a lawsuit sounds extreme, but obviously they're refusing the books because they have something to hide. And after what Mr. Emery said, I can't convince the stockholders who are experienced in business unless I do see the records."

"As for the company records, I'm a director and have an absolute right of inspection."

"Then we won't have to wait until Friday."

"No, now's not the time to demand the records." Dr. Garth sighted through the revolver barrel, then carefully inserted cartridges into the cylinder. "I'll talk with Myerson."

"I'm for that certainly. How about Mrs. Wriston?" When Dr. Garth was slow in replying this time, Adam said in an urgent tone: "Sir, you ought to talk to her."

"The woman's unreliable. We won't have anything even if she gives her word."

"We can't win without her proxy though. Right now the Olins don't need but two hundred and fifty more shares."

"All right. I'll communicate with her. However, if we get the wrong kind of allies early like her and Moon, we may alienate stronger ones."

"Since the Olins are spreading this rumor about me, perhaps we ought to get out a letter to all the stockholders over your signature denying the rumor and explaining our position."

"I thought you'd seen all the stockholders yourself."

"Yes, but my word simply does not have the weight that yours does. That brings up something else, Uncle Ive. I need to start soliciting proxies for the annual meeting—that's just two months away." Adam tried to sound as though he expected no disagreement, but he knew it was a big step, for Dr. Garth would be acknowledging their alliance publicly for the first time. "I wanted to get the go-ahead on having your name printed on the proxy instrument."

Dr. Garth shook his head. "It won't be necessary to have those proxies printed yet."

"I think we ought to get started on them. Of course stockholders can always revoke their proxies, but they would feel more committed once they signed up with us. Also the proxy is worth something as a campaign document. If I could be absolutely sure of attending the meeting, I wouldn't need anybody else's name on the proxy, but of course I can't. If something happened to me, they couldn't be voted unless someone else was assigned the power on the proxy itself." Dr. Garth hardly seemed to be listening, and Adam said in a loud voice: "It's either you—or G. P. Moon."

"Is he the best you can do?"

"Look at the petition. They're mostly elderly women. Or take old Mr. Gainer. An invalid. Not one of them would be up to butting heads with the Olins at the meeting."

"Moon's got no character. You can't be sure the Olins won't buy him back and have him vote these proxies against us."

Adam thought this over. "You have a point. If you don't want your name on the proxy, I'll just have to count on being at the meeting myself."

"All right," said Dr. Garth. In other words he still wouldn't agree to backing Adam publicly. What would he have done if I had just sold him my stock and walked out? It was clear that Dr. Garth had undertaken something he lacked the energy to carry through. His health was making him more cautious, difficult, immovable. Nor did he like being a traitor to the haves in Dun and Bradstreet.

Dr. Garth was still shooting intense glances out the window, but Adam could not see what was distracting him. The seconds dragged on in the quiet room. Adam took a deep breath and said: "Uncle Ive, we've got to be giving some thought to the question of who's going to run the company if we win."

"It's too soon for that."

"There's a big drawback to waiting, besides the fact that the company is losing money every minute that Quigley sits behind that desk. If Quigley renews the present union contract in September, the next president will have his hands tied so he won't be able to get the company out of the red before it's too late. Quigley is not up to negotiation with those professionals the union will send in here, and what I would do is—"

Adam broke off. Now was not the time to try to sell himself as president of The Taurus Company, for Dr. Garth was in no mood to listen.

Dr. Garth snapped the cylinder in place and put the revolver in a desk drawer. "I've had more experience with these matters than you have. I've always won. As you say, we need all the proxies we can get, even from the shyster lawyers and the rest. I'll talk with Myerson, and see if he has any influence that will help. In the meantime tell Moon to drop the lawsuit."

Adam looked over the intransigent body, the hard face, and burst out: "Sir, you don't need to be involved in this hearing Thursday in any way."

"Don't you realize they're inviting you to sue? They either know they can win, or plan to make capital of it in the newspapers."

"They're just playing for time. The business about a bylaw limitation has been knocked down every time it's gotten to court. I don't care for extreme measures either, but we can't win without trying every available weapon. So I'll go ahead with the petition and pay the costs myself."

Adam braced himself as he spoke, and Dr. Garth's hard gaze swung up on him for an instant. His expression proclaimed that he was dealing with a very rash and inexperienced young man who would soon be taught a lesson. Adam felt the gulf separating them was not merely of forty years and a million or so dollars. Dr. Garth's attitude toward him was changing. He tried to think of when the change had begun. Since he had spoken in Herold's favor two weeks ago? More likely since the encounter on the stairs that Sunday afternoon.

When Dr. Garth spoke again, he avoided looking directly at Adam or addressing him by name. "I'll get in touch with you." This was dismissal and Adam got to his feet.

"Is Josephine here?"

Dr. Garth turned his swivel chair and pointed to the window. "Out there on the walk in the garden. Where she used to ride her velocipede." Adam leaned over and saw through the curtains and screen Josephine's dark head over the flowers of the garden. "I wouldn't go out there," said Dr. Garth. "I think she's coming down with flu, and if so, it's very contagious right now. She hasn't been well lately. She gained a little weight when she first came home, but since I left two weeks ago she's lost about five pounds."

"I have to speak with her just a moment."

Adam approached noiselessly from the path leading from the back door. She was sitting in the shade of an apple tree on a garden bench and facing away from him. When she did see him, she recoiled and tried to smooth her hair with one hand. She did look ill, her eyes hollow and bloodshot. "Daddy says I'm getting sick," she said. "You'd better go away."

"He told me." Adam sat down on the bench beside her. "Here's your scarf." The warm air was full of the smell of flowers and the sound of bees. The blooming garden before them had recently had the attention of only half-interested gardeners, and the colors were brilliant and disorderly. Beyond the garden was the mountainous ridge this side of town, and one naked spot where the pavement of the Buttermilk Road gleamed like water. Now and then a nearby bush was shaken by a devil horse, a shiny black grasshopper which by August would be as big as a wren. "How was the bridge game?"

"I didn't feel like playing."

"And you didn't go to the luncheon."

She wouldn't look at him. "I decided at the last minute I wasn't up to it."

"You didn't call me."

"Because I didn't feel like talking with anyone, and you can see I don't want to be cross-examined now."

"What's happened, Josephine? Has she bewitched you too?"

"That sounds like Cato."

"I went right over to see him last night. He warned me about Leah. He said Leah had paralyzed him and that she would make me cruel, but he hoped she would not change you. I see that she is changing you. She's made you dislike me."

"She seems to have made you cruel. You're trying to hurt me."

"You know well enough why I insist on talking with you when it's obvious that you're avoiding me. Because I want to help you. Now tell me what's happened."

"Nothing's happened except for a lot of horrible talk. Also I've just about decided to go away and get a job."

"Where?"

"San Francisco."

"What *did* that woman say to you?"

"Same kind of thing. I still don't know what she wants."

"She wants Cato for one thing," Adam said. "She may only want him back to pull his wings off, but at least she's here because he's here."

"I wish that were all," said Josephine. "She—"

"Tell me." He took her hand, which she tried to withdraw. Her hand felt hot in his grip.

"Let me go. Daddy can see us from his study window."

"Tell me," he said, still holding her.

"She wants money. She asked me if I thought Daddy would disinherit me if he knew about this. She didn't sound threatening; she just wanted my opinion. This is the way she got around to it. She said Cato had quit his job because of me and had given me expensive presents. Now since he was running out of money and she would have no means of support, I ought to make it up to her. He did quit his job when he came here and has given me some jewelry."

"Did she mention any specific amount?"

"She said something about twenty-five thousand dollars at first." Josephine ignored Adam's amazement. "When she started talking about money, I guess I made my first mistake by listening to her, but I was so sick of her—" Her voice trailed away.

"How much jewelry did Cato give you?"

"That watch with the diamond band you've seen me wear, and a bracelet, a brooch, and a pin. I gave them all back to him once before, and he brought them down here and I accepted them again. I've been looking for the right moment to return them again."

"The sooner the better." Adam looked at her wrist to make sure she was not wearing the watch now. "Twenty-five thousand dollars! How much would you say the jewelry was worth?"

"I haven't the faintest idea."

"But not twenty-five thousand dollars!"

"Cato bought the watch at Black Starr and Gorham. The pin and the brooch were made of diamonds from his grandfather's fob and tie pin. Cato had them set for me. All his family's feminine jewelry had gone to Leah or at least through her hands."

"I hope you're not even considering paying her anything."

"I think it would be wonderful if I could get rid of her only for money."

"The point is that you haven't got anything for your money. Anyone who tries blackmail has no sense of honor. She'd keep coming back. As soon as she had worked all the money out of you she could, she'd lose no time spreading this secret. Now I see why she was so anxious for me to leave last night. She didn't want any witnesses to this blackmail."

"She calls it a settlement out of court. Claims her lawyer said she could sue and collect more. Before she left she said that twenty-five thousand wouldn't be enough."

"She'll keep raising the figure as long as you'll listen to her. Let me talk with a lawyer about it."

"No!"

"Just leave it to me."

"No, Adam. They'll follow me to San Francisco, but anyway whatever happens will be a long way from you and Daddy."

"If it happens to you, do you think it would matter to either of us where? She plans to bleed you, Josephine. She's that sort. Going away from your family and friends would just make you more vulnerable, and she could always see to it that her information got back to Mercer."

This argument seemed to make Josephine desperate. "I'll never be free of them."

"Of course you will. You're tired out, and you need to get this

164

in perspective. I think it would be better to keep it quiet of course, and we'll do everything possible to head it off, but as soon as she passed the word, you'd be rid of her."

Josephine's throat muscles were moving, and her eyes growing alarmingly shiny, but her voice was still clear enough for him to understand. "You don't know the whole story, Adam. After you left last night, she said she'll file suit against Cato for divorce on grounds of adultery and name me as corespondent. She showed me a photostat of a deposition—" Josephine turned her face away.

"Did she leave the photostat?" His voice came out a rusty ancient sound. "Let me see it."

Josephine shook her head. "She had us followed in New York."

From the corner of his eye, Adam saw something large and dark in motion. Dr. Garth was coming slowly up the path. "What is it? Josephine, what's the matter?" He spread his big hand over her forehead and eyes. "You need to go inside where it's cooler." She stood up, and Dr. Garth crooked one arm to put around her. She avoided her father's arm and hurried toward the house. Dr. Garth called after her: "Go on up and get into bed, Josephine." As soon as she was out of sight, Dr. Garth turned to Adam. He seemed to be trying to frame a question.

"I'd better go," said Adam.

"You look as though you're getting it too. How do you feel?" said Dr. Garth.

"Not very well." He felt dizzy now with a feeling less like flu than sunstroke. "Josephine!" he kept whispering as he walked. "Josephine!" He saw her face swimming in the sunlight, rouge on her cheeks and lips like scabs, and he was surprised to see his own face over the knuckles of his outstretched hand reflected in the window of his car. He did not remember how he got there. For all he knew he had walked through the solid brick sides of the house.

~~~~~~

26

"Josephine? I've been in Birmingham all day. I telephoned last night, but your father said you were too sick to talk with me. How do you feel?"

"Adam!" She sounded deeply relieved. "Daddy didn't tell me you'd called."

"I've seen a lawyer, a college friend of mine from Birmingham. I'll tell you what he said later. Let me suggest one thing now. Give the jewelry back to Cato as soon as possible and break off with him. Returning the jewelry would be tangible evidence to her that you are through with him."

"Is that what the lawyer said?"

"No, it won't make any difference legally, but he agreed that it wouldn't be a bad idea. Do you want me to deliver the jewelry to Cato?"

"I ought to do that myself. But—" He could hear the sound to her breathing. *"Would* you?"

"Glad to. I'll pick it up."

"Adam, I was afraid when you didn't call—I was afraid this would be too much for you."

"Someone's at the door. I'll see you in an hour."

He hung up and looked at his watch. Five o'clock, and that would be Cato at the door. Before facing him, Adam tried to divest himself of the abominable figure which had taken a place in his mind's eye in order to see and deal with the real Cato Herold. He opened the door. Cato stood there shaking an umbrella—cool-looking, though the day seemed warm to Adam, sprightly and smiling, though to Adam the situation seemed very serious.

Cato entered. "Is Jo sick? I've called there several times yesterday and today, but they wouldn't let me talk with her."

"Dr. Garth's diagnosis is flu, but I think it's the strain of this situation."

"I can imagine, after Leah's threats."

Though Cato had been drinking, he was sober enough. He was shedding that sprightliness which he seemed to regard as a duty and grew appropriately grave. "I called you to come here so we wouldn't be overheard or interrupted," said Adam. "I've talked with a lawyer for a good many hours about this problem, and I wanted to see what you and I could work out."

"You don't happen to have a drink handy, do you? I feel the need of one."

"All I have is beer, and it's not cold. Would coffee do?"

"No thanks," said Cato, embarrassed that he had asked. "What did you learn from the lawyer?"

Adam sorted out what he would say. He had learned that some bad words—meretricious relations, defilement of the marriage bed, adulterous disposition, lewdness—all had a legal meaning, and all were heaped on Josephine. He had choked on what Josephine had told him yesterday, but now he felt old and numb.

"The main thing he told me was what I knew already, that the best course is to keep Leah from filing suit. Do you think there's a chance that she's not serious about it?"

"I don't know. If I had thought she'd even *talk* this way, naturally I'd have behaved very differently toward Jo. You believe that, don't you, Adam? As you know, I've had girls before, and Leah has never made such an issue of it. I still didn't believe her until she showed me one of the depositions."

"There's more than one?"

"I presume there are. I saw one for December twenty-fourth by a private detective."

"What does it state?"

"What do you think it states?" Cato said, offended. "Jo was sick and we couldn't get a doctor. She needed someone with her— it's just circumstantial evidence."

"I don't feel like coaxing this out of you."

"It states that I spent the night in Jo's apartment. Leah claims she has something much more damaging in the works, but she's bluffing."

Adam squeezed his eyes shut. "Where was I? Oh, yes. The point of attack is to show Leah we could get the case dismissed. According to this lawyer, if I can remember—he told me so much it's hard to keep it all straight—there are three defenses which might get the suit dismissed. One is recrimination. That is, if she'd been guilty of some offense which could be grounds for divorce—adultery, say."

Cato had started shaking his head before Adam had finished. "Unfortunately her vices are not sexual. I suppose most of her sins against me would be classified as 'mental cruelty.' "

"Another defense is connivance: if she connived in your contact with Josephine. Had full knowledge of what was going on and consented to it."

Cato grimaced and waved the idea away. "It's no use. Nothing that she does is obvious enough to have weight with a court."

"Have you discussed this with a lawyer?"

"No."

"I have. For heavens' sake, let's see what we can find that may save the situation. I'm not meddling in this affair for the fun of it." Adam paused and deliberately made his tone less sharp as he proceeded. "There is such a thing as passive connivance. If the deposition refers to a date six months back, she has had knowledge for at least that long. So if she didn't protest within a reasonable time against this affair, we may have a case. It's hard to prove, but we've got to find something. I thought that since she was down here and the three of you seemed to be seeing each other socially, it might be possible."

"You saw her that morning at the Garths'. What impression did she make on you then?"

Adam tried to remember. "She seemed to be looking the situation over, I suppose."

"On the basis of that would you say that she was *conniving* in our relationship? Not that you would be an unimpeachable witness."

"No, I suppose not." Adam rubbed his sleep-starved eyes and went on with an effort, keeping as nearly as possible to a flat dull voice. "There is a third defense: condonation. The idea that you repent and she forgives."

"I don't repent of loving Jo, and Leah never forgives."

"The principal evidence of condonation is cohabitation and renewal of sexual intercourse. If you manage that—"

"That would be physically impossible for me, feeling as I do about her."

"Listen to me! When something is worrying you sick, usually it helps to figure out what is the worst that can happen, so I asked my lawyer what that was, and he told me. Not only can she sue for divorce and blacken Josephine's reputation for life, in some states she can file suit for criminal conversation and depending on the humor of the jury collect large damages. Also adultery is a crime, in some jurisdictions a felony. This is not likely, but theoretically it could put you and Josephine in prison. Now if you sleep in the same bed with Leah or even in the same room and try to enter into sexual relations with her for a while, it might head this off."

"The whole idea is sordid and disgusting."

Adam moved to a stool directly in front of Cato and said: "If we could keep her here for a while, Cato, keep her from going to New York and filing, while you go through the motions of making up, it might save Josephine. Living together is prima facie evidence of sexual relations and therefore condonation though it may be rebutted—"

"In the name of God don't use those silly legal terms!" Cato shouted. "Going through the motions is not going to satisfy Leah. Do you think she can't tell how I feel? You are a bachelor. You have a few hours' nodding acquaintance with the law. I have known Leah for fifteen years. Don't you know the greatest actor in the world couldn't make a wife he detests think he loves her?"

"I think you could," said Adam. "Also the appearance of victory over a younger woman might satisfy Leah's pride."

"That wouldn't be enough for Leah. She'd have to have everything."

"You've gone back to her before after an affair. Why couldn't you try this time?"

"Don't you ever let go?" Cato leaped up and retreated to the window at the far side of the room. "The reason is that I've changed, and this is no ordinary affair. She's finally seen that, so she's making trouble."

"Don't you feel guilty about what you've done to Josephine? What kind of man *are* you?"

"If I thought I could do Jo any good without—" He gestured silently at Adam. "If I had even a hope of success—"

"Get along with Leah as best as you can," said Adam. "Sleep

in the same room, if possible in the same bed with her. Get her into the position of condoning before she can go back to New York and file suit."

"I just can't. And what proof would we have?"

"Mrs. Wriston would be our star witness."

"Maybe the connivance point would be better. It's possible that Leah has said things in front of Belle that would indicate consent."

Adam glanced at his watch. "Are you going back to Mrs. Wriston's now?" Cato said he was. "The first move will be to return the jewelry you gave Josephine," Adam said.

"Is Jo coming over?" said Cato, brightening up.

"No, I'll bring them. Let's try the connivance angle all right, but condonation would be better. We could use both. See what you can arrange."

"This is horribly degrading," Cato said and departed.

Alone, Adam prepared to go to the Garths'. As shameful as this affair seemed to him, it also seemed to reflect on his own life, to make it seem empty and puny. Often since leaving Josephine yesterday, he had felt listless as he had during a boxing match when he had taken too many blows in the midsection. Listlessness had given away to a very short temper. In spite of his flares of anger just now he could not hate Cato, but he was afraid of him. He would always feel uncomfortable in his presence and even at the thought of this man.

He thought of that December twenty-fourth of the deposition and he recalled his own Christmas Eve. He was new in Mercer then, had not yet made a beginning socially, and he was not invited to any of the Christmas parties which blazed up the mountainside that night. Someone had asked him if he were going home, and instead of saying: "This is my home," the implication of which was too wistful, he had just said: "I'm staying here." The markets and Duncan Chisholm's office had been closed Christmas Eve, but he had stayed at his desk all day studying financial publications. That night he had been too jaded to work any longer, and he'd gone to a movie. His interest had played out after forty-five minutes and he had driven along Buttermilk Road until bedtime. He had a Christmas package from his sister which he had not yet opened. It would be a fruitcake. It was every Christmas.

The next morning Dr. Garth had asked him to Christmas dinner and mentioned that Josephine had telephoned long distance the day before to say she couldn't come home for Christmas because she had flu. Adam had detected the old man's disappointment even on the telephone.

Adam could hear now, almost like a voice in the room, that vigilant private detective with Sizemore's pink shirt and no face, saying: "I figure she was giving him a Christmas present."

∿∿∿∿∿∿∿∿∿∿∿∿∿∿∿∿∿∿∿∿∿∿∿

27

It was drizzling, and the overcast brought twilight early. When Adam turned into the Garths' driveway, he saw a hooded figure glowing in the pearly gloom of the woods. It was Josephine in a white raincoat. He stopped the car, and she advanced from the shade and got in beside him, throwing off her hood and exposing her fine young head. "You'd better back out instead of going up there to turn around," she said. "Daddy's home and I came down here to avoid an argument about going out. He still thinks I'm sick." She held up a small cardboard box tightly gripped in her hand. "I'm going to return these to Cato myself. I was just weak to think of letting you do it." She avoided Adam's glance.

"Does your father suspect anything?"

"I wish I knew." Hollow-eyed, she watched the road nervously as they drove up the mountain. As they reached the top of the mountain, the misty lights of the town beneath them, she said: "Let's don't go straight there, please, Adam."

"All right. This might be a good time to tell you what the lawyer said. Leah will probably file in New York. My friend wasn't sure about some points of New York law, but his advice was to try to keep her from filing. If she does, have Cato issue a general denial. If you are named as corespondent, you can petition the court for leave to intervene and defend. This means you could have counsel cross-examine witnesses."

"No," said Josephine, shaking her head violently. "No."

"I've asked Cato about any defense he might have that would defeat the suit, and we're trying to go at it from the angle of connivance."

"Adam, don't you want to get out of this?" Josephine cried. "This horrible mess!"

"No. One thing I couldn't do today was answer all the lawyer's questions about evidence and what kind of case she has. If all she has is the testimony of people like Sizemore, it probably won't hold up. You know some of the answers, so you ought to discuss it with a lawyer."

"I dread that."

"Then you ought to show me the deposition, and let me—"

"Please don't make me do that, Adam." After a silence, she said: "What makes me look so cheap is that it was over so soon."

He turned the car up the avenue toward Mrs. Wriston's house. "No use waiting any longer."

"Not yet. This is going to break Cato's heart."

"He's expecting it." He drove down Mrs. Wriston's driveway and stopped the car, and they sat there in silence. The lights of the guest house shone through the slanted blinds. "May I?" he said and took the box from the loose grip of her fingers. Startled, she tried to tighten her hold on the box, but he already had it. Inside the cardboard box, in tissue paper, was a smaller velvet one. "You ought to have a witness as to what was in this box in case it should come up later."

The watch was there, a dazzling rim of diamonds in a nest of satin, and lying in the band were the pin and brooch. The stones of these were of an old-fashioned cut set in gold flowers and shone less brilliantly than he had expected. Cato had not stinted in having them set. There was a bracelet, very delicate, also golden. I should have given her something like this, Adam thought.

She walked ahead of him slowly toward the guest house. Adam rang the bell, and Cato admitted them. As soon as they were inside, Josephine extended the box to him. Cato accepted it without taking his eyes from Josephine's. "How do you feel?" he said.

"Fine," she said automatically.

"I was distressed to hear that you were ill," said Cato. Adam looked from one to the other of them; they stood like sleepwalkers.

Josephine turned to Adam. "Could I see Cato alone for just a minute?"

"Of course. I'll go up and speak to Mrs. Wriston."

As he walked up the driveway, he kept looking back at the guest house windows. The blinds were open, and he could see them standing inside. He had thought the situation could trouble him no more than it already had, but her request had hurt him, quickening the feelings he had kept numb.

Mrs. Wriston answered the door. She looked startled and at a loss for a moment. She was going to a party, Adam decided. Her dark silk dress was cut very low, revealing the soft cranny between her breasts, with which a string of pearls intersected. "Mrs. Wriston, may I speak with you a moment?"

"I'm about to go out."

"It won't take a minute. I'm in a hurry too."

He crowded her into the lush living room and looked out the window toward the guest house once more. Cato and Josephine were still standing a yard or so apart facing each other. He then took a seat across from Mrs. Wriston with a low coffee table between them. Mrs. Wriston was smoking an aromatic cigarette. Adam was well aware that Cato was the best one to talk with Mrs. Wriston, but he couldn't count on Cato. "I suppose you've heard about Leah's threat of a divorce suit."

Mrs. Wriston thought this over and nodded.

"Is Leah here?"

Mrs. Wriston silently gestured toward the ceiling with her cigarette.

Adam moved around the coffee table and sat beside her. The sofa was so yielding that he sank into it and his eyes were on a level with hers, and her half-exposed bosom, even younger than her face except for its abundance, rose and fell just beyond the curling cigarette smoke.

"I think our interests are the same in this matter," he continued in a lower voice.

She raised her eyebrows questioningly.

"My interest is to head off the suit if possible," he went on. "To keep her from filing. If not, to hush it up."

Mrs. Wriston nodded with judicious approval.

Adam restrained himself from going to a window and looking out again and forced his mind into the problem. "I've looked into the legal aspects for some defense strong enough to discourage Mrs. Herold from filing suit. Such as passive connivance—meaning she failed to protest. Cato thinks you may have heard his wife say something which would indicate consent."

Mrs. Wriston shook her head.

"Think back. I'm sure you must recall something Leah has said which would indicate consent or connivance."

Mrs. Wriston brought her cigarette to her lips and enveloped them in a cloud of rich-smelling smoke. Again she shook her head.

Adam opened his lips to speak, but hesitated, baffled.

Then Mrs. Wriston gave her opinion: "I'm not sure they ought to stay together. The marriage does seem a failure."

"But surely you don't want them divorced with all this publicity."

"Well, it isn't my idea."

"Mrs. Wriston, will you help us head it off?"

"Have you talked with Cato about this?"

"Yes, as I just said, he thinks you could help us."

"The poor boy is deeply involved. It's his marriage, after all."

Adam frowned. "You don't think that a divorce freeing Cato, no matter what the cost, would be desirable?"

She shrugged her plump shoulders.

"You *do* know the grounds that Leah is claiming."

"Oh, yes."

"Mrs. Wriston, I don't seem to have made myself clear. Don't you see—" He stopped, for there, only a few yards away, was Leah. Though she was directly in front of Adam, he had not seen her until she was well into the room, and it gave him the feeling that she had materialized there. She advanced with a smile, and Adam struggled against the clasping upholstery to his feet.

"You're not getting anywhere, are you?" Leah said in a mincing tone. "I'll tell you why. Belle knows that taking sides would mean being a witness in court. That's a distressing thought—being in a New York courtroom before a New York jury. They don't like Southerners much there, you know. Belle feels the same way I would. She wouldn't want to be cross-examined." Mrs. Wriston sat still and gazed into the air. "You see, what they try to do is *impeach* a witness for the defense," said Leah. "Now you take my lawyer; very shrewd man but ruthless. When I talked with him about this when I was in New York last week, he was *so interested* in Mrs. Wriston. He was talking about how I could take up residence in a state where they allowed such cases and file suit against Mrs. Wriston for conspiracy to alienate the affections of my husband, and collect big damages. 'Why, the very idea,' I told him, 'she's a friend of mine.' 'She introduced your husband to corespondent, didn't she?' he said. 'Didn't tell corespondent your husband was married. Arranged for your husband to stay with her while he carried on *criminal conversation* with corespondent. She's no friend of yours.' " Leah spoke the legal terms with relish. "Sit down, Mr. Salter." She was walking about the room, making graceful gestures with her hands, her walk displaying the suppleness of her slender, delicate figure, her perfect legs, and tiny waist. It was the kind of figure which Adam would have admired greatly if it had belonged to anyone else, but since it was hers, the sight irritated him. "Then my lawyer said, 'You ought to name Mrs. Wriston as another corespondent. Your husband's been staying with her.' 'Not quite in the same house,' I told him. He said, 'They were close enough to have opportunity. Now all we'd have to prove is an *adulterous disposition* between them, enter a prayer for damages with the suit.' I said, 'I couldn't do that to Belle, she's a friend of mine. Why, I've been a guest in her house.' "

Mrs. Wriston sat very still. She looked suddenly older to Adam, and the exposure of her bosom made her seem soft and vulnerable. Even dressed more modestly she would look to a jury like a woman who might have such a disposition.

"Mrs. Herold," said Adam, "there's no need to make a public display of this in court. Nobody wins that way. There's always recrimination. If you're bent on divorce, why don't you get one in this state on other grounds? There are some very sympathetic judges here and all you have to do is—"

"—perjure myself. You're my witness, Belle. This man, Adam Salter, tried to suborn me."

At this Mrs. Wriston leaped up and hurried toward the door. "Don't go, Belle," said Leah. But Mrs. Wriston, without looking back, cried as she vanished into the hallway: "I have to get ready to go out." Leah's tinkling laughter sounded brittle in the soft room. "That terrified poor Belle. She doesn't want to be a witness to *anything* now. She has a morbid fear of having to appear in court. She's so afraid of old skeletons, like her seduction of Cato nearly a quarter of a century ago. And she's a miser. Belle doesn't spend half her income. Works her servants to death and pays them almost nothing."

"I'm sure you ought to reconsider," said Adam. "I think you and Cato can patch it up. He and Josephine are through."

Leah looked at him with interest. "You want her as unspoiled as possible, don't you? What happens in court won't change the fact that should be most important to you—that they did have intercourse." She looked eagerly into his face with bright eyes and parted lips. "You know that's what happened," she persisted, wide-eyed, with an intense smile. "You don't think it was just something Platonic. You're not that *good,* are you?"

"I'm concerned with facts, not conclusions," he said stiffly.

"But I have proof. Would you like to see it?"

He had rarely been in a position of being treated with malice and helpless to walk out or even to retort. He had to remind himself that in the eyes of the law, the public, and perhaps in reality, she was an injured party whose rights had been abused and who had some claim on his patience as an agent now.

"Cato's had Josephine at her best—when she was fresh and innocent," said Leah. "If she'd been much younger, she wouldn't have enjoyed it so much. Cato caught her when she was just right. But now she's even beginning to look like a woman whose been around. I didn't think so when I first met her. Her face is beginning to change. Perhaps she hasn't deep lines yet, but you can tell where the lines are going to be. I'm afraid when her hair starts turning, as black as it is, the first gray hair will stand out like a glow-worm. Or does she already color it? I had a feeling that you would be the one to get her when I learned that legally you were only a cousin. You may not have Cato's charm, but you have one advantage over him. Do you know what that is? You are the nearest facsimile she could hope to find of her dear old dad."

"I've been told there's a resemblance."

"It's much more than a resemblance. It will be the dearest fulfillment for Josephine. Ah, if you were only a doctor!"

"That sounds like something from the *Cathexis of the Organon.*"

"Did Cato bring that book down here? That's my book." She sat down suddenly. "Yes, Josephine is trying to do with you what Cato tried to do with me. He saw the image of his mother in me. I never saw any resemblance and I could never bear the woman. You should have seen Cato and his mother. They looked just like sisters! Now isn't it a pity—wouldn't it have saved trouble for all of us—if Cato had been a normal homosexual instead of this self-deceiving half-man he is."

"I don't follow you," Adam protested. "And I've never seen any signs."

"You wouldn't, but I know him so well. There are no *signs.*

177

Except—you've heard about Cato's ulcer? It surprised me; I thought peptic ulcers were reserved for men on the make like yourself. You know, men who want to be general manager of something. But I was wrong. Cato's mother tried to force him to become a man too soon, and all his life he's yearned to be dependent on someone—someone big, strong, and rich like Josephine—to regain babyhood, from which he was untimely snatched, to yield to those feminine tendencies which have stirred so much conflict in him. He couldn't let his conscious mind recognize these desires. But alas, his duodenum did."

"Is this from the *Cathexis of the Organon* too?"

"No, this diagnosis came from an analyst of mine and Cato's. Have you ever been analyzed?"

"Psychoanalyzed? No."

"Like most businessmen you are too coarse-grained to need it."

There was nothing to him, in other words, or he would have some interesting vices. As a Southerner with a rural background he was a barbarian to her. "Certainly you are naïve to think you can solve your problems by giving Cato back to me now." Her voice rose and grew shrill. "Cato has spent all his money on this woman. He can't or won't work regularly. I can't just take him, quivering, back into my arms after these indignities. Besides, now that the money's gone, he demands a rich woman." As she talked and even though Adam knew she had no interest in him as a man, her body assumed graceful poses, which seemed to cry out for a compliment or the click of a camera. It occurred to him that he shared her failings: he had not been able to view her as human enough to feel that any human appeal or argument was appropriate.

He leaned toward her. "Mrs. Herold, if this gets into court, the indignities are just beginning. A petition for divorce will be a public confession of failure—yours as well as his." He spoke in a low tone, which grew in confidence as he talked. She had her stare fixed on him. "Such a suit would brand you as spiteful and inadequate— and a loser. If you stay together, you will be in the position of having recovered your husband from a woman who is—pardon me, Mrs. Herold—several years younger than you are and who has money to offer him besides. Also you say this affair is different; what you mean is, your husband is different—no longer promiscuous—a bigger and better man. And once this legal unpleasantness is over, another sort will begin. You will be alone."

"The money's gone!"

"We could make some adjustment in the matter of money."

"Adjustment!" She screamed an explosive nervous laugh. "Adjustment!"

"I mean a reasonable amount," he said in a soothing voice.

"What about the jewelry?"

"Josephine has given the jewelry back."

"When?"

"Just now."

"Is she down there?" Leah opened the glass doors and went out on the veranda. Adam followed and looked down at the guest house. The sky was dark now, and a fine drizzle had begun again. "You are a great arranger, aren't you? Look, they've drawn the blinds. I may call you as a witness for me too."

Adam hurried down the outside stairs. As he passed in front of his car, he saw the red glow of a cigarette through the windshield, and he realized that Josephine was waiting for him there. Josephine had the hood of her raincoat over her bowed head. "We may have to pay her something," Adam said, out of breath. "The connivance angle is shot to pieces, I'm afraid, with Mrs. Wriston no good to us, for the time anyway. Maybe Cato can bring his wife around. Your best course is to keep negotiating with her, don't accept a provocation." As he spoke, he tried by force of will to throw off the thickening weight of heaviness and helplessness. "Just one moment," Adam said. "I want to say something to Cato."

There was no answer to his knock, and Adam opened the guest house door. Cato stood at the window at the far side of the room, his back to Adam.

"Cato, I've just talked with Leah and I think something can be worked out. One thing, don't let her get her hands on that jewelry. She might use it as an exhibit in court." There was no response. "Cato?"

Cato would not look around. He said in a trembling voice: "You've asked too much of me in one day, Adam." He tried to clear his throat. "Would it be all right for Jo to keep the flower pin?"

"No, it would not." Adam stood there for a moment. "Keep negotiating with Leah. And try to get Mrs. Wriston's help."

As Adam got in the car, he said: "Let's go to town for dinner."

"No, I couldn't eat anything now. I'd just like to go home, please."

Adam glanced back up at the house. Leah, untroubled by the fine rain, was still standing on the veranda, silhouetted against the dim light from inside. The sight gave him a feeling, almost a hallucination, which stayed with him on their silent drive back over the mountain, of a bird of prey flying at his eyes.

28

Adam had breakfast at the Mercer Café, the businessman's coffee-house, around noon the next day. He had finally dropped off to sleep sometime after four o'clock a.m., and heat and sunlight had waked him around ten. Sleeping so late made him feel guilty. He should have been out doing something. He had gone back to Mrs. Wriston's last night twice to talk with Leah and had a feeling that someone was inside, but no one came to the door. He had waited a long time. He'd found the guest house unlocked but Cato was gone. Adam had called his lawyer in Birmingham again and asked more questions. His imagination, having devoured all the facts at hand, was acidly feeding on its own lining.

He immediately sensed an emergency, when over the heads of the men who crowded the restaurant he saw Josephine. He arose, and she came to his table. "Have some breakfast?"

"No thank you," she said, out of breath. "Adam, something's happened to Leah. She didn't come in last night." His heart leaped. "She came to our house last night about eleven o'clock, woke Daddy up, and got me out of bed. She was excited and under high pressure. If I hadn't known her, I would have thought she was taking drugs. She said you had agreed to a settlement of money and that was what she wanted to talk about. I said I wanted you present. But she wouldn't wait. She just stated her terms: five hundred thousand dollars. I was exhausted and I told her I wouldn't pay her a cent. 'Is that your last word?' she said. I said it was, so off she went. She wasn't at the house for more than fifteen minutes. It worried me, I knew I shouldn't have flared up like that, so I tried to reach her at Belle's. I telephoned again this morning. She hadn't come in."

"How did she get to your house?"

"In Cato's car. The car wasn't at Belle's either. She didn't get back to Belle's house at all. Her suitcase is still there."

"Doesn't sound good." It took Adam about a minute to decide they couldn't just wait for her to turn up. "Let me check with Clyde Lavender. He can put out a call for the car."

"Leah went out of the driveway so fast I was thinking then she might have an accident. I could hear her tires screeching all the way from the Buttermilk Road."

"She may have had an accident, and the police may not have known where she was staying in town. Excuse me, I'll try Clyde."

He returned from the telephone booth and said, as he sat down: "Nothing reported yet. Clyde's going to call me when he has something." He added: "I was hoping she had met with foul play, but that would just make more trouble. You and Cato would be prime suspects if anything happened to her."

"Adam, I tried to do what you said and not get mad, but it was just too much."

"She wasn't really bargaining. She knew she couldn't get a half million. A blackmailer doesn't work that way. They ask a piece at a time. No, she was just raising hell. I think I'd better see if Cato has any ideas," he said, getting up.

"You haven't finished your lunch."

"I've had all I want."

Outside the sun was hot, and the bright glare off the pavement hurt his eyes. "Would you care to come with me? No, maybe you'd better not." His mind wasn't working well on this information yet. He was still hoping that Leah's disappearance might solve all their problems. "I'll call you when I know something," he said to Josephine.

He drove to Mrs. Wriston's. As he knocked on the guest house door, he was hailed from above. Cato was standing on the veranda where Adam had last seen Leah and came down the stairway to meet him. Adam looked for signs of guilt or of unusual stress, but Cato merely seemed hung over and already healing it with drink. "Where do you think your wife is?" said Adam.

"I haven't the foggiest notion."

"When was she planning to go back to New York?"

"She doesn't make plans."

"Do you think she decided to drive on back to New York without her baggage?"

"I doubt it. She might leave her baggage, but she's a poor driver, and she doesn't like driving. She flew down. I expected her to fly back."

"I think I'll go out to the airport and ask some questions. Would you mind coming along? I'd like to have a word with you."

They got into Adam's car and drove through town to the Clayton highway. "How did you make out with Mrs. Wriston?" Adam said. "Do you think she'll help on the connivance angle?"

"I'm sure she won't. Leah's terrified her."

"Last night Leah asked Josephine for a half-million dollars—or else."

"God in heaven! I don't think she expected to get that much money, though it's hard even for me to tell. She probably just wanted a scene with Jo to make her despair."

"She seemed pretty wild. You don't suppose she did herself in."

"No, it's the people around her who do themselves in." They were passing now between open cornfields with a country store and filling station every few hundred yards. The summer weather had really begun, and the air coming in the windows smelled scorched.

"Where were you last night?" said Adam, watching Cato from the corner of his eye.

"Why, I went to Birmingham last night at the invitation of your rival, Jack Olin, more or less as an escort for Belle. I had declined earlier but decided at the last minute to go. We had dinner at some club there. Belle is enchanted with the brummagem vulgarity of that place. I went in self-defense, really, so I would neither be by myself nor have to spend the evening with Leah. This was the worst morning yet for pit-gazing. I kept thinking—"

"What time did you get back?"

"About one o'clock."

"And your car was gone then and no sign of Leah?"

"That's right."

Mention of the Olins stung Adam: they were working on stockholders whom he was forced to neglect.

"How did your wife seem after we left last night?" said Adam.

"Very tense. I'm afraid she's taken a real aversion to you. Said you were trying to trample her down."

"I couldn't tell I was making any impression at all on her."

Adam turned in at the airport sign and followed the blacktop road along the airfield. "There's my car," said Herold.

"She must have come directly here from Jo last night," said Cato, and the airline clerk inside confirmed it; a Mrs. Herold had left on the 11:40 flight to New York last night.

"Two seats on your next flight to New York," said Adam, and Cato nodded. The next flight left at four-thirty. "That's not much time, Cato."

Outside Cato said: "Wait a moment, will you? Let me see if she's left the keys in the car." He searched the car. "She took the keys with her or threw them away."

Twenty minutes later they were in Mrs. Wriston's driveway again.

"Cato!" Mrs. Wriston in a satin robe called from the veranda. "Call Operator 275 in New York."

"Leah may be on her way back here now," Cato said. He raised his voice. "I'll take it down here, Belle."

Adam cut his motor and waited. He was hot and tired, his mouth dry and body wet, and though he had decided on going to New York, he felt very strongly, from his experience so far, that he could have little effect on Leah. He sat waiting restlessly. Mrs. Wriston came out on the veranda again and watered some plants. This time she wore shorts, and Adam noted indifferently that her hips and legs were slender. Something blooming in the yard was sickeningly sweet.

After waiting fifteen minutes, Adam went inside the guest house. He could hear Cato's voice from the bedroom.

A moment later Cato came in and went for the liquor cabinet without seeing Adam. "Was it Leah?" Adam asked.

"Not exactly." Cato poured himself a drink and took it on the move. He went to a built-in bookshelf, pulled some books aside and felt around with one hand. "Damn!" he said. "She got that jewelry." He turned to Adam. "That was a friend of mine in New York on the telephone. She's filed."

"What?"

"Mrs. Cato Herold has filed suit for divorce against Mr. Cato Herold on grounds of adultery and named one Josephine Garth as corespondent."

"She couldn't have, she's just left."

"She did it this morning. Must have had the petition all ready. She must have decided on it before she came down here. She didn't hear a word any of us said."

"How did your friend know?"

"Hell, Leah's telling everybody. It'll be in the newspapers this afternoon most likely. She'll see they don't miss it. Have a drink."

"Maybe she's lying."

"My friend checked at the courthouse. My friend said it was going to be publicized because of my grandfather."

"All we can do is go on up there and see if we can get her to withdraw the suit."

Herold made a hoarse sound which was between a laugh and a cry of anguish. "How can you be so blind? Don't you learn from what happens to you? If anything, your efforts of last night made the situation worse. It might occur to you that your Neo-Rotarian style of doing things doesn't always sweep everything before it."

"It wouldn't hurt to try."

"The damage is done, man! Can't you get that through your head!" He quieted. "I'm sorry about the Neo-Rotarian crack. I forget that everyone doesn't know her as I do. I've admired your resourcefulness, but this was simply impossible from the beginning. If you go up there and apply more pressure, it will harden her. Give her time to be alone and have a few regrets."

Adam did not accept this as final, but there was no need to take the afternoon plane. He stood up. His flesh felt leaden, and he could hardly get his breath. This is the kind of hot day when things like this happen, he thought. "I'd like to use your telephone." Adam stopped and poured himself an ounce of whisky in the bottom of a glass and drank it warm. Cato was loading records on the phonograph. "A whole half jigger!" he said, looking at Adam's drink. "This is the end of the world!" He flicked a switch, and the volume of music swelled up and shook the room.

"I can't think with that so loud!" Adam said, turning it down.

"Who wants to think?" said Cato, turning it back up.

Adam stopped at the bedroom door. "I'm going to call the newspaper before I call Josephine," he shouted over the music. "You're absolutely sure?"

"You're not going to tell her on the telephone! I'll go out there in a little while and tell her myself."

Adam did not reply but went into the bedroom and closed the

door. He telephoned the *Mercer Times* and asked for a reporter he knew named McEwen. "Mac, this is Adam Salter. Have you had a press dispatch on someone named Cato Herold?"

"Yeah, boy. Hottern hell, too. With Miss Josephine Garth as corespondent."

"Is it going to be in the paper?"

"Yassuh. Tomorrow."

"Is there any way of stopping it, Mac?"

"Not that I know of." McEwen's manner changed, and he hesitated, plainly trying to figure out Adam's interest in the story. "Want to speak to the editor?"

In a moment Adam had Mr. Gurney, the editor, on the telephone. "This is Adam Salter. I understand you plan to run an article about this divorce case which involves Miss Garth."

"That's right" came the clipped unfriendly reply.

"I'm asking as a member of the family. You shouldn't print that. The accusation is unfounded, and it's going to do a lot of harm."

"I'm sorry, Mr. Salter," said the editor, and Adam knew from his tone that this was a familiar form of pressure and greatly resented. "What the article will state is not unfounded, that a petition for divorce has been filed. That's a matter of public record. We're not going to run any details. If the court finds that Miss Garth has been done an injury, we will be more than glad to give equal or greater space to that too."

"That wouldn't undo it."

"This item'll be on news broadcasts and it'll be in the Birmingham papers. It's a story of interest to the public. We would print it if the girl was poor. It simply wouldn't be right to leave this out. If the girl were my own daughter, we'd still run it, believe me."

Adam thought: would you run it if her father owned a chain of supermarkets and bought several pages of ads every week-end? But this was not fair. Dr. Garth was rich enough to make them hesitate about as much as they would. And there was no point in saying something offensive and turning the press against them. "Are you going to be in your office for the next few minutes?"

"I'm going to be in my office for the next six hours, but if you have in mind coming down here to talk me out of printing this, you'll be wasting your time."

"Thanks," said Adam dryly and hung up.

The door opened, and Cato came in. "Could I use your car?" he said. "I'm going out there. I'm going to tell that old tyrant that this was my fault, not Jo's. There's no reason for her to have to stand up to him alone."

"No, you keep away from there."

"All right, I'll borrow Belle's." Cato started away.

Adam overtook him and said: "Listen, Cato, go and you'll make it harder for Josephine and get Dr. Garth mad. My impulse was to go myself, but it's not the best thing. Let her break it to her father in her own way."

Cato stopped and stared. "I'll think about it."

Adam returned to the telephone. He was beginning to realize that Cato was right on one point; the damage had been done, and he himself had to take the blame for part of it. He had gone to Sizemore and thus alerted Leah. He had insisted that the jewelry be returned, and it had fallen into Leah's hands at once. But his biggest mistake had been in negotiating with Leah. The crucial time had been last night when he had the chance to influence her, had her attention for once, but he had been too distracted, too repelled by her, too much in a hurry to get through with it. He had not tried the flattery that she so obviously craved, he had treated her in a businesslike way because he had stopped regarding her as a woman. He had also dispersed with flattery because of a feeling of which he had hardly been aware at the time that such an approach was beneath him. Josephine had put this in his hands, and he had failed her.

He dialed her number, and she answered the telephone. "Josephine, we found her car at the airport. Leah's flown to New York and already filed suit and named you as corespondent. I've called the newspaper. They had a press dispatch about it and they're going to print it tomorrow. I couldn't talk them out of it. You need to find your father and tell him gently before he hears it another way. Would you like for me to come out there now?"

"No, Adam." Her voice was faint. "You're right. I need to tell him."

"I thought of trying to bribe the newspaper, but as they said, it'll be on the radio and in the Birmingham papers. Your father could probably come a lot nearer getting it stopped than I could. Are you all right, Josephine?"

"Yes."

"This seems a lot bigger to you than it will to anyone else, and she's done all she can to you now. I failed you on this, Josephine. I should have done better."

"No, you did all anyone could, Adam. Thank you."

He stood there holding the telephone instrument after the connection was severed, dimly aware of the thunder of the phonograph from the front room. The music sounded like Bach, with a victorious progression of oversized and supernaturally clear sounds shaking the house. It was only an annoyance to him now. What was Herold doing with it? Perhaps getting himself into a heroic frame of mind to undo the catastrophe with a grand gesture.

Josephine was the first hostage against him in the hands of the enemy since his father died. Now he knew his independence and invulnerability were gone. He felt helpless and anxious. For the past weeks he had wanted to marry Josephine. Now he had to marry her. He could not do anything else, whether either of them wanted it or not.

Adam opened the door into the living room, and the music pelted his ears. Cato was gone, and the front door was ajar. Adam quickened his pace. He found Mrs. Wriston in her garden. "Where's Cato?"

"He just went off in my car."

Adam leaped into his own car, backed around, and tore out to the street. Within a minute he was on the Buttermilk Road.

When he turned into the Garths' driveway, he saw in the shade head of him, Dr. Garth's old Cadillac parked, and beyond it was Mrs. Wriston's bright red sports car, stationary and slanting, suggestive of an accident. Adam knew at once what had happened. Dr. Garth had been just returning from a drive, and Cato had overtaken him here. Josephine would not have had a chance to break the news to her father. Adam did not see them at first, only Rutherford, who was burying himself in the job of polishing the Cadillac's tail fins and being deaf, but he whispered hoarsely as Adam passed: "That ain't good for doctuh's heart."

Up ahead, past the gleaming red metal of the front car, he saw Cato and Dr. Garth facing each other. Cato's rising voice reached him. "Of course I take the responsibility for the whole thing. I admit I kept her in ignorance."

Then Dr. Garth's lower voice: "Sir, it means nothing at all to me what you claim responsibility for, especially not now, for you are obviously *drunk!*"

"I don't care what you think of me," said Cato, "but I want your word that you will not blame her or try to make her pay for it."

"My daughter is no business of yours. Now get off of my property."

"I want to see her first," said Cato, looking toward the house.

"Perhaps you did not hear me, sir," said Dr. Garth, stepping closer.

Adam reached them at that point and said: "Come on, Cato. Time to go."

Cato turned to Adam, his face red, and shouted: "This man has just threatened me." He faced Dr. Garth once more. "I suppose you'll kill me. Go ahead. You've already done everything you could to destroy your own daughter!" He turned his back on Dr. Garth and started up the driveway toward the house.

Adam went after him and grasped his shoulder. Cato shook it off, and Adam walked beside him and said: "You're just making a mess for her to clean up. If Dr. Garth dies of a stroke from this fight you're starting, do you think Josephine will thank you for it? Come on back now." Cato slowed down.

Then, without a word he nodded and turned around. Dr. Garth was already in his car, and he did not look at them as the wall of metal and glass passed them with a rush of hot wind.

~~~~~~

29

Josephine opened the door that night before Adam rang. "I'm glad you wanted to come," she whispered. She gave him only a few seconds to admire what so plainly cried out for admiration or to digest the impression of perfume, gay red lipstick, black hair brushed to glossiness, and tight white sweater.

She took his hand and led him through the dining room, where the pale light of one sconce made massive shadows, to the patio, which was lit only by the dim outward penetration of the curtained glass doors. The night air was soft and full of the smells of spring, more like a resort at sea level than mountain country where the breeze on a spring night was usually sharp. The stars of the Milky Way gave an impression of flowing into the valley which was strewn with twinkling lights.

For one who had taken such pains with her appearance she was quick to hide in semidarkness, and he sensed that she could not stand much close scrutiny even from him. "You have that lawsuit tomorrow about the mill, don't you?" she said. "What's it about? Oh, yes, you want to see the books." She talked in a nervous flow. "All this business with me has taken so much of your time." She had run down, and they were silent for a moment.

"How's your father?"

"Heartsick. Oh, he blames Cato. Belle too, but mostly Cato. I'm a little girl who was taken in by the wrong crowd. I encouraged him to think so because I said I hadn't known Cato was married, and I didn't make it very clear when I found out."

"It was easier on your father that way."

"He got Rice Alexander out here within an hour. Mr. Alexander tactfully made the same assumptions that Daddy did. Daddy wants to defend it in court, and I just stalled about that. Mr. Alexander said that it would be easy for the court to put the wrong interpretation on my going out with Cato and that legally it made no difference whether or not I knew Cato was married. Daddy blames Cato, but I can tell he feels that I need straightening out." She was walking around as she talked, her heels making sharp clicks on the brick.

"It sounds as though your father's reacting very well. He's a lot tougher than you'd been thinking he was."

"He used to be tough, but this was a terrible shock. I think it hurt his feelings that the *Mercer Times* is going to print an article about it. He's known the publisher all his life, and he tried to get him on the telephone, but Mr. Everett 'couldn't be reached.' I think he just didn't want to have to say no to Daddy. Some of it is a matter of ego too. Daddy would like to think he's important enough to get this hushed up." Josephine spoke these words with an effort and a hint of tears in her voice. "I guess as much as I dreaded it I had this little-girl idea that once Daddy did find out I was in trouble, he could fix everything."

There was just enough light from inside for Adam to see the contours of her tall well-shaped figure and her dark hair but not her expression. He felt the plastic-covered cushion of a chaise longue, which was wet with dew, and wiped it with his handkerchief. "Sit down."

"Adam, I've been thinking of going to San Francisco, and just coming back to see Daddy once a year and never letting anyone else know I was here, but wherever I go, I'll always be waiting for the story of my life to catch up with me. I haven't anything to look forward to now. I feel too dirty to want anything. I can't even look forward to having children because I'd be thinking sooner or later they'll find out. Maybe when I'm middle-aged, I'll be able to tell myself: but that happened twenty-five years ago."

Adam took her in his arms, his hands gripping her waist, and he knew from touching her that whatever her mood and the situation required of him, it was going to be hard to keep his hands off her. Her perfume had a powerfully sweet sticky smell. "We still may be able to get her to withdraw the suit."

"I'd thought of that. But it won't do any good. I've been seen too much with Cato here."

191

Adam grasped her bare arms and turned her toward him. "Marry me, Josephine, the sooner the better."

"Why in the world would you want to marry me?"

"Because I love you. I certainly could never marry anyone else."

She disengaged herself. "Adam, you make me wonder if you know the truth. Maybe you're like Daddy and think it was all innocent."

"Yes, I think basically you were innocent."

"I'm going to let other people think whatever they want, and I can't tell Daddy the truth—he couldn't stand it, it would kill him— but I have to tell you. I'm not innocent. You just think I am because you can't think of me as an adult. Just like Daddy."

He had already known the truth, but her words chilled him. He had believed that this affair had not touched her because he had managed to keep his worst fears and certainties apart, and the pain he felt made his voice stronger and more compelling. "I have to have you, Josephine."

"This is a trap for you, Adam. Now that I've confessed, you have to forgive. I'm disgraced so you have to save me."

She did not hesitate in replying, and he marveled at her fluency under circumstances which made him speak so awkwardly. Even these bitter words spoken to raise a barrier against him pulled him tighter. "No, I'm not chivalrous."

"I'm afraid of the preacher in you, Adam. It turned out you couldn't save the world, so that missionary zeal is going to save me. Am I making you uncomfortable? I want to. I feel guilty enough. I don't want to have to feel guilty about you too."

"You don't know how you feel, so you think I don't either. You're wrong." He took hold of her again.

"Don't. I'm not the kind of woman a nice man would marry. I'm a mistress type. Aren't you afraid of germs? I've already had two telephone calls."

"About what?"

"One was a ranting preacher, the kind that sobs and shrieks on the radio. He called me a whore and told me to repent. Another was a proposition. The man's going to drive up, blow the horn, one long, two shorts. Come on out."

Adam burned with anger and gripped her too tightly, so that she was gasping for breath, but she made no protest. "I'm going to marry you," he said. He drew her down on the chaise longue and kissed her on the mouth. She pulled her mouth away and lay with her head on his chest, her body resting between his legs. "Tell me you will," he said. She began to shake. She sobbed so that he could hardly understand what she said: "Adam, I've made him into an old man." Then she lay quietly, his hand caressing her hair. Her sobs hurt him, yet he had a feeling of joy which was much more than blood troubled by a spring night and a shapely young woman in his arms. It occurred to him that she needed someone and was therefore allowing herself to be loved, but at the moment that was enough.

She sat up suddenly, and not until then did he identify the tap on the glass. "Yes, Daddy?" Josephine called, her voice unnatural and loud, and at the same moment Adam saw the black shape through the curtained glass.

"You've had a hard day, Josephine, and you aren't completely over the flu," came Dr. Garth's voice. "You need to come in and go to bed now."

"All right, Daddy," she called, standing up, smoothing her sweater and hair. "I'm sorry, Adam," she whispered.

Adam arose, too rattled to comment. The shadow disappeared from the curtains. Adam said after a moment: "Will you marry me, Josephine?"

"Let's see how things look tomorrow."

He kissed her goodnight, and to avoid having to face Dr. Garth inside with possible lipstick smears and the smell of her perfume in his clothes, Adam leaped the hedge into the darkness, landing on the grass with a general shock to his skeleton. "Are you all right?" Josephine whispered over the hedge.

"Will you?"

"Let's talk tomorrow." She did not sound displeased. "Good luck in court."

That night Adam dreamed that he was in a ten-cent store, and he saw Josephine buying a large bottle of perfume, or selling it. He saw the price clearly: 79¢. Across the counter from her was Dean Byroade. Adam woke up and felt for his shirt and put it against his face. The smell of the perfume was still there, the same as in the dream.

~~~~~~

30

The hearing was set for ten o'clock, and Adam and G. P. Moon had agreed to meet beforehand to go over testimony one more time.

During breakfast at the Mercer Café, Adam found the following article in the Birmingham morning paper:

> NEW YORK, May 11. Mrs. Leah Fraden Herold of New York City filed a petition for divorce here today against her husband, Cato Lanier Herold, on grounds of adultery, and named Josephine Garth of Mercer, as corespondent.
>
> Herold's grandfather, John Cato Lanier, was an eminent Shakespearean actor of the New York stage during the early years of this century.

This article, and the prospect of testifying in court, took his appetite, and as he walked toward Moon's office, it seemed to him that the news about Josephine filled the air like band music, that every eye glittered with the knowledge of it.

When he entered Moon's office, Moon said: "I tried to call you." He threw a document to Adam. "Byroade's demurred to the petition, and the hearing's put off to Tuesday week."

Adam, feeling incredulous and thwarted, read through the document. It contained twenty-two reasons why a writ of mandamus should not be issued. Some were to be expected: that the bylaws forbad inspection of the books without approval of the board of directors. Others seemed like pettifogging: "That Adam Salter failed at the time of making demand on the respondent to show proof to the custodian of the books that he was at that time a stockholder in The Taurus Company." Another stated that Adam wanted to see the books for idle curiosity. Some meant nothing at all to him: "It affirmatively appears that granting of the same would introduce confusion and not support substantial justice."

"All this looks like junk to me," said Adam. "Will any of it stick?"

"Nope. But I guess when Byroade threw all that at him, the judge figured he'd better do some more study on the law. This is an unusual kind of case. The last one like it in Sweetwater County was in 1900. Maybe the judge is just a leetle bit afraid of Byroade."

"What's Byroade going to pull at the hearing?"

"Same stuff as he's got here in different words."

"I'm not so sure. He may come up with a surprise. Don't you think it would pay to do some digging on this?"

"Be a waste of time." Moon seemed busy, withdrawn, as though remembering he was doing this work without charge.

"I want to pay you for your time." But that did not have the effect Adam was seeking either. As he kept questioning Moon, Adam realized that it was simply contrary to Moon's nature to exhaust any subject, particularly if it involved reading, and his own insistence was making Moon fidget and breathe wearily.

Adam spent the morning preparing an advertisement for the *Mercer Times* under the heading: WHAT IS THE TAURUS COMPANY TRYING TO HIDE? describing his attempts to see the books and management's steps to prevent it.

That night Adam took Josephine some gift-wrapped perfume he had bought at a drugstore. They laughed about a dozen roses which had arrived with Belle Wriston's card, on which she had written the single word: "Courage." The plump red roses and the message seemed to express very neatly Mrs. Wriston's love of the voluptuous and the highflown. Adam and Josephine were on the patio again, and he could only imagine her flashing eyes and black hair. She moderated her laugh. An article about the divorce suit had appeared in the *Mercer Times* that afternoon, and she did not want her father to hear her laughing, for it might seem that this experience had not chastened her enough. Dr. Garth had been deeply displeased about the roses. Anyway, that just about exhausted the topics they had to laugh about. Adam again asked Josephine to marry him, and again she was indefinite. That evening she gently prevented his embracing her except for a goodnight kiss on the cheek. He hated even more to leave her that night, for he found that when he was away from Josephine, his image of her as pale as a candle flame floated on a dark landscape as though his memory had a winter gloom of old varnish over it, and only being in her presence could expel this deathlike picture.

He went back to Birmingham the next day to confer with a lawyer about The Taurus Company and to study court records of similar lawsuits. It turned out, as Moon had said, the courts hardly ever denied a stockholder the corporation's books, even if he were working for a competitor. A stockholder was not allowed to see the books for improper or unlawful purposes, but it was very hard to prove any such intent. Yet Adam believed that Byroade would come up with at least one new potent defense.

On returning to Mercer late that afternoon, Adam went to see Herold about another pass at Leah. He found Herold lying on a sofa in Mrs. Wriston's guest house. He was unshaven and breathed out a powerful smell of fermentation. A vigorous shaking did not rouse him. Adam wrote a note and attached it to a half-empty bottle with a rubber band.

Herold called at four o'clock in the morning. "She's hiding," he said, thick-tongued, mimicking Adam's Southern accent for reasons of his own. "I hear she's sold the jewelry and spent the money on a trip to Mexico. I'll bet it's her lawyer's idea. You know why? He's afraid of dat old black magic of dat old debble magician, Cato Herold. He's afraid I'll soften her with world-famous blandishments."

"What's her lawyer's name?"

"Marcus Fisher. Don't think you can do anything with that iceberg. I've tried. Fisher won't tell where she is because he knows Leah can withstand anything but blandishments—my bland blandishments." Cato couldn't seem to stop laughing. He was still laughing and choking when Adam hung up. So in the early morning hours Adam gave up hope of affecting Mrs. Herold through her husband.

But with Josephine's permission, he did go to see Rice Alexander, a big untidy mushmouthed Black Belter, whose accent had not been thinned by Harvard Law School. He had recently undertaken a punishing diet and managed to look fat and gaunt at the same time. Adam asked about the legality of trying to buy off Mrs. Herold. That wouldn't be illegal, said Rice Alexander, since it was not a criminal case. He'd talk with Dr. Garth and see if he wanted to spend any money on it, if so he would try to reach Mrs. Herold through her attorney.

Adam was spending his days on The Taurus Company, the fight for control, and also in preparing himself to manage it by learning what the president needed to know. Josephine was taking advantage of this time to read all the hard books she thought she ought to read—*Don Quixote, The Decline of the West, The Divine Comedy* —and getting only a few pages into one before going on to another.

At night after dinner Adam went to see her. She would not appear in public, and they spent their evenings on the patio or driving around the countryside. Blakely, rather subdued, had come to see Josephine once. Josephine was rarely snubbed; instead she received too much attention, most of it from curious women she didn't know well and didn't want to know. A few brought little gifts and tried to steer the conversation with various degrees of adroitness to Josephine's disgrace. Some older women, whose conscious intentions were kind enough, seemed to try to provoke her to tears by insistent expressions of sympathy and urging her to pray for guidance. She refused all invitations and would have declined to see these visitors if Dr. Garth had not pressed her to receive them.

She avoided answering the telephone. Rutherford was growing adept at stopping those hostile anonymous calls. One call did get through that made her very angry. A local sport with shiny gray hair, known as Dude Harper, called Josephine for a "date." He was notorious for pinching at dances and parties, and having seen Josephine's name in the paper, he had thought it wouldn't hurt to try.

Adam and Josephine spent most of Sunday together. In spite of her father's urging she would not go to church. She discussed her feelings with Adam on this point, and as he suspected, she had remained in the church out of loyalty and habit, but as she said sardonically, her Christianity was not strong enough to influence her behavior. Yet she was keenly interested in Adam's religious life, and he realized that she wanted him to be devout. He had to admit that he had gotten an overdose of religion in the seminary, and he hardly thought about it at all now—that he had become, as she concluded, the same sort of Christian as her father.

Josephine did please her father by giving up smoking. She claimed that she did it because Adam did not smoke, but he suspected that it was a penance.

Dr. Garth was very hard to see, and Adam thought this must be his way of showing disapproval of the lawsuit. He had always retired when Adam got to the house, and in telephone discussions of The Taurus Company Adam found to his dismay that Dr. Garth seemed to be getting slightly deaf, especially to any suggestions calling for positive action. He was unwilling, apparently because of his daughter's disgrace, to ask anything of the Taurus stockholders. Fortunately he had reached an agreement with General Myerson before Leah's flight. Eventually Dr. Garth might get around to seeing P. D. Emery and other businessmen in the middle but not Mrs. Wriston. Even mention of her name made him angry. When Adam again brought up the question of having the proxy form printed, Dr. Garth dismissed it and abruptly concluded the conversation.

Once, leaving around midnight, Adam thought he saw Dr. Garth's face in an upstairs window. Adam greeted him, but there was no response. The face hung there with the stony daytime glare of an owl, and afterward Adam avoided looking up at those windows. Josephine said her father was sleeping badly. She sometimes heard him walking at night, and at breakfast he seemed obsessed with prowlers and once asked Rutherford to look for tracks. No tracks were found. One night when the wind was loud, Josephine heard her father outside her door. She found him looking out the front hall window with a revolver in his hand. He had seen something in front of the house—a young man in a black raincoat standing motionless in the moonlight. She assured him it was a dream.

Adam had his own nightmare—a glowing decomposing mill, turning out millions of yards of black towels. Regularly, about two o'clock in the morning, he woke up with a chill of desperation at the thought that the petition might be denied, and he would have no single additional argument or statistic to submit to stockholders.

This fear was what made him get in touch with Lloyd Bowers, the mill's purchasing agent. Adam went to Mr. Bowers' home in the evening when the whole family was watching television. It was an expensively furnished house; the Bowers had good taste. Adam explained that he needed access to the company's books, that he believed that the only way the company could survive was to make reforms by cutting costs in the next few months, and Adam hoped Mr. Bowers could think of a way of helping him. Bowers' forehead wrinkled even more deeply. "Adam, don't you see what you're asking me to do?" He was shaken, and his kindly voice trembled. "You're asking me to betray the trust of Mr. Quigley. Certainly I'd like to help you. Why I've known your family all my life, and your uncle was one of my closest friends, but I just— I can't believe you'd want me to do a dishonest thing." Adam argued that slovenly management was betraying the trust of both stockholders and employees and that there was nothing dishonest about using the company's books for the company's good, but Mr. Bowers could not be moved.

The enemy was not idle. There were two newspaper items in the next week about The Taurus Company. One was a photograph of Jack Olin patting two pieces of partially uncrated equipment. This scene was in keeping, the caption explained, with "the newly inaugurated program of modernization." Adam studied the photograph but could not make out what the equipment was. Monday a news article quoted Mr. Jack Olin, to the effect that The Taurus Company was negotiating with a maker of synthetic fibers. "It's still strictly hush-hush," Mr. Olin said, "but The Taurus Company plans to acquire another firm which has a strong position in the field of synthetics and whose operations will dovetail neatly with our own."

Once more Adam got keyed up for the hearing, had another conference with Moon in preparation, and once more the hearing was delayed. This time Byroade entered a plea to jurisdiction, maintaining that the company was engaged in interstate commerce and was subject to regulation by federal rather than state authorities. This original though far-fetched contention was worth a three-day delay. Moon filed an answer, the issue was joined, and the hearing was reset for Friday.

Adam looked up articles in *The New York Times* and *Wall Street Journal* on proxy fights which Byroade had directed. Byroade had apparently made his reputation by taking over the Erie Machine Company, a large machine-tool maker, twenty-five years ago. The newspaper photographs of that period showed Byroade coarser than he was now, with thicker features, his black hair much lower on his forehead—a face still to be refined in the crucible of success. Studying these pictures, it occurred to Adam that Byroade had been exactly his own age then, and whereas he was an obscure jobless ex-stockbroker, at twenty-nine Byroade had been a celebrity. After the Erie Machine conquest, Byroade had devoted his talents to fending off the kind of raids he had led so successfully before. Adam's study of Byroade's operations disclosed this pattern—careful planning, good timing of publicity artfully brought to a climax, and if the corporation had a reputation for highhanded dealing with stockholders, a dramatic if only temporary reform in this field. Byroade did not rigidly cling to a few favorite maneuvers but suited his strategy to the situation.

The Thursday night before the hearing Adam and Josephine took a drive to get away from the house. She had been to Atlanta that day—for shopping, she said—but she had come back empty-handed, and Adam decided that the real reason was to have her hair set there so she wouldn't have to go before curious eyes in a beauty salon in Mercer.

Adam had often urged her to go out with him for entertainment, movies or a party, for he believed his conversation would be dull compared with Herold's, and he was afraid of boring her, but she didn't want to risk meeting people she knew.

That night was warm and sticky. Around nine-thirty they stopped at a drive-in restaurant for Adam to call Moon and make sure the hearing would not be delayed again. "No, tomorrow's the big day," Moon said.

As Adam was returning to his car, he heard someone call his name. It was Blakely. Apparently she was with Bob Reamer, for he spotted Bob's car on the far side of the lot. "Adam, I know you think I'm neurotic or something after the way I acted there at the Knowlands', and it was especially bad with all this fuss with the Olins that I didn't know about until Josephine told me later." He was surprised at how good Blakely looked—eager, faithful, and unsuspecting—and he felt drawn to her even with the girl he loved only a few yards away waiting for him. "Don't hold it against me, Adam. It was just a misunderstanding." This appealing uprush left him speechless. He had a feeling of waste as he tasted this sweetness he couldn't use, and for a moment he wished he could have them both. Before he could reply Blakely went on: "Adam, maybe I shouldn't say this, but you and I—" Then she saw Josephine in the car, and from that one glance she knew how Adam had been spending his evenings. "Oh," she said, her face full of dismay. "Oh." She turned and hurried away.

"Poor Blakely," Josephine said when Adam got in the car.

"Don't try to give me back to her."

They took a long drive out the highway, ending as usual on the

Buttermilk Road. Josephine was quiet and thoughtful. Adam's mind strayed from the incident just now to the hearing the next morning. Yet he felt very little hope about it; in spite of Moon's assurances another Byroade delay seemed probable.

"Adam, let's look at the Chobot house."

"Now? I don't think we can see anything at night."

"The moon's bright. I want to find out what those Yankees are doing to it. The driveway's just ahead. Slow down."

He turned in between hills of blackberry bushes through a polluted-looking glade littered with paper and beer cans. Farther on, the weeds rose over the hood of the car and fell in waves before them.

"They've already moved in!" said Josephine. He had seen the light too, but the moment she spoke it melted from the windows, and they knew it was a reflection of their headlights.

The lawn was a jungle, but a way had been mashed through by truck tires. "We'd better leave the car," Adam said. "The ground feels soft, and we don't want to get stuck out here."

The moonlight seemed to turn brighter when he switched off the headlights. He reached across her for a flashlight from the dashboard compartment and quickly slipped the other hand behind her waist. As he had expected, she squirmed from his grasp and opened the door. He released her, and as an afterthought, it seemed, she hugged him for an instant. Then she got out of the car, and their arms locked together, they walked slowly on the feeble yellow ring the flashlight made in a broad tire track.

Stepping on what he thought was moss, Adam went through the green scum of a sluggish stream, and one foot was soaked to the ankle. Laughing, he helped Josephine over, and they advanced into deep shadows.

The branches closest to the house were bare and dead, and they stepped into the moonlight again. The upper story of the house presented a baffling configuration of light and shadow. They were only a few yards away when they understood what they saw. "They're dismantling it," Adam said.

"They wanted the brick. It was made in our kiln, and it had that same purple color."

A noise made him raise the light to the skeletonized upper floor, and the tip of the beam fell on a ratlike possum curled around an upright.

"Let's go," Josephine said. "This is depressing."

As they drove back to the Buttermilk Road Adam remembered hearing that old Miss Chobot had often come out on the porch, her white hair girlishly long, laughing and dancing wildly, raising her skirts and showing more white hair.

"I think I got into some red bugs in that tall grass," Josephine said, "and they're about to drive me wild."

"Go ahead and scratch."

They had not gone another quarter of a mile before a man flagging with his arms appeared in their headlights. "It's Jimmy Nabors. He works at the mill." Adam stopped the car. "Hello, Jimmy, what's the trouble?"

"Mr. Salter!" Jimmy's voice was full of relief. "Gosh, am I glad to see you, Mr. Salter. I'm having battery trouble, and I can't get my car started."

"What car?"

"It's up this dirt road a way."

"I'll be glad to give you a push. Get in, Jimmy, and we'll drive you up there." Adam introduced him to Josephine, and Jimmy climbed into the back, saying: "I don't know if you can push me the way I'm situated."

Adam drove slowly up the logging road, weeds strumming on the underside of the car, the singing of crickets growing louder. Jimmy's car, a prewar Hudson, came into his headlights. Josephine caught her breath in alarm. "There's someone there!"

"That's Bobbie Jeanne," Jimmy shouted in embarrassment. "My girl."

Adam then understood Jimmy's predicament. He had brought his girl up this road for privacy, and a weak battery had betrayed him. Jimmy leaped out and went ahead to confer with Bobbie Jeanne. Adam followed. Jimmy's car slanted downhill, the front bumper touching a tree trunk. Adam saw at once that he would not be able to push Jimmy off, and neither had any chain. Bobbie Jeanne, blinded by the headlights, was a slender sweet-looking girl of about seventeen who had lost her lipstick. She avoided looking at Adam.

"Mr. Salter," said Jimmy, worried and earnest, "Bobbie Jeanne's an hour late getting home now. Would it be too much trouble to take us in? I'll get somebody to drive me out with a battery in the morning."

They drove into town, the younger couple in the back seat very quiet, radiating guilt, and answering the sociable comments and polite inquiries from the front seat with excessive respect, putting "sir" or "mam" on their replies. They directed Adam to a modest house, and the two ran up the steps to the door.

Adam and Josephine agreed that they should get Jimmy's car going that night. When Jimmy, panting, returned on the run, Adam told him: "There's an all-night service station on Twelfth Avenue. Let's get your car in tonight." Jimmy protested, but plainly that was what he wanted to do.

They got the battery, and driving back out the Buttermilk Road, Jimmy seemed very eager to explain himself and his predicament to two near strangers. He and Bobbie Jeanne wanted to be married, but he had borrowed money to go to college, and Bobbie Jeanne's father said he had to be out of debt and have a little saved before he could marry her. They figured that if he got an expected ten-dollar raise this fall, they could be married in about a year. Jimmy seemed to be asking for advice and encouragement from two wise old heads. Adam with a laugh finally objected to being sirred and told Jimmy to call them by their first names.

Once more they went up the logging road and by Adam's head-lights installed the new battery. Adam drove back to the Butter-milk Road and waited there to make sure Jimmy was moving all right. Jimmy drew alongside and thanked them. Adam said: "By the way, Jimmy, what equipment was that in the newspaper picture?"

"Oh, that was a couple of lathes for the machine shop." Something more seemed on the tip of Jimmy's tongue, but he only said goodnight and drove away.

"You were nice to go to all that trouble for him," said Josephine. "They seem so much in love, don't they?"

"And mighty young. Especially Bobbie Jeanne. You know, I had a feeling she took a dislike to me."

"No, you just looked like Authority to her. She felt you might turn her over your knee for being parked up there." Josephine sighed. "They made me feel so old. I feel sorry for them wanting to get married so badly and not being able to."

"You ought to feel sorry for me," said Adam, laughing. "I've got it as bad as Jimmy does."

"Do you really, Adam?"

"Worse. And you know it."

"But why? There was Blakely tonight so crazy about you— If you really want me, Adam. All right. Yes."

They were almost home now, and in the glee of the moment it seemed a good idea to wake up Dr. Garth and ask his permission, but once inside the still house, they reconsidered. The hall clock struck hoarsely, the one in the dining room jangled metal adenoids, both saying: it's late, late. Adam would have a talk with Dr. Garth the following evening.

Josephine begged Adam not to leave that night. "This is the only place I mind being by myself. I don't feel like myself here." But it was now past two o'clock, and Adam was convinced that now was no time to risk arousing Dr. Garth's wrath by keeping his daughter up. Josephine remembered that Adam had to be in court in a few hours and agreeably kissed him goodnight.

204

~~~~~~

31

Just outside the courtroom Byroade was talking with the general counsel of The Taurus Company, Mr. Harlow Stubbs. At sight of Adam, Byroade detached himself and came over. "I'm sorry you decided to do it this way," he said in a genial tone. "Are you sure you don't want to wait and get the board's help?"

"I'm sure I want to see the books," Adam said, "and this looks like the only way to manage it."

Byroade smiled regretfully and withdrew.

G. P. Moon was waiting for Adam in the courtroom. "Who are those men over there?" Adam asked, indicating a row of spectators.

"That's about half the Sweetwater County Bar Association."

"What are they doing here?"

"Is the pig's tail pork? They're here to watch Byroade operate. We got an open-and-shut case. They want to see if he can beat it."

Also among the spectators Adam could identify about a dozen Taurus stockholders. Neither of the Olins was present.

The judge appeared, a tall man with thin features and red hair, foxlike in coloring and expression. He could have been any age from thirty-five to sixty. "That's Judge Henry Rivers," Moon said. "Right high and mighty for a man that's coming up for reelection next year too." In a sharp hard voice which cut through the noises of the courtroom the judge announced the case of Adam Salter *vs*. The Taurus Company.

After a conference among the judge and the three lawyers, and a general statement by the judge about the background of the case, Moon put Adam on the stand. He was sworn in and nervously took his place. Byroade, cool and completely at home, sat directly in front of him. Adam knew what Moon was going to ask, but after that Byroade would have his turn. Moon offered in evidence a photostat of Adam's stock certificate.

"Mr. Salter, did you make a demand on the respondent for inspection of their stock and record book and all other company records and if so state to whom you gave the demand and the date."

Stubbs arose and said: "I object on the ground that it calls for a conclusion of the witness as to whether a demand was made, and if so, what the demand was."

"Let the witness state the facts whatever they are," said the judge in a bored voice.

Adam had already decided that Mr. Stubbs was a very dull man and hoped that he and not Byroade would conduct the cross-examination. Fat chance. There were more questions from Moon, and objections from Stubbs, before Adam could state that he had demanded the books and had been refused. Moon entered the carbon copy of Adam's letter to Quigley and Belton's affidavit as evidence.

Now it was the respondent's turn. Byroade got up and advanced toward Adam. There was something catlike about his movements which Adam had not observed before. "Mr. Salter." Byroade's voice was not loud, but it carried well enough for the spectators to hear him. "Were you asking to see The Taurus Company's books on behalf of anyone besides yourself?"

"Yes," Adam said, "on behalf of other small stockholders who have signed a petition calling for more information about the company's affairs."

"Were you making this demand on behalf of anyone besides those stockholders who signed the petition?"

"No."

"Mr. Salter, you bought the stock registered in your name on April 17 of this year." Byroade had a way of asking questions with an air of scrupulous hesitancy. "Did you make any inquiry into the affairs of the company on behalf of anyone else before you became a stockholder?"

"No. I looked into the assets of The Taurus Company to see if the stock might be a good buy."

Byroade nodded gravely. "Now, Mr. Salter." He raised his voice a little, and Adam's throat swelled with apprehension. "Since the company's fiscal affairs are not known to the public, what person or corporation first suggested to you that there might be a speculative profit in Taurus stock?"

Moon leaped up. "I object."

"Objection sustained."

Byroade said: "What person or corporation first acquainted you with the business of The Taurus Company?"

"No corporation did. I was a stockbroker, and customers bring in stocks to be sold or to ask advice about them. This contact is in the nature of a privileged communication, which you will understand, being a lawyer, Mr. Byroade." It was an opportunity to improve his case immeasurably—by revealing Dr. Garth as the man behind him. "A stockholder, whose name I am not free to divulge, discussed the affairs of the company with me, and I became interested on the basis of that discussion."

"You became so interested," said Byroade, his brow lined with astonishment, "that you resigned from your job and have done nothing but deal in the affairs of The Taurus Company for the past several weeks?"

"That's right."

"Mr. Salter, have you negotiated with any competitor—"

Moon objected, and the judge said: "I am going to let him finish his question and then consider your objection."

"Mr. Salter," said Byroade, "have you negotiated with any other towel-maker about your activity at The Taurus Company?"

"Objection."

The judge said: "That question seems relevant in that an affirmative answer would tend to show whether the petition for writ of mandamus is for a proper purpose."

Adam hesitated. Seeing what Byroade was driving at, he was about to say no, but of course that would entangle him. "I have visited other towel-makers to compare their operations with The Taurus Company's. I made no secret of that to Mr. Quigley or anyone else. I have not 'negotiated' with them. What I wanted to find out was why they were making money and our company was losing money with the result that their stockholders were getting dividends and Taurus stockholders were not."

"Mr. Salter, let me ask you just one more time—will you tell the court the name of the person through whose offices you became interested in the affairs of The Taurus Company?"

"No, I have given my word I would not."

"You say you are demanding the books for no one but those on your petition. You are not demanding them for this mysterious party who drew you into the affairs of the company?"

"No," Adam said in a great sweat. Byroade let the exchange hang in the air for a moment before he sat down. He would continue to point at Dr. Garth's shadow, and Moon, who watched Adam step down with a long face, was hampered by this enforced concealment.

"What is this bi'ness?" Moon said desperately. "Good God amighty, man, if that's Dr. Garth you're talking about, get up there and say so!" Adam shook his head.

Mr. Hubert Quigley succeeded Adam on the witness stand. Byroade began: "Mr. Quigley, has Mr. Salter ever discussed anything with you besides asking to see the books and records of The Taurus Company?"

"Yes, Mr. Salter on both occasions when he came ostensibly to see the books of the company discussed our operations and in a bullying way asked for sweeping changes in our management program."

"Did you have the impression that Mr. Salter had been conducting talks and negotiations with any of your competitors?"

Moon objected, and his objection was sustained. It was obvious that many of Byroade's questions, which were sure to be disallowed, were for the stockholders' benefit.

"Would you state whether Mr. Salter referred to any other companies?"

"Yes, Mr. Salter referred to certain policies of a competitor, the State Line Manufacturing Company."

Byroade paused, then said with heightened seriousness: "Now, Mr. Quigley, would you say from your discussions with Mr. Salter that he had knowledge of, or had been in negotiation with, any competitors which he did *not* mention?"

Moon howled his objection, which was sustained.

"Mr. Quigley, what did Mr. Salter say to you on those occasions when he came ostensibly to see the books?"

"I object to the word ostensibly," said Moon. "Relator went to see the Taurus books. That's why we're here."

Byroade turned with a smile and said mildly: "I'm quoting the witness."

"Mr. Salter insisted that we should change our policies from the conservative ones we have followed during my administration," said Quigley. He grew more heated and resentful as he talked. "In other words he was advocating right down the line the ideas of my predecessor, Stewart Baker, and since Baker was fired because he was about to wreck the company with his wild ideas, and he's working for a competitor, I did not believe them, and do not now believe, that he was advocating anything for the good of the company, and since Salter wanted to put back in Stewart Baker's policies one-two-three right down the line, it was obvious that he had been in communication with Baker although he deliberately concealed the fact." Byroade then turned Quigley over to G. P. Moon.

"Ask him what policies he's talking about," Adam whispered to Moon.

Moon did so, and Quigley answered: "Policies of general extravagance in the matter of throwing money around and speculating in cotton and other things which made no sense to me then and do not make sense to me now." Moon apparently did not see the weakness of Quigley's vague reply and did not press the point. Adam writhed with a feeling of an opportunity missed. Moon went on to ask how much money the company was making. Byroade objected that "Mr. Moon's question is calculated to elicit information at issue before the court," and the court sustained him. Moon continued this line of questioning, and Byroade continued his objections. Moon finished by asking: "Mr. Quigley, at the last stockholders' meeting you stated that the company was losing money. If that's so, don't you believe that the situation calls for changes like what your competitors are doing who are making money and for the plaintiff to come up with some such idea wouldn't necessarily mean anything else?"

"I don't believe our competitors would be anxious to help us," said Quigley. Moon let this second-rate retort stand, and Adam ground his teeth.

The next witness for the defense was a surprise: his own Miss Winnie McCaffery—a convert, Adam decided at once, of the suave Mr. Byroade. Stiffly, the flowers on her vast hat bobbing, she mounted the stand. Byroade drew from her a description of Adam's visit to her, and after a meandering indignant testimony, he led her to the point: "Mr. Salter said I was interested in dividends that I need to live on while he saw a quick profit in the stock."

"Did you gain any impression as to how Mr. Salter was to get this profit?" Byroade asked.

Moon objected, and the judge ruled: "Counsel will confine his questions to matters of fact." It seemed to Adam that Moon was objecting at the wrong places, and that Byroade's questions were constructing a convincing picture of him as a shifty gambler.

Moon's cross-examination of Miss McCaffery followed. The line he took was that by "quick profit" Adam meant ten or fifteen years instead of a lifetime.

"Now Miss McCaffery," said Moon, "when Mr. Salter came to you again with this stockholders' petition, did he explain some asset that the management of the company had been hiding from you?"

"He said something about real estate, but—" She paused and looked around the court in confusion. "Mr. Jack Olin said it wasn't worth that much."

"Could he have told you that to make it easier for his agent, Mr. Slocum, to buy your stock?"

Byroade said: "I object. All this is irrelevant." The objection was sustained, and that was Moon's last question.

Byroade had seemed to sponsor the genteel Miss McCaffery with his deference and his understanding eyes, but he looked aloof at the appearance of the next witness, and Mr. Stubbs questioned him. This witness was Arlis Camp, who had been a loom fixer years ago until he lost a hand in an accident at the mill. When Adam had tried to buy his four shares of stock, Camp had explained that as long as he held his stock, the bosses wouldn't put him out of his drink stand, which was owned by the company. He was about fifty but looked older, loud, red-faced, and a show-off.

"Get ready for some lies," Moon whispered to Adam.

Mr. Stubbs asked Camp what Adam had said to him, and Camp answered: "Mr. Salter come to me and tried to buy my stock. I wouldn't sell so he come back later and tried to get me to sign his petition. I told him Mr. Slocum had been trying to buy my stock. Offered me more than Salter. Salter said to me: 'Don't sell. By the time I get through with them fellers I'll give them such fits that they'll be glad to buy you and I out just to get shed of us.' He said he'd been over to the mill, and he was going to stay over there and devil them until they bought him out for two hunnert dollars a stock. It was either them, or another mill would buy him out."

No wonder Byroade had wanted not to appear to endorse the man. Adam was shaken with anger and an impulse to laugh. "He's crazy," Adam said to Moon.

Moon took him then. Moon had been rather courtly in a rural way to Miss McCaffery, but he spoke to Camp in an insultingly distinct voice. "Mr. Camp, what were Mr. Salter's exact words to you about why you shouldn't sell your stock?"

"He said, 'When I git through with them fellers I'll give them such fits they'll be *more* than glad to buy my stock to get shed of us.'"

Moon's posture suggested utter boredom. "But he didn't say who at the mill would buy you out?"

Camp fenced with him, looked at Byroade and Stubbs, got no help there, then cried out: "Why, the owners! Mr. Olin, Mr. Quigley, Dr. Garth, and them."

Moon turned until he almost had his back to the witness. "Mr. Camp, you operate a drink stand near the mill, don't you?"

"That's right. Camp's Place. Got a nice line of snuff too." He looked around brightly for a laugh.

"Does The Taurus Company own the building your store is in?"

Stubbs objected and was overruled. Camp said yes, and Moon said: "Mr. Olin could put you out of business by shutting your store down, couldn't he?" Stubbs objected and was sustained.

Moon then asked Camp whether anybody else had heard Adam make these statements. Plenty of people did, Camp said, but he couldn't remember who. "Plenty of people did, but you just can't remember who they are, so they can't testify that what you're saying is true, is that right? So we have only your word for it?" Moon said with disgust: "That's all." This seemed to Adam Moon's best performance so far.

Adam was shocked to see that Byroade's next witness was Mr. Lloyd Bowers. The latter's face was white, and he would not look in Adam's direction. He began by saying that he testified with great reluctance. After that his cowboy voice was so low that he had to be prompted again and again to speak up, and the judge cupped his hand over his ear now and then and repeated some crucial sentence with harsh emphasis. "All right," said the judge. "You said that the relator, Adam Salter, came to see you and made a 'dishonorable proposition' to you, urging that you falsify information about The Taurus Company so you and he could take over the company and 'milk' it." Moon's questioning could not shake this story.

Camp had volunteered his own lies, Adam believed, but Bowers must have misunderstood him, or Jack Olin must have threatened to fire him if he did not perjure himself.

Moon put Adam on the stand, and in response to questions, Adam gave his own version of the interviews with Camp and Bowers, denied that he knew Stewart Baker or that he had ever thought of speculating in cotton, and specified the policies he had recommended to Quigley.

Moon's argument followed. He had only two points: that no court in the state had ever refused a stockholder the books of a corporation in which he held stock and that his client, Adam Garth Salter—he repeated the full name each time—was a veteran of two wars and "close kin" to a director of the company, Dr. Ivor Garth. Adam knew that Dr. Garth was not going to like that.

Then came Byroade. "The petitioner has been an owner of Taurus stock for a few weeks. He has no grievance as a stockholder of long standing who has suddenly been deprived of dividends. He knew that the company was paying no dividends when he bought stock in it. His purpose, from the testimony of witnesses, is obviously speculative, to harass and embarrass management and to undermine the morale of employees and stockholders. He has spent an astonishing amount of time talking to competitors of the company. Furthermore there is irony in the nature of the last case of this kind to be tried in Mercer. In the case of Curtis *vs.* Bronson Packing Company, the company was ordered to permit Curtis access to the books. Later, when Curtis was tried for fraud in another connection, his activities showed a characteristic pattern of manipulation—of concealment of the stock's value, then puffing it, to the great harm of stockholders. A small company, not covered by SEC regulations regarding disclosure, is particularly vulnerable to a raider who has some speculative gain in view and whose actions may do irreparable harm to the company. Such a raider is not required by law to name his backers, though they be competitors, ex-convicts, or Communists, bent on destruction. But the stockholders must be protected, and for that reason I move that the petition for the writ be dismissed." Byroade sat down to applause from the spectators and the rapping of the judge's gavel.

There would be about a half-hour's delay before the court ruled. "How does it look, G. P.?" Adam said. Moon was bruised but still confident. Byroade, he explained, was just trying to earn his fee.

"Look, G. P. This manager before Quigley—Stewart Baker— was a director of the company, wasn't he?"

"He sure was."

"That's funny. The directors were Baker, Olin, Dr. Garth, General Myerson, and one other. Quigley, I suppose. Did Baker play along with Olin?"

"No, he never suited Mr. Olin."

Adam wondered how with a man like that on the board, Olin had managed to dominate it. If Baker took his, Adam's own position on policy, where was Olin's majority? Perhaps General Myerson had not been so solidly aligned with Dr. Garth as Adam had been led to believe.

The judge returned to the bench, and the courtroom quieted for his ruling: "It is ordered that the respondent in this action, The Taurus Company, by Hubert Quigley, its president, and George Ellis, its superintendent, or such officer charged with the custody of its books and all other records, permit the petitioner, Adam Salter, his attorneys and accountants to inspect the same. It is further ordered that such inspection be held during business hours at the office of the respondent, The Taurus Company, on June 25, commencing at nine o'clock on the morning of that day and without any inconvenience to the transaction of business by the respondent during inspection."

Adam's heart leaped—too soon. Byroade arose and said: "Your honor, respondent in this action plans to appeal the case and prays a suspension of the writ of mandamus until judicial review."

The judge said at once: "It is ordered that the writ be suspended upon the posting of supersedeas bond by respondent in the amount of two thousand dollars. Court is adjourned."

"How long a delay does that mean?" Adam asked Moon.

"It goes to the State Supreme Court and won't be heard until sometime after the beginning of the October term. Could be next year. The bond is for surety for damages if they lose, which they will."

"But that's going to be too late to do me any good, and two thousand dollars is just a drop in the bucket."

"It was up to the judge's discretion if he would suspend the writ or not, and he must have been just enough in doubt about what you were trying to do to suspend it. I'll try to get him to let us go ahead, but it won't do any good."

Of course that was why Byroade was there. So the only way Adam could hope to see the books in time was for Dr. Garth to demand the right as a director of the company.

With the hook of this failure burning in his flesh, Adam cast about for some means to get immediate results. He would not wait any longer, he told Moon as they left the courtroom. He would go ahead and have the proxy forms printed up. He would stop pulling punches with the stockholders; he would tell them how bad things really were at the mill. He would go to see Stewart Baker.

Moon was not listening. His wandering eyes were bright, and he whistled softly to himself. After all, technically, he had just won a case against Dean H. Byroade.

~~~~~~

32

Adam parted with Moon there and turned to the law library adjoining the courtroom. When he entered the stacks, there leaning over a book, smoking a cigarette, and so absorbed that he did not at first look up from his book, was Cato Herold. He was clean-shaven, sober, but haggard. Adam did not speak, and after a moment, Cato saw him. "I see we have come on the same errand," he said, marking his place with a slip of paper. "I'm afraid your local lawyers have no need of New York law and therefore know little about it. So I'm having to fill in the gaps here." They faced each other for a moment in embarrassed silence. "How's Jo?"

"Recovering."

"Good. Process has been served on me. Left at my apartment in New York, a friend tells me. My time hasn't been wasted in here by the way. You know that contact of yours with the detective, and how he seemed promising but dried up? Leah paid him of course, and I've found out why. Not to keep him from tipping you off, but because the testimony of a hired investigator like that has more weight as evidence if he's been paid at the time of trial than if his payment is dependent on the successful outcome of the suit. I've picked up a lot of information like that. Perhaps I could save you some time if you told me what you want to know."

Cato spoke with a relaxed smile as though the law of divorce were a hobby which he and Adam had in common, and this made Adam feel less inclined to talk. "I doubt it. Unless you've heard where your wife is."

"I'm afraid not," said Herold agreeably. He sighed. "I'm afraid it would do no good to find her." He looked at his watch. "Why don't you come and have a cup of coffee with me?" He slid the volume in his hand into its space on the shelf.

Adam had a sudden friendly feeling toward Herold, perhaps because of his own victory last night, and he felt inclined to accept his invitation, but instead he heard himself answering coldly: "I don't have time. I need to know some things today." He glanced impatiently at the books by his head.

"I suppose I ought to thank you for pulling me back that afternoon at the Garths'. You must have suspected that I was afraid of the old man. Not afraid that he would kill me—at that moment I didn't care, I would almost have welcomed it. But I had a feeling about him, you know, like dread of the supernatural. You didn't have eyes to see what I saw, but his face that afternoon was like a window into hell."

"It's understandable that he was upset."

"Upset! If I ever saw murder in a man's face, I saw it then." Cato looked at the floor for a moment, then back at Adam with an odd smile, bright and sad. "Something I've been wanting to ask you," he said, "is who did you say said that about its being a thrilling moment in a man's life when he discovers that he is not Sydney Carton?"

"It was Chesterton, but what a man discovers is that he is not Robinson Crusoe."

"Oh, that's right. Of course. Well, I think I've found all I want here. Sure you won't join me for coffee?" Adam again declined. Cato seemed about to ask another question but only smiled again and said: "Goodbye."

Adam turned his back at once but listened to the sounds of reverberating footsteps and then the shutting of a door. When the sound had died, he looked over the shelves for the volume on proxy forms. His gaze fell on the volume with the protruding slip of paper which Herold had been reading. It marked the case of Thayer *vs.* Thayer, a divorce case on grounds of adultery, and Adam read very quickly until he came to what the court said about evidence in its ruling.

"The evidence by which the act of adultery is proved is seldom direct. The natural secrecy of the act makes it ordinarily impossible to prove except by circumstantial evidence ... The rules which govern human conduct and which are known to common observation and experience are to be applied in these cases as in all other investigations of fact. An adulterous disposition existing in two persons towards each other is commonly of gradual development, it must have some duration and it does not suddenly subside. When once shown to exist a strong inference arises that it had and will have continuance, the duration and extent of which may be measured by the power which it exercises over the conduct of the parties."

Adam knew why Herold had marked the place, for in spite of the reproach it carried, it would be a bittersweet consolation to him for life, just as Adam knew that for himself the words of this long-dead Massachusetts judge would be a curse.

33

As Adam knocked on Dr. Garth's study door that night, he found that in spite of the advantages he seemed to enjoy, he was as nervous as any man is supposed to be in approaching his prospective father-in-law. Dr. Garth was at his desk. Adam had not seen him at close range since the quarrel with Herold, and he was concerned to note that either Josephine's troubles or failing health had made a marked change in the older man's appearance—made his skin look looser and more livid—but what Josephine had said about making him into an old man was not true. He looked neither feeble nor out of his prime.

Although Adam had intended to describe the trial, he decided against touching on a subject of contention. He also discarded some pleasantries and inquiries about Dr. Garth's health, for he was too tense to speak naturally.

"Uncle Ive, you may have noticed that I've been coming for some time to see Josephine," Adam said with a smile.

Dr. Garth said gruffly: "It may seem so to you. However it could hardly have been long. She has been here only a few weeks."

Bad beginning, thought Adam, and he's not making it easy for me. "Uncle Ive, it's been long enough for me to fall in love with her. I want to marry her, and she said last night that she felt the same way. I've come to ask your permission."

Dr. Garth leaned violently back in his swivel chair and stared into the black open window. "Yes, though Josephine did not plead your case—she wisely left that to you—I gathered that this was why I was supposed to be at home and at leisure tonight." Adam smiled until he saw that Dr. Garth was not smiling. "Since Josephine forewarned me, I've given this matter some thought."

Yes, Adam said to himself, and he's better prepared than I am. "Young people regard marriage as a solution to their problems. But marriage solves nothing. It complicates old problems; it creates new ones. Both of you expect marriage to drown out the scandal in which your friend Herold has involved Josephine. But recently Josephine has been seen publicly with that man and hardly anyone else. If you and Josephine are married this year it will appear hasty, and would in fact be hasty. Certainly Josephine's emotions are in a state of turmoil, and since you are interested in her, you perhaps are not entirely detached."

"We shouldn't marry this year?" said Adam. "I was thinking of this month!"

"I had hoped for more mature judgment from you. Such a move would flout convention, and society has ways of making you pay for that."

"I'd think the opposite would be true, that people would think less of this divorce case if Josephine married me and showed that way she had no interest in Herold."

"That is not the conclusion that people would draw. And if your taking Josephine as a wife could save her reputation, then I should have reason to be deeply grateful to you in these circumstances."

"Sir, that's not what I meant!" Adam flushed. He was perplexed that Dr. Garth should introduce this point of family pride to keep him at a distance. Wasn't he, Adam, a member of the family? "Do you think that public opinion is worth primary consideration?"

"I have observed what happens to those who run against it. Taking a little longer view—beyond this month, say—one should use every precaution that the marriage is a success, that there is no shadow on it, for one's own and one's children's sake. Recently I have thought of little but Josephine's welfare, how to get her through this trying period as well as possible. I'd thought of having her visit a maternal aunt in South Carolina, but she must not leave now. It is even a mistake for her to stay completely out of sight as she is doing. People should know where she is."

"There again I don't follow you. I should think going out of town might be good for her, much as I would miss her."

"I am thinking of the future."

"You say we shouldn't marry for a year. How long should we wait?"

Dr. Garth looked at him from sunken encircled eyes. "It would be better to defer a decision until after this divorce suit is out of the courts, and you should put your own business affairs in order beforehand."

"Sir?" said Adam in surprise. "I've been offered several jobs if that's what you mean."

"You are deeply in debt."

Adam looked into eyes which age had made colder than ever and felt a knot of cold in his stomach. He could not immediately weigh this allusion to their joint enterprise, and he did not want to risk a challenging reply.

After a silence Dr. Garth said. "Don't misunderstand my motives. If you have given them any thought, you know that I certainly want to see Josephine happily married and to see my grandchildren."

"Yes, sir," Adam said, getting to his feet. "Goodnight." He half expected Dr. Garth to call him back with some warmer assurances, but the doctor said nothing more. Not once during that talk had Dr. Garth addressed him by name, and his tone had been calm and dry throughout. Adam had taken it for granted that Dr. Garth would welcome him enthusiastically as a son-in-law, if for no other reason than that he would be a permanent bulwark against the Cato Herolds, and now he knew how naïve he had been. He had faced a rich man, a man of authority, and he now saw this allusion to The Taurus Company for what it was. Dr. Garth by that generous arrangement had seemed to treat him, in a financial sense at least, as a son, and this chill statement had been calculated to warn him not to presume on the basis of it.

Josephine, waiting in the parlor, rose to meet him with a smile, but her smile faded as he approached. "What did Daddy say?"

"He said wait."

"Did he say anything to hurt your feelings, Adam dear?"

Adam shook his head.

"Come out on the patio and tell me," she said, taking one of his hands in her own.

"I'd rather that we went out in my car."

"You seem upset, Adam. Remember this has been very hard on him."

"That's what I'm trying to figure—how much difference this divorce suit really makes." The conviction was growing in him that

Dr. Garth's response sprang not from a mood of pessimism but some lifelong position which would not yield to any argument or demonstration.

In the car Josephine pressed Adam further, and he summarized her father's reply this way: "He said that public opinion would be against us if we married soon, that it would be hasty, and that we don't know our own minds."

"You said once you would wait for years."

"I'd rather not. Are you going to leave this decision to him?"

"I've got to consider his feelings, especially after what I've done to him."

Adam had hoped she would defy her father. For a time it had seemed to him that Dr. Garth had little influence over his rebellious daughter, but now Adam wondered if despite appearances Dr. Garth had not been the force which separated Josephine from Herold, and perhaps he was strong enough to separate her from every other man in the world.

~~~~~~

34

Not until Adam saw the newspaper the next afternoon did he realize how well Byroade had managed to turn almost certain defeat to his advantage. Although the body of the article was accurate enough, the headlines suggested that the court had ruled against Adam. Because of Byroade's prominence and his flair for generalization, the trial was reported in detail, with quotation of most of Byroade's motion for dismissal.

That day Adam arranged an appointment with the former manager of The Taurus Company, Stewart Baker, for one week hence, and by five o'clock he had his proxy forms which the printer had rushed through. Only Adam could vote them. He took the first one to Miss Winnie McCaffery, who refused to talk with him. Even those who had signed his petition were harder to see now. His exposé of the condition of the mill, which he had counted on for such dynamic effect, did not interest them much, and his own complex remedies bored them. Not a single stockholder could sit through more than a few minutes of this talk without interrupting with some irrelevant comment or question. They did not want statistics and details; they wanted an instant infallible solution. Their frowns revealed conflict within, and many of those he had counted on said they wanted to think it over.

After several attempts he caught Mrs. Wriston, dressed up, powdered, and scented, just getting into her car. She listened impatiently and said she would mail him her proxy if she decided to assign it to him. As for Chisholm, Emery, and Alexander, he would stay away from them until he had talked wth Stewart Baker.

During that week he got a copy of Byroade's book which a

secondhand book dealer had hunted down for him. Adam read it with such intense concentration that he remembered whole paragraphs word for word. It was manifestly a famous raider's advice to insiders on how to stay in power. One section which impressed Adam was "The Annual Meeting" with a chapter entitled "Ten Questions Stockholders Ask and How To Answer Them." For example:

> *Stockholder:* Mr. Chairman, since the company's losing money and stockholders are doing without dividends, shouldn't officers of the company take a cut in salary?
> *Presiding Officer:* A very good question and one to which your board has been giving a lot of thought. We came to the conclusion that the company's salaries had to stay competitive. A cut would cause us to lose some of our most able men to more far-sighted companies. You see, top salaries represent less than one half of one per cent of the company's gross. Actually since our officers are all stockholders, passing the dividend has meant a cut in income for them too. . . .

And more smooth sweet answers which a badgered or arrogant chairman could substitute for the sarcasm which naturally came to his lips. Byroade always favored the gentle approach: "Don't try to keep the opposition from taking the floor occasionally at annual meetings. This practice arouses resentment and sympathy for insurgents . . . Remember that arbitrary adjournments are often regarded as a sign of weakness in management." There were long chapters on the proxy instrument itself as a propaganda tool and on ways of making the stockholder proud of the company's product.

So Adam was not surprised the following Monday morning to find in the Mercer Bank and Trust Company a showcase with brilliantly colored, professionally arranged Taurus towels. The occasion was a contest to name the color of the yellow towel in the center for a hundred-dollar prize. "Sunburst yellow" and "jonquil" were examples given. It looked like a sales effort, but the customers were too scattered for such a local promotion to be worth anything. This was for the stockholders' benefit, and without doubt the display was a credit to the company.

"They've got 'em in all the banks in town," said someone behind him. Adam turned to see G. P. Moon filling out an entry blank.

"What's your entry, G. P.?"

"Bitterweed yellow. What's yours?"

"Jaundice, I guess."

"Seen this?" Moon asked. Moon handed Adam an envelope containing a market letter from E. V. Chandler and Company, Stockbrokers. Their customers, the letter stated, had inquired about how to vote in the Taurus contest. This sounded unlikely since the stockholders were concentrated in Mercer and E. V. Chandler had no office there. Quigley and Ellis had made a "fine team for the postwar period of internal consolidation" while now Jack Olin was "a top-flight younger executive to spark the company's new phase of aggressive expansion."

Adam handed it back. "A bought statement if I ever read one."

"You see what I see?" Moon drew his forefinger across his neck.

"You mean they're going to throw Quigley and Ellis to us wolves."

"Is the pig's tail pork?"

They adjourned to the Post Office Café, and over coffee Adam spoke his conclusions: "So their new line is that Jack Olin means new management, and any fair-minded stockholder will give him a chance to prove himself. And he won't have that chance between now and the annual meeting. Now my criticism of management is beside the point."

"That's a Byroade trick for you."

"We've got to change targets," Adam said. "From 'management,' which was too vague anyway, to Bascom Olin himself. Sell the idea that he's been the real boss all along, and with his son in, he'll still be boss."

This appealed to Moon, the politician, and he had another idea. "We need to talk with Quigley and Ellis. Quigley's going to retire next year, so it won't make no difference except to his reputation, but Ellis needs to be able to get a job now and then for the next fifteen years. It's sure that nothing we've said about those two has hurt 'em as much as this letter from E. V. Chandler. One of them just might be mad enough to let us have a peep at the books."

"I don't think I can get anywhere with Quigley. He hates my guts."

"And he don't exactly love me after the cross-examination. Can you think of anybody else to talk with him?"

Of course Moon meant Dr. Garth. "Not a chance," Adam said.

"One of us will have to do it." Adam decided that Moon was better suited to this job than he himself was. Moon could be more amiable to someone he did not respect, and if Quigley or Ellis were interested, Moon as Adam's agent would not have to make any promises on the spot. Moon agreed to approach them at their homes that evening.

He reported the next day. Quigley would not believe he was being sacrificed and was hostile throughout. Ellis's pink face turned white at Moon's words and he seemed deeply shaken, but he too refused to consider the proposal.

There was still Jimmy Nabors, and Adam went to his rooming house. He began as he had with Lloyd Bowers by appealing to Jimmy's supposed loyalty to the company's best interests and then asked for detailed information about the company's operations. Jimmy shook his head, and his young face showed great inner pain. Adam worked on Jimmy for nearly an hour. Finally Jimmy cried out: "Mr. Salter, if you don't stop, you're going to get me in bad trouble! Now please. I'm already late for my date."

The next day Adam's new policy was begun with a big newspaper advertisement which attacked Bascom Olin by name and quoted testimony from the trial against him.

When he and Moon looked over the result, Moon groaned and crumpled it up.

"Not so good, huh?" said Adam.

"I'll tell you what you sound like here. You sound like the man who's running fifth in the governor's race. You know you're losing, everybody knows it, so you start swinging like a wild man. Beside the stuff that Byroade's throwing, this ad just hasn't got it."

Adam smoothed out the paper and studied it. "You're right. It has that desperate ring. Some small stockholder might like it, but it's not going to cut any ice with P. D. Emery." He took out a pocket calendar and mentally placed Byroade's moves on it. "Look, G. P. I've been feeling that something was wrong with Byroade's campaign, and this is it. His timing's off. Even by Byroade's book. He says: 'Repetition is good only up to a point. Don't wear the stockholders out by starting the campaign too early and at too high a pitch to maintain.' Not even Byroade's going to be able to come up with something new regularly for the next two months. Take the color-naming contest. It should end only a day or two before the annual meeting, not six or seven weeks before it. Or entertaining stockholders. Mrs. Wriston can stand parties day and night, but people like Duncan Chisholm just don't care much for cocktail parties and late hours."

"'Well, if Byroade's timing's wrong, that's the only mistake he's made."

"I'm going to North Carolina tomorrow to see Stewart Baker. I'm hoping he can help. I still can't understand why Baker, Dr. Garth, and General Myerson didn't control the company. You got any ideas?"

"Nothing, unless Dr. Garth decided he didn't approve of Baker and ran him off. You know how old doc is. If somebody don't suit him, he don't give him any second chance."

Late in the afternoon Adam called on Miss McCaffery again, and she agreed to let him in for five minutes. Adam complimented her on her truthful testimony in court in spite of what must have been great pressure from the Olins (not Byroade) to exaggerate. He reminded her that he had never advised her to sell her Taurus stock to him; he had simply put the facts before her. Miss McCaffery did a lot of the talking. She remembered haughty treatment from the Olins in years past, and she began to suspect that she had been misused, ravished. Though Adam left without her proxy an hour and a half later, she was again sympathetic toward him.

No doubt about it, hammering on that one unpopular target, Bascom Olin, was the most effective course with the smaller stockholders. But Adam had only nine hundred votes now, nearly three hundred fewer than had been represented on the pre-Byroade petition. Many stockholders now said they would come to the meeting and vote in person.

Early that evening, before taking the Buttermilk Road, Adam saw a convertible which looked like Herold's on a used-car lot. Reflections of overhead lights gleamed like necklaces in the brightened paint. Adam glanced inside at the upholstery to make sure. It was Herold's, all right.

He did not tell Josephine about this, for both avoided mentioning his name. Adam kept his proposal of marriage constantly before her, and he could feel in her response a pressure from Dr. Garth which more than matched his own. She had wronged her father and owed him obedience. Adam did not try to force her into a decision. Dr. Garth's reference to money had been enough to

226

make him go slow. He could not even afford to buy her an engagement ring.

The next morning Adam left for North Carolina. He rehearsed the conversation with Baker as he drove, seeing the man across the desk as an older heavier replica of himself. Baker had started working at The Taurus Company at the age of fifteen, and Monroe Mercer had recognized his abilities and promoted him rapidly. By the time he left for the army in 1942 Baker was an overseer, and when he returned, a lieutenant colonel, four years later, Monroe Mercer made him mill superintendent. In 1950 Baker became president of the company.

Baker owed Adam nothing, and the prudent course would be to tell Adam nothing he could use. Adam tried to locate any small but fatal error in the opening and to strike some appeal that would get Baker talking. The most he could hope for was a denunciation of the Olin regime at The Taurus Company. But Adam was curious also. Why hadn't Baker, General Myerson, and Dr. Garth dominated the board of directors and run the company?

The Grasmere Mill turned out to be a modern one-story building surrounded by well-trimmed zoysia, and its manager a pro. Baker had a gleaming scar like a solder patch across his cheek, and a predatory glare in his eyes. His legs were short, his arms long and muscular, and his hands oversized. His was that hard sectionless accent which Adam had often encountered in self-made Southerners.

Describing the situation at The Taurus Company and watching Baker's expression, Adam realized that the latter had agreed to the interview because he was curious about what had happened at the mill since he left. Adam finished with Quigley's statement, that he, Adam, was advocating the policies of Stewart Baker right down the line.

Baker laughed harshly. "Old Hubert's got the bull by the horns, has he? He told me at a textile convention in Charlotte that things were getting better all the time. I knew his machinery, so I invited him to look at what we'd done at a mill we bought in Gastonia. The mill had three hundred E-model looms that were pretty run down. We mounted them on casters and moved them out a section at a time for rebuilding. Steam-cleaned them and replaced worn parts. We're getting less than 3 per cent weaving seconds now with those rebuilt looms. It was right on Hubert's way home, but do you think he'd come? Hell, no. I'm his old boss, see, so he's not having any of that. Death before dishonor." Baker rocked back and grimaced. "Well, Hubert's just about what the Taurus deserves for what it's paying."

"That's why you left? The pay?"

"The pay and the board of directors. I made some mistakes down there myself, or rather I didn't make some changes I should have made. I had worked for two outfits in my whole life—The Taurus Company and the U.S. Army—so I'd never known a mill to be run except the J. Monroe Mercer way, and I guess I hero-worshiped the man. But he got me tied in a knot with that damned union contract he signed his last year there. Twenty years ago he would've eaten ground glass before he would've signed it, and he did it over my protest. I figured out why he did it. Since his coronary, dealing with the union got harder for him—he never did like to deal with anybody as an equal—and that tough boy the union had down there didn't want anybody to try to Big-Daddy him. So Mr. Mercer was going to fix it so he wouldn't have to negotiate any more contracts. A three-year contract—that's very unusual in the textile business. The job loads were so light I think even the workers were disappointed."

"Of course Quigley renewed it after you left. And he's going to renew it again in September, why, I don't know."

"I'll tell you why. Oh, I know that Hubert. He's scared to death of a strike. He can see a striker breaking his windshield with a brick or roughing him up. Once they tear down that dignity, he's afraid there won't be anything inside."

"My impression is that the union people there in Mercer aren't too unreasonable."

"I could have worked things out with the union," said Baker, "but I just couldn't get the board of directors to spend any money on modernizing, and both were necessary if the mill was going to keep making money."

"You were on the board too, weren't you?" Adam said. "This is what I don't understand. The directors were Olin, Dr. Garth, General Myerson, Quigley, and you. Didn't General Myerson go along with you on modernizing?"

"Oh, the general agreed with me. He saw what was needed, but he wouldn't back me up in a real fight against the others. You'd expect a general to fight but not this general. You know why Myerson was so successful in the army? Because he was an expert compromiser. A great team man, see. So with Olin, Quigley, and Dr. Garth blocking it, I couldn't ever get that pocketbook open."

"Dr. Garth!"

"Yeah, like Mr. Mercer, whom he resembles in a lot of ways, Dr. Garth had the idea from 1945 on that a depression was just around the corner. Prices would come down, so we should wait to pick things up cheap. That was the way old doc made his pile. Olin always had been tight, and of course Quigley played along with him."

Adam sat dumbfounded. After a few moments, he said: "Dr. Garth seems to have changed his outlook. He favors modernizing now."

"Is that so? Usually men don't change that much at his age."

"You're right." Dr. Garth had never actually said he favored modernization. Perhaps he only wanted to get Olin's power for himself. Or the entire project might be a vendetta against Jack Olin for courting Josephine.

"What do you see in this for yourself, Salter?"

"I want to run The Taurus Company."

"I know. You've done some security analysis. You've looked at the real estate and you know about the big bank roll. Forget it. It's like the gold in the Spanish treasure ships on the bottom of the ocean. It's there, but you'll kill yourself trying to get to it. Anyway take a few more years and learn the ropes. I'm not saying you couldn't save the company if you had a free hand. Get yourself a good superintendent and you might bring it off. But it'll shorten your life. Look, Salter, why don't you stay over and talk with us in the morning? We've got some good openings, and I think maybe we could work you in."

"Thanks. I've got every cent I own plus a lot of borrowed money in Taurus stock. I'd better fight it out."

"I wish you luck. I didn't get much education, and The Taurus Company's the closest thing to an alma mater I got. When I went to work there thirty years ago, it was a local blue chip. But Monroe Mercer stayed about ten years after he should have retired, and by the time he died, the machines were as obsolete as he was. My last year I got a firm of management engineers to come in and go over the mill. I was going to use their report to squeeze a million or so out of the board for modernizing. The board's stated policy was that they'd approve any new machinery that would pay for itself in two years. Hell, if a machine will pay for itself in two years, you've needed it for ten years.

"You know it's a funny thing about me and Dr. Garth. I thought I was getting somewhere with him about what the mill needed. Now and then I'd ask him to come down and look at some phase of the operation.

"Around Easter the year I left, his daughter was home from school, and she came with him. Tall, built-up good-looking gal—in fact, the best looking girl I ever saw, and I couldn't help staring. I could feel that Dr. Garth didn't like that. I was conducting them to the cloth room, and I opened a door for her, and without thinking I just touched her kinda lightly on the back—you know how you do—just to indicate for her to go on ahead. Not on the fanny or anything, just on the damn back. Maybe it was her waist. Well, Dr. Garth gave me a cold hard look and told me not to soil his daughter's dress. Hell, I hadn't soiled her dress. But believe it or not, he would never come back to the mill after that except for directors' meetings, never listened to another word I said.

"Anyway, getting back—how well I remember the board meeting when I threw the part of the report about new equipment at them. Same old story. General Myerson showed some interest but let himself be talked down. Olin not saying much but pinching pennies. Quigley still a wart on Olin's behind. But Dr. Garth was the one that really killed it. The great stone face.

"Two weeks later the people up here offered me this, a free hand, a profit-sharing bonus, a modern mill, and I jumped at it. Even though the volume here then was about a third less than The Taurus Company's and the salary was lower. I'm making a hell of a lot more now than I did down there. Well, you asked me how to save The Taurus Company. First I'd say get a new board of directors." Baker looked at his watch and stood up. "Sorry, but I'm late for an engagement now." Adam thanked him. There was no point in asking to use what Baker had said. Every shot at Olin would hit Dr. Garth.

That night in his hotel room and on the long drive back to Mercer the next day Adam thought about Dr. Garth. If left to himself he would never get around to supporting Adam openly or demanding his right to inspect the books, which even Byroade could not defeat, for they would show him opposing Baker's constructive program and reveal his wrong prophecies.

So Adam could not leave Dr. Garth alone. He had to insist on an understanding about company policy. But here he was on quicksand, for as far as their agreement went, he would sell his stock to Dr. Garth in a few weeks and step out of the picture.

Adam had outmaneuvered many antagonists not because of superior qualities but because he cared more; because he planned the conversation and anticipated what the other would say, weighed the effect his words would have while the other talked freely, was tireless and could exhaust the other man with negotiation; because his own attention burned steadily while the other's mind strayed from the point at issue.

But he had never felt at his best with Dr. Garth. He had sensed some weakening lack in himself in the older man's presence—a lack of importance. When he talked with Dr. Garth, his usually deep voice seemed to rise in pitch and grow plaintive.

He could see the older man's point of view, but it did not help him. Just yesterday he was one of the younger doctors; he woke up one morning an old man, and his patients were either dead or going to new doctors with steadier hands. He had seen his daughter grown and disgraced. He had felt his powers failing, and if he had managed to doubt it before, he had learned in the past few weeks that he was not going to be one of those lucky old men who retain their health and vigor into their late seventies and eighties. Once Adam's line of action had been defined, it must have seemed to Dr. Garth that Bascom Olin in age, station, and outlook was a more natural ally than his upstart young cousin.

Adam reached Mercer just before dark and found Jimmy Nabors with a big package under his arm waiting for him. Jimmy refused beer and sat on Adam's sofa squeezing the package. "Look," said Jimmy, "I've been thinking about what you said when you came to see me that night. I've been looking around." He fell into silence again. Adam sat down and waited. Jimmy hefted the package and licked his lips.

Then he burst out as though interrupting and protesting something Adam had just said: "I know you think I'm pretty green, Mr. Salter, but I've been working in a cotton mill since I was sixteen years old in the summers, and I was on a work-study program. I came down here because that mill in my home town went broke. So I know the signs." Jimmy got up, still hugging the package. "When this Jack Olin came to work down there, I was glad! Because I thought maybe he could save it. But he doesn't care. Something is left out of him."

Abruptly he thrust the package into Adam's hands. "Here's something from the files Mr. Quigley has been sitting on. There are eight of us in on this. The others have all got families to support, and some of them are too old to get another job if something goes wrong, so I can't tell you their names. I can't afford to lose my job either. I've got to get this stuff back down there before eight o'clock in the morning, or somebody might miss it."

The package Jimmy gave him contained a two-hundred-page report from Robards and Miles, Management Consultants, prepared five years ago for Stewart Baker. "I sure appreciate this, Jimmy, but isn't it mostly out of date?"

"It's still true but worse. Seconds ran 9 per cent then. Now they're at least 20 per cent. You can see by the statistical report for the past year underneath there. There're just five copies of that, one for each director. That's Mr. Quigley's." The booklet contained detailed figures. It would have helped if Dr. Garth had let Adam see his own copy.

"Something else," Jimmy said. "That purchasing agent Bowers is stealing. Taking kickbacks. I'll bet it comes to fifty thousand a year. We get nearly a carload of starch a month, and he must knock down thousands on that one item. That's why he testified against you in court. He's afraid you'll pull the rug off of him. Here're some figures on what the mill's paying for supplies. They're way out of line."

"Jimmy, you understand that for this to do any good, I'm going to have to have to use it on some of the Taurus stockholders."

"I guess that's right." Jimmy was a little scared now. Looking at Jimmy's earnest face, Adam reflected that this was the act of a very young man who hadn't yet learned to let prudence intimidate him, but Jimmy also wanted badly to get married and would suffer from losing his job.

Adam telephoned the Garths' and arranged to see Dr. Garth at eight o'clock that evening. He worked on these reports steadily until then, skipping supper, and arrived at the house ten minutes late. Dr. Garth, Josephine told him, had retired. Her father had seemed in low spirits lately; she hoped Adam's expression didn't mean he had bad news about business for him. Adam spent a half-hour with Josephine, and he was pleased to discover that she had missed him and was delighted to see him.

From the time he left Josephine, Adam spent the next nine hours working on the material Jimmy had brought. The Robards and Miles report was most useful for two basic problems of the company: its wage plan and machinery. Even then when the company had fifty fewer employees than now the force could have been reduced 10 per cent. Some recommendations were outright gifts. Stop paying the Merchants National Bank twelve hundred dollars a year to act as transfer agent.

At five o'clock in the morning Adam admitted that his mind had stopped functioning, and he set the alarm for seven and went to bed. Jimmy came for the reports at seven-fifteen. Now Adam needed to know the prices at which the current backlog of orders had been bid in. Adam knew that if Jimmy could get these figures and if arguments were worth anything, he had what he needed for Messrs. Chisholm, Emery, and Alexander. Mrs. Wriston required another approach—a man with prestige, Dr. Garth, to tell her what to do.

After Jimmy left, Adam went back to sleep. The telephone waked him up around noon. "Adam!" It was Josephine. Her voice was excited and happy. "Leah's withdrawn the suit! It's going to be in the paper tomorrow."

Adam was awake instantly. "This should make some difference to your father, don't you think?"

"It should make all the difference in the world! It has to! I shouldn't have called you, I know how busy you are, but I couldn't wait!" Adam would talk with Dr. Garth that night.

Late in the afternoon Jimmy came back and for forty-five minutes he read off more particulars that his co-conspirators had given him, and until eight o'clock that night, Adam tried to bring a program into focus for The Taurus Company. He then stacked his papers and with stinging eyes and a sore neck and not at all up to facing Dr. Garth, he took the Buttermilk Road.

~~~~~~~~~~~~~~~~~~~~~~~~~~~~~~~~~~~~~~

35

When Adam reached the Garths' that night, Josephine, bright-eyed, threw open the door and hugged him. "This is what's going to be in the paper tomorrow," she said. It was a typewritten version of a news article, about the length of the previous one, stating that the suit had been dismissed at Mrs. Herold's request. There was also a statement by "a prominent local attorney," Rice Alexander. "The law regards the dismissal of a bill of divorce at the request of the plaintiff to be a confession of error on the part of the plaintiff and a vindication of those charged in the bill."

"Why did she do it?" Adam said.

"She took some money. I don't know how much. Daddy won't talk about it."

Josephine took Adam's hand and smiled at him as she knocked on her father's study door. At the rumbling invitation from within, Adam followed her in. Though Josephine had warned Dr. Garth, he looked surprised to see them, busy with some papers, at which he threw a lingering glance before putting them in a leather box. Then he locked the long fingers of his large hands and looked at the young people before him.

Josephine worked her chair over so close to Adam's that her bare round arm touched his sleeve. Adam cleared his throat and began: "We feel that since my last talk with you, the picture has changed completely."

"What Adam means is we want to be married," said Josephine.

Dr. Garth gave her a reproving look for this forwardness and said: "It does *appear* that the situation has changed—that Josephine's name is not going to figure prominently in a divorce court, although Rice Alexander tells me that the suit could be reinstated. Mrs. Herold is said to be a changeable woman. Also Josephine has been seen in Mercer with a man who is now known to be married."

Adam followed the direction of Dr. Garth's glance and saw that Josephine's face was flushed and frowning.

"Moreover," Dr. Garth went on, "I still believe that this turmoil clouds her judgment."

"Daddy, I know what I want to do!" said Josephine with some heat. "And please don't refer to me in the third person."

"It seems that you had very different ideas only a few weeks ago."

Again Josephine reddened and looked darkly at her father.

"You're asking us to wait," said Adam. "How long do you have in mind now, Uncle Ive?"

"No less than a year."

"That's too long, Daddy, and you know it is." Josephine grasped Adam's hand.

"Then let me bring up another point which neither of you seem to have considered. Have you thought of the consequences to your children of a marriage between cousins?"

A silence followed, then Adam and Josephine protested at once that they were only second cousins.

"Let me remind you that this is a subject which you know nothing about," said Dr. Garth, looking at Adam. "There is a well-defined mathematical possibility that if you two are carrying any of the so-called black genes that your children will be disastrously affected." They stared in astonishment as he got up and took a heavy medical book from a shelf. He found his place at once and turned it around on the desk. Adam and Josephine advanced and looked at the book. There was a photograph of a baby without arms or legs. "If you will look at the text," said Dr. Garth, "you will see that this infant was born of a mating of cousins."

"But isn't that freakish?" said Adam, his heart beating fast. "Just what are the chances?"

"If you have several children, the chances are good that one of them will manifest whatever recessive traits you are carrying. I've been a physician for forty-five years and attended thousands of patients. I have seen, especially in the mountain country here, deaf-mutes, monsters of various kinds, obviously from inbreeding. I should like to refer you also to the eighteenth and twentieth chapters of Leviticus in which those of close kin are forbidden to marry. I take those admonitions very seriously."

"My memory of those chapters is hazy," said Adam. "Do they refer to cousins?"

"By implication they do. It is a moral duty to compound the advice therein with our scientific knowledge for the protection of the race. That is the intention of those laws against inbreeding."

Josephine sat without looking at either of them. The medical book with its horrendous photograph was still open on the desk.

"I knew this would be unpleasant and perhaps frightening to you, so I haven't brought it up before. I had hoped that given time you would decide against this marriage anyway. You understand now that I cannot approve it."

"The way I feel about it," said Adam, "is that as much as I want children, I would forego them rather than give up Josephine." Josephine nodded agreement.

"That you should both make a quick and wrong decision on such a question and assume that such an issue is within your power to control is an indication that you are being foolishly hasty."

"I want to marry Adam, Daddy," Josephine said in a thick voice, "I don't want to marry anyone else. I never will."

"Think about it," said her father. "And if you don't mind I'd like to speak to him alone."

"What about?" she said, alarmed.

"About something which would be easier to discuss if only the two of us were here."

She went to the door, paused there, came back to Adam and kissed him on the forehead, then walked slowly out of the room. When she was gone, Adam turned to Dr. Garth. He was bracing himself for some stricture about money, an aggravation of the point Dr. Garth had scored last time.

"What I'm about to say is something that many physicians know, and if they are wise, rarely discuss, but you must know this situation in detail because Josephine has reason to be in a susceptible state, and I'm hoping for more calculation from you." His tone was harsher now with his daughter out of the room, and on certain words like "calculation" he put a drawling emphasis and a taste of sarcasm. "I asked Josephine to leave because a well-bred young lady should not be exposed to such a subject, though it would be fatal for us to ignore it. The Garth family has been close over several generations, and many of the family lived in this small rural community. As you well know, we have kept closely in touch even after we have dispersed. The proverb that propinquity makes marriages is true. Another factor is the attraction of similar persons. This is much truer than the saying that opposites attract."

Adam listened closely and decided that Dr. Garth was saying this with an air of importance and emphasis which it did not seem to deserve. "Yes, sir?"

"The fact that such as this is true would mean that a marriage between you and Josephine is even less advisable."

"I'm afraid I don't follow you. Have other marriages taken place between cousins in our family?"

"Let me give you another example. A family lived in this valley within sight of the Buttermilk Road and once owned land which touched ours. The Chobots. None of them are living now. They were inbred—not always by marriage. At a certain period, over a hundred years ago, such a policy made for an able though peculiar family but it continued to a point of madness and incest and destroyed them. There are few Garths left."

"What is it?" said Adam. "What are you saying? You mean you are advising us not to marry because of the remote chance that something similar occurred in our family several generations back?"

"If it were only a remote chance, I would not have brought it up."

Adam pondered this reply. "Are you under the impression that I know the background of this? It's all brand-new to me, sir."

"You are asking for proof, and in such a matter there never is proof."

Adam shook his head. "Sir, if you have any definite information on this point, I think you owe it to me to tell me."

"Doesn't it seemed natural to you that you are not the first one in the family to have this problem?"

Adam felt like inquiring and protesting further but instead he sat there facing a pair of yellow images, those of Adam and Rachel Garth in their portraits. Those faces fell away, and instead of pictures, as he stared into Dr. Garth's hard eyes, he was occupied with the facts of his own life—how generous Dr. Garth had been with him, how much more he was like Dr. Ivor Garth in appearance and temperament than Professor Ira Salter. But Dr. Garth met him with an aquiline glare—not as a man would confessing a sin. And Dr. Garth believed in sin.

No, Dr. Garth was not his father. What seemed possible was that his mother had yielded to the strong man before him, who could now face him without guilt or regret because he had taken her feeling the duty of the strong to improve the race by cuckolding the weak. How could he mention it so dryly now? Perhaps he had learned to stay cool for the health of his brain and heart. But Adam's face was wet, and he found his arms and legs braced, and his heart rose with the desire to strike back. Even this hard urge was polluted by the kindness the old man had shown him, the favors he had done, the money Adam was to make from him.

Adam made himself sit back as he would strip a suit from a hanger. All was quiet except for the whipping of the curtains and the volleying of his heart. He tried to tear the truth out of the big head before him with his gaze. If there were a strongly moral man who might consider himself on some score above moral law, this was the face he would have.

Without a word he stood, and turning his back to Adam, pulled down the window behind the desk.

Adam leaped forward. "You're going to have to do more than make insinuations to stop me," he said with a shaking voice. "You know that, don't you? You will have to *say* it."

Dr. Garth glanced back at him. It was a measure of his strength that Adam could not make himself speak the accusation. That would be an outrage and would make the old man more dangerous than ever.

The door burst open, and Josephine entered carrying an enormous family Bible. "I've just read the eighteenth and twentieth chapters of Leviticus, and they have nothing to do with us. And I also called Dr. Lawson on the telephone and asked what he thought. He said for ordinary second cousins there would be no objection to marriage."

"I know a great deal more about this family than Lawson does." Dr. Garth closed the other windows. "I'm going to bed."

"Daddy, wait! We haven't *settled* anything—"

Dr. Garth ignored this protest and left the room.

Josephine slipped an arm into Adam's, and they walked toward the front of the house together. "You're soaking wet!" she said.

In the parlor he tried to dry his hands and face with his handkerchief. He glanced up at the ancestral faces and his own warped and gleaming face in the mirror.

"He's always been this way," said Josephine in a low angry voice. "He never would approve of any man he thought I could ever be serious about. Adam, how do you feel? Does what he said change the way you feel?"

"Not about you," he said hoarsely.

"He doesn't know what he's doing. He's actually convinced himself that we shouldn't marry."

"Marry me anyway," he said. She looked alarmed, and he went on: "In this state you have to wait at least three days, have a blood test, but not in Mississippi. I'm going to have to get some money together and make a few arrangements first." There had been no opportunity to talk with Dr. Garth about The Taurus Company, but he couldn't wait for that. He grasped her arms and said: "We'll go to Mississippi tomorrow."

"All right. Tomorrow. I'm afraid to wait."

36

Thunder and rain awakened Adam at four-thirty just before his alarm clock went off. Using the figures Jimmy Nabors had given him, Adam undertook a forecast of The Taurus Company's losses for the next year. The margin on the backlog was not enough to cover overhead, and with the increasing trend of losses The Taurus Company's once big pile of cash would be gone in a year and a half.

At eight o'clock he telephoned Stewart Baker to ask if there were any custom accepted in the textile industry for getting out of a ruinous contract, and Baker said: "Maybe you can get out of it, but the best policy is to honor the contract."

Adam set out a program of reform, proposing job loads and changes in machinery from the Robards and Miles report and adding such items as competitive bids for supplies, which would save about forty-two thousand dollars a year.

The day was cool, and a hard rain, instead of making the air gloomy, reassured him. A fine sunny day would have invited a stroke of celestial irony.

By daylight the black hint that Josephine might be his half-sister seemed unintentional. It would make Dr. Garth an adulterer and a hypocrite, and Adam rejected the idea.

When he telephoned Josephine, her voice was an excited whisper. Dr. Garth was going to a directors' meeting at ten-thirty. Josephine said she had an errand to do and would be ready at eleven o'clock. What was this mysterious errand? She wouldn't say.

Adam visited the offices of Duncan Chisholm, Rice Alexander, and P. D. Emery. Quickly he outlined his program and concluded by saying it could reduce the company's losses by ten thousand a month before Christmas and have it operating in the black in a

240

year. If the present union contract were renewed and if his other reforms were not made, the company would soon have to borrow money or begin liquidation. The distress on P. D. Emery's face gave Adam particular satisfaction, and the other two were visibly disturbed. Adam did not ask for comment but left a copy of his report for each man to study at leisure.

After his visit with Mr. Emery, Adam stayed at the bank to borrow money to finance his honeymoon. The officer he called on let him have five hundred dollars with his car as security. He had decided to delay getting the engagement ring because, as he had explained to Josephine, any ring he could afford now would be too modest for her, but he weakened while buying the wedding band and paid half the five hundred for a diamond ring.

He felt conspicuous and uneasy during these transactions because it seemed quite possible that Josephine would yield to her father's will and not come with him.

It was still raining hard when Adam drove to the Garths' house. Dr. Garth's old Cadillac was gone. Adam went in the back hall and found Josephine in a dark spring suit writing a note. He was bursting with pride. She was his. He kissed her and gave her the ring. She seemed delighted with it. He put her suitcases into his car, and a minute later they were winding up the Buttermilk Road. "How do you feel?" he said.

"Very much relieved." Her words poured out. "I started not to dress until you came because I thought you might say you had thought about it and it was not wise or something like that and then I would feel so foolish all dressed up and jilted, but I knew that was just nerves, and that you wouldn't change overnight."

He laughed. "I was afraid you might not get in the car. Have you had any doubts?"

"Not really, but I feel that we may be struck by lightning."

"I know what you mean. I feel I've forgotten to do something important." But one issue he had not been able to forget. "By the way, Josephine," he said, trying to sound casual, "have cousins in our family ever married before?"

"Didn't you know? Adam and Rachel Garth were first cousins once removed. Daddy blames them for every descendant that's gone wrong. But you can argue just as well from them that cousins *should* marry since our family hasn't turned out so badly. You're not worried about that too, are you?"

"Not any more," he said.

He drove rapidly through town to the Birmingham highway. It was still raining hard. "It's about a five-hour drive to the state line," he said.

They discussed what would come afterward. They agreed they wouldn't go to the mountains because Mercer people went to the nearby places like Highlands and High Hampton. They would go to the Gulf Coast in spite of the heat. After the honeymoon, they would live in Adam's apartment until they could find something bigger.

"Adam, this morning I went to see Belle. I knew Daddy wouldn't do it, so at breakfast I got him to tell me about this mill business you all are working on, and I told Belle what he told me. I remembered that rumor she'd heard, and I wanted to surprise you."

"How did she take it?"

"Here!" she cried, and held up Mrs. Wriston's proxy made over to Adam Salter.

Adam felt very close to Josephine then, so close that he started talking about his business ambitions which he could imagine might not be of much interest to a woman. He reviewed his activities of the past few months in detail. "I'm going to run that mill myself," he said. "I'm going to save it. But don't tell your father yet." Several times he had a feeling that he was talking too much, but when he apologized for the monologue, she asked questions which showed she had been listening with interest.

But she was having fewer spontaneous comments to make as they drove, and she ate hardly anything at the drive-in restaurant in Birmingham where they stopped for lunch. He did not question her about this deterioration in her mood because he thought he knew what the trouble was.

From Birmingham on, they were both quiet. He was so unaccustomed to such self-revelation that all the talking he had done made him feel surfeited and tired. For a time west of Birmingham the rain let up, and they seemed to be between two storms. Josephine leaned forward, cheek almost touching the windshield, and watched the sky as though she really were expecting a bolt of lightning. "Are you worried about your father?" She nodded. "He'll be all right," Adam said. Silence. "Are you sorry we aren't having a big wedding?"

"I'd wanted to be married in church, but now I don't care."

About four-thirty they passed a billboard: *Hydrangea Wedding Chapel, Hydrangea, Mississippi. Rev. Orville Skate. Ceremonies for Lovebirds.* The price was $5 painted in a red heart. "I guess that's sort of a church," said Adam.

So they arrived in Mississippi with no roadblocks, three-state alarms, or tornados. Hydrangea was a town of two thousand with a half-dozen fine antebellum mansions, and a flashy midway of quick marriage for the diseased, the hasty, and the underage. The Reverend Mr. Skate's Wedding Chapel beckoned with a neon arrow jabbing a pulsating red heart. "Let's not go there," said Josephine.

They stopped at a more modest sign of a justice of the peace. Adam felt like asking if she were sure she wanted to marry him but decided not to. If she intended to call it off, she would have to bring the subject up herself, and he was going to try to talk her into going ahead with it.

Getting out of the car and going in ahead of them were a punk-looking boy and a girl about fourteen, both chewing gum, not scared at the prospect of marriage but loaded with ignorance and confidence. Adam felt so nervous that his doubts were chilled into numbness. He saw Josephine's lips tremble as they entered the peeling Victorian house where they were to be married.

They came out fifteen minutes later into a warm drizzling rain. The service was over too quickly, and he felt keenly the absence of friends and ceremony. He was proud of her and regretted that they had chosen such a shabby place. The rain made an early twilight. "I saw a nice-looking motor court back there," he said as they got into the car. "It looked new."

She avoided his gaze. "Adam, let's not stay here tonight. It's so early and I'm so keyed up. Let's go on to the coast. Do you mind? I'll drive if you're tired."

He took a road map from the glove compartment and studied it. The coast was about two hundred miles away. "Biloxi seems about as near as any place. We could stop on the way if something right turns up."

Once when they stopped for gas at a filling station with a grocery store adjoining, he bought a pound box of rice without her knowing it and without himself knowing how he would use it. She bought a package of cigarettes at that stop, smoked one, then threw the others out of the window without comment. She did not want to stop for dinner, but she did not argue. She ate hardly anything. She wanted to drive on and on. As tired as she was and as monotonous as the drive was, it would have been natural for her to fall asleep, but she sat up against the door, ladylike, her skirt well down over her knees.

When they came to a town with an acceptable-looking hotel about nine o'clock and they were only halfway, she still wanted to go on, and he was anxious to please. He did not quiz her about her feelings. She seemed totally indifferent to the scenery. She took an interest in only one thing, and when they reached Biloxi, which was hot even at midnight, she said: "I don't want to stop yet."

He turned under the porte-cochere of a large new hotel. "Why?"

"I'm not sleepy. I'll drive. You can sleep."

"Where do you want to go?"

"Further."

"No. We're staying here."

"Adam, please!"

He did not answer but went inside and registered. He signed: "Adam G. Salter" and added "Mrs. Salter" after being prompted by the clerk. Their room was air-conditioned and new-looking with two double beds. When they were alone, he stood gazing out the big picture window at what he thought must be the Gulf, and she sat in a chair. "Still afraid of lightning?" She made no reply. "What is it?" he said. She shook her head.

He sat down on the bed and put his face in his hands. He was exasperated not because she was depressed and difficult but because she wouldn't explain. He still had the edge of haste against his nerves, an ache in his back, and pressure on the top of his head like a tight lead crown. He felt less like coaxing her to talk than squeezing it out of her.

He telephoned room service to send up a bottle of champagne. This was a dry state, so there was no champagne, but there was bourbon at ten dollars a fifth. It arrived with a pitcher of ice, and Adam poured two drinks as dark red as rust.

"I don't want it," said Josephine, but she took the glass and drank with him.

The whisky heated his stomach and took the points off the briars in his blood. It also loosened his tongue. "Does Herold have anything to do with this tonight?"

"With what?"

"With the way you feel about me tonight. Did you see him this morning when you went to Mrs. Wriston's?"

"He flew to New York a week ago."

"I didn't know that."

"Belle told me. That's why Leah withdrew the suit. Cato went back to her. Belle said, 'He did it for you. I hope you appreciate it.' Cato called me every day while he was in town, and I told him not to call any more, and after that I wouldn't come to the telephone. The day he left he came to tell me goodbye, and I told Rutherford to say I wasn't at home. He did that for me after the way I treated him."

"She withdrew the suit because she was paid off, and he went back to Leah out of habit. He always has after every affair. He has no other place to go."

"No place to go? Do you think Belle wouldn't have been happy to keep him? To give him anything he wanted on his terms. She's been in love with him for years, and she's not the only one. I don't care whether he was sleeping with Belle or not! If that's any comfort to him, I'm glad!" Her voice was thick and unsteady. She got up and poured herself another drink. "That's what I should have expected from you."

"What should you have expected from me?"

"To think it was all because of money!"

"I don't see how I deserved that," he said in amazement. She made no comment. "Something's changed you since last night. Did Mrs. Wriston say something against me?"

"You said it yourself this morning."

"You mean about the mill. Oh. You don't think I should make any money out of a deal with your father. Well, maybe you have a point. On the other hand, I've taken some risks, lost my job, gone over my head in debt, and I'm paying a lot of interest on the money I borrowed."

"What's the first thing you're talking about doing down at the mill? Taking away people's jobs."

"Not necessarily. There's a considerable labor turnover, and I have in mind to cut the force slowly so as few as possible will have to be fired, and it won't flood the local labor market. But even if I had to fire half of them to save the company, that would be the best thing because that would save the rest, and if the company goes busted, they all lose their jobs—"

245

"It's just that I didn't know you were so *ambitious.*" She hissed the last word.

"Ambitious? No, it's not just the money. I want to run the mill because it's a mess, and I can straighten it out." She gave him a dark disbelieving glance. "Why do you think Jimmy Nabors gave me that material from the files? Because the company is dying and he knows I can save it."

"Then why are you doing it behind Daddy's back?"

"This is why. When I started into the Taurus business at your father's request, I thought Bascom Olin was the big obstacle to progress. But I found out a few days ago from Stewart Baker that your father did it just as much harm as Olin did. Your father's been getting ready for another depression for twelve years, so he hasn't wanted to spend the money to modernize. Your father's been sick, he's been avoiding me, and I just haven't been able to get this subject thrashed out with him."

She was close to tears. "When are you going to put *that* in the paper?"

The whisky was making him feel how exhausted he was. "Josephine, I'm not denying I'm interested in money. One reason I want it is for you—just as your father did. You didn't go to Miss Wycherley's School or Vassar or Europe on anything else. The money he's gotten together and you've enjoyed didn't just drift into his hands."

"Daddy's business is saving lives. I know doctors are well paid, and they ought to be."

"Josephine, it hasn't been exactly a secret to you that I've been in the most mercenary of occupations, stockbrokerage, for the past three years. Why did your feeling of revulsion just come out today?"

"I assumed that you had some purpose higher than making money."

"What are the dignified occupations? Besides medicine."

"There are several."

"But not business."

"Some businessmen run their companies for the public good."

"What the hell kind of socialistic talk is this!" He burst out with a sharp explosive laugh. "Businessmen are in the game for money."

"I don't see why you dislike the Olins so much. You're getting to be just like them."

"Listen, Josephine, your father made most of his money by

having it when nobody else did and buying stocks and real estate at distressed prices. I don't see anything idealistic about that. The reason they've made your father trustee of various institutions is that he's got money and knows how to handle it. Look at it this way. Suppose we'd both been poor. Then—"

"Ah. Then you wouldn't have married me."

"You think I married you for money?"

She looked shocked and angry at her own words.

"You know I could have married Blakely, and I'm told the general has as much money as your father."

"That's what fooled me. But I had one thing that Blakely didn't —I was a Garth, and you wanted the house. Well, I never have liked that house, and I'll never live there. Oh! I know you. You condemn me for what I've done because you're so moral yourself but when it comes to money—"

"I don't condemn you!" All this sounded childish to him, but he knew she was not being deliberately ill-humored. "You think I'm so low, so calculating, that I was thinking of money all the time?"

"Why else would you marry *me?*"

"You thought this before we got to Mississippi. Why did you go through with it?"

"It's too horrible to say."

"Say it."

"Because I wasn't *sure* it was just money with you. Because I owed you a lot. And because it was too late to go back. I was afraid the word would be out that we'd eloped, and I couldn't face Daddy and admit we weren't married after the other thing." Her voice sank so low he could hardly hear her last words: "Because I needed to be married. No, I'm not actually pregnant."

"I'll go outside while you undress," he said. This statement caused a desperate widening of her eyes, and he added: "Don't worry. You're safe."

When he returned, she was in bed with the cover to her chin. He took the other bed. Even with the blinds down and the lights off, the room was not very dark. The floodlights outside leaked in under the blinds, and glass jalousies in the door transfused a crackled multicolored light. Although he wanted to know what she was wearing, he avoided looking at her, but from the sound of her tossing he knew she was not asleep.

Thanks, Mrs. Wriston, he thought, thank you very much.

Herold's alleged sacrifice and his own ill-timed talk about business had been what had tipped the balance for Josephine. This act made Herold seem more of a man, and now she was clinging to the idea that he had sacrificed himself for her, which under the circumstances must be very dear to her.

Adam was tempted to think of his troubles as coming from mistakes in timing, that if she had known about this move of Herold's a few days earlier and had had time to digest that, if she had known the details of the Taurus deal all along, then this misunderstanding would not have occurred. But he suspected that it went deeper than a misunderstanding.

He expected her to insist on going home the next day, but when they woke up very early and he asked her, he found that although she answered vaguely, going back to Mercer was the last thing she wanted to do. "You don't feel like facing your father yet?" he said. "Or the public?"

"No."

"Is that all?"

"I don't know."

Neither wanted to stay in Biloxi, so they drove on. When they reached Point Clear on Mobile Bay during the morning, they spotted a car with a Sweetwater County tag and decided not to stay. No place would do. Too much blinding sunlight flooded the gulf beaches. It was always too early, and the heat stunned them.

As they drove down the coast, Josephine's manner changed, and this he saw was the result of a change not of mood but of policy. Although her spirits had not improved and she was all too polite, she was responsive—just as she must have been when she was in college and coming home from Poughkeepsie for the Christmas holidays and some white-shoe college boy struck up a conversation with her in the club car of the Silver Comet.

Adam decided that she had assumed for him some higher ambition than the apparent ones, but the truth was that money had never been a problem to her, he realized, and she had never given it a thought before. Why *did* he want a lot of money? He saw it as a means of freedom and security for himself and his family, a protection against the shabbiness of his childhood and an antidote for the sickening failure of the Salter Webbing Company, but there was no denying that he also saw business as a game at which he believed he was good and which he very much wanted to win. The rewards were not vague, not verbal, not a laurel-wreath consolation prize for half-success. They were universally understood, and they were hard and visible. He usually thought of himself as an idealistic businessman, but her talk had pushed him into the Bascom Olin role he rejected and drawn from him the automatic reference to socialism. Certainly he would never do anything dishonest nor would he give a customer bad advice on stocks for his own ends. Was his code nothing more than that?

He felt that his position was defensible and that her criticism of it came from the ignorance of a sheltered childhood and some liberal professor and did not go very deep with her. Sometime he planned to argue the point with her, but not now because he seemed to be suffering by comparison with two imaginary figures—Dr. Albert Schweitzer Garth and Sydney Carton Herold. In the former, money-getting was dignified, even sanctified by his age, the prestige of his profession, his philanthropies, and the fact that he was her father. Herold was guiltless of the charge of being interested in making money although he did seem willing enough to spend it. Adam framed these remarks as he drove, silently rolled them on his tongue, but even to his own partisan ear the analysis of her father's position sounded offensive, and everything he had to say about Herold sounded cynical and sarcastic.

So he settled for a cool peace all the way to Mercer Davenport's playground south of Tampa Bay, Tarragona, Florida. They arrived at the best time, around nine p.m., when the lights molded and glamorized it and there was no bludgeoning sunlight. Josephine expressed no enthusiasm for the place, and he knew, whether she knew it or not, that she wanted to drive on into oblivion, on down off the tip of Florida, over the highway to Key West and into the ocean.

Tarragona was a winter resort, and most of the big hotels on the Gulf were closed. They stopped at one four stories high and were given a room with a glass wall facing the Gulf and a breezeway behind. The hotel had central air-conditioning, but the room was too warm for him, and he stripped to the waist. The bottle came out of the suitcase, and they had a couple of strong drinks. "Hydrangea seems a year ago, doesn't it?" she said. He agreed and felt like adding that it seemed unreal, that he did not feel married.

Encouraged by her agreeableness, he tried to take her in his arms, and the stiffening and recoil of her body were so manifestly reflexes that he released her immediately, roughly pushing her away. He went into the bathroom and looked at himself in the mirror full of the suspicion which the glass brought to the level of knowledge.

Adam had taken it for granted that his own body if anything was an advantage he had over Herold as being stronger and more masculine, and now he looked at the hoods of muscle capping his shoulders and casting shadows over melonlike biceps, the humps of muscle on each side of his thick neck, the barrel chest and horizontal ridges of stomach muscle as hard as the undershield of a turtle mostly covered by the mat of hair which extended from his throat downward; even his casting of the Garth mouth was muscular. Though his face and neck were dark, his body was too white. It struck him that the slender boyish probably hairless physique of Herold was the one for her. She did not find her husband physically attractive. He crowded close and stared into the mirror until the glass itself seemed to be made of skin and hair, and the sight of it sickened him.

He went into the other room and put on his pajama top at once. Josephine was sitting in exactly the same position. After uneasy glances, she said, looking away: "What are you thinking about?"

"A discovery."

She came over to him and took his big right hand in hers, which were ice cold. "Give me a little more time, Adam."

"You have all the time in the world, baby."

Since he had despaired of having her, instead of being full of pleasant rich suspense, the tension in his body was bitter. The next morning he violated his natural caution, and as soon as possible got such a sunburn that afterward the sun's heat was painful even through a shirt. Josephine seemed no more careful, but her dark skin did not burn. It was the first time he had seen her in a bathing suit since she was a child, and this white nylon suit displayed full curved breasts, small waist, long firm legs. Her oiled skin—he had applied the suntan oil violently to her shoulders and the backs of her legs—glowed with a luxuriant reddish brown, and when she came in from the beach, and he was sitting forward to keep his stinging back from the plastic upholstery of the chair, he could nearly laugh at the thought if he had tried to invent a situation or a

woman to drive him crazy, he could not have improved on either.
He could not help touching her, cupping his hands over her
breasts or kissing her neck, but her response was so sad and lifeless
that he would keep away for an hour or so before trying again. She
tried to be decent and agreeable. The first day she bought him a
magnificent wrist watch for a wedding present. Too magnificent—
he guessed this gleaming golden wafer must have cost as much as
her engagement ring and the honeymoon combined.

They spent four days there as roommates, chums, eating at
restaurants of a holiday festive decor but now quite dead without
the crowds, swimming in the hotel pool after sunset, listening to the
tame growl of the Gulf from their balcony at night. All the while
he bristled with desire and the hope that her deathlike response
would finally turn into a scuffle which might generate in her some
angry heat.

Tarragona was the site of the first really unshakable melancholy
he had known. One incident in particular which he had managed
to put out of his mind for months troubled him. That last day at the
Salter Webbing Company when his father couldn't see that the
venture was doomed, would not listen to failure speaking in its own
true voice, Adam had burst out sharply: "No wonder you've never
amounted—" He had caught himself there, but he could see from
the surprise and pain on his father's face that his meaning was
clear. After he had gone to Atlanta, Adam had often felt an urge
to write a letter to his father and assure him that in everything that
really counted he had been a success, but he had put it off too long,
and for a year after his father's death, he had often waked up at
three o'clock in the morning with the feeling he had to do something, and he would remember with a heavy heart what it was.

The last day he and Josephine went into town across the bay for
lunch and sent a telegram telling Dr. Garth where they were and
that they planned to stay away two more days. It was their first
contact with Mercer. Adam had considered calling G. P. Moon for
news about The Taurus Company, but now those problems re-
volted him. They sent a telegram to his sister announcing the
marriage. Coming out of the Western Union office, Adam halted
with shock, for he thought he saw across the glaring sidewalk the
face of Cato Herold. A second later he knew it wasn't Herold. Josephine had apparently not noticed the resemblance.

The last afternoon they spent in Tarragona, after his embraces had been chilled by her forlorn defenselessness, they were reading, each on his or her own bed. He was reading *Barron's* and she *The New Yorker,* publications mutually disliked. He fell asleep and dreamed about driving out the Buttermilk Road, and the road ended at a beautiful blue lake. The scene filled him with joy and peace, and when he awoke, his shirt soaked with sweat, without remembering at once what he had lost, he was filled with the disappointment and grief he had felt as child on waking from a dream to find that his mother was dead after all.

Josephine was gone. His new watch had stopped, and the angle of the sunlight under the blinds worried him. He went out on the balcony.

She was below, lying on a nylon and aluminum chaise longue, and a blond young man was sitting next to her. The surf and wind kept Adam from hearing what they said. The man was tall and looked about college age. A yellow down grew on his chest instead of hair. He must have said something funny for Josephine laughed appreciatively.

Adam stood there, gripping the rail of the balustrade, waiting and unnoticed. Even this late afternoon sun made his skin smart.

What could they have to talk about all this time? At last the boy arose, laughing, and went up the beach. He had probably just been out walking, seen a good-looking woman, and stopped off to strike up a conversation and see what might happen. When he was about a dozen yards away, Josephine turned and watched him go. Her dark glasses made her look expressionless and cadaverous, with black orbits where her eyes should be. Adam went back inside.

He wanted to ask her what the boy had said to make her laugh so freely when her husband could not, but he knew that the words themselves would not satisfy him. He had seen all there was to it. But now memory of her weakness for Herold frightened him.

He could not help thinking of Blakely then and the peaceful marriage he could have had with her. He had been in love with Josephine, not Blakely, and he had thought that aside from the bodily attraction Josephine was a deeper stronger person who could stand up in a crisis. But now he thought: I won't live in a crisis forever, and I'm strong enough for both of us.

Every thought of Blakely led him back to Josephine at once, and he was still on that subject when she came in wet a half-hour later. She looked a little startled and disconcerted by his stare.

252

"Have a nice nap?"

"Marvelous."

"The water in the pool is too warm," she said, "and so is the Gulf. It makes me drowsy. It's better early in the morning." She walked toward the bathroom as she said this, her butterscotch back toward him.

"Wait!" he said, getting up. "I want to talk with you." She turned with wide eyes, and he knew he had not started casually enough. "What happened in Rome?"

"In *Rome?* Oh." She frowned. "You mean that misunderstanding between me and Daddy. It's a long story. I'll tell you all about it sometime."

"I'd appreciate it if you'd tell me now."

"Why is it so pressing to hear the details this minute? That happened six years ago, for heaven's sake."

"It's pressing, and I'm not just kicking your leg. And would you take off your sunglasses, please."

She took off her sunglasses and spread a towel on a chair and sat on it. She stared at the wall for a few moments. "When Mother and Daddy and I were in Rome, I got in the wrong crowd. Oh, Daddy warned me, but I looked up an Italian girl I had known in school. I should have suspected something. She and her friends worked at night, they wore too flashy clothes. But I was so young, so naïve, somehow their ways became my ways. The very name of the hotel where they worked should have made me suspicious— The Albergo Hotel. I should have known that such an unpretentious name for an Italian hotel must cover something rotten. Even the name of the concierge was suspect. We called her Mama Bordello—"

"Don't devil me!" he shouted. "You know who that sounded like? Mr. and Mrs. Cato Herold. Now tell me the truth."

"The truth would be a dreadful anticlimax with all the sin you're expecting."

"I'll settle for an anticlimax."

She seemed to think it over. At last her expression indicated that she had decided to humor him. "The summer before I went to Vassar I met a nice boy on the boat going to Europe. He was a typical college boy, but the fact that he was just learning to drink made him seem wild to Mother and Daddy. He kept turning up wherever we went in Europe, and in Rome he asked me to a house party. He and some of his college friends had somebody's villa on the Italian Riviera, and his sister and her husband would be chaperones. Daddy was furious at the idea and told me never to see the boy again." As she told it, her attention shifted from Adam to this remembered injustice, and her expression became indignant. "So I went anyway. Just disappeared. It showed that Daddy wasn't even listening when I asked his permission because he couldn't remember the name of the town and had no idea where to look for me. It was a mean childish thing for me to do, and I felt guilty about it for years afterward. Maybe that was why I was such a model girl in college. The house party turned out to be a drunk. I didn't drink then, and I had a rotten time, and after a couple of days I went back to Rome. Mother had insisted that I wouldn't go away like that. She thought I had been kidnaped, and she wanted to go to the police and the newspapers, but Daddy wouldn't let her, and he did his searching for me through private agencies, which were useless. I didn't realize until then how much Daddy did care about public opinion. He did something else that just amazed me. When I came back, he grabbed my arm, and you may not believe this—" Her face reddened. "He actually smacked my behind with his hand four or five times. Remember, I was *eighteen*." She seemed to remember she had told the story under duress and said defiantly: "Disappointed?"

"No."

"Is that all?"

He was relieved but also disappointed because he had hoped to find a key to her behavior in it. "I want to know about you and Herold. When was the last time?"

"The last time what?"

"The last time you slept with him."

Her eyes blazed, and she got up and went toward the bathroom. She stopped at the door. "On second thought you may have a right to know the answer to that. It was the night of Belle's party. The day you met him." She tried to keep her shaking voice steady. "Now can I take a shower?"

"Was he the first one?"

"The only one—ever."

She went into the bathroom, and he sat for a while listening to the water of her shower splashing. He could not keep still long: he felt like kicking the door down, and it was the fear of doing something violent that made him go outside. The air was cooler, the fire had gone out of the sunlight, and the red and globular sun hanging over the horizon gave an appearance of speeding up as it neared the water.

He walked beside the Gulf with his fists clenched. He had been hoping that this was just a misunderstanding that he could clear up, and it occurred to him that theirs might be an unhappy marriage from now on—that nothing he could do would help, that no concession he could make would bring her around. Nor did he feel like making any further concessions. Dr. Garth had been right: they had married too soon after Herold. The thought that she had had sexual intercourse with another man just a few months ago made Adam feel reckless of his life. He did not regret marrying her, for he felt now that he had never had any choice in the matter.

He walked a long way until he had cooled down, and when he turned back, he had stopped hoping he would think of a solution. The sun had set, the sky was turning from blue to lavender-gray, sand in his shoes crowded his feet.

He felt that he was at a disadvantage because of his lack of sexual experience, and he wondered if he shouldn't go ahead and yield to his instincts on the assumption that she really didn't know what she wanted. He considered and rejected the idea of drinking enough so that he could force himself on her without caring how she felt.

But he was really not thinking at all when he mounted the steps to their room.

He opened the door, and there was Josephine, fully dressed, sitting on the bed, weeping. She had a paper sack balanced on her knees. "What did you get this for?" she said. He looked in the sack. It contained the box of rice he had bought and forgotten. "What were you going to do with it?" she said.

"I've forgotten." He sat down and watched her. "How did you happen to find it?"

"I was going to leave you. I was getting some shoes out of the trunk of the car, and I came across this. Why did you have to buy this rice?"

The telephone rang. It had not rung since their arrival, and Adam thought it was a wrong number. Though he was nearer the instrument, she got up quickly and moved around him as though she had been expecting the call, and picked it up. "This is she." She raised

255

her voice. "Yes, Rutherford, what is it?" She listened a long time, parting her lips to interrupt but restraining herself, her face tense and frightened. He watched her, thinking: the old man has a long reach. At last she said: "No, don't worry, he'll never know you called. We'll get there as soon as we can."

She hung up, staring through Adam, and said: "Daddy's had another stroke. The day after we left. That was Rutherford. Daddy wouldn't call us, and Rutherford didn't know how to reach us until the telegram today, but he thought I ought to be notified, so he did it on the sly."

"How bad is it?"

"He's not in any immediate danger. His speech is slightly affected, and some of his movements. Adam, I've got to go home."

"He's not in danger."

"If the situation hadn't been serious, Rutherford wouldn't have called."

"You want to leave in the morning?"

She looked at her watch. "I don't think we ought to wait until morning."

He took her in his arms and sat her down on his knees. She was staring into space and hardly noticed. "Josephine, this isn't our fault."

"It's not yours. He's my father. I should have cared more what happened to him."

He moved her to the bed, got up, and locked the door. He came back and sat beside her and began unbuttoning her blouse. She gasped and gripped his hand. He heaved her on her back on the bed, and she thrashed with her whole body. She was very strong. There was no sound but the grunting and gasping and creaking of the bed. She pushed his face away until he caught her hands and held them locked together over her head with one of his. For less than a minute they tangled as though held by the same skin.

When it was over, she went to the bathroom and stayed for a long time. He lay in the dark feeling brutish and glum. When she came back, he turned on the light and saw that she was silently weeping bitter tears.

~~~~~~

37

It was foggy when they turned off the Buttermilk Road the next night, and when Adam saw the shroud of white fur ahead, it seemed only a lump in a stripe of fog. Then the headlights blacked in the lizard head and rat tail of a possum. Adam spun the wheel to miss it. The right tires clapped the possum down, dropped off the pavement, and the car twisted out of control. Before Josephine had time to gasp, he had it gliding along smoothly again, and the drooping windows of the house appeared through the scud of fog and shadows above them. He had already been excited, and this scare set his heart rapping with insistent pressure.

He stopped the car at the front steps and said: "I'll carry you across the threshold."

"No, not this threshold."

Rutherford came out with a big smile to welcome them and get the suitcases. "How is he?" Josephine said at once.

"Doctor's doing not so bad. He's still in the hospital. They say maybe he can come home day after tomorrow."

They found three card tables set up in the parlor piled with gift-wrapped packages. The fact that people had not waited for announcements pleased Adam because he had feared the town might ignore their marriage. There were a half-dozen tear sheets from the *Mercer Times* of two days ago with a large photograph of Josephine and an article about the bride and groom.

"Where did they get the picture?"

"It's a college yearbook picture. Poor Daddy went to some trouble to make me look respectable."

"Miss Josephine," said Rutherford, his arms full of suitcases, "the ladies from the gif' sto's wants you to come down the first thing and pick out some china and table silver." Josephine looked at the piles of presents and sighed.

Adam considered telephoning Moon, but decided it was too late to take any action about The Taurus Company that night.

They went upstairs to Josephine's big southwest corner room. The windows were open, the Venetian blinds blew inward, and insects buzzed against the screens. The four-poster bed had a sofa at its foot. The room had a ladylike smell of cosmetics over which blew the smell of leaves from outside. On one side were relics of childhood; the giant blue panda looked brand-new.

"What makes that noise?" said Adam.

"I don't hear it. Oh, you mean the attic fan."

"It must have been put in since my time. It makes quite a draft."

Rutherford deposited the rest of the suitcases and said goodnight.

Adam was undressing here, and Josephine in the adjoining bathroom, when the telephone rang. Wearing a slip, she hurried to the closet for a robe and clawed aside her hanging clothes. "I'll answer it," Adam said. He was halfway through the dark hall when the ringing stopped in the middle of a signal. Rutherford was talking angrily in the hall below, and he finished by slamming the telephone down hard.

Then his dark head appeared against the light from downstairs, and he tiptoed through the hall. "What was that?" Adam said.

Startled, Rutherford spun around. "I was just turning off the telephone up here so it wouldn't bother Miss Josephine. That was some mo white trash calling."

For a moment Adam was mystified. "White trash calling?" He motioned Rutherford away from the door to the stairs. "The same kind as before? I thought those calls had stopped."

"They did stop for a while, but something done started them up again."

"Next time call me to the telephone."

Josephine's door opened: "What's wrong? Is it the hospital?"

"Just a wrong number," Adam said, and the door closed again.

Adam turned back to Rutherford. They were standing under the doors to the fan, which seemed to take in everything they said like a huge ear trumpet. "Can we put that fan on a lower speed?"

"Nawsir. You really got to prop them do's open or that fan will grab 'em shut—sound like a shotgun." Rutherford waited politely for a moment, then took a step downstairs.

"Wait," said Adam. There was a lot he wanted to know, and he was too tired now to think of subtle ways of framing questions. "What time of day did Dr. Garth have this stroke?"

"In the morning. When he went to get in the car to go to church, he wasn't feeling right, but he went on. I asked Dr. Garth hadn't I better call Miss Josephine. He said no, but I thought I ought to—"

"You did right to call her. Now, Rutherford, you understand that excitement isn't good for a man in Dr. Garth's condition, and a wedding can be pretty exciting. Do you think Miss Josephine's marrying could have—well, could have gotten him upset?"

"He seemed right calm that day. Jes after he found Miss Josephine's letter he didn't eat much lunch, and he kept looking out the front windows like he might be expecting somebody."

"Who was he expecting, would you say?"

"Maybe looking for Miss Josephine to come back."

Adam thanked him and returned to the bedroom. Josephine in pajamas was waiting for him. "Are you sure that call wasn't about Daddy? Don't keep anything from me, Adam."

As he undressed, he told her what Rutherford had said about her father's outwardly calm acceptance of their marriage. He propped the door open so the fan could draw air through the room, and got into bed beside her. The bed had new mattress and springs, so instead of sinking into a trough in the center as in most old beds, each sleeper could lie on his own firm plateau. He kissed her on the cheek and lay back.

After they had been lying there for twenty minutes, and he thought she was asleep, she said: "Adam, I want to tell you something I've never told anyone."

He waited for a long interval. "What is that, Josephine?"

"Since Mother died, the thing that has worried me more than anything else is that Daddy might marry again. I suppose I've even let him know it indirectly. That was so horribly selfish. If I hadn't been that way, he might have been happier and wouldn't have had these strokes."

"No, you just feel that way because you're exhausted. For one thing, if your father had wanted to marry again, nothing would have stopped him. And he's never shown any signs of wanting to, has he?"

"It's worse than that." Her voice shook. "I sometimes thought I'd rather that he died than that he married again."

"Josephine, your father's going to be all right. I'm sure of it. A lot has happened to you in the past month, and I know everything looks pretty black. It'll look a lot better in the morning, I promise you."

She squeezed his hand tightly, and he sensed that she was trying to hold them together because she felt something pulling her away. The squeeze was a promise, a prophecy, but not an invitation. "I've been very unfair to you, Adam. I'm going to try harder. I'll do better. You'll see."

He lay there exhausted, his skin peeling and itching, overfatigue making him sink into sleep and rise out of it. The fan drawing night into the house made the curtains reach out toward the door, snatched up smells from the outside and whirled them over him. He tried to separate out the smells of grass, boxwood, and trees. He could even smell the scuppernong arbor though he knew it was too far away to reach him here.

Sometimes the big blades of the fan clacked like the arms of a windmill. Sometimes they churned the air like the screw of a ship in water, and that sound, and the sounds of the house itself, like the creaking of a ship's plates, gave Adam the feeling as he floated off to sleep that the house was a ship in motion.

Several times he thought he heard talking but decided it was the creaking of the house from the pull of the fan. Once he woke up with the idea that Dr. Garth was in the room, and he strained to hear, thinking he could pick Dr. Garth's voice out of all those voices which the fan sucked from the walls—not only his voice but his cough, the jingling of his keys, and the clearing of his throat.

Adam was in deep sleep when the scream came. Josephine was sitting up, pointing toward the door. He could not wake her up completely until he turned on the light. What had she seen? A man, she said, hugging him. A waiter. But as she got a little more awake, she said no, a man in black with a clerical collar.

He woke up again at daylight. It was cold now, and he groped his way into the hall to try to find the fan switch. He punched several buttons with mother-of-pearl eyes, none of which was the right one. He went back to bed, and lay shivering, unwilling to wake Josephine to find the switch. He was beginning to understand why she was not fond of this house.

~~~~~~

38

Josephine had already dressed and talked with Dr. Lawson when Adam woke up again. Dr. Garth would come home the next morning. He would sleep downstairs until an elevator could be installed, and Josephine was having a bed put in the study. Dr. Lawson's opinion was that the stroke resulted from an embolism or a spasm, which indicated a good chance for recovery. Very likely, Lawson had told Josephine, Dr. Garth would have had the stroke whatever the external circumstances of his life had been. During breakfast Adam advised Josephine to open her presents, so that no callers would think she was indifferent to what they had sent. "I don't want their presents," she said, "but I suppose you're right."

After breakfast Adam telephoned G. P. Moon and was told that he was in court. He then called Jimmy Nabors. He was staggered to hear that Jimmy was no longer employed at The Taurus Company. He asked at Jimmy's rooming house and learned that Jimmy had gone to his parents' home in Rome, Georgia.

Byroade had been busy; when Adam went to the post office for his mail, he found the box full, and there was a big package for him. The latter contained a handsome set of towels, monogrammed. Adam's had a "S" on it. Evidently sets like it had been sent to all Taurus stockholders.

In his mail was a copy of *Rebel Yell,* which featured an article entitled "New Life at Taurus." It was full of praise of the Olins, especially "able, courageous Jack Olin." Adam found himself described as "sometime stockdealer, Adam Salter." It touched misleadingly on the webbing mill fiasco and stated that many creditors had suffered from the company's failure. The article concluded with the paragraph: "Although Salter claims great influence over Dr. Ivor Garth on the basis of distant kinship, Dr. Garth admits no such thing. Smart Mercer businessmen who know Dr. Garth doubt that anyone can dupe him into being a Hindenburg in spite of advanced age."

This implied comparison of himself with Adolf Hitler made Adam reread the paragraph incredulously. The article managed to cast doubts on Dr. Garth's competence by comparing him with the senile Hindenburg, to whom he did have a physical resemblance, and at the same time to work against Dr. Garth's participation on Adam's side. Most stockholders would not recall the Hindenburg of 1933, but they would identify him as an autocratic Prussian and an enemy. The magazine had gone to press before his marriage. Why bring Dr. Garth into it? Byroade must have decided that Dr. Garth was Adam's ace in the hole, whose support he planned to announce as a dramatic surprise.

The next envelope contained management's proxy instrument. Adam opened this one with interest and found that Byroade had outdone himself. The proxy asked for authorization to start a research and development program; to increase the number of shares from thirty to forty thousand in order to acquire by exchange of ten thousand shares the capital stock of the Galaxy Chemical Corporation ("maker of the miracle fiber, Kolar"); and to authorize a change in the method of electing directors. Just what change was not specified. The accompanying letter announced a luncheon before the meeting at the Nathan Bedford Forrest Hotel, at which a motion picture would be shown. Stockholders had never been encouraged to come to the annual meeting before.

Adam went through this material rapidly but with no special feeling of urgency until he noticed the date of the meeting. That's tomorrow, he said to himself, they've made a mistake. He read on with a quickening pulse and cold tongs on his heart. Management was calling a special meeting because of the need for quick action on the merger with Galaxy Chemical. Now he understood how perfect Byroade's timing had been.

From the postmark the notice must have been delivered the day he and Josephine left for Mississippi only a week ago, and as he remembered it, the law required thirty-days' notice of a stockholders' meeting.

Within five minutes Adam was in the courthouse and found G. P.

Moon in criminal court there. The judge was conferring in low tones with a Negro defendant and his lawyer. Moon was waiting with his client, a duck-tailed boy of the switch-blade set, and Adam leaned over the railing and asked Moon to come out and talk with him. "My case is coming up right now," said Moon. "I can't leave."

"Just one question. Is this meeting tomorrow legal?"

"It's hard to say." Moon's voice sounded strangely hostile.

"How about having lunch with me at the Post Office Café? About twelve-fifteen?"

Moon nodded grimly and turned back to his client.

From a booth in the corridor Adam telephoned his lawyer in Birmingham. He quickly outlined his problem, and the lawyer said he would have an answer that afternoon. Could the meeting be enjoined? That was up to the local circuit court. Adam spent the next half-hour studying the state code. The law definitely required thirty-days' notice, but an amendment allowed a meeting of stockholders in "circumstances of special urgency" with seven-days' notice if a majority of the stockholders waived the usual notice in writing or by participating in the meeting.

On the courthouse steps Adam ran into The Taurus Company's lawyer, Mr. Stubbs, who said he had been looking for Adam and wanted to talk with him about the meeting tomorrow. Adam said he doubted that the meeting was legal. Stubbs assured him that it was; Byroade had seen to that. Management, he said, would allow cumulative voting and the addition of another director to the board if Adam would go along with acquiring Galaxy Chemical. "Do you mean to tell me," Adam said, "that we can get a company with a commercially usable synthetic fiber in production for stock worth less than a million dollars?" It wasn't actually in production but soon would be, Stubbs answered. Had the patents, the know-how, everything. The maddening sensation swept over Adam, as it usually did in Mr. Stubbs' presence, that his time was being snuffed out, exterminated. He said he would think about it and broke away.

Moon arrived at the Post Office Café late, and Adam asked at once about Jimmy Nabors. "Yeah, I understand Jack Olin's got a big drive on down there to root out ehbody that's giving out secrets. Jimmy's the only one they caught so far."

"That boy's not going to suffer because he supported me."

Moon shrugged his shoulders.

"I guess you saw the article in *Rebel Yell*," Adam said. "It surprised me they mentioned Dr. Garth."

"Folks knew you had backing from somewhere. There was already rumors it was Dr. Garth, and when you married his daughter, ehbody sorta got the picture. Byroade was against doing the article that way, I hear. In fact they say Jack Olin is taking over more and more. Going to preside at the meeting tomorrow. He was the one that got Mrs. Wriston's proxy."

"What?" said Adam. "But *I've* got her proxy." Then he saw that Moon had been saving this bit and watching Adam closely for its effect—no sign of great good will.

"Yeah, she revoked it," Moon said. "Jack and his wife really worked for it, wining and dining her while you were out of town. How does that count up? You can't win without her proxy, can you?"

"She can always revoke that proxy again, don't forget that."

"That's going to take some fast doing, with the meeting tomorrow and her being in New York. They say she's got the hots for that Herold fellow and went snuffing after him." Adam scowled and flushed at this reminder of Herold's prowess, and Moon went on: "And don't forget that revoking can work both ways."

"What do you mean, G. P.?"

"Oh, I don't mean me. But you know how old ladies are." He spoke with mysterious emphasis. "But here, I'm forgetting to congratulate you." He turned a cool eye on Adam. "You're a mighty lucky man."

"Thanks," Adam said dryly. "What did you mean about old ladies?"

"Nothing, nothing." After a pause Moon said: "One thing Olin did wrong this week. He offered the stockholders a hundred and fifty dollars a share. It made 'em so greedy now they won't sell at all."

Adam asked Moon's opinion of the proposed compromise relayed by Stubbs, and Moon replied: "I never saw the Olins compromise on nothing unless they had to. It's sure they're not going to do you any good."

Adam said: "We need to round up proxies this afternoon and try to keep our supporters from going to the meeting tomorrow. If they go, even if they vote against Olin, we're licked."

"I'm too busy. I got another case coming up in court this afternoon."

"Then see if you can get Judge Rivers to enjoin the meeting. I sure wish I had known about this meeting before."

"Yeah, I figured you would. I tried to find out where you'd gone so I could let you know. I called out there at the Garths' a couple of times to see if you'd let anybody know where you are. Last time Dr. Garth told me not to call there any more."

"I thought you were acting strange," Adam said. For a moment he was so exasperated at Dr. Garth's tactlessness and what it might cost that it did not occur to him that Moon's mountain pride was hurt. "I'm sorry about that, G. P." He was tempted to explain that Dr. Garth's rebuff was directed at him, Adam, but it would please Moon too much to hear that Dr. Garth in addition to his other troubles had an unwelcome son-in-law. "He's been a sick man, you know." Moon couldn't be placated so easily, for he was sure now where the money behind Adam lay, and that power had snubbed him.

"I know he's sick, and that's not doing you any good with the stockholders." Dr. Garth had begun talking incoherently to himself in church, and people were saying he was too old and sick to trust with the mill. "It looks to me like old doc might be losing his marbles—"

Adam stopped him with a cold glance, then looked away. On the morning of his stroke Dr. Garth must have gone to church as a show of defiance. The humiliation Adam felt made everything darken, and he realized that he still loved the old man.

Adam looked up and saw Moon's yellow eyes on him. "You think I've lost, don't you, Moon?" Adam slapped the top of the table with the flat of his hand. "Listen here. You can run back to Olin if you want to. But whatever you do, I'm going to win. I'm not just kicking your leg, boy."

Moon stared and blinked. "Naw," he said faintly. "I'm with you."

"Okay." Adam looked at his watch. "How about getting to the judge and see if he'll enjoin the meeting?"

In quick succession Adam called Rice Alexander, who was in conference, P. D. Emery, who would be out of town until that night, and Duncan Chisholm, who said: "I'm busy now. If you'll call me tonight, I'll discuss this with you."

The smaller stockholders were not so hard to see, but their manners had changed in a peculiar way. The old ladies like Miss Winnie McCaffery seemed stiffer than ever but looked him over with bright knowing stares. There were no congratulations, no mention of his marriage. Even the pithiest summation of Jimmy Nabor's disclosures hardly held anyone's attention, for all seemed more interested in Adam's person than in what he said. Not one would promise to stay away from the meeting tomorrow. They were pleased with the towels which management had sent them, and they had heard it was going to be a good lunch.

Adam telephoned his Birmingham lawyer again and received this opinion: "I've looked up the statute on stockholders' meetings. It does seem inconsistent. The law on special meetings never has had a real test in court. But if Byroade arranged it, he must be pretty sure the meeting will be valid, and he's got a habit of being right."

The news from G. P. Moon was no more reassuring: "No, the judge wouldn't enjoin the meeting. Oh yeh. Your wife's been trying to reach you. She wouldn't say what for, but she wanted mighty bad to get aholt of you."

The Garths' telephone did not answer, and Adam pondered what he should do. He had been with Josephine constantly over the past few days and so burdened with her dissatisfaction that he had not examined his own unhappiness and apprehension very closely. He had been assuming that he could make the marriage succeed if he could get past some dim event in the near future. Beneath her hostility he sensed that she felt considerable loyalty to him, and he did not expect her to announce that she wanted a divorce. Instead he feared that something beyond her control would take her away. It had seemed that when she was with him in Florida, he could watch her closely enough to hold the marriage together, but in Mercer it could get away from him quickly.

He had suffered that day from an uneasy impression, which he supposed came from the peculiar reception from the stockholders, the change in Moon's attitude, and something he could smell in the air, that things were happening which he needed to know about. He also attributed this feeling to the moving up of the meeting, the customary date of which had previously become so fixed in his mind that the change seemed a violation of natural law. And now, though he knew he needed every minute to dissuade stockholders from attending the meeting tomorrow, he was afraid in his accumulated uneasiness that Josephine needed him badly.

Willie May met him in the Garths' driveway. "Miss Josephine

and Rutherford done gone to get doctuh. She wanted you to come and help."

"But I thought he wasn't coming until tomorrow."

"You know doctuh. You can't stop him from nothing he wants to do."

From the porch Adam saw metal flash through the trees below and Dr. Garth's old Cadillac appeared in the driveway. Adam stood waiting stiffly, his heart beating hard and his mouth dry, as the car moved slowly up toward him. As it drew near, he saw that Rutherford was driving, and he could make out two silhouettes in the back seat. The car came abreast of him, and Adam stepped forward. The car slowed but instead of stopping moved past him around the house. He saw Josephine's face in the near window, and she signaled to him. He followed the car to a stop.

Josephine got out and explained to Adam in a low voice: "We brought him back here so he wouldn't have to climb the steps."

Adam leaned over and put his head in the door to say: "Hello, Uncle Ive. Glad to see you, sir." Dr. Garth, his back turned, was too completely occupied in getting out of the car to reply.

Not until Dr. Garth was out did Adam see how changed he was—stooped, his color unnatural with too much blue in it, the skin of his face dragged downward from the bones. Adam moved around to help, but Dr. Garth avoided his hand. He walked slowly, looking over the back of the house as though seeing it for the first time. Rutherford was trying to assist him at one side, and Josephine, pushing past Adam, went to the other arm. Adam watched Dr. Garth's slow gait for a sign of paralysis, but the impression was rather of stiffness and weakness. Adam followed them into the study where Dr. Garth sat down heavily on the bed. He complained about having to sleep here. It was just until an elevator could be installed on the stairs, Josephine told him. "We're not going to do that," her father said. "It would spoil the finest staircase in the county." Adam took vague warning from this. Previously Dr. Garth would not have hesitated to cut the house in two if it had suited him.

Dr. Garth said something to Rutherford in a low voice, and Rutherford hurried out. Assuming that Dr. Garth would be undressing for bed, Adam turned to go. A two-fingered gesture of his father-in-law's hand stopped him. "Yes, sir?"

"Sit down," said Dr. Garth in a rumbling voice.

Adam glanced at Josephine, who said: "Daddy, don't you think you'd better get in bed?"

Her father expelled his breath with a rush of sound. "This is urgent, and I hope it will do him some good to know what is going on as a result of his actions."

Adam took a seat.

"If you wanted war with the Olins, you've succeeded in starting one, and you picked a good time to go out of town. Why didn't you tell me of your offer to buy Olin's stock?"

"What offer? Oh, down at Chisholm's board room. That was some time ago. I forgot you didn't know about it, Uncle Ive." Adam saw an expression on Dr. Garth's face which showed he didn't want to be called Uncle Ive any more. "It wasn't a real offer, it was a bluff—"

"Do you think I don't know that?" roared Dr. Garth, and Josephine put a restraining hand on his shoulder. He leaned forward and, breathing heavily, said in a flat bitter voice: "You see what you've done now, I hope. By that dishonest gesture you made a fool of Bascom Olin in public. If you hadn't done that, he would not have gone to the lengths he did to get the stock."

Adam recoiled before the glaring eyes and fierce voice. "You mean his getting Mrs. Wriston's proxy?"

"Don't speak that woman's name in my presence again. I'm talking about Rice Alexander and P. D. Emery. They've sold their stock to Olin. He had been pressing them for their proxies. They apparently got together on it. In any case they went through the motions of being neutral by offering it to the highest bidder. Olin got it for two hundred dollars a share." Dr. Garth's discolored face grew darker. "It's not worth that much, and Olin knew it wasn't, but after your goading he had his pride at stake."

"Sir, you said yourself that Olin would always raise any bid of yours on the stock," Adam protested. His own report to these men had been all too effective: he had so thoroughly convinced Emery and Alexander of the company's weakness that they had decided to sell out while they could. "Do you actually think Olin would have let you buy the stock at a reasonable figure?" Behind her father Josephine was frowning and signaling. Adam saw what she meant: he was arguing with a sick man. He managed a smile and stood up. "Well, you don't need to worry about this now. We're still a long way from licked."

"What sense does that statement make? Sit down, I haven't finished talking with you. That is, unless you feel that you need no longer attend to matters of business."

Stunned, Adam sank down into his chair again. He could hardly believe that Dr. Garth was alluding to his having recently married money, but the remark could have meant nothing else.

"I do have one unexpected blessing. While you were out of town, I received word from Mrs. Mercer that she's revoking her trust with the Merchants National Bank in order to vote her Taurus stock in my favor. This is a drastic thing to do, but in spite of it, we don't have the number of shares we need. I told her that you would pick up her proxies this afternoon. That is, if it's not too much trouble." He spoke these words with heavy sarcasm.

"I'll be glad to. With her shares maybe we can block the meeting."

"I don't care what the lawyers say, the meeting's void. The Olins knew Mrs. Mercer might revoke her trust, so they tried to have the meeting first. I've discussed it with Myerson. Forget the meeting." He gave Adam a hard look as though daring him to express the disagreement which he felt so deeply on this point. "How many shares of small stockholders do you have lined up?"

"I couldn't get many definite commitments, but they seemed about equally divided." This was putting the most hopeful interpretation on what he had heard that day.

"Then Olin will win unless Duncan Chisholm votes with us, and he has every reason to support Olin. One other thing. There is a rumor that you plan to make yourself president of the company. Is that rumor founded on fact?"

"Why that's just somebody's guess—probably the Olins'."

"Apparently you did not understand my question. Have you any such intention?"

"Well, I wouldn't turn it down, and I think I'd be an improvement on what the company has now."

"It seems that you have had many plans concerning your personal advancement about which you did not see fit to take me into your confidence." Dr. Garth's biting tone implied the ugliest treachery. "Were you under the impression that I favored this scheme of yours?"

"I was under the impression that you favored saving the company, and I—" Adam caught an imploring look from Josephine.

"But I have certainly not given anyone the idea you supported me as president."

Josephine patted her father on the shoulder. "Daddy, you need to lie down."

"Can I *depend* on you to get the proxies from Mrs. Mercer *today?*"

"Yes, *sir*." Adam waited for dismissal. Dr. Garth turned to Josephine. "Mrs. Mercer says she wants to give a party for you, Josephine. You've always been a favorite of hers."

"Isn't that nice? She sent a beautiful silver service for a wedding present."

"You ought to go to see her too and thank her."

"I'll write her a note. I think it's the custom for people to call on a bride and not vice versa."

"I'm not talking about etiquette. I'm talking about the right thing to do. She isn't well and hasn't been out of the house for weeks. I'm going to lie down now. Send Rutherford in."

Adam walked to the parlor and tried to collect himself. He could hardly keep from muttering aloud the fiery retorts he might have made just now. Considering Dr. Garth's age and ill-health he would never be able to use any of them.

Or was he just afraid of the old man? He had a painful memory of his own father, with his foolish laugh and shabby clothes, before the imposing Dr. Garth, and he tried to think of some moral superiority for himself and his father—the side without money. He reviewed the talk with Dr. Garth the night before the marriage and fought the conclusion he had drawn about Dr. Garth and his mother. It had seemed, when he thought of it since then, even more out of harmony with what he knew, and he distrusted the idea completely. Still the recollection of what Dr. Garth had said enraged him so he could not keep still.

Josephine joined him and said in a tense voice: "Please try to keep off subjects that excite him."

Adam turned angrily. "I didn't bring them up. You know the old man's using his illness as an excuse. Well, I'm not going to take any more bullying from him. It was all I could do to keep from going over the facts of what he's done to the mill."

Josephine recoiled and said more gently: "Remember he's sick. He's so changed."

Adam could not deny it. "He didn't even acknowledge that I was his son-in-law except with that insinuation about money."

"He will though when he's better. Adam, you don't think I told him about your plans to be president of the company—"

"It makes no difference." They stood in silence for a moment. Adam glanced at his watch. "I'm going to Mrs. Mercer's."

"What do you think I ought to do? Should I go?"

"I don't care. Do as you please."

"I don't feel up to it, but it seems to mean so much to Daddy. When are you going?"

"Right now."

39

It took Josephine a half-hour to get ready to go. Adam, pacing in the parlor, could hear her steps on the floor overhead. During that time he cooled enough to regret letting her feel the edge of his anger and to turn his attention to The Taurus Company.

It was certain now, barring some highly improbable change of attitude toward his new son-in-law, that Dr. Garth would obstruct his becoming president of the company. In spite of himself Adam could not forget that this resistance came from an old man in bad health, and that time might remove such an obstacle. The important thing now was to get control of the company into the family.

As for the Mercer estate proxies, revoking the trust was so unexpected and Dr. Garth's attitude so pessimistic that Adam felt there was a catch to it. After some reflection, however, the proxies along with the presents and the party seemed a well-deserved vote of confidence in the family. During that half-hour Adam also came to the conclusion that Dr. Garth must have worked on Mrs. Mercer and had even counted on her support. There was the question of why he had kept it to himself until now. To protect his power against me, Adam decided.

He heard a step in the library and turned to see Rutherford walking toward the study door carrying a big revolver. It was the .44 Magnum.

"What are you doing with that cannon, Rutherford?"

"Doctor told me to bring it down from his room." Rutherford held the gun with his finger tips away from his body as though it were a poisonous snake. "Miss Josephine say she'll be right down."

Adam suspected that Josephine's aversion to the visit was making her slow, but when she appeared brushed and starched, she did not seem unhappy at the prospect of meeting the old lady.

"I've had a few callers today with wedding presents," she said as they rode. "Mostly middle-aged women. Blakely came. Also Vera Knowland and Charlotte Carpenter and that crowd. They couldn't wait, they had to have a look at me."

"You are too hard on them," said Adam. "They wish you well."

"No, Blakely's the only one who came because she likes me."

The sun was sinking into the dying oaks along Beauregard Avenue when they turned under the gloomy shade which surrounded Mrs. Mercer's house. It was the oldest house inside the city limits, built when there was nothing between it and the railroad but a swamp. The town had grown past her and left Beauregard Avenue, like a skin shed by a snake, a street of boarding-houses. Mrs. Mercer would not move and grew hedges seven feet high as dykes to keep the neighborhood out.

A colored man answered the bell and conducted them to a drawing room. The room was full of the impedimenta of a distinguished family. One portrait of heroic size in a Confederate uniform was of General George Swift Grayson. Another represented a handsome tall woman with dark eyes and hair, Mrs. Mercer herself.

The colored man reappeared and showed them across the hall to another series of large rooms which extended the length of the house. At the far end was a shrunken figure, an old woman dressed in black with a blanket around her legs. Silently she watched them approach. Josephine walked ahead of Adam, and smiling, said warmly: "It's so good to see you, Mrs. Mercer." She leaned forward to kiss the withered cheek but something warned her, and she halted and half turned, saying: "This is my husband, Adam."

Mrs. Mercer's voice—strong, ringing, mannish with age—cut short Adam's greeting. "Here are the proxies, Mr. Salter." She extended an envelope to him. Adam hastened to take them and thank her. He got close enough to see that the brown eyes fixed on him were still keen.

"You've been so sweet," said Josephine. "The silver is lovely."

"I suppose your father told you about the reception I intend to give."

"Yes, and I think that's just too kind—"

Mrs. Mercer's cold voice cut her off. "I'm not doing these things for you. I'm doing them in spite of you, for your father, whose heart you have broken."

Josephine stood still for a moment, her face growing red, and her lips parted to make a reply. Then she turned and walked out of the house.

Mrs. Mercer gave Adam one curious contemptuous glance, then looked past him, her curiosity satisfied, her contempt rewarded.

"The suit has been withdrawn, mam."

"Your wife brazenly appeared in public with another woman's husband."

"Has it occurred to you that Josephine was not told he was married?"

"Even so, her behavior was inexcusable."

"I think you put too much stock in rumors, Mrs. Mercer."

"What I know is a matter of public knowledge. Good day to you, sir. Your wife is waiting."

Adam was not out of her sight before he realized he still had the proxy envelope in his hand. The desire to refuse it made him stop at the door. He opened the envelope and saw that it was not his own proxy form but a typewritten one which gave Dr. Garth and General Myerson the power to vote the shares. They were not his to refuse. He was just picking them up for Dr. Garth, and he would worry the sick man further by making a gesture with them.

The butler with a low bow opened the front door for Adam, and he went out into the twilight. Obviously Mrs. Mercer regarded him as a hanger-on of the family, a nonentity, an instrument to make an honest woman of Josephine. Couldn't she look at him and see that wasn't the case? And did even the hired man she thought he was deserve to be treated so abruptly? She had made up her mind about him before she saw him—that is, if she saw him at all. She would not live long enough to change her opinion of him.

He could do nothing now to defend his wife against this, and at that moment he hated the town of Mercer, and all in the world he wanted was enough money to buy and sell everyone here—the Olins, the Mercers, and the Garths.

Josephine was waiting in the car. "Don't let it worry you," he said. "She's just a mean old woman."

"No, that's the way they all feel. The others just can't afford to be that blunt. They have something to lose. That's the way they would all treat me if they weren't afraid of Daddy. You know why those women came to see me today really? To see if I were pregnant. I think Blakely even is afraid of me." Driving with one hand, Adam reached over and squeezed her hand. She pulled loose and said: "Don't pity me."

"Pity you? Do you think this is just happening to you?" He let her out at the front door of the Garth house and handed her the envelope. "Give these to your father, please. Go on and have dinner. I'll be back later."

Mrs. Mercer had presumably explained her animus against Josephine, but her words made him sense something hidden. Once more he felt that he had been in the dark since he came back, walking on the heels of some open secret—a secret only to himself and Josephine.

It took some backing and craning to find G. P. Moon's house in the twilight. Moon, chewing, answered the bell and said brightly: "Come in the house and have some fried chicken and buttermilk."

"Would you mind stepping outside, G. P.?"

Moon followed Adam to the curb.

"What is it I don't know that's been going on?"

Moon took his time about lighting a cigarette before he answered: "I'd have told you earlier but I figured it wasn't no use ruining your peace of mind unless I had to." Opening his mouth wide, he blew out a wobbling globe of smoke. "Somebody's giving out the details of the Herold divorce suit."

"What suit? The suit's been withdrawn."

"Somebody's not letting that stop it. I don't guess I have to tell you who."

"What do you mean by 'details,' G. P.?"

Moon took a deep breath and burst out: "Somebody's showing around photostats—depositions, a copy of the bill, and some stuff."

"Don't people realize they're forgeries?"

"They *look* real," said Moon, "being certified and all. People say Dr. Garth fixed the whole thing with money."

"The whole thing? Me too. Is that it?"

"Well, Jack Olin plays rough. Could be the old man doesn't know about it, but both of them are mighty used to having their own way, so maybe neither one of them cares how he wins."

"It doesn't sound like Byroade," Adam said, and Moon agreed.

The headlights of a passing car fell on Moon's face, and Adam could not tell whether the expression he saw was of scorn for the cuckold after the fact or brotherly feeling for the opportunist who had managed to marry an heiress at a discount.

"I'd like to see those documents, G. P."

"I wouldn't if I was you."

"G. P., I believe if you wanted to badly enough, you could find me a set of those documents in fifteen minutes. You're that ingenious."

Moon meditated. Then he moved toward his car, saying: "You wait here."

Ten minutes later Moon returned with a bulky worn envelope, the contents of which Adam examined by the dome light of his car. Among them was a copy of the bill with check marks to guide the reader to the nights on which Cato Herold and one Josephine Garth had committed adultery. December 24, December 25, January 3, January 17, and "succeeding occasions." He was about to go on to the attached depositions when two photographs slipped out of the envelope. One of these was a picture of Josephine and Cato walking abreast on a city street.

He might have taken the other photograph himself—almost. Cato and Josephine were in his convertible just as they had been beneath the Garths' windows, but here one of Cato's hands was inside her low-cut dress. Over his shoulder was her ecstatic face. In the background was the Myersons' lakeside cottage. It must have taken a great deal of patience to get such a photograph, evidently taken by infrared flash, for it showed both faces unmistakably.

Adam thrust these papers into his pocket and got out. Moon was waiting. "There's no doubt that the Olins were the ones who're spreading this?"

"Is the pig's tail pork?"

"Where does Jack Olin live?"

"Now hold on, Adam. I wouldn't go up there and make any trouble. He's awful handy. He's been hoping for years somebody would swing on him. He'd be right glad if it was you."

"Where does he live?"

"He built a house on Mimosa Lane. At Tulip Tree Drive."

As Adam drove to Jack Olin's house, he traced in his mind how these photostats got to the Olins. Leah must have met Jack through Mrs. Wriston—another reason for Mrs. Wriston's shunning him. This was a very personal attack, for Jack had known Josephine

276

well. But *he* was the object. The Olins were making an example of him. As a matter of policy they were crushing him, to show who had power in Mercer and discourage any rebellion in the future.

The house was old brick trimmed in white, split-level, and clinging to a large steep lot. A grinning picture window returned the grin of the city lights below. Now he was high over the smoke of Olin factories, and the smoke he smelled here came from steaks cooking over charcoal. A half-dozen cars parked along the curb indicated that the Olins must be giving a party.

Adam rang the bell and waited. The party noise must have kept them from hearing him ring. He kept his thumb on the bell.

Jack Olin's wife, Dorothy, more pregnant than ever, opened the door and greeted Adam with an inquiring ladylike smile. She did not seem to remember him. "I want to see Olin," Adam said.

His tone made her frown. She turned and called back over her shoulder. "Jack. There's someone here to see you."

Jack Olin came to the door and looked through the screen. "Yes?"

"I'd like to have a word with you."

"I have company. What do you want?"

"Come on out here, or I'll come in after you."

The noise inside dried up. Adam heard through frantic whispering the word "police" and Dorothy Olin pleaded: "Don't go out there, Jack!" The screen opened, and Jack Olin stepped outside. Several faces crowded against the screen.

"Do you want to have it out here or do you want to go somewhere that's not so public?" Adam said.

Olin led the way around the house to a sloping turfed back yard. They were followed by the five men from the party. The windows of the house threw enough light to see. Adam took off his coat, and so did Olin. "Jack'll kill him," one of the spectators said.

Ben Knowland stepped forward and said to Adam: "I'd advise you, buddyro, to get out of here before you get your butt beat bloody." But like the others he was eager for some excitement, and because Adam had come there truculently to start a fight, they were saved from having to feel any sympathy for him.

Adam moved around him and advanced toward Olin. The shape the latter's broad shoulders gave his white shirt stood out against the dark. "Did you think I was just going to keep still and take it?" Adam said. "What kind of man did you think I was?"

"It didn't make a damn with me what you were."

As mad as he was, Adam felt some reluctance, a sickness in the bowels at the thought of hitting the other man. He had boxed just enough in college to know he was not fitted for it. His reflexes even then had been too slow, and he had lacked the instinct to finish off his opponent. He hadn't had a fight since childhood, and the tableau before him did not seem real. Adam hesitated only a few seconds, but that was too long. Jack Olin said loudly to the others: "This is just more bluff. The guy is all mouth. Come on inside." He started to walk past Adam, and Adam grabbed at the front of his shirt.

His hand was knocked upward, and knuckles in quick jabs struck his stomach and jaw. The ground rammed his back, the lighted windows tolled like bells, and Adam lay gasping for breath. He tried to shake the bloody mist from his head as he pushed himself up.

He had just time to get his balance before another blow came out of the dark and crushed his nose. Adam staggered. A fist smacked his ear. He fell forward, and something hard and sharp embedded in the ground struck his cheek over the bone—he did not know how sharp until he felt the blood wetting the side of his face and running off his chin.

Pushing with his hands, he got his grudging legs under him. A fist burst into his face. He grabbed at the arm but it tore away from him. It was like a moving part of a machine. He had nothing but pain in his face, the taste of blood, ringing in his head. Still haven't hit him, he said to himself. Yet he felt a soul-sickening wish taking hold of him—that the fight were over though it would mean he had lost. When he heard a spectator call out to Jack that it looked like he had won and to let up, Adam hoped such an idea would prevail. He felt a great nausea at the idea of being hit again. He tried to squeeze up some fuel, but his reasons for fighting were now flat and remote. He had not imagined its happening that way.

Though he knew now there would not be an opening, he moved against the bent-armed boxer's crouch. He made a circle to be level with Olin and threw himself into the next blow, grabbing with his hands.

That fist drove into Adam's chin, and he went flat again. The next few minutes were hazy. He was knocked down several more times, he lost count of how many. He was taking longer to get up.

He would work his way to his knees and forearms, then push himself up with his hands. Jack stood there fresh and springy, his shirttail neatly tucked in, his fists ready, and as soon as Adam got up, the fists did what they were trained for, and Adam went down hard.

The haze thickened, and there was a waxing and waning in the volume of the spectators' talk and some laughter. Adam realized he had been down for some time. He felt a sharp pain in his ear, and he realized that Olin had his ear lobe between thumb and forefinger and was leaning over him and whispering: "Now listen. Get off my property. And I don't want to see you again or the whore you married."

Adam grabbed Olin's arm. This time his hands closed on cloth and flesh, and the two men rolled down the sloping yard. Adam rammed his head into Olin's face, locked his arms around the rib cage, crushed with his arms, lifting the other's body to tighten his grip. Olin clawed at his face and eyes. A thumb with a strong nail dug into the open cut in Adam's cheek. Adam felt the flesh tear, and he let go. The pain kicked off some action inside him, and fire played over him and devoured the pain.

For a moment they were both trying to regain their feet, and Adam snatched one of Olin's moving arms from the air, and with a leveraged jerk drove him face forward into the grass, at the same time throwing his weight on the other's back and neck.

Olin rolled under him, and Adam planted his knees on Olin's arms, and digging his fingers into his scalp, beat his head again and again on the ground.

A babble of voices swept over him, and hands tugged at his arms. But they had to pull Adam off, and just before he let go, he drove his fist into the brimming mustache of red blood.

He got up with clenched fists and turned on the others. Wide-eyed, they backed away. He had not fought a clean-looking fight, and they did not admire him, but they were afraid of him, and that was all he wanted. They turned from him to Olin, who was gasping and bubbling on the ground. Adam staggered up the yard, and Olin's wife, swollen and awkward, cried out and ran past him. She'll remember me next time, Adam said to himself.

A child was crying inside the house, and Adam wondered how much Olin's children had seen. He had given them nightmare food, and he had left the grown folks something they wouldn't forget.

His arms trembled so that he could hardly drive, but he got himself to his apartment. He was caked with blood and dirt, and he needed some stitches in that torn cheek. He was relieved that his teeth were all in place though one in front felt loose and a molar was sharp to his tongue.

Some strong drink might help, but he didn't have any, and anyway his stomach was too excited to take it. He washed his face carefully, and the soap burned like acid.

He lay on his bed with the lights out. The telephone rang twice that evening, but he did not answer it.

He had been looking for an enemy. He had thought at times it might be Herold, and that day he had picked Jack Olin, but now he knew he hadn't finished anything, for he did not even have the cleaned-out feeling of vented hate. Because his enemy was not an Olin, but Dr. Garth.

~~~~~~

40

Sweating, Adam woke up to the taste and smell of blood. His bloated cheek was throbbing, and the swelling pulled the skin of his whole face tight. The bedclothes were stiff and evil-smelling against his mouth.

It was about five o'clock in the morning. At the moment of waking he had a thought which drove him out of bed: that Josephine would think that he had left her because of Mrs. Mercer's and the town's rejection of her.

The bathroom mirror reflected a purple and misshapen face. He should have had a doctor attend to it last night.

Outside the gray air of morning twilight was full of the noise of birds. He drove through a deserted town to the Buttermilk Road. The east was growing flesh-colored when he turned up the Garths' driveway, and a light was burning on the porch.

The front door was locked, and so were the doors to back hall and kitchen. The other entrance led from the patio to the dining room, and he squeezed through a gap in the hedge, getting his shirt and hands wet with dew. This door was locked too. Josephine and Dr. Garth were both sleeping on the other side of the house, so a little noise wouldn't wake them. Adam took off a shoe and broke out a pane of glass with it, reached through, and turned the inside catch.

He went through the dining room to the hall. By the increasing brightness through the fanlight he saw his way to the stairs. The attic fan was still straining at the depths of the house as though choked by the shutting of all the doors and windows.

Boards creaked, the library door opened, and Dr. Garth stepped out. He was fully dressed. He peered around the hall, and Adam silently pressed back into the shadows. He hoped that Dr. Garth would decide he hadn't heard anything and go back to bed. Then Adam saw the gun in Dr. Garth's hand: the Magnum. He thought of its bone-destroying thunder and held his breath. Dr. Garth turned so slowly that Adam decided he was sleepwalking. His jaw was slack, and an expression of dread disfigured his face as though he were still walking through a nightmare. Dr. Garth stood there perfectly still, the gun held poised, the barrel level. He looked in Adam's direction, and it seemed impossible that he would not see him, but after a long stare, Dr. Garth backed into the library doorway.

Adam gave him plenty of time to get back into the study. When the floor had stopped creaking, Adam took off his shoes and went upstairs.

Josephine stirred but did not wake up, and Adam thought she had an expression of extraordinary purity. He swallowed some aspirin he found in the bathroom, put on nightclothes, and lay down beside her. He remembered the documents were still in his coat, and he ought to destroy or hide them, but he could not make himself get up again. The annual meeting would be in a few hours, and he ought to set an alarm clock. He went to sleep in the babel which the suction of the fan pulled from the walls.

He did not sleep soundly but against scudding bitter dreams of loss and defeat.

Sunlight flicking his eyelids awakened him. The fan was off, and the curtains flapped in a mild breeze. He squirmed for a comfortable position and knew from the pains which he discovered like nails in the bed that he could not be comfortable for a long time.

The blinds were closed, but the sunlight leaked through at the edges. He turned from the light and on the other side of the room saw Josephine combing her hair. For a few moments he kept still and admired his beautiful tainted wife. As she combed, she was thinking hard, spasmodically biting her lip and looking at her watch.

When he stirred again, she put down her comb and sat on the bed beside him. "How do you feel?" she whispered.

"Rotten. As though I'd been drinking seawater."

She frowned nervously. "Daddy can't come upstairs of course. Maybe you'd better go down and let him look at that cut on your cheek."

"No."

"He's different today. I talked to him about being so hard on you yesterday. I may have said too much. He's not going to say anything critical to you." She took Adam's right hand gently in both of hers and looked at the skinned knuckles. "Adam, please try to get along with him. He doesn't want to be old and difficult."

"I don't want him to see this."

"He already knows about the fight. It's all over town. Nobody knows you were hurt this much though." She scrutinized his face. "That's a bad cut. I know it's sore. It's infected. I'd let Dr. Lawson sew it up. Daddy's hands shake too much. How about breakfast?"

"Maybe later."

"Adam, did you come in through the dining room last night?"

"Yes. Sorry I had to break the glass."

"But I left the front door unlocked for you!"

"No, it was locked. All the doors were locked."

"That's strange." She put a cool smooth hand on his cheek. "You feel awfully hot."

"What time is it?"

"About eleven-thirty," she said, and he raised up in panic. "You're not thinking of going to that meeting today, are you?"

"I have to." His head throbbed at the thought.

"Don't you dare. You're sick." She looked at her watch. "Daddy wants me to go to the bank to get everything in his safety deposit box. He's picked today to burn a lot of old records and letters."

"Don't let me keep you. I'm all right."

"I hate to leave."

"Oh, I see. It's him you hate to leave."

"He's strange today. He asked me to call the minister, and when he came out, Daddy had changed his mind and wouldn't talk with him. Adam, why it's worrying him I don't know, but he's brooding about the idea of your becoming president at the mill. Couldn't I tell him, please, that you've given it up?"

"But I haven't. Of course it's not up to me. The directors will choose the new president. I hope I can sell them on choosing me."

A look of despair came over her face. She stood up. "Dr. Lawson's coming in a little while, and I'll leave word for him to come up and see you. If there's anything you want, ring the bell in the hall. I'll tell Rutherford not to bother you."

But she didn't go. Staring at her wedding ring and pressing her thighs against the bed, she said: "It may seem a little late for this, but I've been so wrapped up in myself and so worried about Daddy that I've been a terrible bitch to you. When you didn't come home last night, I wondered if maybe what Mrs. Mercer said . . . But I realized you weren't that kind of man, and that I was lucky to have you for a husband. I promise you that I'm going to be a good wife if it kills me."

"Then come to bed," he said, putting his hand on her hip.

She smiled wanly and patted his hand. "Idiot. As sick as you are. I don't want to be such a good wife that it kills *you*. Now stay in bed. I've got to run."

As soon as she was out of the room, Adam got up. His head swam, and he immediately lay down again. He would rest a few minutes, but he couldn't let himself doze off. He was feeling too bad to be very elated about what she had said, but it gave him some satisfaction to remember it.

He lay with his eyes closed. A June bug flew into the window screen and made it twang. Faintly he smelled the smoke of Dr. Garth's papers burning. Willie May was walking around the house and burst out with a few bars of mournful song. Adam heard Josephine's car motor start, and he pictured exactly where she was, going down the hill, turning, going up the Buttermilk Road.

He tried to work himself to the point of getting up. He had to see Duncan Chisholm before the meeting. It was hard to sort his arguments, and the violence of last night threw a shadow over everything he might say.

He became aware of a sound in the hallway and tried to identify it. Someone was walking slowly and heavily. Maybe it was Rutherford carrying a trunk or a heavy piece of furniture on his shoulders.

From under lowered lids Adam saw two blazing eyes in the doorway. He caught his breath. It was Dr. Garth. He advanced into the room, his tread making the glass shake.

Adam's impulse had been to protest Dr. Garth's climbing the stairs, but an ill-understood feeling of caution made him keep perfectly still with his eyelids almost shut.

"There is dirt in it," said Dr. Garth. Adam made a pantomime of waking up. Dr. Garth set a stainless steel tray on a bedside table and removed the lid. "The wound will scar."

The tone of Dr. Garth's voice indicated that he was holding himself in check, and Adam resolved to do likewise. "Sir, I appreciate it, but you shouldn't have come upstairs," he said, his voice cracking.

Dr. Garth grasped Adam's face in a big hand and turned it to catch the light, throwing his own head back to sight through the lower lens of his bifocal glasses. Then he released Adam and wet some cotton with a bottle of orange liquid. He applied it roughly to the cut on Adam's cheek, and Adam gritted his teeth at the sting.

"It is very near the brain." Dr. Garth assembled a hypodermic syringe and thrust the needle into the red rubber seal of a bottle. Adam looked from the fluid drawn into the glass barrel to the steel tray which contained a dozen shiny surgical instruments. "I'm all right," he said. "What's in that bottle?"

"Your cut will require more treatment than can be given here," said Dr. Garth.

"Look," said Adam. "It's very likely the meeting today will be legal. I've got to go to it instead of lying here." The effort of sitting up made the blood pound in his ears. "What's in that hypodermic?"

Dr. Garth leaned close, breathing hard, and Adam moved his head to avoid the needle, but a strong cold hand pressed his head against the pillow. "Procaine. Keep still." Dr. Garth's breath was like the air of a hospital.

Adam turned his eyes down to see the trembling point of the needle blur and disappear into the edge of the wound. He felt the steel slide into harder tissue, then withdraw. The needle struck again, numbing as it went, and hit the bone over the sinus. When it came out again, Adam put his arm up to fend off another shot. "I don't want any more treatment," he said.

"This arrangement must suit you," said Dr. Garth, "seeing that you do not seem to want to get well." He set the needle down. "I am going to buy you out today. I will pay more than we agreed for your stock. The premium will be great enough to compensate you for the additional expense and inconvenience that may be caused you by going to a public hospital instead of camping here where my daughter will feel obliged to nurse you. The added burden of your being on her hands will injure her health. When you are well enough to be discharged from the hospital, I shall expect you to convalesce in your own apartment. Is there anything about this arrangement that you do not understand?"

"No, I think I understand it."

"I'll have to ask for your word in writing so that if there should be any question about it in the future I shall have something to remind you what our agreement was."

"I suppose that Josephine will stay here and look after you."

"That is her duty, yes. Now is everything clear to you?"

"Don't you think you've isolated her enough already?"

"She belongs in this house, my house," said Dr. Garth. "It *is* my house. You seem to regard it as a family relic to which you have some right. I saved it from rot. If I hadn't, sharecroppers would be living here now, and keeping pigs in the dining room. I did not save it for you."

"If I go, I will take her with me. You've blamed others, including me, for what's gone wrong at the mill although Stewart Baker tells me that you've hurt the company more than anyone. But my real sin has nothing to do with the mill. It's that I'm Josephine's husband."

Dr. Garth faced him. "I know men your age. Some of the best families in Mercer have brought me their daughters unmarried and pregnant. There was nothing that I could do. They had once been pure girls, but now they were soiled and ruined. Their parents would rather have seen their daughters dead."

"What does that have to do with me? I *married* Josephine."

"Married her to degrade her and use her money for selfish ends. You took advantage of her. She was too young to know what you wanted."

"Too young! Josephine is twenty-four years old! You accuse me of these sins, but you even tried to make me doubt my mother's chastity to keep me from marrying Josephine. I once loved you like a father, but I know better now."

Dr. Garth's eyes burned with hate. "I had thought I had offered you sufficient profit for you to conduct yourself in an honorable decent way. It appears that I misjudged you."

"This is the same old story. If you don't want to hear something, you just stop listening." Adam got out of bed. "But listen now, hear the truth, and you will know it is true. Your daughter is an outcast. Everyone in town who has the slightest interest in this matter including Mrs. Mercer knows all about the Herold case and Josephine's part in it. Everyone but you." Adam walked to the closet and pulled out the bloody jacket he had worn the night before. "You are a senile old man, but I don't believe you have outlived your principal vice." For once Adam's voice sounded not plaintive in Dr. Garth's presence but firm and deep. It hardly seemed to be coming from his own lips. He took out the envelope of papers and photographs and handed them to Dr. Garth. "Look on your daughter's nakedness. At leisure. Not here." Dr. Garth turned his back. His face made a rippling drowning reflection in the far mirror. He hardly seemed aware of Adam's presence, but Adam went on:

"And while you're looking, look into your daughter's face, and see if she does not feel, in spite of herself, that you've already lived too long. Ask her." The sight of the twisted mouth and burning eyes in the mirror made Adam wish with all his heart that Dr. Garth would go ahead and die.

Gripping the envelope in his hand, Dr. Garth walked slowly from the room.

The bed tempted Adam, but it was getting late. He shaved with trembling fingers and dressed. The wound felt bloated and numb but was more livid than ever, and Adam applied a big bandage to conceal it.

He slowed down as he passed between the columns on the porch. He had acted cruelly toward a sick old man, and though it seemed that Dr. Garth had deserved it, Adam felt an impulse to go back and try to undo what he had just done, not leave it this way even for a few hours, but some of Dr. Garth's words came back to him, and he pressed the feeling in as though deliberately tightening a muscle in his heart. He started his car, saying to himself: I can make peace when I get back. I'll be calmer then.

~~~~~~

41

When Adam arrived at the Forrest Hotel, the private dining room was dark except for a square of moving color projected on a screen. The scene was of the Taurus cloth room where pretty girls handled stacks of bright towels. As soon as his eyes adjusted to the darkness, Adam tried to tell from the heads against the colored screen how many stockholders were present and who they were.

The music shifted to a marchlike tempo, and the camera framed a man in the middle distance coming out of the mill. He locked the door, and as he turned, the camera drew closer. It was Jack Olin, and the sight of him made Adam's face ache. The sun was setting, for the new vice-president worked late. The camera rolled with him as he walked, holding his handsome face against a golden sky. The narrator, with the stirring voice of *The March of Time,* was saying: "Once more the men who make American industry great meet the challenge of the future with strength and courage . . ." The young executive kept walking, his face against the sunset. He looked tired but undaunted. The band music swelled up, the hero came to a stop, and the camera tilted to catch an American flag waving behind his head.

That was the end, and after a decent interval, the lights came on, and Adam found himself in a room with several dozen clapping blinking stockholders. G. P. Moon came over and said: "Not a dry eye in the house. Hey you look right green. You all right? Well, anyway, Jack Olin won't be able to make it today," Moon said with satisfaction. He gestured toward the front of the room with his thumb. "They figure old man Bascom Olin might blow his stack, so Byroade's going to be chairman of the meeting."

"That's bad news." Adam stood up and looked around the room for Duncan Chisholm, aware that his own battered face attracted some glances. "How did they seem?" Adam said, surveying the crowd. "Will any of them leave, do you think?"

"Not one. Olin's got a quorum easy by my count."

Byroade was talking intently to Bascom Olin. Many Olin satellites were here, from the big ones like Calvin Davidson to the little ones like Arlis Camp. This kind of support gave Olin close to a quorum among his own shares and employees.

"There's Mr. Chisholm." Adam circled to where Mr. Chisholm was sitting alone and asked him to step outside for a moment. Mr. Chisholm glanced at the clock and reluctantly followed Adam into the hall.

"I'm going to protest the meeting, and I want your support."

That's what I was afraid of, the thin face seemed to say. "No, I've decided to remain neutral."

"Then will you leave?"

"No, I told Byroade I would serve as inspector of the election."

"If you stay, it will assure them of a quorum."

"I have no obligation to take sides in a free-for-all," Mr. Chisholm sounded slightly angry, and Adam thought: The issue was under his skin before I got here. "There have been things on both sides I haven't liked."

"You mean my fight with Jack Olin. I had to do that. You know why."

"I *don't* know why."

Adam tried to select his words carefully before going on. "I mean the photostats he was sending around." Adam felt a darkening of the spirit at the thought that he, and not the Olins, had showed these papers to Dr. Garth.

"The Olins weren't circulating those photostats!"

"Who did it then?"

"I looked into this unsavory subject because I had to make sure the Olins weren't responsible. It seems to have been Mrs. Wriston under pressure from Mrs. Herold."

"I don't believe it," Adam said, but he knew Mr. Chisholm was probably right. "Anyway, Jack had it coming."

"That is your affair, not mine. I hear the Olins are offering to compromise with you. That's what I'd do if I were you."

"Do you really believe they'd give up any of their power?"

Mr. Chisholm uncovered his wrist watch. "It's almost time for the meeting to begin—"

"I know the Olins are good customers of yours, Mr. Chisholm," said Adam, consciously advancing to dangerous ground. "Does that mean you will let them put you in a position of approving everything they do? I don't just mean about Jack. Sure, I lost my temper, and I seem to have been wrong. I mean all the Byroade tricks, like the article in *Rebel Yell*."

Mr. Chisholm said in a cool voice: "I tried to head this off, you know. I warned you. Let me remind you, you are trying to make money out of this proxy fight. That's why you are here. Now you urge me to renounce my own business interests in favor of yours."

"No. For a principle."

"May I ask what principle is involved?"

"You once said you would support the best man available to run The Taurus Company. What you're doing in effect is supporting Jack Olin. The principle is let the best man run the company."

"As far as I know, he's the only candidate for that job."

"I'm a candidate."

"Why he's had ten years' experience in the textile business and you've had less than two. Moreover I used to think you had a cool head, but what you did last night makes me doubt that."

"Would you really pick him over me?"

Mr. Chisholm glanced at his watch again. "I'm sorry, but I'm due in there now. I really have taken into consideration these things you're bringing up, and my decisions will be made according to my conscience."

"In that case, I'm not worried, sir. I knew you wouldn't let them turn you into an Olin man."

"Now hold on! I won't have you putting this kind of pressure on me!" Mr. Chisholm turned abruptly and preceded Adam through the double door.

Moon was waiting for Adam inside. "Mr. Chisholm's staying," Adam said. "That assures them a quorum. He seems to think that Jack didn't send those photostats around."

"Yeah," said Moon, avoiding Adam's eye. "They say now it was Mrs. Wriston. Of course Jack could of put her up to it. But I'm afraid the fight didn't do you no good. Up to last night Jack was in the wrong. Now they feel kinda sorry for him."

Adam looked over the crowd. He could not delay a decision any longer. Either he must stay and vote, or walk out and try to take enough stockholders with him to prevent a quorum. Right now he did not feel like fooling with them. He had to make himself care. All he wanted now was to lie down.

Moon tapped his shoulder. "Hey, I thought you said General Myerson wasn't coming."

The general was standing just inside the door, and Adam went to him at once. "Dr. Garth indicated that you had agreed to stay away."

General Myerson said with some exasperation: "What I said was that my lawyers believe the meeting *is* regular."

"I plan to protest the meeting. Will you leave with me?"

"It would be better to stay and vote. Do you have Dr. Garth's proxy?"

"No, or Mrs. Mercer's either. If we could get enough stockholders to leave—"

"We have no hope of preventing a quorum."

"Then I'll have to stay too. Will you call Dr. Garth and tell him we need those proxies? I can't do anything with him."

"Is Dr. Garth well enough to come today?"

"No, but he could send proxies. You're empowered to vote Mrs. Mercer's stock."

The general glanced at the wall clock. "It's past time for the meeting to start."

"I'll slow things down here until you get back."

General Myerson hesitated, looking at Adam with distrust and with outright disdain at Moon just beyond him. Plainly he did not want allies of this kind. "I'll ask him." He turned and strode out.

"Testing . . . one-two-three-four . . . testing." Quigley was self-consciously speaking into the microphone. The volume of sound would have been great enough for a football stadium, and possession of the microphone would mean that the chairman would always hold the floor. Byroade was still talking to Bascom Olin. Adam waited until he had finished and gotten up. "I'd like to discuss this compromise I hear you're offering," Adam said to him.

"It's too late."

"Is all you have in that proposal cumulative voting and a sixth director?"

"Those are the main provisions, yes," Byroade muttered, and he brushed past to speak to Quigley.

Adam returned to his seat. His aching head made him feel

stupid, and Byroade would have all the right responses by experience and instinct.

Quigley said into the microphone: "The bylaws provide that the chairman of the board of directors shall appoint the presiding officer at all stockholders' meetings. We are fortunate in having Mr. Dean H. Byroade to serve today as chairman." Byroade stood up to light applause and faced the assembly with a smile. Mr. Ellis, he said, would be secretary of the meeting, and Ellis presented some documents from the Merchants National Bank to show that due notice of this meeting had been given stockholders.

Moon got up and said: "I object that due notice was *not* given stockholders, and I object to the way this thing is being handled instead of the usual—"

Byroade's electronically strengthened voice filled the room. "I'm sorry, you are out of order. There will be a time for discussion and motions from the floor."

Moon persisted, and Byroade's voice rushed over him: *"You are out of order, sir. Please be seated."*

Adam could detect an annoyed reaction among the stockholders nearby and signaled to Moon to sit down. "The crowd's with Byroade," he whispered. "Better wait."

Ellis was saying: "Mr. Chairman, here is a list of stockholders of record who are entitled to vote at this meeting." He then proceeded to call the roll. When he came to General Myerson's name, Adam stood up and said: "I'd like to ask that we wait for General Myerson. He's just stepped out of the room."

"We'll have to proceed," said Byroade. "Mark General Myerson present, please, Mr. Ellis."

Byroade then called for proxies. He explained that a stockholder's latest proxy superceded any given previously, and a vote in person canceled all proxies. Olin got up and thrust his handful into Ellis's face. Olin moved with the rigidity of pent-up rage, his encircled eyes shunning all others. His mouth was drawn tight. It was the mouth of a man often in the wrong, who knew it and didn't mind it.

Adam nervously felt the proxies in his breast pocket. When he stood up this time, a quick ebb of blood from his head darkened the room, and he had to support himself on the back of a chair.

"There's the general," Moon said.

General Myerson drew close and said to Adam: "I told Dr.

Garth what the situation here is, but what he'll do I can't tell you." Instead of taking the empty chair beside Adam, the general moved on and sat in the next row, and Moon grimaced knowingly.

Adam went to the front of the room, the floor feeling a long way below. The undertone of talk quieted, and he was aware of hard stares. He delivered his proxies to Ellis, knowing many of them would be worthless because of the presence of stockholders who had assigned them to him.

Byroade announced. "Mr. Duncan Chisholm has kindly consented to serve as inspector of the election again this year." While Ellis administered the oath of office, Adam whispered to General Myerson: "What's the story of Galaxy Chemical Company?" The general mumbled his reply, and Adam gathered that the general opposed the merger.

Byroade asked if a quorum was present. Mr. Chisholm said there was. "In order not to delay very urgent business, let us waive the reading of the minutes of the last meeting," Byroade said.

Adam leaned forward and asked General Myerson if this matter were up to the chairman, and the general answered that the minutes must be read if anyone requested it. Moon overheard this and leaped up. "Mr. Chairman, I demand a reading of the minutes."

Byroade, looking displeased, told Ellis to read them. As Adam had expected, they contained nothing important, and during the reading, he kept turning to look at the doors behind him.

"The first item on the agenda," Byroade said, "is a research and development program for the purpose of improving and broadening the company's line of products." This was one hundred per cent stockholder relations, and Adam was going to let it pass, but Moon was on his feet again and in spite of Adam's whispered warning, protested the program as a waste of the company's money. Byroade seemed willing to give Moon more rope, but the latter's voice brought back his role as a tormenter of witnesses to Arlis Camp, who stood up, wild-eyed, and pointed at Moon and hollered: "That feller's trying to ruin the company!" A sharp exchange between Moon and Camp and a general hullabaloo followed. Byroade rapped with his gavel, and when quiet was restored and Adam got Moon seated again, Byroade said: "The next item is to vote on the authorization of ten thousand shares of additional stock in the corporation to acquire the capital stock of the Galaxy Chemical Company. Mr. Olin will present the details of this motion."

Olin growled into the microphone: "As your chairman, I strongly recommend that you vote *for* this merger. It will place The Taurus Company in a strong position in the field of synthetics. Galaxy is a good company with sound finances as you will see by the sheets Mr. Quigley is passing out. Several companies are bidding against us, so today was set as a deadline for us to decide whether we want it or not. If we don't want this wonderful bargain, somebody else will snap it up. The current ratio . . ."

Adam glanced at the printed sheet and listened for a weak point, but the report had been carefully screened. He felt hot and sick, and he could not keep still. His gaze moved from his watch to the double doors and back again. Olin went over the balance sheet at high speed and finished with a discouraging scowl: "Any questions?"

Adam got up and said: "Would you please read the names and addresses of stockholders of Galaxy Chemical."

Olin waved a sheet of paper. "These are not local stockholders, and the list wouldn't mean anything to this meeting."

"We'd still like to know who owns the company."

Moon shot to his feet. "I demanded a written stock vote on this question."

"Since there has been another request for the list to be read, would you please accommodate the minority, Mr. Olin," Byroade said. "I hope the others will bear with them."

Olin was right: the names meant nothing to Adam. He had been expecting some Olin satellite or Olin-controlled corporation to turn up among the stockholders, but of course Byroade was too agile for that. There were nine stockholders. When Olin had finished reading the list, Adam said: "Does Mr. Olin or any of his family or any corporation in which he is a stockholder have an option to buy any of that stock?"

Byroade bowed slightly to Olin, who replied without looking at Adam: "The answer is *no*."

Olin might be lying, but Adam thought it more likely that he was still underrating Byroade, who would have assured without leaving fingerprints that Olin would soon own most or all of the stock of Galaxy Chemical.

"Mr. Olin!" Adam shouted. "Do you deny that this Galaxy merger is a device to give you control of The Taurus Company?"

Olin, eyes bulging, turned on Adam, but Byroade interposed his sharp voice. "Mr. Salter, if you have any facts to support this imputation, state them. Otherwise, we shall proceed."

"Without proper notice how could anyone have time to gather the facts?" Adam looked around. The faces turned toward him were impatient and hostile. "Don't you see what the Olins are doing?"

Byroade drowned him out. "You are out of order, Mr. Salter!" After so many Byroade smiles, the Byroade frown was formidable.

"The Olins haven't changed," Adam said. He turned to the stockholders and saw with horror that his speech was damaging his cause by each word. He sat down.

"Now the matter of the election of directors," said Byroade when the room was quiet. "That cumulative voting be adopted, as Mr. Salter has proposed." He pronounced "Salter" with a grimace and the brittleness of distaste. "That one new member be added to the board of directors making a total of six, and that the board be divided into three classes, one class to be elected annually, the present board to be classified according to a vote of the majority of the present directors." It sounded like a compromise up to the last clause, but of course it was an old Byroade trick. Cumulative voting with a classified board would allow the Olins to retain control even lacking a majority, but Adam knew that he could not by a statement from the floor make the small stockholders understand how. Byroade opened the floor to questions and gave courteous but not very illuminating answers as to how the new system would work. "If there is no more discussion, we will now vote on these proposals."

Adam arose and said: "I favor cumulative voting but not with a classified board. That would mean that you'll only be able to vote on two directors a year, and if this present Olin-dominated board classifies itself, the ones up for election this year will be the only two directors not under Olin's thumb. Then Olin and his subjects, Quigley and Ellis, will be invulnerable for at least another year. Cumulative voting will make it worse because it will mean an organized minority can concentrate its firepower on those two seats." He could tell that his talk was failing with the restless crowd. "Listen! I know it sounds complicated, and it's supposed to. If you vote this system in, you'll wake up to find you've voted even more control out of your hands and into Olin's."

"Mr. Salter," said Byroade, "what are we to make of this newest position of yours? You claimed not long ago that you favored modernizing the company's products, yet your attorney has just objected to the research and development program. You talked about diversification, but now that the company has an unparalleled opportunity to expand into a very promising field, you oppose it. You demanded cumulative voting, and now that we have tried to work something out to make such a change feasible, you oppose that also. You have made an unsubstantiated charge reflecting on the integrity of the board of directors. The only conclusion we can draw is that you are a troublemaker indifferent to the company's welfare."

Adam whispered to General Myerson: "Will you back me up on this?" The general twisted in his chair but would not speak. Adam's head was full of arguments, but he had already presented them to each stockholder again and again. He had a good case, which he had not presented well enough, and the stockholders did not want to hear any more dull details about what was wrong with the company. Adam got up and shouted: "I am not reflecting on the board of directors in general! I am accusing Bascom Olin of trying to keep control of the company by trickery!" He expected to be interrupted, but he caught sight of Byroade's face, on which there was a cool smile, and his eyes beneath his black brows seemed to say: talk on. Adam swallowed hard, and gesturing too much, he did talk on. "You're making your choice this afternoon between life and death for The Taurus Company. September your labor contract comes up for renewal again, and I've told you what continuing your present contract means. Next year at the increasing rate of losses your cash will be gone. This company is facing the same fate the Liberty Mills did. The Olin administration down there hasn't been management. It's been a bunch of pallbearers. If Bascom Olin keeps control of the company, and he's had control since 1950, the company will die." Adam was aware that he was repeating himself, and he made a futile effort to think of some fresher argument: "You all know what I want for the company is new life, and I can give it new life—"

Olin got to his feet, and those around him tried to hold him. Byroade in alarm stepped forward with some soothing whispers, and Adam heard Olin's rasping voice: "If he thinks he can get away with talking off to me, he's crazy! When I get through with him, he's going to think a truck hit him—"

The doors behind them banged open, and all heads turned to

look. Josephine stood there with an envelope in her hand. The stockholders had not expected the sight of the pretty young adulteress and turned to stare. Adam grew hotter with embarrassment at her attracting so much attention. Even her beauty shamed him. He went toward her, ridden by a compulsion to place himself before her and protect her well-curved body from their stares, but as he drew closer, he sensed from the cast of her haggard face that she was too anxious to care about the crowd.

He reached for the envelope, but she whispered: "Daddy said these are for General Myerson." The general was approaching, and she held out the envelope for him. Byroade was the only person in the room who did not know who she was, and he looked perplexed at the expectancy of the crowd and the extreme emotion on Olin's face. All eyes followed the envelope from her hand to General Myerson's. "What's wrong? Are you all right?" Adam said.

"It's Daddy," she whispered. "I'm afraid, Adam. Please hurry home." And she was gone.

The general took the contents of the envelope out and examined them as he walked slowly through a silent staring audience to the front of the room. Byroade's expression sharpened as the significance of Josephine's errand occurred to him, and thinking fast, he turned to the microphone, but Olin's rough voice came first: "Those proxies are too late to be voted at this meeting!"

General Myerson presented them to Duncan Chisholm, who studied them while the others crowded around. Olin snatched at the proxies, but Chisholm handed them to Ellis and said distinctly: "The bylaws provide that any proxies received before the closing of the polls is announced can be voted, and as inspector of this election, I rule that these proxies be accepted." Byroade answered that the office of inspector was a ministerial and not a judicial office, that acceptance of these proxies violated the spirit of the bylaws, and such, and Chisholm argued back vigorously. Adam advanced to joint the controversy, but before he reached the group there, they dispersed, and General Myerson said as he passed Adam: "They're to be voted."

Quigley and Stubbs went through the room distributing ballots. Adam, waiting for his ballot, recalled his speech just now. It had been full of heat without inspiration, as Byroade had expected, considering Adam's physical condition. That was why he had let Adam keep the floor.

Adam received his ballot and marked it, skipping the box on

the research and development program, voting against the Galaxy merger and against changing the method of electing directors. Moon observed him and marked his the same way.

The ballots were collected and delivered to Duncan Chisholm. "Are all ballots in?" he said, looking around the room. "The polls are closed." He sat down and examined the ballots, cross-checking for duplicate and canceled proxies with Ellis's help. Then he took the approved pile and ran up totals on an adding machine. Adam watched, a bubble of ice in his heart. After the quiet just now, the clicking of the adding machine seemed to set off a rising clamor in the room. Moon lunged about in his chair nervously and said: "Old doc shoulda come himself instead of sending his daughter. That would of helped. He's not that sick, is he?"

Mr. Chisholm stood up, and silence fell again. "The results of the balloting are as follows. For a research and development program: in favor, 17,502. Against 25." A cheer from the crowd. This meant that General Myerson like Adam had decided that this issue was not worth voting on.

"For the merger with Galaxy Chemical Company, 14,511. Against: 15,115. For a change in the method of electing directors: 14,449. Against: 15,105." The crowd gasped.

Adam hardly comprehended this until Olin thundered: "Those totals are wrong! Count them again!"

"I will ask Mr. Ellis to count them again," said Duncan Chisholm, "but I believe they are correct." Ellis nodded unhappily.

An uproar broke out. Olin pushed Duncan Chisholm aside to get to the ballots. Adam too believed that an error had been made, and he looked at General Myerson and G. P. Moon for some confirmation of what he had heard. This is the way victories are, he thought. They don't come at the right time to feel them. Something struck him in the side of the head; it was Arlis Camp, walking on the seats of a row of chairs, who had bumped him accidentally with his elbow in an effort to get to Moon. Camp shook his fist in Moon's face, and Moon threatened an ultimate soul-shattering lawsuit.

Adding up all his votes—his shares, Dr. Garth's, General Myerson's, Mrs. Mercer's, Moon's, plus a hundred shares he had by proxy from small stockholders, Adam isolated five hundred votes which he could not account for. His gaze moved over the room, and stopped on Duncan Chisholm. Then he knew who was the owner of those five hundred shares.

He moved to Duncan Chisholm's side and said: "You voted with us, didn't you?"

"We had better adjourn this meeting, and not try to do any more business today."

"But why?"

"To allow time to work out a compromise with Olin."

"Compromise? We can elect the board of directors. We've *won*."

"By a very slim margin. Don't you know that in a short time Bascom will buy a few shares and get control out of your hands? And look at Byroade. I know him well, and it would be naïve indeed to think he accepts this as final. His next move will be to sue you, charging fraud in the solicitation of proxies, and he'll destroy your reputation before he's through."

The sight of Byroade was sobering. Adam said: "Let's see what the general says."

They summoned General Myerson and retired to a corner of the room. Moon, mindful that his shares had been indispensable to victory, crowded in with them. Mr. Chisholm repeated what he had said to Adam and added: "This isn't just personal with Bascom. He's trying to protect Sweetwater Pipe which is a highly leveraged company. Now we must arrange it so Bascom can save face, and allay his fears about control of Sweetwater Pipe."

Adam had a feeling of closeness to these three men, each of whose shares were necessary, as though power over the corporation had descended about them like a cloud. "What do you say, general?"

"Duncan's right. And I think we ought to have Dr. Garth in on this. What do you say to calling him and getting his opinion?"

Adam's inner response to this suggestion was violent. "I don't think so. Not now."

"It might cheer him up to know how the vote went," said General Myerson, "but I'll leave that to you, Adam. I'm convinced we ought to work something out with Bascom."

G. P. Moon said: "I'm for twisting Olin's tail while we got the votes."

"I'll have to go along with Mr. Chisholm and the general on this, G. P.," Adam said. "Let's adjourn the meeting."

They returned to their places. Most of the stockholders looked confused, but not Olin. He had seen Mr. Chisholm's ballot and fixed him with a fierce stare. Then he sat down, his mouth drooping, and planned universal revenge. Chisholm and Byroade talked intently for ten minutes, during which Byroade, for once discomposed, gestured angrily. The latter then spoke to Olin, who gave a curt nod. Byroade's face smoothed, and through the microphone he asked for a motion for adjournment to August tenth. Moon leaped up with that motion, was seconded, and it carried easily.

Moon grabbed at Adam's sleeve. "I want to talk to you about me and The Taurus Company."

"Not now, G. P. I've got to go. Something wrong at home."

"You're not going to forget me, are you?"

"You know very well I can't under the circumstances."

The answer seemed to delight Moon.

Adam went through the air-conditioned hotel lobby and out to the sidewalk. The sudden heat and brilliance made him dizzy, and swaying, he stood trying to remember where he'd parked his car.

"Adam." It was Duncan Chisholm's voice. Adam turned. "This doesn't mean that I'm supporting you for president."

"You don't think I can handle it?"

"You could with able subordinates. But Bascom won't have it. The board, on which you no doubt will have a seat, should bring in a good manager from outside."

"But a good one like Stewart Baker wouldn't take the job as long as Olin's so close to control. And I want mighty bad to run it myself."

"I have another suggestion which will run counter to your instincts—to liquidate the company."

"No sir." Adam tried to think through what Mr. Chisholm had said. "I'll bring Mr. Olin around. After all we've got the power now. Excuse me, I've got to hurry—"

"Think it over. I'd hoped you'd give that idea up about being president, and since taking sides in this will probably cost me Olin's brokerage business, you ought to come back and help me make up for it."

Adam thanked him with a wry smile and took his leave. That's at least three who don't want me for president—Chisholm, Olin, and Dr. Garth. As he drove out the Buttermilk Road, he thought about what he would say to Dr. Garth. He would not make an issue of running the company today, but he could use the victory just now to make peace and offer a belated soft answer.

Mr. Chisholm's warning worried him, and so did another aspect of the situation. When he did run the company, Dr. Garth as chairman would be both boss and father-in-law, a combination which would in this case mean maddening interference. But the feeling of apprehension which seemed to center in his throat came from memory of Josephine just now.

He felt a little nauseated and cranked the ventilator open to get more air on his face. Some of the adhesive tape had come loose, and he pulled the dangling bandage off. The breeze on his deadened cheek gave the feeling of a hole there big enough to put his thumb in.

Even from a distance he noticed something out of the ordinary about the front of the Garth house. It turned out that the front door and screen were open. Both were always kept shut on a day as hot as this to hold in the cool night air. Adam mounted the steps and saw through the dark hall that the back door was also open. A hot wind was blowing through the house, pushing the screen back with steady force and bending it hard against the hinges.

Both the parlor and library were deserted. So were the dining room and patio. Adam went upstairs to the bedroom, which was just as he had left it. Returning to the hall, he called Josephine's name. He crossed over to Dr. Garth's bedroom and knocked softly. There was no answer, and he opened the door. The room was dark, the blinds drawn, and the old tobacco smell which met him was so strong that he was sure that Dr. Garth was inside, sure enough to take a step back and call softly: "Dr. Garth?" No one was inside. He was drawn to the room in spite of the dust and shadows, but turned away.

He descended to the kitchen and found there a pan of rolls ready for the oven like a relic from Herculaneum. The room was very hot. "Rutherford!" he called. "Willie May!"

Returning to the hallway he heard a tapping sound, light but insistent. The sound came from Dr. Garth's study. He knocked there and put his ear against the door. The tapping continued inside, but he heard no answer to his knock. He opened the door. The weight of a Venetian blind cord was blowing against the wall.

He walked through the house once more, very softly now, and he felt reluctant to raise his voice. He went out the back door to the garden and thought he saw someone walking in the arbor, but it was only a bunch of vines tossed by the wind. The wind was blowing hard, and once more from the pines on the ridge he heard the roar of the phantom football crowd. It had a marked rise and fall, he imagined, like the swelling roar for the run of a long-dead fullback. Then the sound fell in disappointment as the run was called back.

Dr. Garth's car was not in the garage, but Josephine's was. Adam tried to think of what had happened. It was now about four o'clock. Josephine could have come to town in Dr. Garth's car and made another stop before coming home. But where were the others?

When Adam went back into the house, he smelled food burning. The kitchen was filling with greasy smoke. He turned the oven control to *Off* and flipped open the oven door. He took a gust of hot smoke in the face, and with his handkerchief wadded, he pulled out a pan of blackened roast.

Moving faster now, he went toward the telephone in Dr. Garth's study—not yet sure whom he would call. The drawn blinds made the room so dim that he had picked up the telephone before he saw the blood in Dr. Garth's chair. There were pools of it on the desk top and on the floor. Under the desk kneehole was a revolver. Adam stooped and picked it up.

The gun was sticky with blood, and he put it down. The blood made a trail of spots and shoe-shaped tracks away from the desk into the dim hallway. He followed, his pulses jolting and his entrails withered. The trail made a spotted arc around the staircase and out the back door. He remembered now seeing some spots outside and thinking they were oil. There was a muddle of footprints in the soft dirt around the walk, of which he could make nothing except that they seemed to lurch from side to side and were very deep. The bloodspots ended on the pavement near the garage. He stood staring, unable to think of any explanation except that the bleeding had been stopped or that the bleeder had ascended into the air.

A familiar voice which he was too shaken to identify called to him from the study. He went back inside, hardly aware that he was wiping his sticky hands on his clothes, and at first, blinded in the dim indoor shade, he could make out only a streaked silhouette. "Hello, Adam." It was Clyde Lavender examining the revolver. "Thirty-two on a forty-five frame. Funny that a doctor, with all the drugs he could get that would be painless, would use a gun, isn't it? And knowing all he does about the human body—"

"What's happened?"

"Dr. Garth shot himself. They took him to the hospital. He was still alive, but they didn't give him much time. Shot himself some place in the body. Heart, I guess." As he talked, Clyde flipped the cylinder out. "It could have been an accident, but I've seen a lot of these cases, and—"

Adam did not really see the road between the house and the hospital nor did he think anything except get there, get there, get there.

The hospital receptionist directed him, and the corridors and strange faces flashed past him. The stroke of his heart was charging the blood through his body and now and then a fragment with it about how Josephine had tried to reach him and couldn't. The door opened as he approached it, and Dr. Lawson stepped out. For an instant, before he recognized Adam, he put up his hand to forbid him to enter. Adam pushed past and saw Josephine with dry staring eyes, and this side of her, with a red stain on the sheet, was Dr. Garth, his mouth open and his jaw slack. Adam thought: but I had something to tell him.

Adam turned to Dr. Lawson, whose lips formed the words: "He's gone." Adam had not needed to be told. Death filled the room like black gas. He moved around the foot of the bed to Josephine. She was gripping her father's hand with both of hers. Her face was as white and empty as his as though the same blow had struck them both. Adam put his arm around her shoulders and squeezed her.

She shifted her shocked stare to Adam. "Leave us alone," she said. Her eyes in her blurred face were like smoked cracked mirrors.

Dr. Lawson led Adam into the hall. What undertaker? Adam didn't know. He was aware that he was hearing words of explanation and advice regarding Josephine which he could not follow. "Let's go next door and let me look at that cheek," the doctor said, and Adam did so. While Dr. Lawson prepared the instruments, Adam had time to reflect on Clyde's remark that Dr. Garth with his access to lethal drugs had chosen a gun and how in spite of his knowledge of anatomy he had not killed himself at once. So death was not the only thing he had wanted.

Dr. Lawson gave Adam antibiotic tablets, and after more Novocain, he trimmed the cheek wound with scissors and closed it with nine stitches. "Go to bed," he said. Adam with a smell of antiseptics in his nostrils and his cheek heavy like a chunk of frozen dirt went to rejoin Josephine. He dreaded that room, but the bed was empty and Josephine was gone.

He came out of the front door of the hospital, a snowman walking on a needle of snow over a chasm. He could not get rid of the feeling that they had been very hasty about taking Dr. Garth away. He had been alive so recently. Were they sure he wouldn't speak again?

He saw the old Cadillac, and the thought flashed on his mind: "Why it's Uncle Ive's car. Uncle Ive's here." A dark figure approached him. It was Rutherford, and when he drew close, he took off his cap, and Adam saw tears in his eyes. "Miss Josephine's done gone to stay with Miss Blakely," he said.

Adam asked Rutherford how it happened. About a half-hour after Josephine left the house, Rutherford heard a shot. He and Willie May had gotten Dr. Garth out to the car, how Adam didn't know, for Dr. Garth weighed over two hundred pounds. That was when Josephine arrived, and she and Rutherford took him to the hospital. Willie May was afraid to stay in the house by herself. "I know how she feels," Adam said. "Did he leave a note?" Rutherford hadn't seen one. Adam realized his questions were torturing the man. "Go on home, Rutherford," he said.

~~~~~~

42

When the muffled voices and sounds of car motors stopped that night, Adam was still sitting alone at the Garths' dining-room table, a telephone at his elbow, the doors closed against the visitors whom the minister and his wife were receiving in the parlor. The nerves in Adam's cheek were coming to life against the bandage, and his throat was sore. He had been there all that hot evening notifying relatives by telephone, making arrangements. Josephine's aunt and uncle were coming tomorrow from South Carolina. The funeral would be the day after that.

Across the hall in the library was the coffin containing the dead man. Adam had arranged this for no better reason than that it seemed fitting. The coffin pressed on his mind like a heavy clamp, and he felt constrained to take it into account in every move.

Adam had searched Dr. Garth's office for the Herold documents and photographs, in vain, but he had found a recent will of Dr. Garth's, which left everything to Josephine.

Next to the will was a file marked "KIESELGUHR," which contained correspondence with an industrial geologist who had been directing soil analyses and core drillings at Kieselguhr for Dr. Garth. A letter of March 31 stated that only a few hundred yards from the old ore pit there was indeed one of the largest and purest deposits of diatomite or kieselguhr in the world, ranging up to a thousand feet in thickness. A letter from the executive vice-president of Malco Products, Inc., manufacturer of industrial chemicals, offered to buy the property outright or lease it and pay a handsome royalty. These letters were all addressed to Dr. Garth at the Buttermilk Road, and none mentioned The Taurus Company. So this was Dr. Garth's secret.

Adam could not put The Taurus Company out of his mind. The greatest obstacle to his becoming president was gone. It would depend largely on Josephine. His own shares would be needed to protect hers; he might sell only enough to the Garth estate—at a profit—to pay his note and keep the rest. Or he could sell his and Josephine's stock to the highest bidder and thus deliver his supporters into Olin's hands.

Or they might liquidate the company. That would satisfy most stockholders and mean over a hundred thousand dollars profit for himself. But he could not forget Jimmy Nabors and the others who had helped him and who had not taken him for a mere liquidator. He would keep the company running, and with Josephine's stock he would become president.

Undeniably during the past few weeks his own plans had by degrees taken into account the money she would inherit. The house around him had been the heart of two fortunes, and he had envisioned building a third and greater one from it.

He felt sick and exhausted, and though he could not make himself get up and put his papers away, he knew he had done all he could that night. Sitting at that big mahogany table, he had an overwhelming sense of the ugliness of life, which he identified as the first smell of his own grave.

Once again he telephoned the Myersons and asked if he could come there. "Josephine's asleep," the general told him. "She's full of sedatives."

"Well, could I come over in case she wakes up?" Adam said.

"I wouldn't," said the general. "You know how you seemed to upset her this afternoon."

It had taken Adam nearly an hour that afternoon, after Josephine had refused communication with him through that locked bedroom door, to realize that he would have to make the decisions for her—select the coffin, designate the clothes for burial, decide when the funeral was to be, make arrangements with the preacher, name the pallbearers.

Stiffly he walked out on the porch. The moon was setting. To the east there was a great confluence of blackness over Kieselguhr.

It seemed very late, but the golden scepters of his glittering wrist watch pointed to eleven o'clock.

He had been holding to a far-fetched hope: that Dr. Garth's death might have its bright side, that the loss would unite him and Josephine by bringing out her need of him. But he remembered with a shudder how strange and raucous her voice had sounded through that locked door. Josephine might lock herself in and start acting like a crazy old woman in the Garth house—a house as haunted as the Chobots, for Josephine could haunt it herself.

"Mr. Adam?" Rutherford stood in the doorway, asking if there were anything more he could do. He added: "Now that doctuh's gone, ain't nothing to hold me. So I'm going on to Detroit."

"When will you go?"

"I don't know when I'm going exactly but I'm going," he said vehemently. "I'm not going to stay here for the rest of my life. I'm going to take my family and board that train for Detroit."

"Will you give me some notice, Rutherford?"

"Yes, sir, I'll give you plenty of notice."

When Rutherford had gone, Adam again searched Dr. Garth's study. Rutherford had cleaned it up, but Adam held his breath there, for he felt that he was breathing death.

He went around the downstairs room checking the windows. After he had felt the window locks, he turned on more lights. The furniture and even the walls did not look substantial to him now, but like crusts of soot which would crumble at his touch. Strange, he thought, that this house can be so dark when Kieselguhr could draw in all the world's shadows.

He detoured around the library, but the great mahogany coffin lured his glance, and through the glass lid, he saw an inanimate pink cheek. He was pulled forward, and with sleet in his blood, he looked down at the big dead face. The jaw seemed at the wrong angle, and the skin translucent. It was not Dr. Garth but a good likeness. Adam backed off until the face had dropped away from the level of his gaze. The coffin seemed to match the furniture of the house very well.

Adam took the Kieselguhr file into the parlor, where the air was sticky with the smell of flowers. His eyelids were twitching and eyes stinging, but he studied these papers again. This was a Miocene deposit of marine origin, he learned, and he noted how pure the various specimens were, how large the deposits, how highly Standard and Poor thought of Malco Products.

He spent almost an hour going again and again through the file, then sat with his head wavering and the far side of the room out of focus. The attic fan bathed him in warm air and the sweet smell of flowers.

Dr. Garth had been right: the house had his stamp on it. Adam thought of the arbor outside with its gravelike proportions and its winy smell of death. A giant's grave, he imagined. His chin was sinking to his chest. His mind moved to such thoughts as the possibility that the soaking of bricks under water had made the house harder to illuminate since they consumed the light. The room was progressing and misting now, and the fan made the flowers dance and grin.

He found himself driving along the Buttermilk Road and when he thought it must go on forever, the road ended at the Chobot house. From there he looked out on Kieselguhr, and Kieselguhr was a shrunken sea. Through this dream, mixed with dreams of the dead, their faces pressed against the windows around him, his heart beat with a stroke of semaphoric warning.

A pair of rats peeped out from the shadow boxes around the ancestral portraits. Adam jerked and cried out, and the rats disappeared in a splash of gray sparks. A sound which was now being repeated had waked him. Someone was trying to get in the front door.

He twisted with a grunt of pain and looked at the slowly gaping door. Into the center of his webbed field of vision came Josephine. She did not see him at first. She leaned back on the heavy door to close it. Grief had hollowed her cheeks and made her eyes puffy. Coming toward him, she said: "I called Cato and asked him to come down here. Do you want to hear any more? Cato said he would come, but that I should turn to you. Also, if he came, Leah would file suit again. Cato has a kind heart, but he didn't want to come. Maybe he feels so guilty about what happened here that it's just too painful for him, but I believe the real reason was that he was out of trouble and he didn't feel up to any more right now. He kept saying he would come if I needed him, but I realize he wasn't what I wanted. I called him because I blamed you. I should have blamed myself."

"No, your father and I had an argument this morning."

"About the mill? I want to put your mind at rest about that. I have some money that Mother left me—just about enough to buy the stock from you. I wouldn't want you to lose anything because of us—"

"Do you think I care about that now?"

"—but I want your word you'll give up this idea of making yourself president of the company. That was Daddy's wish."

"You don't have to ask me. You've inherited your father's stock in the company, and you can vote that stock any way you like."

"I want you to give it up of your own accord. That shouldn't be so hard. You've won so much in such a short time. General Myerson says you won at the meeting today."

They stood facing each other. "No man in his right mind should want that job," he said. "The richest man in town and the smartest lawyer in the state will be trying to knock me out of it. No professional who's in demand like Stewart Baker would touch it—not with Olin just a few shares from control. It just means a lot of hard work for me, and the easy thing would be to do as you say. Don't you realize that right now I'm dying for work that doesn't depend on Garth money? Before you said anything tonight, your father managed to put a curse on that job for me. Just thinking about it makes me want to vomit—"

"Then *give* it *up!*"

"It doesn't have to be settled tonight."

"But I want to know what you're going to do. I think I'll understand you a lot better. I'm sure you don't feel like talking, you look awful, but I've got to know."

"All right. I'm not only asking for the job, I'm asking for a completely free hand. It's either me, or some fourth-rater like Quigley who hasn't the will to save it." Adam rubbed his stinging eyes. "Don't try to decide now. Wait a few days."

"If there's one thing I'm sure of, it's that Daddy wouldn't want his estate used to make you president of that company."

"That's right. So now that you've taken his wishes into consideration, I'm just asking you to make up your mind. He didn't want me for a son-in-law either, remember?"

"But he didn't *say* that!" She sat down, biting her lip. "Don't make me do this, Adam. You're all I've got. You're the one I can depend on—"

"This is no time for us to be quarreling about business, Josephine."

She stole a glance at him, then quickly looked away. "You're right. It doesn't have to be settled tonight." And he knew he had won again—that she would come around.

He had always insisted that his life meet certain conditions of justice and logic. Now Dr. Garth's money would make it possible for him to enforce and even raise his specifications, just as the same money had given this power to Dr. Garth. He was surprised to discover that this prospect made his heart even heavier.

He patted her lightly on the shoulder, and to avoid his touch, it seemed, she got up and went to the wall doorway. "I've told myself again and again it was an accident when he was cleaning the gun." Her back was to Adam. "Do you think it was an accident?"

"It could have been. He wasn't the kind of man to take his own life."

"But he did! Why?"

"I didn't help. During the argument, I did and said the cruelest things I could think of."

"What?"

It would relieve some pressure now if he could disgorge it all, but he said, after a moment's thought: "Imagine the worst, and that's it."

She dropped it there. She did not want her ugliest suspicions confirmed, for she wanted to be able to forgive him. "No, he was cut off from us. You know what the last thing he said to me was. It was in his study. He looked at me a long time and said: 'This room is too dark. Perhaps it would be more cheerful if the woodwork were white.'" She turned and walked slowly across the room.

As she passed before a window, Adam noticed that the darkness was growing gray. It was nearly five o'clock. Already Dr. Garth seemed long gone like an emperor calling his last garrisons from the Danube.

"At the Myersons—" Her voice grew thicker. "I kept thinking that I needed to see how Daddy was feeling and—" She was blinking her inflamed eyes and swallowing hard. "Where is he?"

"He's in there, but I wouldn't—"

She turned and gasped at the sight of the coffin so close in the flowers and shadows of the library. Fearfully she moved toward it, and Adam followed. His palm lightly touched her back, but she shrank from him, and he stood back.

She advanced and looked down at her father's face. Her lips moved, and she shook her head. Then she turned and covered her face with her hands, and Adam stepped forward and put his arms around her shaking back. "The thing I can't stand is how he felt there at the last," she cried, "and I was in the room not twenty minutes before getting those proxies, and he couldn't even tell me about it."

Choking and struggling with grief, she pressed against him. He wanted to say that he would give anything to have her father back, but that was too trivial to bother her with. He was reminded by the sight of her face, white and haggard and not so young nor pretty at this moment, that in spite of everything, madness or death, it was the face he would always love.

"Adam," she said, disengaging herself and picking up her pocketbook, "this came out of his pocket in the hospital. I want you to have it. He would have wanted it that way. At least he would have if—" Her voice trailed away, and watching Adam's face with bright wet eyes, she took a ring of keys from her pocketbook and held it out to him.

Dr. Garth would want it that way? Under no circumstances. Still Adam wanted her to keep that worn but useful phrase.

"I don't think he would, Josephine."

She grasped his hand and closed his fingers over the keys.

But what about Herold? He wanted to ask though he already knew the answer. She could no more give up Herold in a single night than he could give up his craving for success, or the Garth mouth, or his love for her. So the ghost of a living man would join the Garth ghosts, but unlike the others, which were immortal and which for Adam at least had grown stronger that night, Herold's would gradually lose its power.

Adam and Josephine went around putting out lights. She showed him where the fan switch was in the hall. He turned off the fan, for the house was cool now. Then he took her hand, and together they climbed the finest staircase in the county.

ABOUT THE AUTHOR

Thomas Turner was born at Oxford, Alabama, January 28, 1927, and spent his childhood there and at Anniston. He attended the McCallie School, Chattanooga, Tennessee, and graduated from Princeton, 1949, Phi Beta Kappa, summa cum laude in history. He studied writing there in R. P. Blackmur's course and at the University of Alabama in Hudson Strode's course.

Mr. Turner has published stories in *Harper's* and various literary quarterlies, and the stories have been reprinted in *O. Henry Prize Stories, 1959,* and *Best Articles and Stories.* One story has been printed in a Japanese textbook edition and produced as a play on the Canadian Broadcasting System. He has also had jobs in textiles, farming, food processing, concrete manufacture, and has worked for the Federal government. He is now working in real estate development. He is married to Caroline Dale Carter of Williamsburg, Virginia, and has one daughter.